THE COMING OF AMOS

THE COMING OF AMOS

BY

WILLIAM J. LOCKE

Author of "The Morals of Marcus Ordeyne,"
"The Lengthened Shadow," etc.

This story is a free trip to sunny,
olive-shaded France, an inexpensive
gamble at Monte Carlo, and above all,
a sun bath, a riot of blueness and green-
ness and glow, which are far better than
plot and far above all character weaving.

NEW YORK
DODD, MEAD AND COMPANY
1924

THE COMING OF AMOS

THE COMING OF AMOS

CHAPTER I

I HATE excursions and I abhor alarms. Once they were more or less to my taste; now, at forty-five, I've had enough of them. I ask little of Providence beyond the peaceful existence I have somewhat laboriously assured myself. If I paint half a dozen portraits a year, I can live in comfort. If I sell, during the same period, a few landscapes, impressions, sketches or what not, I can live in affluence. Even if I choose to be bone idle, I can sit in the sun all day and sleep in a warm bed all night and have enough food to keep me alive. I own this villa at Cannes, perched on the top of a cliff with nothing in front of my broad windows but the southern sea and sky and the long Esterel of ever-changing beauty. I am king in my castle. I seek no other position that fate or financiers or governments could offer me. Let me paint when I choose, bask like a lizard in my tiny rock garden full of cactus when I feel that idleness would be good for my soul, summon hither whom I please for mutual entertainment, descend, when the humour takes me, into the pleasant throng of humans, and all my very modest desires are entirely satisfied.

But do you think I can get this minimum that I crave? No. There is always something coming along to disturb my nicely balanced equilibrium. The Perfect Egoist would be able, in most cases, to withstand the shock; but that is an ideal of character which I shall never attain.

1

Just as I shall go down to my grave as the Imperfect Painter, so shall I go down as the Imperfect Egoist. It is of my struggles towards Perfection, my rebuffs and my despairs that I propose to write. Also, in consequence, of the exasperating doings of a lot of people, notably those of my step-daughter Dorothea, my nephews, Claude Worthington and Amos Burden and the Princess Nadia Ramiroff. There is also a personage of the name of Ramon Garcia.

As you gather that my story is, technically at least, autobiographical, you must allow me to explain myself further, with as little tediousness as I can. Hitherto you only know that I am a painter, a step-father, an uncle and the associate of a Russian princess, striving hard towards an ideal of gentle egoism. The matter is complicated when I say that Captain Claude Worthington is the son of a Bishop, that the Russian princess is an enigma, and that I am a widower. All this needs explanation. You don't even know my name.

It is:

David Fontenay, Associate of the Royal Academy.

I passed my boyhood in a close ecclesiastical atmosphere. My father, the parson son of a dean, had married an archdeacon's daughter. My great-grandfathers were parsons. My father, an Honorary Canon of Bristol, was also Rector of a near-by county parish. The family, on both sides, were in easy circumstances. Our society was mainly sacerdotal. It thought in Church, it talked in Church, it lived in Church. It admitted only the laity who also thought in terms of Church. To my boyish mind Church was the one thing in the world that mattered. My sisters, much older than I, took interest in nothing else. Amiable young men belonging to the privileged laity aforesaid came with their arts and their

fascinations and went away not so much spurned as un-
regarded. The home was Church-bound. But as cat
will after kind, as the wise Touchstone remarked, so will
a healthy parson's daughter. My younger sister, Muriel,
fell in love with my father's brilliant, just ordained curate,
who, having walked away with all the honours that
Oxford could propose for competition, was obviously
marked out for preferment. *Explicitur episcopus.* My
brother-in-law, the bishop, is explained.

Muriel was the intellectual. She loved the paraphernalia of sacerdotalism and was gathering material for a
treatise on vestments when Thomas Worthington arrived.
It was the putting of their heads together over this pretty
pedantry that led to the putting of their hearts together
in the common way of mortals. Need I say that a stalwart young bachelor parson was the best man? I remember that he cast eyes of amorous decorum on my
elder sister Dorcas and that he went away sorrowing,
for, as I afterwards learned, he had great possessions
and was a fashionable vicar in Kensington.

Dorcas would not look at him. She was a girl of
strong character, who took her religion seriously, and
hated the polished shell that enveloped the yolk of piety.
She was the only one of the family who dared to hold the
Church in disrespect. My father, kind, bland man, in-
dulged her in her theological waywardness; he had his
reasons; she was immensely useful, in that she carried
on, with singular efficiency, the poor side of the rectorial
administration. My father only grew alarmed when he
discovered that she was promulgating Calvinistic heresies
among his parishioners. He became more alarmed when
he learned that she was attending the revivalist meetings
of a firebrand of an itinerant preacher by the name of
Burden. When she came home one night and calmly as-

serted that she had found Jesus and was saved, my good
father was profoundly shocked. He sent her to bed to
think it over. She thought it over to such purpose that
the next afternoon she ran away with the man Burden,
leaving a letter to say that she would marry him within
the shortest interval permitted by the law and then sail
with him to the centre of Australia to convert the blacks.
The whites, she remarked, were not worth converting.

In my father's old-fashioned way of the aristocratical
parson, he would never allow her name to be mentioned
in his presence. The social mésalliance perhaps he would
have condoned; but in mis-allying herself ecclesiastically
she had committed the unpardonable sin.

So much for Dorcas. She faded out of my boyish
memory; all the more because she was dour and un-
sympathetic and so rubbed my sins into me that I began
to love them for their own intimate sake. There was
some thrill in being a vivid sinner; none whatever in
colourless virtue.

I believe this made me frightened of the hereditary
career that my father had mapped out for me. I was
condemned to goodness all my life. My dismay grew
blacker and blacker as my public school revelations of
the great world grew more and more alluring. I didn't
want to walk about in a black coat and preach sermons
and go on reading, for ever and ever, Church services
which I already knew by heart. I wanted to wear gorgeous waistcoats and coloured socks. I craved the
generous lustiness of physical existence. And I wanted
to paint. Who ever heard of a parson painting? The
old monks, of course. They had little else to do. But
a modern parson's time was too fully occupied. And
paint I must. Most of my pocket-money I spent on
materials. I painted during every leisure hour I could

steal from compulsory study and compulsory games. I painted everything paintable, woods, leaves, cows, boys, ships, bunches of carrots. I painted my own reflection in a mirror. I remember trying to interest my father in my daubs. His approval was urbanity itself. Such accomplishment tended to the amiable recreation of a cultivated mind. His sister had painted agreeably—it was in the family. I glanced round the library walls adorned with my late Aunt Eliza's water-colours and shrank as if from the menace of a Family Curse.

In my arrogance I said: "But I'm talking about real painting, father."

I can see him now looking at me above the gold eye-glasses which he had put on to inspect a small and sticky canvas, and waving a hand to the walls.

"And I, my son, am talking of genuine talent. Not —er——"

With his white, soft fingers he flicked my picture an inch or two away from him. It was no good.

A year or two later, when I left school, I had the battle royal. Poor old chap, I must have caused his narrow but exquisite soul infinite pain. The recalcitrance of man, equally with the peace of God, passed all his understanding. Here was I, inbred in the Church, consecrated from my birth to its service, practically (in his own mind) ordained in my cradle and now stolidly refusing to have anything to do with Holy Orders. Didn't I believe in God? Of course I did. In Christ? Certainly. In the Church? Yes. In the sacredness of the Priest's profession?

"For those who can hold it sacred," said I. "But I'm afraid I can't."

"Why?"

In my callow priggishness I replied:

"I'm much more interested in the sacredness of another profession—Art."

He gave me up and summoned my brother-in-law, Tom, from the important Midland living to which he had already been preferred, to reason with the renegade. Tom, a little, brisk man, with the face of a humorous dog, turned me inside out in a quarter of an hour. Then he dragged me into the library.

"Well?" said my father.

"He'd make the very worst kind of possible beast of a parson," said he.

My father made a gesture of despair.

"It's terrible," he groaned.

"It isn't," cried Tom cheerily. "He'll be a much decenter Christian outside than in. Heaven isn't a close corporation for the clergy. In fact I believe there's quite a little clique of them in the other place."

My father opened his eyes wide.

"Yes," said Tom. "And David will join it if he takes orders. Personally, I would rather see a painter saved than a parson damned."

I'm sure my father thought that the brilliant young Vicar of Middleborough was talking blasphemy. But he asked meekly:

"What would you advise?"

"I'd send him to Paris at once to learn his trade."

My father gasped. The old ecclesiastical world seemed to be clattering down around his ears.

"Paris?"

"Where else? The young devil has got the gift. I've seen his pictures. I'm not a fool—I'm a bit of connoisseur—and I keep up to date. I assure you, sir," he added after a pause, "I know what I'm talking about."

He did. The present Bishop of Bradbury is the most

all-round man I have ever come across. He is one of those weird beings who react to every form of human activity. A creature with all kinds of brain-cells working simultaneously. A marvellous, encyclopædic fellow. Why he chose to become a bishop is a matter between himself and his God. Anyhow, at this particular interview he grinned like a dog, and routed my father with the Divinity of Common Sense.

That is why, to this day, I love Tom, the bishop. I think I know him better than my sister Muriel, who always loves to feel herself on the heights. Tom doesn't care a hang whether he is on the heights or in the depths. He is equal to both. But I think he is at his best on the mid-slopes of a generous humanity.

So my father, almost in an obfuscated dream, sent me to Paris, where I learned my trade.

He has been gathered to his clergyman fathers long since, dear old man, and walks serenely in Elysian Fields with the sweet sound of church bells for ever in his ears. My mother, a fragile sphinx, as she always was, still lives in the dainty retirement of the Somersetshire hills.

One more member of my family may here be explained, Dorothea. She belongs to my brief and wondrous married life which has nothing to do with this story. My wife, when we married, was a widow with one little girl. After five years she died. The little girl is now a young woman of twenty-three. She runs, in partnership with another independent young person, a funny little shop in South Molton Street, where they sell cushions and embroidered bags and such little vanities at disgracefully exorbitant prices. We are the very best of friends and companions, when she can tear herself from her criminal commerce and come to visit me at the Villa Esterel.

I don't know but that the recent world convulsion,

through the midst of which I went like so many millions of others and which now—so long ago does it seem—produces nightmares only in my sub-conscious mind, has not directly brought me to that serenity in which I hoped to achieve the Perfect Egoism. A bullet through my lung, exiling me from the fogs and the damp and the sunless slush of London, cut short as successful a career as ever was the lot of a young painter. A similar accident of peace would doubtless have made me curse my fate. But the late Abomination of Abominations had one great effect, in that it stripped a man of vanities and made him see himself soul-naked. Otherwise why should I have come out of it with the clear knowledge that I was not the miraculously endowed painter of women that I, in the first place, and the Royal Academy, in the second, thought I was? There certainly occurred an amazing transformation of values. For one thing, during those years, in tedious intervals of inaction, I returned to the open-air joy of my boyhood's daubing; to setting down on canvas the actualities of ghastly beauty or, for spirit-soothing contrast, the loveliness of untouched wood and stream. The facile portraiture of dainty women seemed an idle thing. I became conscious of an insincerity in my art; and insincerity in art is the living death. I had the knack—and I have it still—of the photographic likeness. I had the colour-sense, the costume sense, that women love. I established a bravura, sweeping, rapid *genre* of my own, as effective as you please; but it was shallow, a trick as certain to come off as that of a con-juror; as easy as lying. It had not the stern and patient paint by which alone the Great Ones expressed their im-mortal meaning. . . .

Out of evil cometh good. *Ex tenebris lux.* And this is the light that has come on me out of the darkness, shining on my nakedness which I seek to clothe in humility. And this is why I fear I shall never be the Perfect Egoist whose standard is always inside himself. My confounded standard will persist in being outside. Instead of damning Velasquez for an antiquated pedant, as your born Egoist would do, I would give my soul to be able to paint a square inch of his wonder.

Instead of entertaining myself with my reactions on other people, I am exasperatingly conscious of their reactions on me.

I should be so happy on my cliff in the sunshine if people would only leave me alone. I am quite a sociable man; but I want to be sociable in my own times and seasons. I'm no misanthrope. I love my fellow-creatures. But I like to love them in my own way. They expect me to love them in theirs: which is unreasonable. At every turn I find some block in my egoistic path.

Last year I grew a pointed Vandyke beard—auburn just streaked with the faint grey of the early forties. I thought I looked distinguished. Wavy hair which I let grow longer than usual; dark blue eyes; not bad, regular features—I was rather pleased with myself. Like this, said I, I can paint in the Vandyke manner. Then arrives Dorothea. I meet her at the station. She gasps. Holds herself aloof from my step-paternal kiss.

"For God's sake, Daddums, take it off, and cut your hair. You look like a Chelsea Horror in the Café Royal."

I murmured something about the slavery of shaving.

"If that's all there is to it," she said in the lamentable modern vernacular, "I'll shave you myself. But off it comes."

I shuddered and obeyed and resumed the military cut and the clipped moustache of my war service, which I suppose will be the hirsute scheme of my visage till the day of my death.

How can one be the Perfect Egoist with such people around one?

I have said that I paint a few portraits a year. My reputation is so far sustained that I can count on commissions from our visitors in Cannes, and from the generality in September and the beginning of October, when I rent a casual studio in London. But, whereas once I could rattle them off with gay insouciance, like the lightning fellow who tears off strip after strip of portraits at a Palace of Varieties, now it is a matter of considerable agony of soul. I can't flatter the confounded women. They must look just as my awakened conscience dictates. And they must sit long and often so that I can work in the stern honest paint. Two or three blazing idiots of critics have deplored my change of style. The masterly touch of the two, three brush strokes and hey presto! the thing was done—had vanished. I had sunk into conventionality. Triple idiots! There's only one convention of which I have been guilty and that is the eternal convention of every conceivable form of Art: Sincerity; and the toil and anguish that it means.

Oh! I suppose I'm a perfect damfool of an Egoist. But all the same, why can't they leave me alone?

And yet, when one is left alone, and desires to pursue the most egoistic of motives, the poor human creature is unaware that he is not only looking for trouble, as the phrase goes, but craving it, insisting on it, not being happy until he gets it.

Thus in my roundabout way, I am arriving at the beginning of my story.

There's not a portrait painter alive who does not

occasionally paint for love, without question of money. A face, a personality gets hold of you, haunts you. You must make the spiritual translation of it on canvas, or you will have missed a masterpiece. You have the desire, comparable with nothing save the blind sexual impulse of procreation, to create. You see your subject, man, woman, child—sex is indifferent, my reference merely analogical—and out of it you must make your vehement creation.

The little Princess Ramiroff—Nadia—has crossed my path, in the most conventional of social ways. She has pale golden hair, fascinating features with a touch of the Kalmuck type, and blue, green hazel, grey—no, mainly green—eyes in which vibrate from second to second all the sorrows and despairs and all the joys and mischiefs of the world.

"Will you sit to me, Princess?"

"What an honour!"

"What a privilege!"

And that is how Nadia comes into the story.

CHAPTER II

BEHOLD me painting her.

There are two or three things which she can't understand. First, why it is that I don't pitch my easel in the great drawing-room, with its open south-west view of nothing but sea and sky and the long purple Esterel melting into the blue. There, says she, she can drink in beauty; with beauty would her soul be filled, and her face would be the register of the gladness thereof. I have to explain to her, in simple terms, such things as diffused light, tones and values, and why it is that the cold purity of my north-east studio, without any distracting view at all, is the only light in which to paint the human face. I don't think she quite believes me. It is either too much trouble to transfer my clutter to the drawing-room, or I'm a disagreeable person who dislikes the sun. So she wears a little mocking smile on her face—the most adorable thing she can do, from my point of view, although she knows it not—and yawns and wonders, out aloud, why on earth she ever consented to undergo so uninteresting an ordeal. She can't even see what I am doing. I put a swing pier-glass behind me, so that she can view both herself and the canvas. She is horrified. Nothing resembling her can ever proceed from that chaos of smudges and smears—the stern honest paint foundation on which I will live and die. Whereupon I shift the mirror so that she may find delectation only in her own mutinous reflection.

Another matter to her incomprehensible is my tyrannous choice of costume. She was all for sitting to me in an evening confection of greens and coppers and bronzes in which, under electric light and against the background of rioting colour provided by other women, she looked a magnificent little person; but in the cold glare of the studio a green, copper and bronze confection and nothing else.

"How," I ask, "am I to get the gold of your hair and the green of your eyes and the pinks and coppers of your cheeks, as delicate as the bloom of a peach, if I have to hide them all with this barbaric tawdriness? I'm painting the Princess Nadia, not a fashion-plate to advertise Monsieur Poireneux—no peace to his soul!"

"I will wear, then, my mauve dress."

"Which sucks the colour out of you. You will wear the black dress I saw you in last week."

We argue. She calls me horrid names. But I prevail.

"I will wear my pearls."

Her pearls are historic. Poor dear, she lives on them, selling one at a time, so that the famous necklace is shrinking fatalistically like the *peau de chagrin* of Balzac's story.

"If you think, Princess, I'm going to waste my precious time——"

"Precious time—bah! You amuse yourself all day long."

"If you think I'm going to waste the precious time"; I say sternly, "which I can devote to my own amusement, in the niggling and most laborious occupation of painting pearls, each one having its individual iridescence, you're very much mistaken. Besides they're of no pictorial value. And," in answer to a grimace, "your skin properly painted would make every pearl in the world look trumpery."

"Flatteur, va! You only want to save yourself trouble."

We both were right. We laughed. We are the best friends in the world.

"What you can wear is that wonderful chunk of jade brooch of yours, in your corsage."

She came meekly on the day of the first sitting with the costume in a suit-case. When she appeared in the studio, I took her to the pier-glass.

"Look at yourself."

"Poor little ghost," she said dismally.

I don't care what she thinks. It is I who am painting her. She is exquisite. I wish I could paint her in words. You see the sheer pale gold of her hair—a bit rebellious owing to its fineness of texture; the light bronze of her eyebrows overhanging great eyes which according to light and mood wavered exasperatingly between hazel and green; the complexion, now of a pure blonde, now of peach sun-warmed; the delicate high cheek-boned, some-what broad contour of face; the humorous full-lipped young mouth; the dainty chin; and her small head set on a dainty neck, which flows into free curves of shoulder and bosom; to use the word again, a dainty creature, ancestrally hybrid of the Frisian hordes and the Tartar tribes that have made the Russian of the last few hundred years. Yet she is no wisp of a fairy, golden-haired thing. Although slightly built, she has an admirable solidity. The flesh proclaims itself in terms in which the modest and the generous are at courteous pains to yield each other precedence. . . .

Beautiful? I don't know. There is a puggishness about her rebellious nose which would disqualify her in a competition of Classical Beauty. And yet, this infernal little nose with its tip, cocked up in the air, destroying the perfection of her gracious modelling, makes for her fascination in a painter's eyes. . . . This, and the baffling combination of olive and peach and mother-of-pearl of her skin; and the alternating shafts of gaiety and shadows of sorrow which, passing across her face, are but indexes of the wavering fortunes of some strange warfare in her soul.

Who is she? A widow. Heroine of a Russian tragedy that has come to be regarded as conventional. Married young, a child, during the war, she managed to escape like so many other women, with her jewels, from the land where her husband was murdered and his property confiscated. Last year she took permanent refuge with her aunt, her mother's sister, who married in the beautiful long-ago an Italian councillor of Embassy at the Court of St. Petersburg, the Marchese della Fontana. They have a villa in Cannes on the Croix de Garde. He is a crumpled little old man; she, the Marchesa, a horse-marine of a woman. It's a dull and fusty villa, save late at night, when there are all kinds of goings on, and Nadia has the air of a flower growing among lichen. Nadia, I must tell you, is in the early twenties, about the same age as my step-daughter, Dorothea.

But to return to the portrait, the only thing with which I am concerned; for, otherwise than artistically, what concern have I with attractive young women?

She has grown used to the mirrored reflection of herself in her black dress with the huge Chinese monster carved in exquisitely coloured jade in her corsage. It is the repeat of her eyes. There she is, all golds and greens and nacre, with the black to set it off.

"What do you think?" I ask her.

"*Pas mal——*" but she is obviously pleased with herself.

"You'll admit that a mere man can sometimes be right."

"I don't admit it at all. No man's ever right. It's the artist, not the man that I yield to."

Once she asked: "What are you going to do with it when it's finished?"

"I'll exhibit it this year at the Royal Academy in London. After that I will lay it humbly at your feet."

She expressed her thanks prettily enough; but behind them were signs of dismay. What was she, a poor little wayfarer living in an Innovation trunk to do with a three foot by four oil painting of herself?

"You can hang it up in the Villa Miranda."

Her eyes narrowed, as she looked at me.

"Your pictures are worth a lot of money?"

I made the appropriate gesture conveying a modest sense of my market value. She nodded her head in appreciation.

"When I travel I take my property with me. I don't leave it at the Villa Miranda."

"You mean the Marchese——?"

"I mean," she said, "that you will put your picture wherever you like in your home and give me permission to come and look at it whenever I like."

"Princess," said I, "this house and all that is in it is yours."

With an ironical grimace she quoted the Spanish formula: *"A la disposition de Usted."*

"If you don't take care," I laughed, "I'll put it at your disposal in a very blunt English fashion—and both of us will be infernally sorry."

"Oh! A declaration!" she flashed amusement.

"Anything you like, if you'll only keep still while I'm painting you."

"Oh," she said, "I'm just a subject and not an object."

"Madame la Princesse," said I, "is whatever Madame la Princesse pleases to be."

I rose and did the portrait painter's cat-crawl around the canvas, scanning it from all angles.

"The frivolous woman is snubbed," she remarked.

"Utterly and hopelessly," said I.

I sat down again. The impudence of her nose would not come right. One stroke revealed it as a deformity; another as a classical feature which robbed the portrait of likeness. I rubbed the nose out altogether, trusting to a future illumination, and putting on my heaviest frown worked on the gold of her hair. She was impressed, thinking, like most sitters, that I was intent on some fleeting expression of eyes or mouth, and sat stock-still. When the sitting was over, she came round to review progress. In her eyes there was none. There was retrogression, owing to the smudged-out nose.

"And it is for this that I've been wasting this beautiful morning of sunshine when I might have been walking with my dog on the Croisette. *Viens*, Chouchou, and see what thing Monsieur has done with your mother."

Chouchou, a cynical orange Pekinese, who had been asleep on a far-off cushion, sat up at this appeal, yawned and cocked his little lion head to one side. She snapped her fingers.

"Viens!"

But he wouldn't. The celestial dog of China suffers no mortal dictation as to his comings or goings. All he did was to wave a serene squirrel tail over his back. She addressed him in French.

"Viens, I say. Was it for this that I took you out of Russia from the Bolsheviks who would have killed and eaten you?"

He cocked his head again, at a different angle, as one who held in derision all the Lenins and Trotskys of the universe. Set in the midst of his tawniness, just below the ironical black eyes, gleamed his black, little Mongol nose. . . . Talk about the eagle beak of the Duke of Wellington, the fantastic appendage of Cyrano de Bergerac, the exquisitely haughty line of Cleopatra's organ —no nose on earth could so express the don't-care-a-damnativeness of disdain as that of Chouchou.

"My dear Princess," said I, with a sudden inspiration of which she could not guess the source, "take Chouchou on your lap and sit for another ten minutes. I may be able," I added, barefacedly mendacious, "to paint him in."

Delighted, she swept the adorable bit of superciliousness from his cushion, and, returning to her chair, posed again. And I worked once more on her little disdainful Mongol nose.

She sat, sweetly contented, thinking that I was painting in Chouchou, against the black of her corsage. Poor dear, how should she know that the painting of dogs is a specialist's gift? While she held him against her bosom in what she thought to be his most fascinating attitude, I was intent on her nose.

Time passed.

There entered, canary vested and black sleeved, my valet de chambre, François.

It was one o'clock, and Amélie (my cook—and his wife) wanted to know whether she should serve the déjeuner for Monsieur that was commanded for half-past twelve.

One o'clock? The Princess Nadia rose in dismay, clutching an indignant Chouchou, who barked his gastronomic appreciation of the flight of time.

"My aunt also lunches at half-past twelve.   Why didn't
you tell me?"

I made apologies and offered a seat at my frugal table.
At least there was sunshine in the wine I could set before
her, and nothing but view of blue sea and sky from the
dining-room window.   Being hungry, she accepted.   Being a woman, and as such, curious as to the details of a
lone man's establishment, she would have accepted in any
case.   We lunched charmingly.   To the lone man's table
she lent an all too rare graciousness.   Free from the
austerity of the studio and the consciousness of strange
processes of creation, she expanded into gaiety, rattled
off piquant paragraphs of the social chronicle of the
villadom and casinodom of Cannes, and ate and drank
with the youthful gusto so pleasing to an elderly host.
During the meal I confessed abandonment of my project
of painting Chouchou.

"It was only to keep me quiet?"

"That was all."

Hence followed naturally an argument on the cynical
guile of man and the more subtle wiles of woman.   In the
former, it appeared, there was always a certain brutality,
an April Fool coarseness.   For instance, the recent dup-
ing of herself and dog.

"Bark at the horrid man," she commanded.

The Pekinese, on the chair by her side, upturned a cold,
glazed eye.   Having lunched delicately and fully, he had
no further concern with the superficial whims of mankind.   We laughed, in light mood.   François served
coffee and liqueurs.   Nadia lit a cigarette.

I shall always associate Nadia's delicate lighting of the
cigarette with the Troublesome Event.

It was at that moment that I heard an impatient voice
and something like a scuffle outside, followed by the

throwing open of the door and the appearance of a gigantic young man behind whom François flashed gesticulating.   The gigantic young man wore a bowler hat, which even in that instant of amazement I noted was too small for his head, and gripped in his hand the most ancient extant of Gladstone bags.   Simultaneous with his incursion, I rose with a——

"What the devil——?"

He cut me short.   "You're Uncle David, ain't you? That feller was wantin' to take away my bag.   I ain't going to give it up until I'm sure."

He grinned—a wide, disarming grin.   Apparently he had not lost his temper with François.   He was merely asserting his right of entry, in the most good-humoured way in the world.   In a dazed way my mind went back to a similar type in the waiting-room of a little Texas station, years ago, who had lounged up to me with the same fatuous grin and asked me for the funny page of the Sunday paper I was reading.   The Texan's billycock hat was too small for him.   Like the Texan's, my visitor's clothes were shrunken and sun-stained, his linen frayed, his uncouth hands glazed over freckles.   I frowned.   But he stood there with his grin, transparent honesty.

"My good fellow," said I, "you're making a mistake. You've come to the wrong house."

He looked around, as though to identify it, and shook his head.

"If I have, Mister, I'm sorry.   I thought you were my uncle, David Fontenay."

"I'm Mr. Fontenay," said I; "but who the deuce are you?"

"I'm Amos Burden," said he, "and my mother's dead and I've just come from Australia."

"Good Lord," said I; and, in order to gather my wits

together, went on: "Take off your bag—I mean your hat
—and sit down."

My mind, cranked up, began to whirr. This must be a
son of my sister Dorcas who ran away with the itinerant
preacher. A vague memory, a casual line in a letter a
quarter of a century old crossed my brain; a letter from
Muriel to me in Paris: "Dorcas seems happy in her
extraordinary way. She writes me that she has a baby."
From that day to this I had heard no more about the
baby. I had forgotten there ever was a baby. Dorcas
had become a dim abstraction, apart from the actualities
of my existence. Now, apparently, poor woman, she was
dead and this was her son, possibly the baby brought, for
one fleeting instant, within my horizon.

During the swift period of my wit-gathering he had
deposited his bag on the floor, himself on a chair tugged,
with some noise, from the wall, and his bowler hat on the
luncheon table. Nadia, still in her black evening dress—
she had been too hungry to change—leaned back in her
chair, watching him amusedly through the clouds of her
cigarette smoke. Before I could speak again, I saw him
catch her eye and gape at her. No doubt she was something for an Antipodean to gape at—considering the hour,
two o'clock in the afternoon. I had never before realized
the imperative conventions of times and seasons. In the
studio she was but a model; in the evening she was a
perfectly costumed woman of the world. In the golden
light of this January afternoon, she seemed to be entirely
nude save for the wisp of black chiffon scarcely veiling
her bosom.

The young man, as I say, gaped at her open-mouthed,
then turned to me with staring blue eyes and grinned.
He stretched out a long pointing arm.

"That my aunt?"

She flushed to the roots of her pale gold hair; less, I fancy, from outraged modesty than from suppression of hilarious emotion. I recovered swiftly.

"Madame," said I, in what I hold to be my grand manner, "is the Princess Ramiroff. Princess, may I present Mr. Amos Burden."

He did not rise from his chair which he had brought near the table, but just stared at her, as though flabbergasted by the title. She leaned forward with extended hand, every kind of enchanting malice in her eyes. Suddenly he gripped it in his huge paw.

"How d'ye do, mum."

He held on to her until I saw her wince. Meanwhile, in his brain, a worrying thought found expression.

"I beg your pardon, but I suppose I ought to have said Your Royal Highness."

She smiled sweetly, as she strove to withdraw her crushed fingers.

"I'll tell you exactly what to call me when your uncle allows us to be better acquainted."

This gave me an opening.

"In the first instance, young man, you've got to give me some proof that I am your uncle."

He released the hand of Nadia and regarded me more in indulgence than in indignation.

"You're Mister David Fontenay, ain't you?"

"Yes," said I.

"And you had a sister, Miss Dorcas Fontenay, what married my father, Mister Ezra Burden? And her father was the Reverend Edward Fontenay what lived in Great Shepperton, Somersetshire?"

"That's him," said I.

"Then you are my uncle," said he amiably, "and what's the good of saying anything more about it?"

"What indeed?" cried Nadia, with one of her crystal laughs. "You have the most delightful uncle in the world. I only wish I had one like him."

"I wish he'd give me something to eat," said Amos. "I've had nothing since seven o'clock this morning."

I rang the bell, ordered François to provide food for monsieur, also to remove monsieur's bowler hat from the table. Nadia took the opportunity of asking him to send her maid up to the dressing-room. Amos eyed him suspiciously as he disappeared with his property.

"I got a letter," said he, routing one out from a greasy note-case. "Mother wrote it just before she died. Said I was to give it to you."

I exchanged a glance of permission with Nadia and opened the letter. It was of considerable length—but it was from my sister Dorcas. Politeness forbade my reading it at that moment, so I put it in my pocket. At any rate, there seemed no reason to doubt that this gigantic young savage was my nephew.

"When did your poor mother die?" I asked in a more conciliatory tone.

"Five months ago."

"Dear, dear," said I. "I'm very sorry. But"—after a perplexed pause—"how did you manage to find out my address?"

"Aunt Muriel. I wrote to her, you know, as soon as it happened."

"But how did you know I was here?"

"Folks are generally supposed to be where they live, ain't they?"

"I mean, I might have been in England."

"Well, you ain't," said he.

The Princess laughed, extinguished the stub of her

cigarette on the ash-tray and rose.   Naturally I rose too.
Amos remained seated.

"The Princess is going."

"Oh," said he.

She smiled on him graciously.   "No, don't get up.
You must be tired after your long journey from Australia."   And she disappeared through the door which I
held open for her.

I followed her into the hall and regarded her with the
wrinkled brow that denotes a craving for sympathy.

"It's rather alarming, isn't it?" said I.

"Enchanting!" she cried.   "When will you let me
come round and play with it?"

"Never," said I.

She tossed her head and gave me her hand to kiss and
tripped upstairs to find the maid who should array her
in the decent garments of the afternoon.

"Young man," I said, on entering the dining-room,
"it seems to me you have a good many things to learn."

"Mother said I was to come over here and learn 'em,"
he replied amiably.

"The first thing is that you mustn't remain seated when
a lady gets up."

"Oh," said he.   "Yes.   I'll try to learn that."

"Would you care to have a wash up before lunch?"
I asked.

"What for?   I washed this morning."

Then it was I who said: "Oh!"

François appeared with the beginnings of the meal.

"What will Monsieur drink?"

"Tea," said he.

"No wine, whisky and soda . . . ?" I asked.

"Never touched the wicked stuff in my life."

I let the adjective pass.   Our acquaintance was far too

young for me to begin a temperance argument. He plunged with voracity into his food and engulfed two eggs *sur le plat* and a roll almost before I knew they were there. Then he attacked a great dish of ham and beef and galantine.

And, while he ate, I smoked a reflective cigar and watched him.

He was not ill-looking in his lumbering way. His features, heavy and coarse, were redeemed by blue eyes of a childlike innocence behind which gleamed the possibility of a shrewd intelligence. His hair was black and bristly and stood up straight on his head and came down to a peak on his forehead. Like his hands, his face was glazed by the sun over the freckles of a lifetime, so that it was impossible to determine his original complexion. He had great breadth and depth of shoulders, and beyond his shrunken sleeves protruded thick hairy wrists.

Either he was too ravenous for speech, or it was not his habit to talk while eating. It was only when François brought the tea—the finest China, which I and those of my friends who really love me smuggle from England—and he sipped it, that he spoke.

"What's this stuff?"

"Tea."

His features expressed disapproval. "Don't you know how to make tea in this country?"

I remembered youthful reading of wild life in the bush.

"I'm afraid we haven't got a billy."

"Thought not.   And it hasn't drawn."

"I think I understand," I said. He craved black Ceylon, syruppy, potent, boiled in a pot and left to stand for several hours. He should have his abomination; he who had the impudence to call my wine wicked stuff.

"To-morrow, I'll give you what I think you'll relish."

He raised his eyebrows and grinned innocently.

"Ain't I going to have supper?"

"Do you drink tea at supper too?"

"Why yes."

To anticipate a few hours' history, I may say that I gave him, at dinner, his throat's desire. The brew would have killed the most hardened Mothers' Meeting in an English parish. He smacked his lips and pronounced it good. His inside must be as muscular as his biceps.

He ate, as I said, vastly of the cold viands. I noticed that he spat out the first mouthful of potato salad, the unfamiliar oil not suiting his palate; and when he came to a newly cut wedge of Gruyère cheese, fresh, with the little dewdrops in the holes, I thought he might reject this also. But he liked it, cut off chunk after chunk which he conveyed to his mouth with his fingers, until he had devoured the whole. François, judge of time, like the excellent servitor that he is, coming in with the coffee, blinked drunkenly at the empty space where he had left a demi-kilo of Gruyère. But, well-trained, he recovered his nerve.

"*Monsieur, desire-t-il du café?*"

Amos looked at me, jerked an interrogatory thumb at the dainty cup—I have a choice Sèvres service——

"Coffee," said I. "I hope you'll find it stronger than the tea."

"My sakes," said he, with a laugh. "Do you folks call this coffee?"

He tossed it down. His throat must have been of triple brass; for Amélie would sooner die than serve coffee imperfect in temperature. He grinned again.

"That gets a feller," he admitted. "But I'd like some more. In a big cup. Big." He looked up at François,

and with his hands indicated a vessel about the size of a
bowl of gold-fish.

François questioned me mutely. I said to him in
French:

"One of the *bols* that you and Amélie use for your *café
au lait* in the morning."

François retired bearing with him the impression that
the world had gone mad. I learned afterwards that he
put it down to the war.

My nephew, Amos, leaned back in his chair, with a sigh
of content.

"I hope you've enjoyed your lunch," said I.

"Thank you, Uncle David," he replied. "I've had a
square meal."

I pushed the box of cigarettes towards him and opened
my cigar case.

"No, I'll smoke my pipe."

He pulled out pipe and pouch and soon the azure coast
reeked with obscenity of odour. It was a gorgeous day
and the big south-eastern French window was wide open.
I rose and threw wide the western casement through
which came the freshening breath of the Mistral. Then
carefully selecting a chair out of the draught—I beg you
to remember my cultivation of the Perfect Egoism—I
addressed him blandly.

"My dear fellow. An hour or so ago, I was practically
ignorant of your existence. Will you kindly tell me why
you are here and what I can do for you?"

I could not be expected to clasp my newly found
nephew to my bosom; there is nothing inherent in mere
nephewdom to rake frantic emotional chords; and this
particular nephew who, by putting his horrid hat on my
lunch table and spitting out on his plate an unpalatable
potato and spurning my exquisite Ceylon tea—to say

nothing of his behaviour to ladies, his ungrammatical speech, his nerve-shattering accent, a blend of White-chapel, the slums of Greenock, the New York Bowery and the Larrikin quarter of Sydney—betrayed an unimaginable ignorance of social usages, was not one to stir one's soul with the trumpet call of family pride. He had fallen, I confess, into my neatly ordained life, like a hulking disaster. I looked on him with the blackest and most sardonic disfavour.

But my outward urbanity I am sure you must admit.

CHAPTER III

I OUGHT to have known that he was coming. I was warned by my sister Muriel—the one who married my good friend, the present Bishop of Bradbury. On receipt of the news of Dorcas's death—the sisters had been in vague correspondential touch, a letter every five years or so—Muriel had written to me. But alas, in my pursuit of the Perfect Egoism, I have never been able to nerve myself to the self-sacrificing effort of transliterating Muriel's letters. I have told you how Muriel, the intellectual, first found common ground with her husband in the Treatise on Vestments. She was also an authority on Missals. In her early days she seemed to be a posthumous child of the Gothic Revival. She out-Pugined Pugin, who was in his grave long before she was born, in her enthusiasm for the recreating of dead and gone Gothic things. All this was very harmless. Her excellent husband knocked, so to speak, the crockets and the gargoyles off her, and she became a model wife and mother. But one thing he could never cure—the handwriting which she invented for herself in those Gothic days. Her manuscript was beautiful; it was clerkly; it resembled the twelfth-century parchments, deeds of land, Acts of Parliament and what-not, which you can consult in the Record Office. If you learned the cursive characters, all well and good; if you didn't, her communications remained an enigma. Now, even though I had acquired this esoteric knowledge, I seldom tried to decipher her epistles. The fact of her writing in a strong bold hand assured me of her health. When I needed any special information, I wrote to Tom the Bishop, who gave it to

me by return of post in a dictated typed reply as clear as
his own mind.

Muriel did announce the coming of Amos. I turned
up her letter later, and there, lying in wait for me all the
time, was the undeciphered news she had received from
Australia. I tried to explain this to Amos; but all I
could get out of him was:

"Fancy folks getting letters and not bothering to read
them!"

"My boy," said I, while he was smoking his awful pipe
and drinking his French peasant's breakfast bowl of
black coffee, "I've met many hundreds of Australians
in my life, but I've never come across one quite like
you. For goodness' sake tell me something about
yourself."

I was justified in my adjuration. The Australian of
good family—and the Fontenays are of as good blood as
any in England—has breeding and education. He talks
the King's English. Even the roystering privates whom
I had come across during the war showed signs of supe-
rior sophistication. My nephew Amos was a puzzle.

"Hadn't you better read mother's letter first?" said he.

It appeared to be the only human, polite and common-
sense thing to do. I took the letter from my pocket.
Childish memories were revived by the clear spiky un-
compromising handwriting. It was all the clearer, as she
had evidently taken the pains of a person who has grown
unfamiliar with the handling of a pen.

"Do you know what's in it?" I asked.

"No. Mother was never much of a talker."

I spread it out and read:

"Dear Brother David——"

The invocation gave me a curious sense of remoteness.

"Dear David"; yes. Even "My dear Brother," but "Brother David"! I did not know myself.

It went on:

"I have not written to you before, because you were a child when I left home, and your heart was unawakened to the Grace of our Lord Jesus Christ. What you are like now I don't know, but I hope and pray earnestly that you have found Salvation as I have done and the certainty of eternal communion with God. My dear husband found Peace many years ago, and as he has no relatives living, and as I am going to join him very soon, you are the only man of the family alive to whom I can write concerning my only son, Amos. The doctor who came to see me yesterday, after a long and weary journey up country, told me I was suffering from pernicious anæmia and prescribed treatment and remedies that I cannot get in this wild and lonesome place. So my days are numbered. I am ready, after a long and toil-worn life, to look into the face of my Saviour, the Lord Jesus Christ.

"I cannot but think that our dear father's son, whatever errors of dogma he may have been trained in, is a good Christian man, and it is in this belief that I commend to him my only son whom I have done my best to keep unspotted from the world.

"I find it difficult to express myself, having lived apart for so many years, from what, in our worldly days, we used to call civilisation. The words come slowly, and I am very weak and tired and longing for the Eternal Rest in the arms of our blessed Lord. What I want to say is this:

"Last night, after I guessed my sentence from the doctor's lips, I lay awake all night thinking of my boy, Amos, and probing my conscience to learn whether I had done my duty by him or not. A Voice came to me saying that I had not. That in keeping him by me in the wilderness, under the pretence of sheltering him from the temptation and sin of the world, I had been acting from selfish motives. I had trained him, since his beloved father's death, in the Fear of the Lord; but, owing to the incessant toil which has been our daily lot since we came into possession of our first piece of land, he has received no other education. And so my conscience tells me that I have sinned by failing in my duty towards my son, and my repentance now assures me of God's divine forgiveness.

"Amos is twenty-five years old. He has never left Warraranga; he has never seen a town, not even the poor little township of Jacksonville to which one of our hands went to fetch the doctor. The Voice tells me that it is not right that he should remain here all his life without subjecting himself to the discipline of the world. For possibly, when I have passed away, and my influence fades, he may be tempted by the rough men who work for us to seek the excitement and the pleasure of the towns. I would far sooner send him, after my death, into the great world of Europe, under sure guidance, and yours, dear brother David, is the only guidance that I know.

"If he was poor in the world's goods, my pride would not allow me to ask such a favour, but thanks to the Everlasting Mercy, we have prospered exceedingly. I own many square miles of arable land and pasture, and heads of cattle and sheep in quantities unknown to you in England. I have drudged my life out for my dear son and put away money almost unthinkingly into the bank. At this time of writing he has no notion that he is a wealthy man. Bit by bit I have saved. Besides the land and stock and crops managed now, under Amos and myself, by Joseph Judge, a close friend of my husband and a devout Christian, there is something like fifty thousand pounds lying at compound interest in the Commonwealth Bank of Australia."

At this point I gasped and glanced at the uncouth inheritor of wealth, who, elbows on table, regarded me with the blue eyes of bland innocence, smoking his filthy pipe.

I read on:

"As I have made my will, being a woman of business, leaving him residuary legatee, after a provision (a quarter share in the estate) for Joseph Judge, and a few bequests, Amos will be a rich man, how rich he will not know until after my death. It is my earnest desire that he should learn to spend these riches in the true service of God, and unless he receives the education and the knowledge of the world, its snares and its dangers, which I have culpably neglected to give him, I do not see how he can be expected to do so. . . ."

Here a first portion of the letter ended. Under a date a couple of days later, she resumed:

"I have spoken to Amos and laid upon him my commands, which he faithfully promises to execute."

This sentence was written in the old spiky hand, with innumerable quivers, betokening the vehement will of the dying woman. But what followed dwindled gradually into illegibility. She scribbled until her powers failed and the end was a meaningless scrawl. But what she wrote sufficed. He had promised to come to Europe for five years, to seek me out, and place himself under my tutelage. After that there was nothing but the half decipherable incoherence of the Calvinistic Faith in which she had lived and died.

I put the letter back in my pocket.

"Your mother must have been a great woman," I said.

"I got her photograph. Like to see it?"

He produced his greasy letter-case and fished out a card.

"A feller come last year taking likenesses. Said he had a swell business in Jacksonville. I guess it's good."

Good! No doubt it was. But it shocked me through and through. What was I—fourteen?—when Dorcas ran away. I had my boyish memories of her—a tall, eager girl, fresh complexioned, an ordinary young lady, attired in the conventional taste of the period. I held in my hand the picture of a gaunt, worn, hollow-cheeked elderly drudge, in an amorphous print cotton gown. Her thinning hair was tied in a skinny knot behind. The hands, showing plainly against the skirt, were gnarled with toil. . . . Before my mind flashed the vision of my other sister, Muriel, when I had last seen her in the autumn—fresh and unlined, with plump arms and shoulders emerging (just within the limits of decorum set for wives of modern bishops) from a pink chiffon bodice; and round her neck were great fat pearls. But Dorcas! So have I seen faded and broken portraits of miners' mothers which wounded soldiers showed me during the war. How could sister of mine and Muriel have reached this stage of social—what other word can there be?—of social deterioration? I looked again at the grim face. It was that of Dorcas right enough; with her long determined chin and her steady eyes that could glow and harden at once.

"Yes," I said gently, handing the photograph back to Amos. "She was a remarkable woman!"

"She could do anything from holding prayer meetings to shearing a sheep or building a shack. None of the men could touch her."

"And your father?" I asked.

Father, it appeared, had been all for religion. He had gone out with the intention of taking the Gospel to the Bushmen of the interior. But when he reached the Never Never Land he found that all the blacks with whom he came in contact were already converted, while those few remaining unconverted were inaccessible. My sister Dorcas must have loved the scrubby, fiery little man with a great passion, to have acquiesced in this ignorant absurdity. Labouring in the vineyard of the Lord, he called it; which meant working with their hands for sustenance, for they took little with them, while they preached their fervent doctrine to all who would give them a hearing. As far back as Amos could remember, it had been Mother who had held command. It was she who had schemed, planned and directed. Although he spoke of Father with filial awe, as of a great and holy man, I suspect the late Mr. Burden of lamentable incompetence in worldly affairs. It was Mother who gradually bought the sheep and the cattle and the land, who paid the hired hands, who designed the new rude buildings, who sold the wool and the corn, at the same time as she cooked the dinner and scrubbed the floor and made and mended for husband and son. Not that this man Burden was idle. He must have slaved hard. But he had no thought of piling up riches in this world; to earn his

bread by the sweat of his brow was the divine ordinance;
having earned his crust, both his conscience and his
worldly desires were satisfied.

"But he was a one-er to preach," said Amos enthusiastically—the slang word seemed an echo of long
past decades and lands infinitely remote. "If he couldn't
get nobody else to preach to he would preach to mother
and me. I wish you could have heard him, Uncle."

I replied gravely that I should have been much edified.

"You would," said he.

Reading between the lines of Amos's artless narrative,
I surmised the tragedy of the vehement, ineffectual little
man; a born preacher, driven by the spirit to one of the
waste places of the earth where there was no one to
preach to. He had died ten years ago—"of the fever,"
according to Amos, possibly worn out by the thwarting
of his passion.

It was Mother who had taught the boy to read and
write and cipher. How did she find time for it? Amos
guessed she could find time for most things. Beyond
that he had had no schooling. From his early childhood
he had taken his part in the daily drudgery. He had no
other conception of life.

I got all this out of him gradually by discreet questioning, for he was far from loquacious. Description was
beyond his powers. To this day I have the vaguest picture in my mind of the wealth-producing wilderness
which he had left. I had nothing to go upon but the
portrait of Dorcas, his hands, his speech, his manners.
Dorcas's letter was explanatory but not descriptive. . . .

The red winter sun was sinking behind the Esterel in
a pomp of royal purple, when I raised the sitting and
conducted him to his room. He looked round the pleas-

ant red-tiled chamber, its asperities softened by a Persian rug or two and, with a grin, admitted that I had snug quarters.

"I daresay you'd like to rest or go out for a stroll," said I. "Anyhow, dinner's at half-past seven." And I added unreflectingly: "You can dress or not, just as you like. I generally do."

He regarded me in a puzzled way.

"Dress?"

"Yes," said I, "evening dress."

"You mean change my clothes?"

"Of course," said I.

I showed him the bathroom and fled.

He turned up for dinner in riding-kit, old and worn. I had told him to change, and he had changed into the only other costume he possessed. I am perfectly aware that clothes are but externals; but after all they connote a more subtle philosophical significance of life than was dreamed of even by Carlyle. Entering the drawing-room punctually at half-past seven, Amos stared me up and down in my dinner-suit.

"Well, I'm blessed!"

"Why?"

"Are you going to give a party?"

"No," said I.

He wrinkled an uncomprehending brow.

"Do you stick on those things every night?"

It was far from my heart to hurt his feelings. He had floundered into the room like a confident, ungainly dog. So I said, with what I believe was a kindly smile:

"You must have seen practically everybody like this on your voyage home."

He shook his head. "Not a one," said he.

"What line did you come by?"

He mentioned the line, gave me the name of a famous ship. I was more puzzled than ever.

"Do you mean to tell me that no one on board dressed for dinner?"

Obviously he didn't know what I was talking about. An idea struck me.

"You came first class, of course."

"First class?—Na-ow!" His features grimaced a humorous scorn of the suggestion.

"Second, then?"

"Na-ow. Why waste money in foolishness?"

He had come steerage! He, with fifty thousand pounds, not invested, but in drawable, tangible paper equivalents of fifty thousand golden sovereigns, lying to his credit at the Commonwealth Bank of Australia. Just think of it! Fifty thousand liquid pounds!

I had learned from François, in the meanwhile, that the ancient Gladstone bag constituted his sole luggage and that he had trudged with it from the station, up the hill. I learned too that he had found his way to the villa by showing all and sundry a dirty piece of paper and following the direction of pointing fingers, for of French he knew no word.

At dinner, which he called supper, being convinced that he had dined at two o'clock, he ate with heartiness of appetite, but with suspicion of new-fangled food. As I have said, he thoroughly enjoyed the decoction—it was more than an infusion—of black Ceylon tea. His table manners were of the most primitive. He used his fingers largely in place of a fork, and wiped them on his clothes instead of the napkin, as to the use of which he seemed to be at a loss. Every minute, in order to understand this nephew of mine, I had to recall the photograph of my grim eldest sister in her print cotton dress, who had cut herself adrift from the gentle life whereof napkins were a symbol. Finger-bowls beat him altogether. At the sight of them he muttered queer religious euphemisms of oaths. As an object lesson I hastily dipped my fingers in; he was evidently struck by the futility of the performance. I swear I caught in his eye the unspoken thought:

"If you want to have a wash, go into the washhouse and wash—but finnicking about with tips of fingers is too blamed silly for words."

During the meal conversation languished. My questions elicited monosyllabic replies and my observations no response whatever. As at lunch, he was silent. It struck me that among primitive races dining was not a social art, but the intense satisfaction of an appetite. It had been his life-long custom to come into the rude homestead at meal-times, with the hunger born of open-air toil, and to fling himself into his seat and attack the coarse food set before him, as the dog rushes to his platter, therein to be soul-absorbed. He sounded, however, a disturbing note, at the beginning of dinner, when the soup was set before him.

"Ain't you going to ask a Blessing, Uncle?"

I had a second's bewilderment. I had travelled far from the childhood days when, in my parson father's household, we put our hands together and asked to be grateful for what we were about to receive. In my worldling's world the suggestion was pathetically, accusingly grotesque.

"It's the custom, on this side," said I, "for everyone to ask it silently." And with an air of profound meditation, I peppered my soup as though casting the incense of prayer.

"Let us get at things," I said, when he had recovered from the concentration on food, "what are your plans?"

"I ain't got any," said he, "Mother said you were to make 'em for me. She died rather sudden, as you know, so I didn't have much time for talk. But I promised to come to live with you for five years, Uncle David, and as Mother said, get my education."

There was no getting away from his transparent honesty. I'm afraid my lips curled in a humorous smile.

"That's your idea, is it—to come and live with me for five years?"

He wagged his big head.

"I promised Mother," he replied.

During my gasping, my cigar went out. Absent-mindedly I relit it from the little silver lamp. I made a wry face and crushed it down on the ash-tray. His shrewd eyes watched me. He said:

"Cigars ain't much good. They're a toss up. Why, I once paid fourpence for two cigars, and the second one I had to put down just like that. A pipe's much safer."

Perspiration beaded my forehead. What point of contact had I with the fellow? How could I tell him that, in my pursuit of the Perfect Egoism, I smoke only Corona Coronas imported direct from Havana, at fantastic cost? I could only acquiesce gravely with his proposition and light another. I must say in vindication of my hospitality, that I had offered him my cigar case, but that he had preferred his pipe.

"Thank heaven," I thought, opening the window to let the rankness curl over the unoffending Mediterranean, "as he can't have had the wit to smuggle, his supply, wherever he got it, will soon be exhausted."

I had to return, however, to the main theme of conversation.

"You reckon to be with me for five years?"

He nodded sagely. "It's a long time."

"A damned long time," said I.

I saw him wince. I asked ironically:

"Do you object to my saying 'damned'?"

"Mother wouldn't allow anyone in the house to say 'damn' or 'blast' or 'bloody.' "

"Why?"

"She said it was blasphemy."

"And how many were you in the house?" I asked, in pursuit of information.

"About fifty!"

"Fifty!"

My brain reeled for a moment in the process of assimilation of a new idea—I must leave this little narrow painting life of Europe and get some kind of conception of the primitive wilderness. I repeated:

"Fifty? In the house?"

He grinned wide.

"Why, of course. How do you think they would get food if Mother didn't cook for 'em?"

I didn't know. I vaguely suggested wives. Apparently wives at Warraranga were at a premium. The vast majority of shearers and cattle-riders had left their peculiar and individual specimens of the Eternal Feminine behind in some township where such things were to be had as beds and hairpins and frying-pans and other conditions of female existence. As far as I could gather, the vast sheep—or cattle—run of Warraranga was exploited by temporarily celibate labour, my late sister having no use for female encumbrances. The men came in droves from the township to work for a particular season. Dorcas fed them in a bare tin-roofed hut, furnished with rude trestle tables and benches. Sometimes there were

more than fifty, according to Amos. It all depended on
the season. They seemed to sleep under other tin-roofed
shelters. There, of course, they could do and talk as
they listed. But in the eating-shed—that is my own
conception of the dreadful place—Dorcas ruled absolute.
Did her quick ear, as she threaded her way through the
maze of eating men, catch a foul or blasphemous word,
she pounced on the offender and cast him out into the
wilderness that intervened between Warraranga and the
spot where he had his more or less permanent being.

Please bear with me if I give an entirely erroneous picture of Warraranga. Through my lack of enterprise the
wilds of Australia are unknown to me. For aught I
know they may be as sophisticated as Peckham Rye.
This is a story, not about Australia, but about myself.
My imagination can only record the impressions made
on it by Amos's peculiarly unpicturesque narrative.

Amos, however, I know.

He winced at my casual "damn."

His delicate-eared upbringing is no doubt very good
for his soul, but I'm afraid, if he does not get used to a
little light blasphemy, his path through the social world
will be painful.

The question of the five years still lurked at the back
of our talk. But he did not revert to it. Knocking out
the ashes of his pipe against the heel of his boot, he
declared himself to be sleepy and ready for bed. I asked
him at what hour he would care to breakfast.

"When do you generally have it? Half-past five—
six?"

I pictured myself facing him before dawn across a
breakfast-table laden with eggs and bacon and beefsteaks,
and shuddered.

"It's the custom in this country for people to breakfast

in their own rooms," I explained. "Also rather later than you do in Australia. Don't you think eight would be a good hour?"

"Crikey!" said he. "What do you do before then?"

"Sleep," said I.

He remarked that it was a funny country, and gripping my hand in his painful clasp, bade me good night and sought repose.

I wandered up to the studio, which is cosy at night, with a great log fire burning on the hearth. For a long time I sat there staring into the flames, the most embarrassed Egoist on earth. What in Heaven's name was I to do? If he had been a normal young Australian of decent upbringing, the problem would have been comparatively easy. But he wasn't. He had the habits and manner and speech of a coal-heaver. He was devoid of anything approaching education. Even the practical education in knowledge of strange cities and strange peoples provided by the war had been denied him; for his mother, holding war to be infinitely wicked, had retained him by her side. In the social—you may call it snobbish —sense of the word, he was impossible. And here was I holding my niche in the fashionable little world of Cannes. It was a grotesque and exasperating situation.

Of course I could repudiate all responsibility and send him about his business with good advice. The Perfect Egoist would have done so, to a certainty. But somehow I could not disregard the message of the dead woman in the print gown that was my sister. I read her letter over again, two or three times. . . . Also, if Amos were an uppish, contradictory, disagreeable beast I might salve my conscience with the argument that the task imposed on me was beyond human accomplishment. But good nature, simplicity, trustfulness, all the best doggy virtues just oozed out of him. I couldn't turn him out of doors into a friendless Europe. And yet, the problem remained: What the devil was I to do with him? Who could advise me? Impelled by the instinct of the helpless male, I ran over a list of level-headed women of my acquaintance in Cannes. And then the brilliant idea occurred to me. I would turn him over to Dorothea. She must leave her embroidered-bag shop and come out immediately and take charge.

I wrote to her there and then a letter that would have melted the heart of a far sterner vendor of embroidered bags than Dorothea—sealed it, stamped it and took it downstairs to the slab in the hall to be posted the first thing in the morning. After which, with the exhilarating feeling of a coward's duty done, I went smilingly to bed.

CHAPTER IV

I RANG up the Princess Nadia early in the morning to put off the sitting. She pouted audibly. Wasn't she really to be permitted to play with the bear? I replied that my studio, with which alone she was concerned, lay apart from whatever private menagerie I chose to keep. To-morrow, when she came, the bear would be chained up. On her dignity, she gave me to understand that I must not reckon on her sitting to-morrow or ever again, if I were so high-handed in my proceedings. As an ultimatum I briefly told her to attend to-morrow at half-past ten, and rang off. She must learn that painting is not a frivolous amusement.

I was not in the mood for work. In spite of the hopes I entertained of Dorothea, Amos weighed heavily on my mind. I found him sitting on the gravel in my little declivitous garden, reading the Continental *Daily Mail*. He had been up since dawn and, having raided the kitchen for eatables, had gone for a stroll, to stretch his legs. From his account I imagine he had strolled to the Cap d'Antibes and back. He had walked, he informed me, because, having searched the villa precincts, he couldn't find a horse. When I informed him that nobody rode in Cannes, his jaw fell in stupefaction. He ejaculated: "Golly, what a country!" I explained that all who could afford it and many who couldn't went about in motor-cars. He sniffed. They had motor-cars in Warraranga; stupid things that were always bursting their insides. Give him a horse. Or a horse and buggy. To change the conversation I asked him, casually, if there was any news in the paper.

"It beats me," said he, tapping the front page, "what's it all about?"

I glanced at the headlines. Germany and the Reparations and the endeavour of England and France to come to an understanding.

"But I thought we had taken Germany."

"What do you mean?" I asked, puzzled. "How could we take Germany?"

"We won the war, didn't we?"

"We did."

"Then if we didn't take Germany, what did we take?"

What did we take in fact? What answer could I give to this primitive mind? If I told him that since the armistice all that the Allies had struggled to take was precautionary measures against each other, he would not have understood.

"We're trying to take Germany's money to pay our war expenses and damages to property and so on, but she professes not to have any. The French Government says she has: the English Government says she hasn't. Hence the squabble. America declares she has nothing to do with it. President Wilson said that America went into the war so that the world should be free for Democracy. Democracy has it now, all hands down. Democracy can do whatever it pleases, but it hasn't the remotest idea of what it pleases it to do."

The young man rose lumberingly to his feet, an unsightly figure in his shrunken sun-stained clothes, a string of a black tie beneath the flannel collar of his flannel shirt, and his foolish little black bowler hat perched on the top of his great head.

"I'm an ignorant bloke, Uncle. Mother said I was. That's why I promised her to come to Europe to get education. There's this war. I've tried to figure it out,

but the *Jacksonville Courier* didn't seem to know much.
Fellers came back to Warraranga from Gallipoli and
France with all sorts of tales about war and I was just
'shamed I hadn't gone—but Mother wouldn't let me—and
I listened to them; and I know that millions and millions of men were killed. But what the whole blamed
thing was about I don't know. All I know is that we
licked the Germans and I thought we had taken Germany
—and it seems we haven't. . . ."   He reflected for a few
moments. "Seems as if we got licked," he said rumina-
tively. "Mr. Judge, that's our manager, you know, when
we came to fix up Mother's money, explained that we
had to give away a lot of what we earned out of the place
to the Australian Government to pay for the war. It all
seems wrong somehow."

"Everything at this moment is as wrong as it can be,"
I admitted. "The whole world's upside down."

"Whose fault?"

"Germany's."

"And this feller here"—he tapped the quotations from
the speech of an eminent statesman—"says we must let
Germany be prosperous again. It beats me. I sometimes wonder what the Lord's a-doing of."

"The Lord?" I queried.

"When Sihon king of the Amorites and Og the king
of Bashan went against Israel, He didn't let 'em grow
prosperous. He wiped 'em out and had all their cities
destroyed."

He shook a perplexed head. Whereupon I sat down
by his side and endeavoured to explain the European
situation.

Later I scuttled him off to Nice in the car with a view
to clothing him in garments of good repute; but the only
things I could get ready-made that would fit his huge

frame were some shirts and a soft felt hat. The idea of being measured and fitted for clothes amused him. In Warraranga when his suit was wearing out beyond his mother's power of repair he would send to Jacksonville for a "No. 12," and that was the end of the matter. To choose stuff, colour, pattern and cut had never occurred to him. The suit he wore was his Sunday best and he had had it for five years.

"If I have to dress up like all them folks," said he, indicating the throng of loungers on the Promenade des Anglais, "it'll cost a lot of money. Seems silly."

"You can argue that out with Dorothea," said I, "and I'm sure you'll come off second best."

I felt sure that, for Amos, fear of Dorothea would be the beginning of wisdom.

On our trip I took the opportunity of sounding him as to his financial notions and arrangements. They were vague. He had about fifty pounds in notes and an un-touched cheque-book of whose magicality he was inno-cently certain. In Warraranga he had no dealings with money, his mother having held the tightest of purse-strings. Until her death she had allowed him ten shill-ings a week, most of which he had saved. Even though he had spent some months going through his affairs with Mr. Judge, sole executor, he had not grasped the stand-ard of his fortune. Hence his steerage passage and the purchase—for three and sixpence—of his dreadful billy-cock hat. No wonder poor Dorcas, when she discovered that living for ever was not the lot of mortals, shivered with apprehension as to her son's future, and commended him to the guidance of a man of the world. Once he discovered the meaning of wealth, far beyond the com-mand of ten shillings a week, Heaven alone knew what would become of him. God knows what would have become of me, sophisticated young worldling that I was, if I had found myself at five-and-twenty with fifty thousand pounds lying at the Bank. Verily, I believe, I should have vermilionized the cosmos!

Amos, however, was docile. I took him, on our return to Cannes, to my bank, guaranteed his Australian cheque for a couple of thousand pounds and thus fixed him up an account for temporary needs. The disposal of his fortune was a matter for future consideration.

In describing these earliest impressions of the coming of Amos I have been forced to dwell on externals. They were the astonishing aspects of him which blazed before my bewildered vision; and I do not know how otherwise to set him down before you. In the great things, Honesty, Truth, Kindliness, he resembled any ordinary decent human being. In the little things, which added together make a total of appalling vastness, he was as far removed from any polite circle as an Esquimau. It was not merely a question of manners. It was a question of blank ignorance of conditions under which the civilized world existed; conditions not only social, but historical, geographical, artistic, religious, economic. At first he could only display himself objectively by behaviour, and subjectively by ingenuous revelations of his history and by uncouth comments on his present unfamiliar environment.

Some days passed. I painted hard at the Princess's portrait, conducting myself towards her in the severest professional manner. To her enquiries as to the bear, I replied that he was in Nice fitting himself out with a new skin, which was mainly true. I fulfilled various social engagements, luncheon and dinner, and in the intervals

kept an eye on Amos, who appeared to be perfectly contented. In Warraranga he had scornfully driven an
antiquated Ford car that buck-jumped over irregularities
of road surface and a motor lorry that made roads for
itself. Here, in my garage he picked acquaintance with
my chauffeur, Maxime, and a bright 20 h.p. French four-
seater which revolutionized, in a day, his idea of motor
transport. So much so, that one afternoon, crossing the
Croisette, on my way home to lunch, I had to skip, in
the most undignified fashion, out of the path of a furiously driven and unhorning car, which, within an ace of
killing me, after skidding through violent application of
brakes, turned with the apologies of a scared Amos. So
much so, as well, that the following day, wishing to use
the car, I sauntered into the garage to find that where
once had been an engine, there was nothing but an amorphous heap of bolts and screws and rods and magnetos
and carburetters. On the bench, swinging his legs and
smoking a cigarette, sat Maxime; and Amos, sweating
and blackened, spanner in hand, was playing the devil
with what remained of the chassis.

I shouted: "What the blazes are you doing?"

Amos grinned. "Don't you be afraid. We'll stick it
together again. I had to find out what makes the blamed
thing go."

Although I was put to some inconvenience, I could not
but commend his earnestness. Monsieur was an excellent mechanic, said Maxime. Well, he had worked all
his life with his hands. Monsieur, continued Maxime,
with the respectful familiarity of the French chauffeur
who has seen the war and the world, had already begun
to learn French, at his instruction. *Tenez.* He put a
grinning Amos through his paces. *Boulon. Chambre à
air. Jante Pneu. Vilbrequin* . . . also *Bon jour* and

Bon soir and *Comment allez-vous?*   I sauntered off content to leave the two together.   Amos arrived somewhat contemptuous of a nation which did not speak English; it was beginning to dawn on him that they have a right to their own language which it might be useful for him to learn.

I found him during these few days less of an embarrassment than I had feared.   He was a most tractable and obedient creature.   I think he regarded me as the Vicegerent of Mother on Earth.   The hours of daylight he spent mostly in the open air or in the garage.   When darkness came, he sprawled his great bulk about the drawing-room and wagged his head over any illustrated English weekly that happened to be on hand.   As far as I could make out, the only books he had ever read, apart from the Bible, were "The Pilgrim's Progress" and "The Fairchild Family"; also Adam Lindsay Gordon's poems of which the surreptitious copy was eventually seized by his mother and cast into the fire as ungodly.   He read with great difficulty.   As on the first evening of his arrival, he retired to bed soon after dinner.

My painting caused him great puzzlement.   Evidently he thought nothing of it; but his native shrewdness told him that it must deserve serious consideration.   He compared unfavourably my unfinished portrait of the Princess Nadia with one or two photographs she had brought to show me and had left lying about.   The photographs were much more like her.   As for my landscapes, he could not correlate my interpretation of Nature with Nature itself.   Besides, he could not see the use of it. This magic coast of azure awoke in him no sense of beauty.   It was merely strange, almost risible in its difference from the plains of limitless horizons whence he

had come.   On the Corniche Road he said it was funny
to feel as if you were always going to fall off.   The
mystery of blue sea and grey rock and white towns gleaming in the golden air moved him not at all. . . . Yet when
I made a quick charcoal sketch of him, one afternoon, he
was delighted.   To him, it was my masterpiece.

Still, for all his big dog's docility, I let day follow day,
still continuing not to know what the devil to do with
him.

I am exceedingly fond of my step-daughter, Dorothea;
but never was I more glad to see her than when I caught
sight of her sensible head poked out of the train window
at Cannes station.

She is brown-haired, rosy, plump and capable; fairly
tall; and, unlike her partner, she doesn't dress like a
heathen embroidered-bag-merchant.   She is of the modern world, very neat and spruce.   She wore an iron-grey
coat and skirt and a silver fox round her throat, and between that and a cocky little tam-o'-shantery red hat, her
honest face shone pleasantly.   At the end of this London-
Cannes journey I feel like a sick rag and know I look it.
She was all exuberant youth, trimmed and tidied and
unfatigued.

She glanced around among the hurrying passengers and
porters.

"Where is he?"

"Who?"

"The young man of the Stone Age.   Oh, I am disappointed."

"For the present I'm keeping him in the garage."

She passed her arm through mine.

"Is it as bad as that?   Poor old Daddums.   In your

letter I couldn't disentangle the truth from the picturesque. You're a bit of an artist in your way, you
know. I'm dying to see him."

Maxime possessed himself of her hand-luggage, and
arm in arm we descended the steps and passed through
the underground passage on our way to the exit side.
For a moment she forgot Amos in the joy of the South.
How lovely it was to smell garlic again. She had been
standing by the open window almost since Marseilles,
drenching her senses with the perfumed blue and gold of
the Midi. Dirty yellow fog in London; raw mist in the
Channel; cold rain in Paris. Then darkness, nothing-
ness, the rumble and clatter and the deathly silences of
the train. Sleep. Sudden shafts of light between blinds
and window jambs. Up with the blinds—she had travelled with a Nice-bound woman who had never been South
before—and then the world flooded with the young laughter of the morning sunshine, and afterwards the Mediterranean and the aching beauty of its azure promise.

"There's nothing like it in the wide world, that first
glimpse of the sea before Marseilles. Oh damn——.
Pardon, madame," said my young woman, who was for
sailing through the barrier without delivering up her
ticket for which she must search her bag. "Nothing in
the world," she continued ecstatically. "It *is* a promise.
Talk about syrens singing!"

We entered the car. Maxime threw the rug around us.
Yes, he had Mademoiselle's dressing-case in front. Had
he ever forgotten anything belonging to Mademoiselle?
Yes. That basket of figs two years ago at Saint-Jeannet.
He threw up his hands. Ah! Mademoiselle was unfor-
giving. She commanded. Not straight home; up the
street and out by the Carlton so that she could have the
sweep of the Croisette. In laughter we started, as-

cended the busy rue d'Antibes, the Bond Street of the
Riviera, Bond Street not even in miniature, with its silly
narrow pavement and its silly narrow roadway, and the
lure of its luxurious shop windows—and on to the Croisette, the sea-front of Cannes. Dorothea clutched my
arm. Wasn't it wonderful, the redemption of the morning's promise? Even I, hardened to the coast's eternal
loveliness, drew a quick breath of wonder. To the east,
the green island of St. Marguerite stood on a sea of ultramarine, insulting in its challenge; and, as the eye swept
westward, the pride of dying splendour softened in the
light of a pure amber in which the still obedient sea
melted into sunlit tones of purple and pale mauve, washing the quais above which rose clear in yellow and red the
terraces of the Souquet, the old town, surmounted by its
two square towers, that have watched for centuries, across
the infinitely changing sea, the coasts of Africa and its
romantic perils. And behind and beyond, in serrated
gradations of menace, pleasantness and comfort, dwindled
to a smiling point the long line of the Esterel, dark and
mysterious save for a bastioned forefront of tender olive.
A couple of white sails flecked the eastern ultramarine.
In the oily mauve of the west, bleached by the sun,
floated one little boat, with one little man handling
an oar in the stern. And in the port the tapering
masts of the yachts stood out in delicate tracery against
the sky.

"Tell me brutally that I'm an idiot to spend my days
in a fusty little shop in South Molton Street," said
Dorothea.

I obeyed. She laughed, the best and most understanding of friends.

"I suppose you know I've sent word to Claude to come
along," she remarked casually.

"Claude? Hasn't that young warrior got anything to do yet?"

This was my other nephew, Captain Claude Worthington, the son of Tom, the bishop, and my sister Muriel, who on vague pretext of health had wandered pleasantly about the coast for the past two seasons. Fortunately for everybody, Muriel had not commended him to my semi-paternal care.

"He's selling Dutroyen cars in London. They're going like hot cakes, he tells me. I gave him the idea to come down and sell them to the English and Americans on the Riviera."

"Dorothea, Dorothea," said I. "How many residents or birds of passage are going to buy Claude's cars?"

"None," she replied cheerfully. "Does it matter?"

"I see that young man yet standing behind your embroidered-bag counter."

She laughed. "I wish he would. We'd grow rich."

"You're utterly devoid of conscience, Dorothea," said I severely. "But hitherto you have observed certain rules of discipline. I expect you to continue. Claude is not going to have the run of the Villa. He can come to tea once a week."

"He'll go off his head with joy," she murmured.

I continued. "I didn't take the trouble to send for you so that you could dance at the Casino with Claude Worthington."

It's well from time to time to put these young women in their places. She regarded me demurely.

"That's awfully clever of you, Daddums." Then after a pause, "How does Amos dance?"

"You'll see," said I.

The car tore up the steep rue Georges Clémenceau,

the new unimaginative name for the old rue de Fréjus, and stopped at the Villa. We leaped out. François opened the door. Between respectful expression of delight at seeing Mademoiselle and a certain excited agitation, his speech became unintelligible. I gathered, but paid no attention to, an announcement that there was a monsieur in the salon, and, throwing open the drawing-room door, entered with Dorothea.

There was a gentleman in the salon, a thin, shifty-eyed, would-be smartly, but seedily, dressed fellow of forty, sprawling before the fire and smoking (I nosed it before I saw it) one of my Corona Coronas. And on the other side of the fire sat Amos, in his shirt-sleeves, the discarded coat and waistcoat on a distant chair.

At the sight of the standing lady, Amos rose, according to promise. The other man rose too. Amos smiled pleasantly and ducked his head.

"This Cousin Dorothea?"

"Yes," said I curtly. "But will you kindly introduce me to your friend."

"Captain Foljambe," said the seedy man.

"I met the Captain in the Croisette," Amos explained.

"I happened to be in temporary difficulties," said Captain Foljambe hurriedly. "And between one gentleman and another—in fact—" he turned to Amos—"You have my address—Guards' Club. I won't intrude any longer. Good-bye."

Amos was about to grip him cordially by the hand when I interposed.

"Wait a bit. You've been giving this person money?"

"A trifle, a trifle," said Captain Foljambe. "Enough to get to Paris, where I have heaps of funds. Between gentlemen——"

"How much?"

Amos regarded me for a moment, and then flushed brick-red.

"You mind your own business, Uncle David. Here's a poor bloke down and out. Knocked down in the streets of Monte Carlo and robbed of everything—watch, jewellery, bank-notes. The poor fellow hasn't eaten for two days. Walked here—was going to walk to Paris on an empty stomach, eating nuts and blackberries. 'Naked and hungry you've taken me in.' That's the Scriptures. So Ameely's cooking him a meal of ham and eggs. And he's a gentleman, a captain in the Guards." He challenged me. "Haven't I the right in this country to help a fellow-creature in distress?"

"For a man who hasn't eaten for forty-eight hours," said I, "Captain Foljambe is managing to do very well on a strong cigar. Also officers of the Guards usually have credit that can tide them over temporary difficulties, and they know they can't gather nuts and blackberries from the hedges in January. Furthermore, an honest man cleaned out at Monte Carlo can always get the *viatique* to take him home. How much have you advanced to this gentleman?"

"Only his second-class fare to Paris—a thousand francs," replied Amos.

"The second-class fare to Paris is two hundred and fifty francs," said I.

I held out my hand to the seedy crook in expressive gesture. Dorothea, without being told, put her finger on the bell-push. Level-headed girl, Dorothea. The man hesitated. Evidently the ingenuous Amos had not advised him of my cynical existence. François appeared. Said I:

"Will you give me the note, or shall I telephone to the Commissariat of Police?"

"Your friend's story is not quite accurate," said Captain Foljambe—"I mean in matter of detail. But still—to avoid unpleasantness—as between gentlemen——"

"Confound you!" I cried, "if you say that again I'll have you locked up at once."

He fished in his trouser pocket for the thousand franc note, handed it to me and swaggered out of the room, followed by the vigilant François.

Amos passed his great hand over his upstanding hair. "D'ye mean that that educated, pleasant-spoken feller's a crook?"

"An honest man would have defended himself," said Dorothea.

"I suppose you're right, Miss," said Amos.

He made a turn or two about the room and then threw himself into a chair.

"By Gosh! Did you ever hear of such wickedness!" And after a pause, "Such a kind, nice feller. Talked like anything. Knew Australia too. Sent out specially to organize artillery in Melbourne before the war."

Dorothea smiled. "Curious job for a Guardsman, wasn't it?"

"I dunno, Miss," said Amos abjc ¹⁻ʳ

I made an impatient step—the credulity of the fool was unimaginable. I began.

"You——"

Dorothea, still hatted and fur-coated, waved me a swift arresting gesture. I swallo... d my wrath. Amos sat, bent forward, his head bowed in his hands. The wood fire was burning low. Dorothea took his coat and waistcoat from the chair and touched him on the shoulder. He started up.

"It's getting cold," she said. "In this treacherous climate it's dangerous to sit in one's shirt-sleeves."

He lumbered to his feet. She smiled at him before she made him turn so that she could help him on with the garments.

"Besides," she said, "you look so much nicer."

He shuffled round, buttoning his waistcoat.

"That true?"

"Solemn true," she smiled.

"My dear," said I, "you've been travelling God knows how many hours and you're longing for warm water and soap. Everything's ready for you. Go along."

"I think I will," she said. And to Amos: "I'll see you later."

He grinned at her. Impatiently I snapped my fingers.

"Open the door for your cousin."

He obeyed in some perplexity. She swept graciously past him. But as she went I heard him say:

"Don't you think I don't know what you meant when you said I looked nicer."

There are quite interesting cells in the brain of Amos.

CHAPTER V

I AM convinced that the forties are the golden age of man. Then only can he gather the golden apples of wisdom. By fifty he has either exhausted the crop or it has withered into semblance of that of the Dead Sea.

My ripe wisdom counselled the summoning of Dorothea. Naturally, it justified itself. After a few days Amos followed her about like a bereaved puppy who has found a new mother. There was something pathetically absurd in his submission. She could have taught him dog tricks and he would unquestioningly have performed them. Various suits of clothing having come from the tailor's, she showed him how and when to wear them. She imposed upon him her dainty choice in neckties and handkerchiefs. She made him purchase a clouded cane and instructed him in its nice conduct. This apanage of attire amused him greatly; for what was the use of a stick purposed to beat neither beast nor man? She trained him patiently in table manners. She took him to her coiffeur in the rue d'Antibes, who reduced to civilized proportion his riot of black, upstanding hair. On occasion, she sent him upstairs to wash his hands or brush his nails. So, I remember, did his mother, Dorcas, send me when I was a little boy; that she did not adopt the same procedure with Amos was a symptom of her strange social deterioration. Now Dorothea, however, took maternal charge. When I marvelled at her vast impudence, she said that one must do a thing thoroughly or not at all. How a grown man could brook her domination I was at a loss to imagine, until I hit upon the solution of the apron-strings.   All his life had he been tied to them; he was used to them; knew not where he was without them; and evidently found those of Dorothea more pleasant than those of Dorcas.   Consequently, to my external eye, he grew in grace day by day.

Occupied with my work and social duties, I saw little of Amos.   Why should I have seen more?   He was perfectly happy, in the perfectly capable hands of a young woman who was having the time of her life.   Instead of wasting her life in the embroidering of vain bags, she was devoting her art to the embroidering of a real live raw product.   I am afraid—so implicit was my trust in Dorothea—that, ever so little, I neglected him.   You see, when she went about visiting her friends, of whom, in Cannes, she has many, she set him some task devised by her feminine ingenuity; the learning by heart of a poem by Wordsworth or Rupert Brooke, or a page of French verbs; or the perusal of a chapter of a Book of Etiquette which she had purchased *ad hoc* in London, and, by manuscript corrections had warped into conformity with the usages of folk of ordinary sanity; or a series of errands among the vanity shops of this Vanity Fair of a place.   Then, of course, her friends came to the Villa, chiefly to tea.   I gathered that, acting under her instructions, and actuated by his own shyness, Amos silently filled the background and handed cups of tea and eatables with the awkward precision of the trained animal.   Dorothea, as I have said, was enjoying herself prodigiously.   I had her word for it.   Periodically, *en tête à tête,* she joyously reported progress.

Once—fruit again of the wisdom of the mid-forties— I let fall a remark:

"As you know, my dear Dorothea, I'm not given to

fulsome flattery, but you're not devoid of attraction for the Untutored Savage. As a very modern woman you can't be unconscious of a truth so blatant."

"You talk like a book, Daddums," said she. "A book written in the nineties. That was when they rediscovered the fact of sex and made a terrible hullabaloo about it."

"To continue to speak in that archaic tongue," said I, "it is the primordial instinct of animal life. Amos dates much further back than the 1890 epoch. He belongs to any old age you please—when men were men."

Perhaps she caught the serious note in my voice; she twisted her head and looked at me out of the tail of her eye.

"What do you mean, Daddums?"

"Exactly what I say. Here is the primitive animal confronted with a desirable female of his species. That proposition is nineteen-twenty enough for you, isn't it?"

"Quite," said Dorothea. "But it's a self-evident proposition applicable to any two young people of the present day."

"By no means," said I. "You young modern people have developed a sexual code of intimacy. If not, the world has never known such moral corruption——"

"Daddums!" she cried, indignantly.

"Yes, my dear. You're the heiress of all the ages——"

"In the foremost files of *The Times*," she said mockingly. "You can't shock me. Go on."

I went on. What Dorothea doesn't know, as far as knowledge goes, isn't worth knowing. But there's all the world of difference between knowledge and wisdom. There was once a majestic poet—just quoted—world-famous in his day, but now despised, who put the whole matter in a nutshell: "Knowledge comes, but Wisdom lingers."

"What I'm trying to get at is a thing that the cumulative experience of all the centuries hasn't taught you. There's an infinite difference between the primitive man and your modern dancing partner.   I warn you, my dear, for your guidance, that Amos hasn't danced his sex away."

She sat down with some deliberation on a chair close by and fixed me with her candid brown eyes.

"Really, Daddums, you've put before me an original idea."

I rose and waved a middle-aged hand.

"Well.   That's what it comes to, doesn't it?   You modern young dancing people—either you're corrupt, which I don't believe for one moment—or you have your tacit, unbreathed, yet recognized convention of asexuality. You have reduced yourselves to such a state of physical unsensitiveness that all sorts of complicated factors have to come into play before two young dancing things fall in love with each other——"

"You're perfectly right," she assented frankly. "We've progressed.   We're centuries ahead of your 1890."

"And Amos, being centuries behind, isn't a party to your convention."

"I see," she said.   "Your argument is incontrovertible. But really, dear, you make things rather difficult for me. Oughtn't you to have thought out this Freud-ish situation before you sent for me to dry nurse him?"

Holding me in a helpless corner, she smiled in gentle derision; then broke into gay laughter.

"I'll put Amos in training and make him dance from morning to night."

"Dorothea," said I, "you're nothing but an incorrigible hussy."

The entrance of François, announcing a new sitter, the Comtesse d'Orbigny, put an end to this conversation.

Madame d'Orbigny is a beautiful and wealthy American, married to an elderly Frenchman of distinguished family and of impeccable breeding, and hides a world of neurosis behind a studied exterior which, I am certain, she characterizes to herself as poise. In short, a feminine type of peculiar interest to the portrait painter. I was painting her professionally: not for joyous foolery, as I was painting the Princess Nadia.

Which brings me to Nadia.

A day or two after this she came to the studio, all smiles.

"*Mon cher*, I have met the bear on the Croisette."

"Dorothea has to let him loose sometimes," said I.

"But he is a beautiful tame bear. I love him."

In her picturesque way she described the encounter.

It was a forenoon of sunshine, all pale gold, turquoise and ultramarine. Down the broad pavement by the sea came the Princess, followed by the tawny Pekinese, Chouchou. In my perfect Cannes there is no such thing as the vulgar crowd of promenaders who make an ant-crawl of the Promenade des Anglais at Nice, or of the front at Brighton. The Croisette is used as a discreet and pleasant lounge. A thousand cubic yards of luminous isolation enveloped Nadia as she walked eastwards by the sea. Suddenly dashing into this cubic space at six perspiring miles an hour rushed Amos, his clouded cane over his shoulder as though a wallet at the back should have been suspended. He all but trod on Chouchou and skipped aside and stumbled. The shave from accident brought him to a halt and made him cry:

"Good Gosh!"

Chouchou barked his aristocratic indignation. The Princess smiled and extended a gracious hand.

"I thought I was never going to see you again, Mr. Burden."

"Gosh!" said he. "It's Your Royal Highness. But you look different. You were——"

"Yes," she interrupted, with that mocking little smile of hers, and with expressive hands—"I was."

"Oh!" said Amos.

"I don't always go about in low-cut evening dresses in the day time."

"I thought you did it because you were a princess, Your Royal Highness," said Amos.

"I'm not a Royal Highness; I'm—or I was—a Serene Highness; but everybody calls me 'Princess,' just as you'd say 'Mrs. Jones.'" She glanced around. "Don't you think we might sit down?"

She led him to a green garden seat that faced the gold and azure splendour of the sea; whereon they sat, with a whipped-up Chouchou between them.

"I don't understand, mum," said Amos. "Ain't you a king's daughter?"

In answer to her wrinkled brow of question he went on:

"I thought all princesses were kings' daughters."

"My husband was the great-great-something-great-grandson of the Emperor Peter the Great."

"Golly!" said Amos. "An emperor's a bigger boss than a king, isn't he?"

She sighed. "There's only one emperor left in the world now."

"Who's that?"

"Your king. King George. The Emperor of India."

"That's the war. It was bad for emperors, wasn't it?"

"Yes, very bad. You see, the war has changed everything."

In a few words she sketched her fallen fortunes. He listened open-mouthed. Never had she listener so sympathetically entranced. She had no need to pile up agony. Her simple tale of murder and anguish and terror was tragedy enough.

He turned and clamped her little shoulders with his great hands, regardless of her Serene Highness-dom, and cried:

"Good Gosh! And there are men living that have done all that to you. Tell me where they are—and they'll have to reckon with me."

What happened after that I don't quite know. It was the dramatic end of Nadia's story, and she was too finished an artist, in her way, to spoil it by anti-climax.

"So, you see," she said, "the poor little exiled Princess has found a champion out of a fairy tale to restore her to her kingdom. That's why I say I love him."

This talk took place at her last sitting. At the end of it she was pleased to express her approbation of the portrait. Apart from pictorial value, it was a good likeness. The mutinous little Tartar nose that had given me so much trouble had come out deliciously right. I was boyishly delighted with it. And the good patient paint had finally interpreted the baffling mother-of-pearl over peach-bloom of her flesh; and I had caught, I know not how, the sorrowful mischief in the hazel and green elusiveness of her eyes.

We stood, side by side, looking at the canvas. Presently her hand crept under my arm.

"It's strange," she said, "I feel like a re-created being."

I smiled down on her and asked her what she meant.

"You know well," she replied with a little pressure of

her fingers. "That is just as much of a living thing as I am; so there are two of us, and of one of us you are the creator—and in that capacity I am afraid of you, you whom I tease and jest with. That is the Nadia who has seen sad things which she strives to forget and who tries to smile at the unknown things that life holds for her. You must forgive all my foolish words and frivolous behaviour of which I am now ashamed———"

"My dear child," said I, drawing her arm close to my side—the moment was not unemotional—"if you hadn't been just your adorable self all through the sittings, how the deuce do you think I could have painted you?"

"*Mais encore*———" she began.

"But yet," I interrupted, "if you had got it into your head that you were going to be re-created, as you call it, you would have sat solemn, with a face like Madame la République Française who mourns on every monument in the country."

She sighed. "I suppose you know best, *cher maître.*"

"Of course I do," I laughed, "—in painting. It's my trade. But all the same, I wouldn't have you afraid of me for anything in the world."

She turned up her delicate face. "And why?"

"Perfect—friendship—casteth out fear."

"And you wish so much to be friends with me?"

"Would I have spent my heart on that if I didn't?"

"That's true," she said, and took a cigarette from a box on the table. "I'm glad. I have not many friends. And, in Cannes, a woman like me can have many enemies."

"Let me meet them," said I, "and———"

"And they'll have to reckon with you?" Her face lit up with merriment. "That is what Monsieur Amos said. So I have found two champions in one day."

Have I or have I not a sense of humour? I don't know. All I know is that, in my heart, I damned Amos to the full extent of my efficiency.

She came up to me again—she had, I forgot to tell you, slipped on the black evening gown, so that I could have my last critical survey of values—and laid her fingers on my arm. She can be childishly caressive when she pleases. On the other hand, I have seen her freeze up into the iciest little green glacier at the approach of the undesirable. Only a few nights before had I seen the phenomenon—in the Casino, when she stood talking with one Ramon Garcia, a Latin American of sorts, a friend of Madame d'Orbigny, and received everywhere. I didn't like the fellow, oiled and perfumed and bejewelled and moustachioed, with manners too good to be true; but I shivered in sympathy with him as he drifted away, frost-bitten from head to foot. . . . Nadia, I say, came up to me—a quick cloud veiling the mischief in her eyes.

"Seriously, *cher maître*, I value your friendship above everything. Things are difficult for a woman in my position. The slanderous tongues. Sometimes it seems even worse if I continue to live with my aunt and my uncle than if I braved everybody and lived alone. It is not gay at the Villa Miranda—you know."

I did. It wasn't at all gay in the home of the old Marchese della Fontana, where bridge was played for high stakes from afternoon to midnight, and where tables of *chemin de fer* and roulette found frequenters till the early hours of the morning.

She drew up her slim figure. "There are people who know who I am, yet who dare to treat me as though I were an adventuress—*déclassée*. There are men whom I can't trust. There are women who hate me—I don't know why except that I am young and pretty and attractive. I play at the tables and I win, and there are black looks all around; I lose, even the value of one of my precious pearls, and I see in their hearts they are rejoicing. *Ah, je suis bien seule. Aidez-moi—voulez-vous?* You can do it with your artist's power here and your English probity."

I don't know whether she talked French or English. She used to run indiscriminately from one language into another. Now I come to think of it, I seem to hear the echo of the phrase: *"votre fière probité anglaise."*

She stretched out at full length her bare shapely arm, that melted, undisturbed by strap, into the curves of shoulder and neck, and looked at me, her body swaying, her head at an appealing half-turn. I took the hand held palm downwards, and, bowing over it, kissed it, in conventional manner, below the wrist.

"My dear Nadia," said I, "you can count me always as your most obedient and loving servant."

"I am sure I can," she cried. And before I knew where I was, she broke the pose, put up her lips so close to me that I felt her breath on my cheek, and whispered: "You are the man I love and trust most in the world." After which she bade me gay adieu.

I stood again and looked at the practically finished picture—there is little else to do besides the finishing off of the background—and wondered, in spite of my conviction of living in man's golden age of wisdom, whether I had been wise, I will not say in wasting, for no time devoted to artistic creation can be wasted, but in expending so much of myself on this portrait of the Princess Nadia. She had complained once that I treated her only as a subject; whereby she meant a living abstraction, only important in so far as she could be translated into terms of paint. She was perfectly right, at the time.

She was a subject and nothing else. I have explained
how I had been driven to paint her. . . . Was she still
the same to me? I knitted my brow at the question.
How much self-expenditure had I bestowed on the trans-
ference to canvas of the green and amber mysteries of
the Princess Nadia Ramiroff, and how much on the very
warm and human bit of flesh and blood that was Nadia
herself? There was nothing at all subjective in the lin-
gering touch on my cheek of warm breath, the sound of
sweet words in my ears and the fragrance of her near-
ness in my nostrils. And, I swear that her eyes looking
at me mockingly out of the canvas said:

"My dear David, I don't in the least see why you
shouldn't make a fool of yourself, if such is your good
pleasure."

And those were the eyes that I myself had painted.

It was with some reluctance that I showed the picture
to the Comtesse d'Orbigny at her next sitting. Of course
she had heard of it. Things have to be done in a very
dark way, in a very dark room, on a very dark night, not
to be heard of on the Riviera. And even then the black-
beetles come out and whisper them to the flies and the
flies buzz them about the kitchens, and from the kitchens
they come to the drawing-rooms distorted through the
successive prisms of black-beetles, flies and kitchen folk.
Everyone on the Côte d'Azur, although we had bound
ourselves in a mutual oath of secrecy, knew that I was
painting the Princess Ramiroff. I had to stand the portrait on the easel for Madame d'Orbigny's inspection.
It pleased her to fall into platitudinous ecstasy. What
it was to be a great artist! How he taught the world
the things it heeded not! No one would ever have suspected all that soulfulness behind the poor little Princess,

who seemed to do nothing but gamble and dance—and yet, looking at the portrait, one guessed what the little thing had gone through—those Bolshevik horrors. It made one shiver to think of them, if her story was true. Luckily she had escaped. Of course there were people in Cannes who declared that neither her title nor her pearls were real——

"My dear Comtesse," said I, "anybody in Cannes with a real title or real pearls—No. Any little lady of nothing-at-all can have real pearls for the asking from the millionaires of Latin America—but anybody of real *noblesse,* to whom the Almanach de Gotha is not a vain compilation, knows that the Princess's title is authentic and her pearls—historic—are genuine. The Russian Grand Dukes, here, may accept out of courtesy, and perhaps political necessity, the acquaintance of all sorts of cosmopolitan people, but they don't receive on a plane of equality spurious Russian Serene Highnesses. It's just as idiotic as to suppose that King George of England would invite a gentleman calling himself the Duke of Shoreditch to Buckingham Palace. So, if you hear this cruel and beastly slander again, just refer the slanderer to the Grand Duke—or"—I lost my temper for a moment —"or, hang it all, to me."

The Comtesse d'Orbigny—once Rosamund Leete, daughter of Senator Joseph P. Leete of Arkansas—raised her beautifully shaven eyebrows.

"My dear David Fontenay, what a tirade! Why fire it off on me? My title's genuine, I suppose—and so are my pearls. Gaston's got parchments that carry him way back to Charlemagne, and I've got a warranty for my pearls from the Rue de la Paix. I haven't the slightest doubt as to the poor little Princess—I was only deploring common gossip."

"Why do you persist in calling her the poor little Princess?"

I was irritated—perhaps at the condescension of wealth. Nadia had behind her the tradition of centuries. Madame d'Orbigny's grandfather slept with pigs in a Galway cabin. That I know. My old friend, Sir Patrick Murfree, owns or used to own the cabin. He is eighty now, and lives in Bury Street, St. James's; but he remembers the emigration of barefoot Daniel Leete; and to this day in and out and round about the cabin are uncles and aunts, grand and otherwise, and cousins in all degrees of affinity, of this very interesting and beautiful but hybrid product of Ireland, Scandinavia and the United States. For it was the clever son of the ignorant peasant, deriving his brains from a Swedish mother, who had made the Leete millions. Of course Rosamund, having nothing to do with Irish grandfather and Swedish grandmother, claimed pure American descent; which everyone, save perhaps representatives of the New England or Southern families, was prepared to grant her, not caring one way or the other; and which I granted her with all the good-will in the world, when she did not question the unquestionable antecedents of other people.

The Comtesse d'Orbigny replied, with her rather tired smile:

"I won't, my good friend, if you want to have all the pity to yourself. People who know her well say she's most fascinating."

"Those are the very people," said I, "to go to for accurate information."

But somehow I felt that I had bungled matters. Madame d'Orbigny would go forth and proclaim to Cannes that I was in love with the Princess Nadia Ramiroff. *Quod erat absurdum.* Damned *absurdum.*

So I swore, in my vain self-confidence. For what regard could I, a man getting on to fifty, have for young women in their twenties, save that which was purely paternal? Youth to youth was the eternal law. Middle age (man's) to—well—say to the mid-thirties when a woman has learned to be comfortable. Not that I wanted a woman at all—in the way of romantic conjunctivity. That was all over; I had lived my life. As I remarked in the opening pages of this confession, I desired nothing in the world but to be left alone, as I was.

Hitherto my name in Cannes had been coupled with that of women by not even the frailest gossamer breath of gossip—to say nothing of scandal.

And now I had sent out the Comtesse d'Orbigny with a pretty story.

CHAPTER VI

MY nephew, Claude Worthington, obeying Dorothea's behest, turned up in Cannes with a bright pea-green Dutroyen two-seater torpedo, in which he rattled all day up and down the Croisette, making a noise like an up-to-date summons to the Day of Judgment. He placed an order for one of the same kind, on the second day of his arrival, with a very young English stockbroker who had won forty thousand francs the previous evening at Monte Carlo. To Dorothea he proclaimed in exuberant mood:

"At this rate, dear old girl, I'll be selling a car a day, and my fortune's made."

She turned to me—it was at lunch, to which meal, in spite of my embargo, she had summoned him—

"Won't you be his second customer, Daddums?"

"Do, sir!" he cried enthusiastically—like all the best of the old fighting army he had carried on the tradition of respectful address to his seniors—"you'll never regret it. We're the only people who can give you first-class material for the price we ask. It's our secret. It's a Rolls-Royce engine at Ford cost."

His eyes twinkled; my eyes twinkled in ironical response; so did Dorothea's. But Amos, sitting opposite, bent his brows:

"Why do you tell such lies?"

Claude is fair and slim and fresh-complexioned and wears a little blond, curled-up moustache, a tortoise-shell rimmed monocle and (when in France) the ribbon of the *Légion d'Honneur* at the buttonhole of his perfectly cut jacket. He flushed angrily.

"What do you know about it?"

"I ain't saying nothing about Fords," replied Amos. "I seen 'em in Warraranga. But Maxime, Uncle David's chauffeur, took me round to a garage the other day where a pal of his had a Rolls-Royce. And I went all over the engine, bar the part that's sealed up. And I looked inside yours just before dinner"—to Amos, dinner was always the term for the midday meal—"so I do know what I'm talking about, and that's why I want to know why you're telling lies."

"Claude was only joking," said Dorothea.

"Of course I was, you silly ass," said Claude.

Amos rose and towered over the table.

"Don't you call me no silly asses, Cousin Claude, or you and me'll see which is the silliest ass."

Exerting authority, I rapped my knuckles on the table and bade him sit down at once. He obeyed, with a sideways swaying of his head and shoulders, for all the world like a bear under menace of the stick. He jerked his thumb towards Claude.

"I know nothing about selling motor-cars. But I know a blamed lot about selling horses."

"So I suppose," said Claude, recovering his equanimity, "if a joker came to Warrawhat-you-call-it and said he'd got a foal out of a winner of the Oaks by a Derby winner, you'd have called him a very naughty man."

"Mother was all for Christian forbearance," Amos replied seriously, "but if a feller told such a lie about a horse he wanted to sell, only half of him would have got out of Warraranga."

"Then I suppose your sense of humour would have been tickled. You'd have laughed like the devil."

"There's nothing to laugh at in lying and cheating," said Amos.

I had to intervene again, for the sake of peace.

"My dear Amos," said I, in the authoritative tones of the father in "The Swiss Family Robinson," "you've come to Europe to get education. You have to learn that over here people mean only a certain proportion of what they say. Claude didn't expect us to believe his Rolls-Royce and Ford story, and we knew that he didn't. No more than you expected us to believe that a detected horse crook in Warraranga would have left the station cloven in twain from skull to crutch." My gesture was expressive beyond possibility of mistake. "But there was a basis of truth in what both Claude and yourself have said and Dorothea and myself have quite appreciated it," I smiled. "I think we may regard the incident as closed."

For the time being peace was established. But I foresaw trouble between the two young men; and, as the days passed, my prognostic was justified. In spite of the virtues of meekness and humility inculcated by my sister Dorcas, Amos betrayed, when occasion warranted, a disposition distinctly bellicose. It even seemed that Dorcas countenanced the severe man-handling of offenders and that heads in Warraranga were punched on mild provocation. Claude complained to Dorothea, with an old warrior's artlessness, that he went about in terror of his life. He couldn't always be refusing challenges to single combat; one of these days he would be driven to accept, and the Battling Bushman would pound him to protoplasmic jelly. He wanted to live and dance and drive about in motor-cars and possibly marry her, Dorothea. To be swept up in a dust-pan and put in a coffin did not appeal to him as an aim in life. Dorothea, on enquiry, learned that there had been disputes: one, particularly, during the course of which Amos had threatened his cousin with physical violence. Amos had chosen to criticize Claude's mode of living; briefly, had taunted him with not having done a stroke of work in his life. Every man had his duties.

"What about the war?" asked Claude.

"I know nothing about the war," said Amos.

"You took damn well care not to," Claude retaliated. Claude was young. He was irritated by the sanctimonious suggestion of duty which is as poison in the nostrils of the ordinary young Englishman who will face (as he has recently faced) Hell without a quiver, but will be almost physically sick if told to do it to the tune of "God save the King" or "Rule Britannia," or under any stereotyped whip of sentimentality. To talk to Claude about abstract duty was almost as indecent as to refer to his sexual impulses. So, angrily he flashed perhaps an unworthy taunt. Then, of course, Amos blazed out in righteous indignation.

"All I know is that during the war I did seven men's work every day, and if you say I was a coward I'll blame well bash your pretty face in."

"As my beauty is my only worldly asset," replied Claude, "I'll admit that you're as brave a chap as ever skipped."

Claude, narrating this to Dorothea, continued:

"He growled like a bear and turned away. But I was scared stiff."

Said Dorothea: "It was beastly of you to rub it in about the war. If he had gone for you, I shouldn't have pitied you a bit. You were just asking for it."

The young man fumed. "Why had he the infernal cheek to tell me I was wasting my life doing nothing?"

Whereupon Dorothea declared that Amos was afflicted with a mania for telling the truth, and dismissed a sore and uncomforted young man.

"But I dressed down Amos," said Dorothea to me.

"Wouldn't it be more modern, my dear," I remarked, "to have said, 'I told him off'?"

"You forget, my dear Daddums," she replied, "that we belong to a post-war world and are going back to classical English."

She smiled her ironical, affectionate smile. Things are upside down nowadays. Love is akin to pity. She pitied me because she loved me. Otherwise she would have regarded me with unemotional serenity as a parchment record of a faded past. But she honoured me with her tales of Amos and Claude; relating that which could be comprised within the limits of my understanding and suppressing that which was not good for me to know. Of her own joy in driving this tandem of wild and ill-assorted cousins, she said no word.

I was glad when Claude, having temporarily exhausted the car-buying possibilities of Cannes, betook himself and his pea-green two-seater to Nice, to spread the glad tidings of the Dutroyen car through that simple and Dutroyen-reeking town. He went with an open exhaust of foul smoke and profanity. Instructions from an unqualified imbecile firm had to be obeyed.

"But thank Heaven, sir," said he, "I can run over to Cannes in half an hour."

With such confidence did Puck declare his capability of putting a girdle round about the earth in forty minutes. But I was a middle-aged Oberon out of sympathy with Puckish vagaries.

"Ah, my dear fellow," I sighed, "after all there was something very satisfying and romantic in the old-fashioned post-chaise or diligence. You had all the gay adventures of the road, and when you started you never knew at what time you would arrive."

Said Amos, who happened to be present at the leave-taking:

"I'm with you, Uncle David. With us, in an ox-waggon, it would take a day."

It is astonishing how the lower emotions sharpen the wits.

Claude in Nice, Dorothea devoted more pains to Amos. The time had come, said she, to take him out and show him the world. He made his début at a *thé dansant* at the Casino, a guest of the Crawley-Johnstones, friends of Dorothea. . . .

I was reading over the drawing-room fire, having no ear for jazz-music and therefore unappreciative of dancing teas, when in rolled Amos, who had only left, accompanied by Dorothea, a short while before. I looked up from my book.

"Hullo! Back already?"

He moved uneasily from side to side. Yes. That wasn't the kind of place he was accustomed to. He couldn't breathe. And the blamed noise. And the women dancing. Like a lot of painted harlots.

"Excuse me," said I, "weren't Dorothea and her friends dancing?"

"Oh, I see what you're driving at—but I can't help it. To see modest girls behaving like that made me sick."

So he had just risen, and without a word of excuse or leave-taking had walked out of the crowded room into the open air of virtue.

"My young friend," said I, with some acerbity, "the worst of the Christianity which your excellent father

preached and your good mother practised is that it misses
some of the essentials of Christ's teaching. 'Judge not
that ye be not judged' is a divine maxim which I don't
think is written in letters of gold outside the meeting-
house in Warraranga.   Now we are in Cannes, the most
civilized town in the most highly civilized country in
the world and the centripetal point of all this civilization
is the Casino Municipal—and its unwritten motto is the
maxim I have just quoted."

"Yes—but doesn't that mean shutting one's eyes to
any old sinfulness and saying it's none of my business?"

He was perfectly right; but I didn't tell him so.   On
the contrary . . .

"No," said I.   "You have passed a judgment on the
dancing ladies in the very strongest terms, and you have
included in it my daughter Dorothea and Miss Lucy
Crawley-Johnstone, who certainly were not committing
any old sinfulness, as you call it.   They are merely following a code of manners the result of an evolution unknown in Warraranga.   You have judged without knowledge and without charity and so you are held, at the present moment, round that tea-table on the dancing floor, to
be an amazingly rude and impossible young man."

I continued my lecture.   To obtain revision of this
judgment he must return forthwith, with some social
excuse.   He had suddenly remembered the sending of an
important telegram; he had recognized by the entrance
staircase a childhood's friend whom he had not seen for
twenty years; he had forgotten to kiss me good-bye and
had returned to do so.   The terms of the apology didn't
matter; but back he must go.

"I ain't going," said Amos.

I grew angry.   "You're going out of this house this
moment," said I.   "Either to the Casino or wherever

else you damn well like. If the Casino, you can come back: if not, you can't. I won't have you."

I felt rather a brute and a sophistical hypocrite. To this primitive mind trained in Ezra Burden's ignorant, half-mystic, half-Judaic misinterpretation of Christianity, with no knowledge whatever of social usages, still less of that which is more delicate, namely social sanctions, the sight of the rabble-rout clothed in Bond Street and the rue de la Paix of modern Maenads, Bacchantes, shepherds, fauns, dancing to the delirium of the saxophone played by the great god Billy Pan, must have been a spectacle of stupefaction and affright. It was Sodom and Gomorrah. It was Babylon. It was the court that took its colour from Queen Jezebel. I was sorry for him; but he must go either the way of Warraranga or the way of Cannes; and only in the way of Cannes, figuratively speaking, could I be of any use to him. To some extent, I relented.

"I'll go back with you and see you through."

He shambled silently out of the house with me and eventually through the crowded restaurant to the Crawley-Johnstone's tea-table. I made his excuses. A most important message for me which he had forgotten. My hostess smiled on him and pressed upon him tea and cakes. But he refused and glowered at the packed square of dancers—men and women, youths and maidens, tightly clasped together, each pair of bodies swaying as one to the barbaric rhythm of the music. Dorothea passed, dancing with the nondescript Crawley-Johnstone boy and caught my eye and pantomimed expressively. A comfortless quarter of an hour was in store for Amos. I smiled reassurance and talked to Mrs. Crawley-Johnstone —there were only the three of us at the end of the long table strewn with the litter of temporarily abandoned teacups and straw-furnished glasses and lonely cigarettes sending up their blue spirals of smoke.

Presently Amos gave a gasp and a start, and instinctively I clutched his arm as one grips a dog about to spring. I followed his gaze of anger. There, clasped dreamily in the arms of the South American Ramon Garcia, swept by the Princess Nadia Ramiroff. I, myself, frowned. Not long ago I had seen him wilt before her, shrivelled and frost-bitten; but now his oiled and curled handsomeness radiated the triumph of one, not forgiven, but forgiving. He looked down, with abominable homage, on her upturned face. A glance fixed, for me, her arresting picture. A close-fitting black velvet hat crowned the pale gold of her hair and set off, under the electric light, the mysterious green of her eyes and the skin that I had been at such almighty pains to paint; she wore a knitted black silk frock, short at legs and arms, relieved by a girdle of gold. She looked adorable. Doubtless she felt it. Certainly she was losing herself in the passing moment. She danced divinely; so I admit did her polite rapscallion of a partner; divinely, be it said, in pagan reference, like the ministrants of the Fifth Muse. Into terms of Helicon and Castaly they translated the rhythms of Central Africa, and I was lost for a moment in wonderment at the sheer beauty of their movement. She passed with a half smile of dreamy recognition and soon was swallowed up in the whirl of dancers.

Amos sat with his elbows on the table breathing heavily. I talked, at the top of my voice, to Mrs. Crawley-Johnstone so as to be heard above the jazzaphonic tumult, about any rubbish that came into my head, and at the same time kept the corner of my eye on Amos. The dance ended; but at the enthusiastic encore came the band's immediate response. Dorothea sailed by, this time without deigning a look in our direction. And in her turn, there came into our view the Princess and Ramon Garcia. The kind and comfortable and elderly Mrs. Crawley-Johnstone drew politely, but quite unnecessarily, Amos's attention to the couple.

"That's the Princess Ramiroff. I always say that when those two dance together they simply wipe the professionals off the floor."

Amos turned his great head and growled.

"I don't like it."

"Why?"

"I hate the way the feller's clawing her about. It isn't decent."

This time it was Mrs. Crawley-Johnstone who gasped and started. I too. The suppressed ferocity of his speech betrayed far more than puritanical and impersonal disapprobation of modern dancing.

Our hostess drew herself up and replied frigidly:

"I can see absolutely nothing to object to."

"I can," said Amos.

I led her, by a gesture, beyond earshot of the glowering Amos.

"My dear friend," said I, "we ought to have warned you. . . ." I went off into indistinctly heard explanations and apologetics.

"But why should he have his knife," she asked, "particularly into Garcia, who is the least—well—the most exquisite dancer? Does he know him?"

"No. But he knows the Princess."

"Oh!" said she, and with a little smile hovering round her lips, turned to the chin-on-elbow planted Amos whose narrowed eyes were piercing the maze of dancers, obviously in search of the offending couple.

Fate ordained that the end of the dance should bring

that same couple to a stand immediately in front of us. Señor Garcia bowed in polite salutation. I, of course, rose to my feet; and to his, at an angry sign from me, stumbled Amos. The Princess's hand—although it is recognized in Cannes as being outside our English code of etiquette, but because I wanted to impress my bear of a nephew with some sense of courteous behaviour—I kissed in correct foreign style. Only once before had I done so, somewhat romantically, on the day of her last sitting in the studio.

"*Cher maître,*" she laughed, "one does not often see you in this den of frivolity. What good angel has brought you?"

I waved a hand towards Amos. "This one," said I.

She turned to him, smiling graciously, flushed with the perfect dance which had put her for the moment into good humour with all the world—and unconsciously held her hand out high. He gripped it, red as a turkey-cock, and suddenly, as if in desperation, pulled it roughly to his lips and kissed it with a great smack that seemed to resound through the Casino. With a little indrawn breath of apprehension, she snatched it away. The conventional approach of lips to wrist is one thing, the passionate salute on bare flesh is another. But she held her ground.

"You're not dancing?"

"I should think not," said he.

"Is it because you cannot dance or because your principles object to it?"

Have I said that she has an adorable way of her own of speaking English?

He bent down—and I saw his great hands clenched by his side. "I object to it. I hate it," he replied.

"But you wouldn't if you danced with me. Some day

you will. I'll make Mr. Fontenay give you lessons."

By this time the young Crawley-Johnstone boy and
Dorothea and the rest of the dancing party had drifted
to the table and hurriedly went on with their unconsumed
refreshments. The Princess, caught away from Amos by
various greetings, embraced the company in a nodding
smile and retired with Ramon Garcia. As she did not
dance again, I suppose she went off to the baccarat
rooms.

After another dance the party broke up. We three
walked home beside the little port all silver in the young
moonlight towards the black twinkling mass of the Souquet silhouetted against the western sky. Dorothea, her
arm linked in mine, talked of the evening's loveliness. Of
the bit of moonlit cirrus in the quiet sky: of the points
of lights in the yachts against the quai and the mysterious
dark tracery of masts and spars. Amos, hands in
trousers pockets, and shoulders hunched, trudged silent
by our side. Dorothea, I could see, was bent on punishment; and I felt peculiarly disinclined to converse with
him—and it was not only because I agreed with Dorothea
in her opinion that wholesome correction was part of a
sound educational system.

Amos spent the next few days in profound and solitary
meditation, which I very wrongly attributed to sulkiness.
You see, in that early period of our acquaintance I could
not gauge his candid integrity. He went off, as I know
now, on day-long rambles into the mountains, filled with
remorse for unwitting offence against those from whom
he had received loving kindness, and fired with the de-
termination to comprehend the true nature of that offence.
He left the house at six in the morning, and, on his return at night, went up straight to his bedroom. At first

we were greatly concerned at his absence from the meals which he was in the habit of consuming with such vast appreciation. Any other of our young friends, with money to burn, we should have judged according to our worldly standards. Was there not Monte Carlo, with its strange goddesses, abstract and otherwise, only fifty kilometres away, singing in the Eastern Italian wind its eternal allurement? But we knew that to this allurement Amos was deafer than were the companions of Ulysses, with their wax-stopped ears, to the songs of the Syrens. For the latter knew all about the Syrens, whereas poor Amos was entirely ignorant of their existence.

Yet what was he doing all day and half the night?

It was I who put forward the theory of the fit of sulks. Dorothea with clearer vision said:

"I believe he's jolly well ashamed of himself, and doesn't know how to meet us."

"It's for you then, my dear," said I, "to hold out the helping hand."

She rose—we were at dinner and François was out of the room—and came behind my chair and clasped my chin and cheeks in her two palms.

"You can only be spoken of in superlatives. Not only are you the very dearest Daddums in the world, but you're the most accomplished transferrer of responsibilities that has ever been created."

Whereupon she kissed a spot on the top of my head which, with mendacious exaggeration, she calls my bald patch.

"If you think," said I, with all the dignity I could muster, "that he'll come to me with his tail between his legs, you're very much mistaken."

"Oh, he won't come to you, my dear," she declared, "he'll come to me."

"Didn't I practically say so, before you took away my character?"

"He has got all sorts of things on his mind, all sorts of incomprehensible things," she said very seriously, after she had sat down again. "We must make allowances. Why, even a dog coming into a strange house has to sniff round the walls and furniture, so as to get the hang of it. How much more a human being—and, Daddums, Amos is a jolly intelligent human being—who is suddenly planted in a strange universe. Amos is sniffing. He has done something we think wrong. He's sizing it up." She threw out her hands. "Oh, I can't go on with the dog metaphor. The human soul gets beyond it. Anyhow, I'm not going to shoulder your responsibilities and tackle Amos."

She took a decided mouthful of *haricot verts*.

"My child," said I, "you're a contradiction of Ossa piled on a paradox of Pelion."

"Not a bit," Dorothea retorted. "I'm exhausting myself in telling you that Amos will come to me of his own accord. He's not coming to you, because he looks on you as a sort of god of this astonishing pagan land, Baal or Dagon, or whatnot. He has a sneaking adoration for you but doesn't know whether he's committing the sin of idolatry. Darling, don't you see that he's all ends up?"

Gravely eating my *haricots verts*, I admitted the disequilibrium of Amos's philosophy of life.

"Besides," she went on, in her young, and I must confess, in her perfect wisdom, "you're a man, like himself. In any case he wouldn't want to humble himself before you, when there's a woman about. He'll come to me all right in his own good time. Always provided——"

She paused, leaned across the table and tapped my

hand with her medial finger, fixed me with her brown
eyes at the back of which gleamed a mockery entirely un-
becoming a respectful step-daughter—

"Always provided he doesn't unbosom himself first to
the Princess Ramiroff."

I assumed my perfect expression of the man of the
world.

"Why, my dear, should Amos neglect the most charming and sympathetic member of his own household and
seek advice from a comparative stranger?"

She laughed her young, delighted laughter.

"Oh, Daddums, don't you know? Why, it jumps to
the eyes! Amos has fallen madly in love with Nadia.
Oh, darling!" Her eyes and hands and smiles and all
the feminine thing that was Dorothea flooded me in
triumph. "A great artist like you—and so blind! Oh,
poor dear old darling Daddums!"

Then again she paused, with a brow knitted ever so
little in perplexity.

"Darling, I thought you would be amused. You with
your sense of humour——"

"My dear," said I, "the sooner we begin to abandon
the idea of Amos as the toy savage the better."

She persisted. "But isn't it funny? Nadia and Amos.
Beauty and the Beast. Isn't it romantic?"

"Not at all," said I. "It's absurd. Let us drop the
subject."

In this house my will is law. Dorothea dropped it
with the unconcern of a monkey dropping the peel of an
orange which it is eating.

"Daddums," said she, "you are so clever—I wonder
whether you'll explain to me what Einstein's theory
really is."

I looked at her sternly.

"His theory is that rays of light which we once thought so straight are all bent and warped like the processes of the female mind."

"That," said she, "is the only lucid explanation I've ever had of it."

The following evening I was rung up by the Princess Ramiroff.

"Is that Mr. Fontenay? I want to ask you a favour.— Oh, yes, I know that your life and all that is at my disposal—but it is a question of the poor bear who is so unhappy. . . . Yes, he knows he has behaved badly. Let me intercede for his forgiveness. . . ."

And so on and so forth. When I could get in a word or two—

"How do you know all this?"

I could hear the silver notes of her laughter at the other end of the line.

"When an exiled Russian meets a bear, her national emblem, it's natural that she should make a friend of him and feed him with honey. But say you forgive him."

"Oh yes, I forgive him."

"Thanks. I'll send him along to you for dinner. *Au revoir!*"

She rang off.

She would send him along for dinner. He was there with her at the Villa Miranda.

A sudden fit of unreasonable anger overtook me. Anger against Dorothea for being right. Anger against the Princess for encouraging the fellow. Anger against Amos for his colossal impudence. And anger, raging and violent, against myself for being such an utter fool as to be angry.

CHAPTER VII

O N fine mornings—and, in this Land of Enchantment, most mornings are fine—I take my coffee
and croissant on the red-tiled, sun-baked balcony of my bedroom. What though it be winter, a thick
dressing-gown and warm slippers are ample protection
against any lurking inclemency; and there I sit over the
fragrant meal, my eyes absorbed in the never satiating
beauty of the only three things visible, the sea, the sky,
the line of the Esterel. Sometimes I dream of painting
the blue morning in its baffling light; but as yet I dare
not. . . . My old friend, Sir Lawrence Alma Tadema,
once got near the soul of the Mediterranean in a tiny
picture "In Blue Ionian Weather." I saw it long ago,
before I had set out on my travels. It dealt with in-
tensities—indigos, cobalts that caught your breath and
made your heart ache. It spoke Ionian truth: but had
no relation with the blue of the mornings here which was
both my unceasing joy and my despair. To express it,
even crudely, one would need at least a hundred shades;
no palette would be big enough for careful preparation,
no brain could be swift enough to mingle pigments ordi-
narily set in order to capture the ever-changing values.
There are blues and nothing else, sea and sky and mountain: a chromatic scale of blues from the deep Ionian to
what seems to be pearl-grey but is only murky blue in
travesty. Not the suggestion of another colour to give
guidance to the eye: often not even the flash of the white
or brown sail of a fishing boat: just blue and blue; the
sky azure; the sea deepening towards the west into ultra-

marine; the long line of low, delectable mountains standing out dreamily in pure and pale turquoise and their
bases swathed in a paler haze through which the villages
of Théoule and La Napoule shimmer aquamarine. No
common earth can be viewed from my balcony. I live
in a blue ether of illimitable tones of blue, in the pure
light of infinite space.

And then later, under the kisses of the golden sun, the
blue mists melt from the Esterel and the tender greens
peep shyly forth, and the little clusters of houses far away
re-clothe themselves in the pale mystery of marble
palaces.

But it is the early morning symphony of blue that I
love; for it strikes within me chords of past regrets, past
dreams, past longings, and sets my heart once more aching for a perfected beauty of existence of which, after all,
it is but the eternal symbol and the message.

So sat I on my balcony the morning after the return
of my poor prodigal.

He had come down to dinner the previous evening,
half sheepish, half defiant. To have figuratively slain
the fatted calf would have signified too great an appreciation of his foolishness. We received him as though nothing had happened. . . .

I learned later that of the things undreamed of in his
philosophy, fatted calves were the most remote. He had
expected sharpened tongues, such as his mother was wont
to greet him with after the rare absences from the station
wherein he had sown his mild wild oats.

I could see him wrinkling a perplexed brow, when he
was received by Dorothea's laughing gossip and by my
own unreproachful demeanour. As I have had reason to
remark, Amos was not garrulous at meals, the stoking of

the furnaces of his great frame being a matter of too deep a preoccupation. But when Dorothea had retired, and I had lit my cigar and Amos his pipe, he blundered into speech.

"I've been rude, Uncle. I apologize."

"My dear fellow," said I, "it's not a question of rudeness; it's merely one of not quite understanding our ways, which must seem strange to you after Warraranga."

"Yes," he said, "blooming strange." He looked in a far away manner at something on the wall over my head. "I wonder whether I ever was in Warraranga. Somewhere on my way here I saw a wallaby in a cage. . . ."

I interrupted him. Why let him develop the melancholy parallel? "Would you like to be back in Warraranga?"

"I dunno," said he. "Perhaps the wallaby wasn't a case in point. He was sure of his bellyful, and the cage was big and he could jump about just as he darned well pleased——"

"So can you," I smiled.

"No," said he. "I jump on people's feet and they holler out." He reflected for a moment or two and continued: "No, I don't want to be back. Leastways not yet awhile. We have no women out there like the Princess—or Dorothea." And after another of his pauses—"I didn't know there were such women in the world."

"Such women," said I, with a reminiscence of Steele, "are a liberal education to a young man."

He bent forward eagerly and brought his great hand down on the table. "That's just what it is! Just what I've been feeling and not known how to say."

"But half a dozen are better than two," said I, "and twenty are better than half a dozen."

"Ah!" said he, doubtfully.

"Some will teach you good things, and some bad. There are all kinds of sides to life which a man must learn if he's going to hold his own in the world. It'll take you about five years to get a superficial working knowledge of them, after which you can look around and fall in love and marry without dooming a pair of human beings to too great misery."

"Ah!" repeated Amos.

As a contribution to the discussion the remark lacked brilliance. But his mental processes were obvious— the inverse of my arithmetical proposition, carried a step further to the principle of one being better than two.

At this point Dorothea entered, cloaked for outer revelry, announcing her intention of joining the Crawley-Johnstones at the Casino. A cheque that had come in that day from the fraudulent embroidered-bag shop was burning a hole in her pocket. She must gamble or she must die.

"Gamble?" cried Amos.

I laughed. "What was I saying? Here's a young woman who will teach you some of the necessary bad things. Go along with Dorothea. All right—if you like," I added in reference to my step-daughter's mute imploringness. "I'll come too."

We whisked down to the Casino, where after the formalities necessary to gain Amos his card of admission to the *Salles de Baccara,* we entered the lofty, discreet rooms, where the idlers of Cannes congregate in full season.

It was the first time his eyes had rested on such a scene. There was the elegance of the whole imaginable social gamut from princes of the great world porphyro-genitic, born in the purple, to little princesses of the half-world, born in the gutter.   The nobility and the baseness, the scorn and the greed, the laughter and the despair of France and England and America attired impeccably, so that one knew not fair sinner from fragile saint, or states-man from criminal, sat or stood or moved in pell-mell jumble and jostle.   The conglomerate value of the pearls on women's necks and the diamonds about other portions of their persons would have paid for the war, were it not that if all were thrown on the market together, not even South America, already pearl and diamond glutted, could have bought them. . . . But in the eyes of barbarous youth (as, indeed, in those of middle-aged and sophisti-cated man) bare shoulders, bosoms and arms crowned by heads of loveliness, gleamed more astonishing and precious than all the precious gems wherewith they were adorned.   To Amos, the spectacle was that of his first vision of the Princess in her low-cut evening gown multi-plied a thousandfold.   He gaped around at one woman after another.   I held his arm.

"My boy," said I, "if you set properly about it, you can learn here in a month more than you could in two years elsewhere," and I introduced him to Mrs. Blenner-hasset, a charming young widow with a past *sans re-proche* and a future apparently *sans peur.*

She fanned herself.   "How do they manage to make the air in this place so dry?"

"Mrs. Blennerhasset," I said, "is panting for cooling streams.   Take her into the bar"—I pointed down the room—"and let her drink."

"How you understand us!" she said.

I whispered into Amos's ears—I was trying a bold ex-periment.

"For God's sake give the waiter a five-franc tip.   Thus you will acquire merit in all eyes."

Of course, I know I ought to have devised other education for the sacred charge, my nephew. I ought to have sacrificed my pleasant life and taken him to London and accompanied him on instructive courses through Museums and Historical Monuments and arranged for him to attend lectures on whatever they may lecture about in South Kensington, and trotted him round the various sermon-famous churches (so as to broaden his mind) from the City Temple to Farm Street, and gathered together around my table—tea and dinner—such strenuous young intellectuals as my middle-aged contemporaries have managed to procreate, and generally given him all the advantages, within my command, of the Higher Thought and the Lower Corporealism. I am perfectly acquainted with the weight and the velocity of every stone which you may throw at me in rebuke of dereliction of duty. But, to my pagan mind (for which please remember the responsibility of Dorcas, my sister, and his mother), the principle involved in the pursuit of things that one ought not to do and the neglect of those which one ought to do has always appealed to me as that of the perfected existence of the free and enlightened man.

Therefore I make no apologies. Dorcas desired her son to see the world. I was showing it to him as it was my privilege to see it.

While conversing casually with friends, I found that our entry with our gigantic and brawny young barbarian had caused a mild sensation, report of him having already run through Cannes. I must introduce him to all kinds of fair ladies; I must bring him to innumerable tea-parties, to lunches in more reasonable numbers, and to a few dinners. Had I accepted I should have been bear-leader in ordinary for the rest of the season.

Mrs. Blennerhasset led him back to me: then drew me

aside. Her face challenged the Æschylean ocean in the countless ripple of its smile.

"He's a dear. But do tell him it's unnecessary to order a quart of champagne for one poor stray woman, while he drinks nothing himself but tepid water out of a carafe. Of course, I didn't know anything about it till the waiter came with the open bottle."

"I ought to have told you he was bred in the Bush."

"So I gathered from his conversation. What's 'bred in the Bush'—it sounds like a proverb—but I can't find the tail to it. Anyhow, take care of that young man. He has got the sins of us all on his conscience. It will break down under the weight one of these days and then his own sins won't matter." She paused, then said suddenly: "Can you lunch with me on Tuesday?"

I passed a hand over a reflecting head. Tuesday, Tuesday? Alas and alas! I had promised the day to a distinguished Royal Academician, passing through Cannes, whose life's dream, apparently, it had been to be personally conducted by one who knew through the old hillside towns, Biot, Vence, Saint Pol du Var. Tuesday was his one day.

"I'm sorry, but it doesn't matter," she replied cheerfully. "I only asked you out of politeness, for I'm sure Mr. Burden will be much more amusing without you."

I bowed her my hundred thousand thanks. She waved them aside.

"I'd sooner have him by himself. The young man looks on you as the great Panjandrum, the Omnipotent Conundrum——"

"You have a pretty wit," I interrupted.

"Madame," said a discreet attendant coming up, "there is a vacant place which I have reserved at the five louis table."

"I fly," she said. "Sorry you can't join us. Nadia Ramiroff will be there, and that fascinating villain, Ramon Garcia, and one or two others. Yes"—to the beckoning attendant—"I'm coming."

Madame d'Orbigny swam down the centre aisle and smiled her greeting.

"Won't you introduce your handsome nephew whom everybody's talking about?"

"Do you want a drink?" I asked.

"Good heavens, no!"

"Then I'll bring him to you."

She looked horrified—pardonably mistaken, I must confess. I have found that the humorous side of me is often hidden from other folk. I reassured her.

"He's the totallest abstainer that has ever abstained since babyhood."

I moved a few steps and clutched Amos who, head and shoulders above the crowd round the table near by, was gaping unintelligently at the wicked game. I made the requested presentation, and having left them sitting on one of the round central settees, gracefully retired from their neighbourhood in quest of Dorothea. I found her at one of the small tables gloating contentedly over a stack of green hundred franc plaques and red louis counters. I watched her win for a while. At last:

"My dear," said I, "the air is stale, the company's flat, and a continuance of your game, I'm sure, will be distinctly unprofitable. I would suggest our all going to our comfortable beds."

"Leaving when I'm having the luck of my life? No, no. My last bank, I passed eight times."

I lifted polite shoulders, commended Amos to her speedy care when she should arise penniless, and made for home. Perhaps I should have stayed if Nadia had been there. But she had gone to Monte Carlo. Ramon Garcia, chance encountered, volunteered the information, which was like the fellow's suave but swaggering impudence. She had gone, he said, to play the great game—*Trente et Quarante*. Alas! There was no stopping her. I replied stiffly that I would not permit myself the liberty of criticizing the movements of the Princess Ramiroff. He agreed.

"Precisely! But ah! she needs friends."

"She has them, Monsieur; good night," said I in a very bad temper.

The insolent Ecuadorian or Patagonian or whatever he was!

I passed by the settee. Amos had gathered somehow another (figuratively speaking) fair dame, Miss Challenor, an international lawn tennis player, who prided herself on the fact that every ounce of flesh on her body —and it might well be measured by ounces—was pure muscle. She looked like a bit of old string with a knot tied at the end of it for a head. The two ladies talked across Amos, who, striving to be polite, turned his heavy face from one to the other with the regularity of an automaton.

I approached, made my obeisance and adieux. To a restive Amos I said:

"You're in the best and most adorable of hands. Besides, you've got to look after Dorothea when she has lost all her money."

Oh, the joy to get out of the evil-smelling, all but drugged atmosphere, into the pure, crisp air. The moon stood serene in the heavens and the rippled silver gauze of the sea crept into the harbour. I walked down the avenue of plane trees among the soft and dreamy shadows and turned up the hill.

I know not at what hour Dorothea came home. I can trust her with untold latch-keys. In London, where she lives in a flat over her embroidered-bag shop, she can appear with the milk if such is her good pleasure. That she is at liberty to do the same in Cannes makes for the charm of our mutual relations. If I sat grimly up for her, she would loathe me. And I hate being loathed.

So I went to bed, putting out of my mind the happenings of the day and thinking (a sure way of inducing sleep) of the amazing picture I could paint on a "five league canvas with a brush of comet's hair."

It was on my balcony, in the blue and pale gold of the morning above recorded, that I thought of the previous evening, although there was no great matter for reflection. The only teasing point was the luncheon party to which Amos was bidden as the fellow guest of Nadia and Ramon Garcia.

I lit my after-breakfast cigarette, and I noted that the spiral of smoke from the end was only a few tones lighter than the blue mist swathing the Cybele bosoms of the Esterel.

An infernal noise at my bedroom door caused me to turn round and crane my head. It was Amos, who had burst in unceremoniously. He strode across the room to the balcony, the most dissolute, overnight figure I have ever beheld at nine in the morning. He was still in dinner costume. His collar was crumpled, his tie somewhere round the back of his neck, his stiff shirt-front a grimy and creased disgrace, with buttonholes bursted from studs, his unshaven cheeks a dingy reproach. He plumped on the table a packet which looked like letters enclosed in strained yellow elastic bands.

"I've got 'em," he cried. "I take you to witness that

I've got 'em.   I don't want to be had up for robbery.   I ain't got anything else."   He held up his hands *kamerad* fashion.   "You can search me."

"What the deuce is this all about?" I asked, fingering the packet.

He pounced on my hand.   "No, no.   You're not going to read 'em, Uncle.   I haven't.   Have you got a big envelope and sealing-wax?"

"Of course I have," said I, impatiently.   "But I don't keep them in my bedroom.   Ring the bell for François. No, wait a minute, and explain yourself.   You obviously haven't been to bed, and if you hadn't been house-trained by your excellent mother, I should say that you've been making a beast of a night of it."

At this point, after a tap or two and a reconnoitring glance through the door ajar, there entered Dorothea in white tennis kit, fresh as the morning.   I rose from my chair.

"What the——"

She cut me short, speaking as she crossed the floor.

"Yes, I know, Daddums.   What the blankety-blank-blank is the meaning of this female intrusion?   It's about Amos.   He hasn't been home all night."   Then, as she stepped on to the balcony she saw him.

"Oh, it's you, is it?"

"Yes, it's me," said Amos.

"You haven't been to bed?"

"My dear, if he had, would he have arisen and re-invested himself in this——" I waved a hand.

She nodded.   "Yes, in this——" and caught the eye of Amos, who stood sheepish and self-conscious.   She addressed him in the stony manner of the offended modern young woman.   "I searched the whole Casino for you, and when I went to the door the commissionaire

told me that a monsieur answering your description—as
you were last night—had already gone."

"If you'll give me time," said Amos, "I'll tell Uncle
David all about it."

"And not me?"

Amos grew dull crimson and swayed his body in his
funny bear-like way.

"No, Cousin Dorothea."

"If your story is as disreputable as your appearance,"
she countered acidly, "this is certainly no place for me."

She went out, her head in the air and a little curl of
disdain at the corners of her lips.

Amos's eyes followed her till she disappeared through
the bedroom door, and then he turned to me with a
puckered brow.

"She thinks I've been painting the town red; but I
haven't. You must tell her I'm not that sort."

Again I asked what the dickens he had been up to and
what were the letters which he desired to seal up in my
presence. He scratched his head and gave me to understand that not having breakfasted he was a-hungered and
a-thirst. I rang for François, and bade him bring eggs
and coffee and sealing-wax and croissants and set another chair for Mr. Burden on the terrace.

The silver and blue of the morning ripened into gold
and azure. A little wind from the west, a touch of
Mistral, swept the mist from the Esterel and the folds of
the mountains stood out green and olive, and the mystery
faded from the old town on the Souquet which laughed,
in its new clear beauty, at its late illusion.

And there in the sunshine, with intervals for vast refreshment, he told me the following amazing tale which,
for the sake of economy of narrative, I supplement with
details learned later, and relate in my own fashion.

CHAPTER VIII

YOU will remember that I left Amos at the Casino sitting between Madame d'Orbigny and the lawn-tennis lady, who conducted across his body a vehement conversation. From this constraint he suddenly extricated himself in his artless way. He got up, grinned at them and walked off. Miss Challenor, it seems, was deeply offended and called Amos an uncivilized boor; but Madame d'Orbigny told me that it served her right for her execrable manners in screaming tennis shop which the poor boy could not understand, and in which she herself was entirely uninterested; if she, Madame d'Orbigny, had been a man she would have given her the same lesson.

Amos, freed, lurched about seeking Dorothea. He found her at her table, still winning. Let her turn the corner of another thousand and she would stop. But he mustn't stand over her glowering his puritanical disapproval down her back. He would bring her bad luck. So he moved off and stood among the crowd around the "big" table, looking on at the incomprehensible game in which vast sums of money changed hands at every deal of the cards, and striving to reconcile the hideous wickedness of the proceedings with the otherwise virtuous lives of those who took a part in them, such as Dorothea, Mrs. Blennerhasset, then seated with a pile of thousand franc notes in front of her, and the entirely adorable Princess Ramiroff, self-proclaimed the most notorious little gambler on the coast.

Once, as a boy, lured by Satan, he had given a station

hand sixpence to put on a horse. The animal romped home at forty to one. The baser sixpence was transmuted into a glorious golden sovereign, wealth beyond the dreams of his boyhood's avarice. But his mother discovering it one day—by dint of fumbling with his emblem of El Dorado, he had worked a hole in his breeches pocket and it had fallen with a chink on the wash-house floor—and learning whence it came, threw it with anger into the fiery furnace beneath the copper—it was washing day—and told him that so, if he pursued his evil courses, would his soul burn in Hell. He had believed her words for many years. From infancy he had been trained in what to most sane folk is the humorous eschatology of the late Dr. Watts. No "Little Bo-Peep" or "Little Jack Horner" for his baby lips to lisp, but the invigorating poem:

"There is a dreadful Hell
Of everlasting Pains,
Where Sinners must with Devils dwell,
In Torment, Fire and Chains."

Even now in his manhood he could not free himself from the literalness of this physical damnation. If he had been liable, but for his mother directed by God's grace, to the eternal torture of continuous combustion—he had always imagined a soul in Hell to be like a bit of asbestos, always red hot and never consumed—for staking his poor little sixpence on a horse race, what unimaginably awful penalties were being incurred by these pleasant folk who gambled for thousands of sixpences every day of their lives?

The spectacle of this concentration of deadly sin dazed and baffled him.

And there was also the great Drink Question. I had

wormed this out of him in the course of many conversations. His mother, etymologically accurate, had informed him that alcohol was an Arabic word meaning "The Devil." But she had also assured him that, in so terming spirituous liquor, the Arabs had been directly inspired by the Almighty. In this faith Amos had lived until he came to Cannes. There he found us all, decent, God-fearing folk drinking (in moderation) alcohol, or The Devil, in all sorts of alluring forms. . . . That evening I had sent him away with Mrs. Blennerhasset to quench her thirst, he had asked—so she told me:

"What will you take?"

Idly she had replied: "Oh, anything mildly alcoholic."

Whereupon Amos, the docile, remembering my various lectures on petty meannesses which proceeded, not from lack of generous impulse, but from sheer ignorance of values, rushed to the bar and ordered the most expensive alcoholic liquor he could think of, which was a quart of the best champagne.

He had no doubt that, socially, he had done the splendid thing. But, morally, had he not been guilty of great wickedness?

At the General Store at Warraranga owned and controlled by Dorcas, no liquor was allowed to be sold. Furthermore—such is the impression which Amos's references to his home have made on my confused mind—she would make occasional raids on the men's quarters, and whatever bottle of whisky she discovered, she would smash upon the floor as a stumbling block and an offence to the faint-hearted. How she managed to die unmurdered will be an insoluble mystery for the rest of my life.

This is by the way. We return to Amos standing unbeautiful, and clothed in the none too perfectly fitting

dinner-suit of the Nice tailor, in the alien throng, eating
his conscience out in foggy bewilderment. By degrees he
edged (or barged) his huge frame to the front rank behind the chairs and surveyed the nine high players. Directly opposite sat Ramon Garcia, who, as was obvious
even to his inexperienced eye, was losing heavily. The
sentiment of hatred being forbidden by the Evangelical
creed in which he had been nurtured, he regarded the
South American with a puritanical disapprobation, compared to which hatred would have been fulsome fawning.
At the uplifting, on the croupier's spoon, of every
staked packet of ten thousand franc notes, Amos felt like
an Israelite of old witnessing the destruction of his enemies. He grew excited, exultant. When the wretched
Garcia lost a bank of five thousand at the first banco he
was inclined to shout: "The sword of the Lord and
Gideon!" and physically consummate the man's discomfiture. But he was restrained from so doing by his recent lesson in civilized deportment. As he watched, his
shrewd brain grasped the principle of the simple game,
and he intelligently followed Garcia's varying fortune,
and presently he became absorbed. Inspired by Gide-
onite wrath, he willed him to lose. Garcia lost and lost.
Amos, concentrating on the sinner, did not notice the
mischievous glances of Mrs. Blennerhasset sitting two
places in numerical order below, who was winning and
winning. Scarcely even was he conscious of that com-
municable tension of the spectators of high play. He
lived intensely in himself, in his almost entranced desire
that ruin should fall on the unutterable curled and ironed
foreigner, who had held in his profane arms the sacred
body of the princess of his dreams.

If there is anything in luck, in mascotism or anti-
mascotism, one might have reason to believe that Amos,

towering his great bulk above the table, had the most
maleficent of influences on the occupant of the seat on
whom his unswerving eyes were fixed.

Eventually Garcia surveyed the green cloth in front of
him, bare of everything save his match-box. He made
a brave show of relighting his cigar before he rose from
the table. But Amos noted that the cigar had not caught
and that it was only a gesture of bravura on the part of
the man.

A vague middle-aged personage dropped into the gambler's chair. Amos became conscious of a touch on his
arm. It was Mrs. Blennerhasset. She smiled on him
kindly.

"You've brought me good luck. Look." She held a
wooden bowl filled high with plaques and notes. "Let
me change this, and then I'll stand you a drink out of
my winnings."

He followed her to the change desk and thence through
the crowded room to the bar, by chance almost empty.
They sat down at the first table by the door. The white-
coated barman took the orders. No champagne this
time. Orangeade. Mrs. Blennerhasset, after the way of
the woman of the world, when she is a man's hostess,
slipped the note of settlement at once into the bar-
assistant's hand.

"What peace," she said, "after that bear garden."

But Amos did not hear. Beside themselves there were
but two couples in the place. One on the high stool by
the bar itself, the other in the far diagonal corner, under
the lee of the turn of the bar. And at this couple Amos
glared.

They were Ramon Garcia and the Princess Ramiroff.
She was wearing the black dress in which I had painted
her and in which Amos had first seen her, and she had

round her neck her precious rope of pearls. She looked white and ill. Garcia turned towards her, almost eclipsed her from sight. But Amos saw. On the marble table stood idle, untouched, straw-furnished glasses. The pair conversed in low tones, almost in whispers, the man apparently insistent, the woman frightened. Picture her small, fragile, delicate, in her nothing-at-all of a black bodice, golden-haired, green-eyed, the wonder of her skin just a flat tone under the electric light, and her mobile little mouth quivering as she spoke.

Mrs. Blennerhasset, always indulgent woman of the world, laid a commanding touch on Amos's arm, so that he had to turn.

"Do you know the Princess?"

"Know her? Why, of course I do," said Amos. "Do you?"

"Why, yes." The lady smiled. "She's the dearest thing in Cannes. But I don't quite care for her friend."

"Oh," said Amos.

Whereupon he leaped up, barbarically disregardful of his hostess, crossed the room, and stood in front of the pair, the newest product of Latin America and the oldest product of Russia. Ramon Garcia rose with the perfection of ironical courtesy. Amos, ignoring his existence, stretched out his huge paw to Nadia, and as soon as her hand mechanically extended was grasped, he held it in his vast grip.

"Come over to us, you'll be more comfortable than you are here."

Dragged upward to her feet, she fumbled with her words.

"But I'm with Señor Garcia."

"I don't care who you're with, you're coming with me."

The couple on the stools, a young man and a little lady

of no account, seemed to find relief in the incident from the boredom of their temporary companionship. The young woman giggled loudly. Amos turned sharply round and catching a responsive grin on the young man's face, conveyed the impression of being an unsafe butt for derision; whereupon the young man hastily hid all his grin and as much of his face as he could in his long tumbler of iced drink and, like the Arabs in the poem, silently faded away with his partner.

Meanwhile Nadia, still in the grip of Amos, was led to Mrs. Blennerhasset, by whose side she sank in bewilderment. The South American, in furious anger, swung Amos violently by the arm, to which motive force our young giant responded slowly, like a rock turning on a pivot, in answer to the pressure of a secret spring. Señor Ramon Garcia apostrophized him in his semi-barbaric French. Amos stood stolid until he paused for breath. Then he said:

"No *comprennez*. Talk English."

It was like a douche of cold water. Garcia sputtered a few words, then pulled himself together.

"We will talk English to-morrow, sir," he said slowly. *"Madame la Princesse,"* he bowed low, *"votre très obéissant serviteur."*

"If I kicked him into the middle of that first table there," said Amos, gazing through the open door at the departing figure, "I suppose there'd be a row."

"There would," said Mrs. Blennerhasset. "But why do you want to kick poor Garcia?"

"You said you didn't like him, and neither do I," replied Amos. He grinned. "I don't know what he was talking about, but he looks the sort of joker that carries either a gun or a sheath-knife in his hip-pocket. From the way his moustache curls, I should think it's a knife."

He loomed large over and above the two seated women. The little Princess, dead white, stared, with strained face, across the table.

"I don't understand. Why have you made an enemy of that man?"

"Because he's no friend of yours. Any silly fool could see that. He was bullying you. Now, wasn't he?"

Mrs. Blennerhasset rose tactfully. An irresistible spirit moved her to go and lose her winnings. No. She laughed with an arresting gesture. She had no need of escort along the Road to Ruin. Nadia swept after her for a few paces.

"For God's sake, my dear——"

"Of course not. Not a word. You can trust me."

Nadia returned to Amos.

"She's a good woman. Anyone else, and you would have made a fine scandal in Cannes."

Amos, who had been holding his great bulk in gladiatorial defiance, suddenly collapsed. His shoulders sagged.

"You're not angry with me, are you?"

The feminine principle in her could not repress a wan smile.

"What you have done is not that which usually happens in good society."

"I don't care about society," said Amos. "I care about you. Let's sit down."

"Ah, no! I must be going home. I am tired. I went over to Monte Carlo to dine with some friends from here. I do not think your uncle knows them—the Valentine Montgomeries—Sir Valentine, you know. He became famous during the war for supplying the allied armies with the funny little metal things you stick into boots for the laces. They have that big villa on the Californie

—the Villa Yildiz. It's supposed to be the Yildiz kiosque in miniature——"

"I don't know what you're talking about," said Amos politely.

Nadia passed her hand over her eyes.

"Neither do I. I'm so tired. After dinner I went into the Sporting Club and lost twenty thousand francs in a quarter of an hour, and then they drove me back here."

"Why did you come here instead of going to bed?"

The Princess shrugged her shoulders and looked wide of him.

"You came to meet that blamed Dago," said the direct Amos.

She shot a swift upward glance. "What makes you say that?"

"You do," he replied.

"I must go home," said Nadia.

"How are you going?"

"Anything. Cab—taxi——"

"I'll take you. I'm not letting you take any risks with Mr. Garcia. You're safe with me. You can bet your life you are."

He grinned broadly in the pride of his youth and his strength and his adoration. She said yieldingly:

"That will be very sweet of you."

"Sweet?"

"Is that not right in English? I mean kind, charming——"

"Aw!" said Amos.

They passed through the rooms into the vestibule. Dorothea, dependent on his escort, was blotted from his mind. The young savage, in temporary possession of the desired female of the species, was too exultant to have a thought for any other. Nadia guided him in the path whereby wraps and hats and coats could be recovered.

A myrmidon brought up a taxi.

As soon as they drove off together, he asked:

"What made you so scared at that blamed Garcia feller?"

All of a sudden she broke down and began to cry and sob and shake her small frame hysterically.

"My Gosh, Princess, what's it all about?" cried Amos.

In the circumstances, the ordinary man, with heart and honour free, would have put his protecting arm around the weeping wisp of lady and drawn her to him—and then God knows what might have happened. But Amos, dumbfounded, let her weep. He made various attempts at consolation.

"If that feller's hurting you, I'll skin him alive. Just tell me."

So had he offered to be her champion against all the Soviets of Russia; with the same serious confidence and lack of rodomontade. His comfortable voice seemed to reassure her, for she eventually dried her tears, and when, after the short drive, the taxi drew up outside the Villa Miranda, she held out her hand with a smile. But Amos said:

"I want to hear about that feller Garcia."

She wavered for a moment, her foot on the first step. In the keen air of the starlit night she stood out clear against the gloom of the house, a fur-clad wraith with a halo of pale gold. She inclined her head so as to get a glimpse of the ground floor windows on the left from which gleamed a strip of brightness.

"They are still up. Come in."

He dismissed the taxi, opened the door with the key

she had fumbled for in her bag, and followed her into the villa.

In the large well-lit drawing-room the bridge tables were occupied. At one sat the Marchese della Fontana, wizened, white-moustached, distinguished. At the other the gaunt and forbidding Marchesa, aunt of the Princess. A third had evidently just been abandoned and two men hung round, smoking cigarettes. At the entrance of Nadia and Amos they came forward.

"Ah, Princess——"

"Now we can get our four; the Willoughbys have gone, having cleaned us out."

"No, old chap," cried the other, "don't say that. It was you who insisted on the last rubber."

"It doesn't matter. We can carry on again."

A simultaneous interval for deal happening at the two tables, Nadia made formal presentation of Amos, after which host and hostess sped back to their places. On the vacant table one of the men spread out the cards.

"Let us cut for partners."

"I am sorry," said Nadia, "but Mr. Burden, I know, does not play bridge and I am too tired."

"Not play bridge?" asked the man who had bewailed the defection of the Willoughbys, turning to Amos. "Then what do you play?"

"Nothing," replied Amos.

"Oh, come," said the other, "it isn't bedtime yet. We must do something."

They were both fairly young, in the middle thirties; clean shaven; one an American, somewhat rosy, the other an Englishman, long and lean. They had been introduced respectively as Mr. Cyrus Spedding and Captain Thompson. Spedding, who had deprecated the reflection on the Willoughbys' honourable conduct, laughed pleasantly:

"We must get something out of Mr. Burden, anyway."

"I don't play cards," said Amos.

"Of course, if one can't afford to lose——" began the Englishman.

"If I wanted to, I could lose a darned sight more than you can," said Amos.

He was a bit off his balance, the first squiring of dames being an experience disequilibrating to a temperament so ingenuous. Besides, in spite of his ignorance of the world, the two men awakened within him a certain antagonism; yet not the same as that awakened by his cousin. He disliked Claude Worthington exceedingly; but he grudgingly recognized in him the pure breed. With these two men something was wrong; just as something had been wrong with the crook who had caused his first disillusion in the great world, and with the unspeakable South American whose insolence towards the Princess he was in this house to learn.

"I'll take you on at anything you like," said Thompson.

"I, too," said the American.

Said Nadia, troubled: "One of these tables will soon be up and you can cut in."

"No, I'm sick of bridge. Spedding and I are out for your friend's blood."

Amos's young pulses throbbed with anger. That was not the way to talk to Her Serene Highness, the Princess Ramiroff. He said:

"I've never touched a card in my life. If it's a game of skill, you'll do me down, and I'm not having any. But a game of chance——"

"Right," said Thompson. *"Chemin de fer."*

"That's the game they were playing at the Casino?"

"You've guessed first time," said Spedding. He turned to the Princess. "Would you mind telling me where we can find the shoe and the counters?"

"I'll bring them," said Nadia, very dignified, and she moved away.

Obeying a swift glance, Amos followed her to a cabinet at the far end of the room.

"I'm sorry—I thought we could step away into my uncle's *cabinet de travail*. But how can we? And what are you doing? I scarcely know these people."

"It's all right," said Amos. "If I lose, I lose like a man. If I win, I win. But I'm not going to be sneered at by any Englishman or Yankee, especially when you're about."

She shrugged helpless shoulders and handed him shoe and cards and counters, which he brought to the table. They sat down, Nadia by Amos's side.

"As Mr. Burden does not know the game, I will guide him."

So they began to play, at first with varying fortunes, afterwards with a steady trend of luck to Amos, the neophyte. He sat as a man bemused, held in the thrall of the unprecedented excitement. The wickedness of the act he forgot, conscious only of foes in the two men, of insult to the fair lady to be wiped out in this, the only way. It was also thrilling to find that magic in his fingers which turned up the winning cards, eights and nines, almost at will. The losers played wildly, as angrily as common manners permitted. Amos, unaccustomed to the etiquette of the gaming table, grinned his delight.

At last the bridge table rose. A little clock on the mantelpiece struck two in a shrill silver tone. Amos's opponents cried an end to the game. It was certainly not their night out, they said. Counters being redeemed,

Amos found himself the winner of a great sum, and the jacket pocket bulged with bundles of notes, which he thrust in untidily.

"You'll give us our revenge another night," said the American.

"No," said Amos. "I only played to-night to amuse you. I ain't going to do it a second time."

"It's usual among gentlemen," said the English-man——

Amos pricked up his ears. The sound of the word had a ring of unpleasant reminiscence.

"I don't hold with gentlemen," said he, "who are out for other folk's money."

The little Marchese sped from the group of leave-taking bridge players, whose attention had been drawn to the dispute.

"*Mes chers amis*—my dear friends"—he began. "Surely there seems to be a little misunderstanding——"

"No, there ain't," declared Amos, drawing out the pocketful of notes. "These fellers want to win back the money I've won from 'em. But I ain't going to keep money got this way. Not me." He clamped the mass on the table and turned to Nadia, who stood uncomfortable, half frightened, but not unadmiring: "Princess, give that to the poor Russians starving here in Cannes. Them what you've told me of——"

"So that if these gentlemen claim their revenge—" she smiled brightly.

Amos burst into a guffaw. "They can go to the Russians."

"That puts an entirely different light on the matter," said Captain Thompson.

Mr. Spedding agreed. "I guess it does."

"All the same," said the Englishman, "I can't help feeling that we've been butchered to make a Russian holiday."

"In my country, Captain Thompson," said the Princess with her prim little Russian accent, "people have really been butchered to make a holiday."

She held up her little head very proudly. No Thompson, even though he commanded a troop of Household Cavalry, should sneer at the tragedy of Russia.

"A joke's a joke, Princess."

"When it is not a gibe," she said.

Suddenly she became aware of a dead silence. The chatter of the bridge party clustered around her aunt, the Marchesa, had ceased. She turned to the little crowd, her two hands full of the notes:

"One does not get such a gift for our Russian poor every evening in the week. You will pardon me for being somewhat—what you say?—*émotionnée*."

A lady came forward, saving the situation.

"But who is the benefactor?"

"My good friend, Mr. Burden, from Australia." She introduced Amos—"Mrs. Weingartner."

"German?" asked Amos.

The lady smiled unhappily. "American. Pittsburg."

"How d'ye do, mum?" said Amos.

Whereupon, after perfunctory bows to the Princess, the company stood for a frozen moment and then, under the smile of the little old Marchese, melted away.

The two were left alone for a moment.

"If you were not such a good, kind, strong bear I should sometimes be very cross with you," said Nadia.

"Gosh! What have I done wrong now?"

"You must not mention the word 'German' to anybody on the Riviera. Don't you know that Mrs. Weingartner was *née* Mosenthal? *Américaine pur sang*. And that her husband fabricates as much steel in a year as would make a bridge from here to New York? And apropos of bridges, that she is the very worst bridge player in Cannes? Ah, my friend, you have made a monumental *gaffe*."

"What's a *gaffe?*"

"It means that you have put your foot in it with my uncle, the Marchese."

"Gosh!" cried Amos, a million miles from comprehension.

The Marchese and his wife came in through the open door. They both looked old and haggard, and had heavy, baggy flesh below the eyes. Nadia ran towards them, her arms outstretched.

"My dear ones, you are too tired for any words. You must go to bed. I have to talk to Mr. Burden about the distribution of his generous gift."

"It would be interesting to know how much it is," said the Marchese with a courteous bow.

Nadia waved an expressive hand in front of her face.

"That you will never know, my dear uncle."

He smiled indulgently, bade the younger folk an apologetic good night, and disappeared with the Marchesa.

"Are you not tired too?" asked Nadia.

"You are," said he. "Anyone can see that. I suppose I ought to go. But I didn't come here to play cards. I came to learn about that feller, Ramon Garcia."

"Yes," she said, "but you cannot help me. No one can help me." Her eyes rested for a moment on the piles of notes. Then she went to the table and counted them deliberately. She turned to him with an enigmatic little smile. "Perhaps you have helped me more than you know. Good night."

But Amos, the simple man of the fixed idea, returned to Garcia.

"He doesn't count," said the Princess. "It is nothing. He was only rude and I was angry."

Amos sat down deliberately on one of the chairs by a card table.

"I suppose lots of women cry for nothing; but not a woman like you. I ain't going from this room till you tell me what this feller has done to you. You don't like him. Uncle don't like him. And you can bet your life I don't like him. I can't see as how he has got any friends."

"Oh, but I assure you, he has got a great many—and very powerful friends. He goes to all the best families in Cannes."

"They must be gumps to have him," said Amos.

Nadia shrugged her shoulders and fingered the now carefully folded pile of notes. Again she held out her hand. Amos rose, stuck his hands in his trouser pockets and towered over her. She rushed towards him imploringly.

"Oh, go. Please go, my dear friend. Believe me, I am not anxious. I can arrange everything now."

"Why now?"

"Because, as I said, it is nothing important. Women are sometimes hysterical. It will be all right."

"Nothing can be all right with a feller like that," Amos persisted. "He's wrong all through. I want to get to the bottom of it."

So they argued for a good while longer. She was too exhausted by an emotional day to exert the ordinary wiles of women. Perhaps instinctively, too, she knew that on this fanatical cherisher of the fixed idea they would be of no avail; and a fixed idea, that of knight-errantry to the death in her defence, which could not but appeal to her feminine inmost. All she could do was to fence in desperation, so as to guard the secret of which she was ashamed. Now and then shafts of anger flashed from her at the uncouth would-be dragon slayer who had unwittingly delivered her from the power of the monster. On Amos, however, both arrows of wrath and poor little smiles of seduction fell blunted. His heredity spoke. I can imagine a poor wretch under process of conversion at the hands of the zealous Ezra Burden breaking down finally, and saying in his ignorant and worn-out way:

"Yes, damn you. I'm saved."

In circumstances of discipline I can picture a single-minded, adamantine Dorcas.

At last, exhausted by the unrelenting tyranny of his purpose, the artificial product of the centuries that was the princess fell into hopeless shattered pieces and the primitive little Russian, Nadia, spat out:

"If you want to know, he has one, two, three, four, five, six"—she counted on her outstretched fingers—"of my letters. Foolish letters I wrote a year ago. I want to get them back. He is a *goujat*—a wicked, horrible man—I know now. He will not give them to me. He will only sell them. And I have not the price to pay for them. I play to-night to win the money and I lose twenty thousand francs. There! That is what it is. You force me to tell you." She reeled. "Oh *mon Dieu! Mon Dieu!*" and threw herself, a tiny crumpled up little heap in the corner of a couch, thrust away by the side of the wall.

Amos stood still for a few moments, then went up to her and put his great paw on her shoulder.

"Don't you worry, Princess."

And when she raised her head out of her weariness and her shame, she found that he had gone.

What happened to Amos for the next five or six hours even he had but a dim notion. He merely obeyed his physical instinct and walked hard; walked anywhere, unconcernedly, his mind a-whirl with the sensations of a young man's lifetime crowded into a single evening. And the whole experience had been a crescendo of emotion. There had been the hatred of Garcia; the intensity of the spell he had put upon him so that he should lose; the sudden rescue of the Princess from his evildom; her passion of tears; his first flaming into deliberate sin at the gaming-table; the diabolical thrill of success. At last, her confession; the maddening sight of the poor little shrivelled heap of that for which he would give his soul, in the silken corner of the yellow and red striped couch. . . .

Whence he had picked up the fact that the depraved and detested Garcia dwelt in the great Riviera Hotel, on the slopes behind the town, he knew not; but it was as fixed a certainty in his mind as the facts that God was in His Heaven, and the Devil in his Hell. Finding himself in front of the gates at about four o'clock in the morning, he appears to have reasoned with himself, and decided that this was but a reconnoitre; and so, cognizant of the enemy's position, he went forth, darkling, into the unquestioning hills. It was a thing that a drunken man might do. Now Amos had never touched alcoholic liquor in his life, but a man may be drunk on other things than wine.

It was respectable morning when he entered the hotel. The brass-buttoned, clean-shaven, sleek-haired personnel of the swept and garnished hall—chasseur, lift boy and night porter (the majestic concierge with the cross-keys on his collar not having yet arrived—yet the last mentioned having obviously shaved himself in his sleep) surrounded him with the courtesy of the servants of a perfectly conducted palace.

"I want to see Mr. Ramon Garcia." French hands went up, but voices responded in English. Mr. Garcia could not be up yet. It was very early.

"It's a matter of great importance. I must see him at once. What's the number of his room?"

Someone said: "36."

"I will send the chasseur to awaken him," said the night porter.

"I don't want a kid to wake folks. I can do that myself," said Amos.

Probably the concierge, who was due for duty an hour or so later, would have assumed his ambassadorial manner and exercised his smiling but authoritative tact, and Amos would never have reached the room No. 36; but I am afraid that night porters are the failures in their highly diplomatic profession, otherwise they could not be compelled to blink in daylight. Also, there is this to be said about it: Amos was honesty incarnate. In his vast British face lurked no suspicion of guile. He was also very bulky and very much in earnest. He waved away the lift boy.

"I'll find it," said he. "I don't want to be carried upstairs, when I can walk, and I've got eyes."

So Amos strode up the carpeted stairs, and looking to right and left, soon arrived outside room No. 36.

Now in the most modern hotels a shut bedroom door is a door automatically locked, so that the key-forgetting tenant, arriving, say, on the sixth floor, after lift hours, and seeking to gain entrance to his chamber, becomes a victim to the most amusing state of human madness that an unkind spectator could possibly be privileged to observe. "In the misfortunes of others," Monsieur le Duc de Rochefoucauld is supposed to have said, "there is always something that pleases." The general statement is cynical. But in the case suggested by the present particular proposition it would be a very dour personage who, the more profane the language of the locked-out tenant, did not find therein the greater entertainment. But in many hotels which have not yet arrived at this humorous perfection, bedroom doors can be opened from the outside, unless they are deliberately locked or bolted from within. And of such comfortable and older palaces was the one in which Amos found himself.

Ramon Garcia not having thought to bolt or lock his door, Amos marched straight in.

It was a little north room. The outer shutters and the windows being tightly closed, it was almost pitch black. Amos turned on the electric switch by the door.

"Hi!" said he.

"——"—all kinds of things—cried Ramon Garcia, springing out of bed.

But, before he realized that he had landed on his feet, he fell with a thud to the floor. For Amos, having purchased in the town a length of fine rope, had made a lariat, slip-noose at the end, and cast it over his unsuspecting enemy, so that, tightening around his ankles, it upset his equilibrium. Whereupon Amos, like a gigantic bear, heaved himself upon him, and then began the struggle. Garcia fought like a wolf, tore at Amos's collar in order to get a strangle-hold, and ripped his shirt open so that he became an after-offence to the morning; but Amos's strength quickly prevailed. He tossed him bodily over on to his front so that he lay prone, and then treating him as though he were a parcel, tied him round and round with the cord and turned him face upwards. At the first cry of rage and affright, Amos lifted his great foot above the head of the prostrate man.

"You make another sound and I'll jump on your darned face," and as an earnest of his unalterable intention, he pressed his heel with terrible lightness on the features of Ramon Garcia, who lay, a hideous, trussed figure, in pink pyjamas, between the bedside and the door. In discreet tones he spat the hell of his soul at the half-comprehending disturber of his peace.

"Sh!" said Amos, with uplifted foot. "Sh!" and he went deliberately and threw open the glass windows and the outer shutters, so that the pure light of the morning flooded the room.

"*Mais qu'est-ce que vous voulez enfin?*" asked the trussed man, who began to realize that his assailant was no common bandit, but the nephew of the eminent artist, Mr. David Fontenay, and the abominable champion of the Princess Ramiroff.

"You said last night that we'd talk English to-morrow," replied Amos. "Now's your chance."

"What you want?" came from the floor.

To the English question Amos gave no answer, for his eyes rested on a despatch case lying open on the table by the window, a key, one of a bunch attached to a key-chain in the lock. The case was filled with papers, among them a bundle of letters neatly tied together, which, with a grin at the perfect ease of the proceedings, he put into his pocket. You must remember that Garcia lay supine on the floor by the further side of the bed and could see little but the ceiling.

"Again I ask you what you want?"

Amos strode round and stood over him scowling unpleasantly.

"I want you to keep yer ugly mouth shut, you blackmailing son of Belial. Shut tight—now and for evermore. Understand? If you don't, there won't be much left of you. And you'll hop out of Cannes by the first train—no matter where it's going to. See? And it's no use your hollering now, because when I get downstairs I'll send somebody up to untie you. You can believe my word. But if I hear you hollering, I'll come back and jump. You can believe that too. So good-bye."

Whereupon Amos flung out of the room and down the stairs, told the unemotional night porter that Mr. Ramon Garcia needed his immediate ministrations, and, buttoning his overcoat over the dreadful remains of his evening linen, walked home.

The sun was blazing hot when Amos had ended his sketch of this extraordinary story, all the substance of which I had extracted from him by the Socratic method, and the full details of which, as I have before stated, I only gathered later, and all of which, to repeat my phrase, I have recounted in my own way for the sake of economy of narrative.

"You didn't tell him what you had come for?" I asked.

"No," said Amos.

I took up the packet that lay where he had put it, among the breakfast things—the letters were folded lengthwise—and absentmindedly glanced at the visible strip of the outer one. Then my brain began to reel. I slipped the letter from its elastic bands and very hurriedly my eye swept its four pages.

"My dear boy," said I, "this is not the Princess Ramiroff's handwriting."

He bent forward. His voice failed him, and a very funny little sound came from his open mouth.

"Wha'?"

"It's written in Spanish and signed by a lady called Luisa, whom neither you nor I have the honour of knowing. What's going to be done about it?"

Amos looked at me blankly.

"I dunno," said he.

CHAPTER IX

THERE was only one course for a reasonable man to follow. Consider the circumstances.

Amos had made violent entry into a technically unoffending man's bedroom, assaulted him, tied him up, threatened him with hideous injury, and stolen his private correspondence. The gates of a French prison yawned for him. Not a word could he say in justification of the brutality of the offence. Not even could he plead a woman's honour, for if he did so there would be a search for the woman, and Cannes would find her and then there would be the prettiest mess imaginable.

At any moment a rabid South American, accompanied by the hitherto hidden terror of Cannes policedom—I once saw something resembling a sergent de ville here, but he may have been a Customs official, or a postman—might be ringing the house down. It was only a question of time, for though we are leisurely in Cannes, we are more or less sure. Amos must be an immediate fugitive from justice. There was no other way out.

While Amos, scared, went off to change his disreputable raiment and pack his bag with necessaries, I dressed swiftly and rang up an Agency. When was the next steamer from Marseilles to England? I had the idea that once on a British ship he would be safe. Providence, I learned, had arranged that a P. & O. boat, homeward bound, was due that evening. The clerk asked whether I needed tickets. I rang off abruptly. I would make arrangements for Master Amos at Marseilles. I ordered Maxime to stand prepared with the car at the garage door, on the road by the sea, to which one descended from the garden by rude and winding steps.

We met in the hall. Amos, unshaven, untubbed, hurriedly cravatted, gripping his ancient Gladstone bag; myself, followed by François with a small valise, in case I should have to stay the night; and, emerging from the drawing-room, where she had been strumming the piano, Dorothea. She looked from us to the baggage and from the baggage to us.

"What in the world——?"

"We're having a little trip—a motor tour," said I. "To show Amos the country."

Her lips reproduced the little curl of disdain which marked them when she had swept out of my room.

"It's as bad as that, is it?"

Amos dropped his Gladstone bag, which he had been holding as unconscious of its weight as is a woman of the rubbishy thing in which she carries her powder-puff and lip-stick, and strode a pace to her.

"You think I've done something blackguardly. I haven't. Uncle'll tell you. Now, have I?"

"Amos, my dear," said I, "is very much like the Knight who, going to rescue the Princess from the Dragon, has made a mistake and abducted quite a different lady—very possibly the Dragon's own legitimate wife."

She counselled me to talk sense, as is the way of modern youth unversed in classical allusiveness.

"And who is the Dragon, anyway?"

"That feller Ramon Garcia. I went into his bedroom this morning and knocked him about and tied him up with a rope and left him, and I thought I had taken what I was looking for, but I hadn't. And I've made a hash of everything, and Uncle says I've got myself in the wrong and I'd better beat it as soon as I can, if I don't want to be jailed."

The smile lit in Dorothea's eyes spread gradually over her face.

"Ramon Garcia—tied up with a rope! Oh, tell me more."

"We can't," said I. "The car's below to run us to Marseilles where Amos can take ship to England. Every minute's precious. Good-bye, my dear."

Dorothea is a woman of quick decisions. She planted herself in front of the door of the drawing-room, through which one must pass to gain the garden and the downward garden path, and spread out her hands in a barring gesture.

"Let me go with Amos to Marseilles and see him through." Then she whipped me by the wrist into the drawing-room. "You're the dearest of all dears, but you're not Amos's age. You'll make the poor boy think he's a horrible criminal. He's scared to death of you, like all sorts of people who don't know what a pet lamb you are. Let me go. I'll fix him up. Besides, I love motoring and you loathe it."

She was right. I have never found pleasure in the mere process of locomotion. Also, she would be a far more agreeable companion than I, to the unfortunate Amos. Again, of Dorothea's capability I had no question. I see her, in a future life, conducting poor lost souls to snug quarters on the banks of Acheron. She had done something of the sort during the war at Waterloo Station. But——

"But, my dear," said I, "it's a matter of valuable time. Why the police aren't here is a mystery."

"Then why on earth are you wasting the valuable time?"

She laughed, ran out into the hall and caught up her fur coat and bade Amos come along.

"But if you have to stay the night?"

"There's a tooth-brush shop in Marseilles. On the right-hand side of the Cannebière as you go down to the Quai."

We went through the drawing-room. Amos said, lamely:

"Cousin Dorothea, I'm sure I can get to England by myself."

"I don't see how you can help it, unless the ship goes down," laughed Dorothea. "But I'll see you safe on board that ship at Marseilles."

We went through the little rocky and cactus-filled platform that serves as my garden and down the declivitous path to the road—the Corniche d'Or, by the sea. The mystery of the morning azure had hardened into startling blue and gold. The green line of the Esterel stood silhouetted against a sky of deep turquoise. The lazy surf of the Mediterranean fringed the strip of sand on the other side of the road. Maxime, rug over arm, waited by the open door of the car. François, wasp-vested, as becomes the French valet-de-chambre in morning livery, stowed away old Ezra Burden's Gladstone bag. The travellers took their seats.

"You haven't told me," cried Dorothea, "where Amos is bound for when he gets to England."

"I'm consigning him," said I, "by telegram to the care of the Right Reverend the Lord Bishop of Bradbury."

They drove off down the golden road.

"Thank Heaven," I cried, "he has been able to show a clean pair of heels."

I watched the car disappear, and turned to the side entrance and mounted the narrow rocky stairs. And

then I became aware of a sense of loss and loneliness.
It was not that I missed Dorothea, great as was my affection for her; besides, she would return that night or
the next morning. I felt a gap in my life made by the
flight of this hulking innocent, and a curious remorse for
non-fulfilment of common duties. Surely, if I had taken
him well in hand he would not have tied up Ramon Garcia and threatened (by no means idly) to jump on his
face. If I had not made myself an artist in the devolu-
tion of responsibility, I should now have been standing
by his side in manly defence, instead of smuggling him in
haste out of the country. I was the most broken reed
that strong-handed sister ever trusted. First I had sent
for Dorothea. She, poor child, had done her best. Now
I was packing him off to the mercies, quite tender in
intention, I was sure, but dubious in execution, of my
sister Muriel, and to the general supervision of a busy,
non-pietistic bishop in a manufacturing diocese. Like
as not Tom would tell him that Adam and Eve and the
serpent and Noah were all solar myths and that no intelligent being nowadays believed in the eternal frying in
Hell of folks who had behaved naughtily during this life
of continuous temptation. On the one side, the Right
Reverend Tom would shatter the foundations of his
simple faith and on the other, Muriel would seek to in-
vest the wreckage in incomprehensible social frills.

Why had I, who alone (so thought I in my arrogance)
could gauge his psychology, not carried him through this
ordeal and so won, not only my self-esteem but the devotion of youth so precious to son-less, sensitive men who
are fading into the sere and yellow leaf?

I mounted to my studio. A block of fresh clay had
just arrived. I am a painter, as you know, by profession,
but I amuse myself, frankly as an amateur, now and

then in the practice of the sister art. I regarded the lump with ironical distaste. Such human formlessness, said I, had I to my hand to mould as I wished. I had neglected it. And now it is flying from French justice at the rate of sixty kilometres an hour, accompanied by a young woman, the partner in a rag and bag shop, the workings of whose mind are as sealed a book to me as those of Medea or Clytemnestra.

And the pure, honest, direct simplicity of Amos! It was an education in life—painful perhaps—but no education can possibly be free from the fustigatory principle—it was an education to behold him sweep away social sophistries with a wave of his ham-like hand and delve to the bedrock of mortal values.

I had missed the golden opportunity of fashioning a wonderful human being.

"Damn!" said I, as I threw a wet cloth over the clay.

That done, I became aware that damning was but a futile occupation. All my responsibilities had not been laid on the shoulders of Dorothea and Tom, the Bishop of Bradbury. I had connived in a felony. I had procured the criminal means of escape. The proceeds of the robbery with violence were in my possession—the packet of letters in the neat, convent-taught, character-less Spanish handwriting, signed "Luisa," containing God knows what secrets that might exist between man and woman. I had thrust them in my pocket while dressing as the best place, temporarily, to put them. I dragged out the packet. It was about four inches thick. Nadia, according to Amos's story, had confessed to half a dozen indiscreet letters. Written on thin lemon-coloured paper, in violet ink, this was the correspondence of a life-time. Why had not Amos taken these matters into consideration before pouncing on the preposterous bundle? Well, I suppose that, even in these days, if knight-errantry were a matter of pure reason, dragons would have a fat time.

Still, there was I with the accursed bundle; and there was Ramon Garcia, after having applied what unguents he could find to the weals left on his body by Amos's rope—you may be assured that Amos had not trussed him tenderly—storming the Commissariat of Police and bringing down upon us the awful punitive powers of the French Republic.

If there is one agonizing process that I dread more than all others it is the sudden making up of my mind. I subjected myself to this mental purgatory and passed out unscathed. I went out, descended the rue Georges Clémenceau, found a taxi by the Casino and drove to the palatial hotel where Ramon Garcia dwelt. It would be now a matter between us two—man to man. I had the letters from Luisa, he the letters from the Princess Nadia. I hoped for the best—a question of courteous exchange; but I was prepared for the worst. Blackmail can only be met by a brave front. In my elderly way, too, I felt the thrill of knight-errantry. Most open, indiscreet, generous of women—such was my little Princess Nadia—I could think no harm of her. I could blame her, of course, for putting herself into the power of an unscrupulous villain; but no more than Amos had I the remotest doubt of her candid innocence.

I felt prepared to endure any kind of physical pain in her service. In my exalted mood I pictured myself standing intrepid while Ramon Garcia fired off revolvers at me.

The taxi deposited me at the foot of the stately steps of

the hotel.   A smiling chasseur threw open the doors.   I crossed the hall and the concierge, an old friend of mine, advanced in smiling greeting.

"Monsieur Ramon Garcia?" I began.

"Monsieur Garcia is not here, sir."

"I suppose," said I, "he has gone to the Commissariat of Police."

"I don't understand—why should he go to the police?" asked the concierge urbanely.

"My nephew, Mr. Burden, was here this morning."

"So I have heard," said the concierge.

"Eh bien?"

"He was here and he went away."

"And the night porter?"

"He has gone off duty for some time.   If you wish to see him, Monsieur Fontenay, I will tell him to call at your villa."

"Do," said I.

The concierge retreated to his table and made a note on his block.

"And Monsieur Garcia?"

"Monsieur Garcia left Cannes by the morning train to Italy."   He turned to the conducteur discreetly effacing himself in the shadow.   "It was for Milan you took the ticket for Monsieur Garcia?"

"For Milan," said the conducteur.

"When?"

"This morning."

"Monsieur Garcia seems to have come to a sudden decision," said the concierge.

I looked from one man to the other in amazement.

I asked stupidly whether he had taken all his luggage. The concierge smiled.   Of course.   And his address in Milan?

"I am to keep his correspondence until he sends instructions," said the concierge, who, in spite of our old friendship, began to show signs of polite boredom at my interest in Señor Garcia. Besides, a fussy lady holding an envelope without a stamp was striving to attract his attention.

I nodded a lame *"Merci, mon ami,"* and walked obfuscated out of the hotel and drove to the villa.

It was astounding. I had expected to find a fiery South American dragon snorting flaming vengeance; instead I had news of a baffled adventurer running away as hard as he could. Suddenly I threw myself back on the taxi seat and broke into the shrill laughter of reaction. Here were the two protagonists of the morning's drama, the aggressor and the aggrieved, flying for their lives from each other, one due west, the other due east, with never a chance of meeting, apparently, unless they, in their respective directions, circumnavigated half the globe. What could be more comic? I laughed up the villa steps. François opened the door.

"Le déjeuner est prêt, Monsieur."

I had forgotten all about lunch. It was amazing how the time had flown since Amos had interrupted the peace of my early breakfast. I was hungry. I sat down to a sound and serious meal, postponing, for digestive reasons, too profound conjectures as to the motives of Garcia's flight. When I had finished my coffee and was halfway through my cigar, it occurred to me that the flight of Amos was now rendered unnecessary; further, that he might be recalled. I summoned François and bade him bring me telegram forms. With these I dallied for a while. I had printed "Amos Burden"—if you present English telegrams in the most beautiful cursive script at a French post office they will render it into a choice transliteration of Syriac—and an artistic "P. & O. SS." when I was brought to a halt by the reflection that either the Agency had failed to give me the name of the steamship or that I had forgotten it. François must ring up the Agency. But it would not be open till two o'clock. That is the curse of this otherwise delectable country. I never feel called upon to transact any business except between the hours of twelve and two. And between twelve and two every office and shop is shut. You might just as well try to ring up your great-grandmother in her tomb as an office in France at one o'clock. While ruminating I prolonged the curve of the last "S" into some sort of a caricature of Amos. It came out rather well. I must have spent about half an hour over the silly thing.

Then said I:

"Why should I stop him? England is quite worth seeing. Its abominable climate in February is good for a pampered young savage's soul. Bradbury is an educational contrast to Cannes and a more violent change of mentors than from myself to Tom, the Bishop, no young Telemachus could be privileged to experience."

I sharpened my pencil, a nice fat B.B., and worked further on Amos, cursing the ruled lines of the telegram form and my own folly in starting the fascinating game. But when you see a real live thing growing under your fingers, how on earth can you stop? François put a tentative head through the door, desirous of clearing away. I waved him to perdition. Presently he reappeared. Madame la Comtesse d'Orbigny awaited Monsieur in the studio.

Then I remembered I had given her an early appointment for a final sitting. I rose, my head full of Amos on the telegram form, and went up to carry on what at that moment I characterized as my dreary task. I shuddered at the thought that, had it not been for Dorothea, I should have gone to Marseilles. For if one does carry on a trade, no matter how dreadful, one should make it a point of honour to be bound by its rules.

With regard to Amos, I went upstairs reflecting amusedly on the change of a problem when viewed in a pre- and a post-prandial light.

Meanwhile, though the immediate problem of Amos was solved, there remained that of Ramon Garcia. Why with every technicality of justice on his side, had he fled so precipitately, leaving Amos in possession of the stolen letters from the unknown Spanish lady signing herself "Luisa"? Perhaps the Princess would help me. In answer to my telephone call, the Marchesa della Fontana informed me that Nadia had again gone over for the day to Monte Carlo. There remained, for immediate enquiry, only the night porter of the hotel. He came, with a dark smile on his face.

"Monsieur desires——?"

I quickly informed him that Monsieur desired to know what took place when, at Mr. Burden's instructions, he had mounted to the chamber of Monsieur Garcia.

"He commanded me," said the night porter, "to send up his breakfast and his bill and to obtain a first-class single ticket to Milan. Also to have his luggage brought down."

"Is that all?"

"Yes, Monsieur Fontenay, that is all."

I drew out a hundred franc note. He smiled again. He was a gentle, melancholy man, with a smile-worn face. He held up a protesting hand.

"Monsieur Garcia was exceedingly generous."

I pocketed the note. If there's no loyalty in bribery and corruption, the sooner bribery and corruption end the better.

"So you will say nothing?"

"Nothing—unless——"

"Unless what?"

"The police," said he. "I made that a condition."

"*Merci, mon ami,*" said I, ringing the bell. "François will give you a glass of wine."

Thus did the night porter thicken the mystery. He had mounted, met the extraordinary sight of the occupant of Room 36 lying on the floor, tied up from ankles to shoulders—obviously the act of the giant who had visited him—and instead of being told to fetch the police, he had been paid a large price to hold his tongue. He had told no one; not even the concierge, the suavity of whose demeanour, at first suspect, I now felt sure was that of entire innocence. Three people alone, apparently (myself and Dorothea apart), held the secret of the disgraceful scene: Amos, the night porter and Garcia himself. For the purchase of this secrecy from the night porter, Garcia must have excellent reasons. It could not be sheer vanity. Besides, there was the bundle of letters, that infernal bundle of letters, written on thin yellow paper in violet ink, folded lengthwise, tied up with string and measuring some four inches thick. They lay where I had tossed them after lunch, during the sitting of Madame d'Orbigny and my interview with the night porter, on my studio writing-table. I balanced the packet in my hand. The letters might give me the word of the enigma. I have a little Latin, more Italian, considerable French. Without knowledge of the language I can, therefore, make out the gist of written Spanish. I gingerly put my thumb into the middle of the bundle and bent back the folded sheets. There my eyes rested on the beginning:

"Adorado Ramon mio, alma de mi vida."

No! I rose, unlocked the little safe in which I keep my few important documents and threw the bundle in and locked the safe up again. It is impossible to read a woman's love-letters, even though written to so impossible a villain as Ramon Garcia.

Dorothea turned up with the car the following evening, and the information that she had invoiced Amos to Bradbury, per steamer and rail. Though he was the most gentle and innocent bear in the world, she announced, his most poignant regret on leaving France was that the laws of the game had prevented him from jumping on Ramon Garcia's face.

"I'm only wondering," said I, after a while, "what your uncle and aunt will do with him in episcopal circles."

"The only thing I'm afraid of," said Dorothea, "is that his eccentric passion for truth may make them hate one another."

CHAPTER X

IT was the wretched end of a March day of cloud and mist and wet Italian squall. So had been its predecessor. Usually I laughed at folks who cried out against a day or two of rain and foul weather. We were, said I, the spoiled children of climate. I recognized the beneficence of rain. It made things grow. It quickened the mountain torrents which gave us our supply of electricity. In my time here I have longed for rain. For, towards the end of a season of drought, artichokes are worth their weight in paper francs, the electric light goes out and the hotel lifts cease going up. All is not gold that glitters in this golden land. The blustering Italian rain coming over sea and mountain is a very good thing. But the rain, like all forces of nature, proverbially blind, will not see when you are in the mood for it. It dashes down, not when you are sated with sunshine, but tactlessly, just in the hour when your heart craves the sun and all its comfort.

On this particular March day I sat in my studio, if not comfortless at least uncomforted—a victim to cosmic grievance. Everything was for the worst in this worst of all possible worlds. I was as lonely as might be a companionable hippopotamus in the Serpentine; Dorothea had gone back to her rag and bag shop; young Claude Worthington having found only one customer on the Dutroyen infested coast, the youth inebriated with success at the gaming tables before alluded to, had been despatched by his firm to Holland wherein to spread the glad Dutroyen tidings; Amos was still in Bradbury ap-

138

parently attuning his mind to a reconciliation between
his aunt's bare shapely arms and his uncle's lawn-sleeves;
the car, afflicted by some sort of gastric trouble, couldn't
run; and Maxime was away in Normandy attending the
funeral of his step-father's grand-aunt, in whose testament he had the Frenchman's eternal hope of being mentioned. I had finished my season's commissions. An
ancient and picturesque villain, with a head like Mistral
the poet and a nature as unseductive as Mistral the wind,
whom I was modelling in clay, for want of something to
do, had, with cold alcoholic cynicism, unsuccessfully dis-
puted the path with an autobus the day before; and I
had been alternating this diversion with some sunshine
sketches of the little seventeenth-century hill village of
Biot, when down came the rains and put an end to it for
the time; and before me lay a letter from the Town
Clerk of some awful place in Lancashire, I think it was
Chootle, inviting me to visit it and paint the Mayor
in his robes and chains for an honorarium—they re-
gretted the literal signification of the word—the Town
Clerk must have seen better days—of a hundred
guineas.

The wind whisked outside; the rain beat against the
windows; the Mediterranean thudded on the shore like
Niagara let loose and stopped and let loose again at ten
seconds intervals. Within, all was as still as death. The
sense of entire isolation overwhelmed me. A younger
man would have rushed out, braving the miserable rain,
with some objective of companionship—a friendly house,
a dancing tea, the Casino—last refuge of the destitute
opulent. But the lone man in his mid-forties, with all
old desires satisfied, with newer and all but unformulated
desires vaguely and incomprehensibly craving satisfaction,
foresees no solace in drawing-rooms or dancing teas or

Casinos, and, shrinking from miserable rain, is thrown despairingly back upon himself.

I don't know whether I am much of a painter. I sell my pictures. I make a good livelihood. People flatter me. My brother artists have recognized me so far as to admit me into the Royal Academy. I do my honest best. The wonder of the joy and anguish in my work I would not exchange for whatever thrill there is in any other avocation under heaven. But I am not obsessed by it. The grip of it relaxed, I am, I think, just a simple sorry human being seeking simple human things. All this apologia to lead up to my vehement protest against the cant theory of the artist's essential celibacy. One has heard it suggested that an artist's art is his wife and his wife his mistress. It is but a foolish analogical lie. An artist may marry a fool of a woman who may make hay of his life; but so may a doctor or a stockbroker or a pork butcher. So do women of fine impulses and aspirations marry fools of men. . . . Yes, it is cant, the speciosity, in this case, of arrogance, which, when looked into, wilts into shrivelled garbage this theory of the artist's holy espousal of his art. A male artist is essentially a man, and a man needs a woman to accomplish his manhood, just as to accomplish her womanhood a woman needs a man.

I declare that I, a painter in love with my work, granted by the world the proud title of artist, sat lonely there, that afternoon, consumed by an awful hunger for a woman.

For that is what it came to. That was the element into which, sitting before the wood fire in my studio, while the storm raged outside, I resolved all my greater and lesser grievances.

Once there had been a woman. A joy and an inspiration.   My every brush stroke was an appeal to a Celestial approval.   And, laughing up her sleeve, the Celestial half knew she was guiding my hand all the while.   But that was all over and finished, dead and buried, with only the tenderness of it preserved in lavender and laid in an innermost shrine rarely unlocked, and then in wistful reverence. . . .

I wanted neither young Claude Worthington, nor Amos, nor Maxime, nor François, nor my deceased Mistralesque model.   I was not sure, at that moment of self analysis, that I wanted Dorothea, though my hurt Egoism made me view her defection in a severe light.   Yet she had been supremely logical.   Her filial duty accomplished to the best of her ability, she had very gracefully handed in her resignation.

"My dear," I had pleaded, "your rag and bone shop being in perfectly capable hands, you can't possibly leave me in these afflicting circumstances."

"My dear," she retorted, "your gradual allusive depreciation of my business corresponds with its actual going to the devil while I'm not there to look after it.   You sent for me because you were afflicted with Amos; and now the infliction is removed, I can't see where the afflicting pathos of the situation comes in."

She had me cornered.   What could I do?   Pride forbade an appeal *ad misericordiam*.   So Dorothea went with all the honours of war and peace and everything else.   She is the best young woman in the world.   But why, a week after she returned to the joint management of her immoral emporium in South Molton Street, did she accept an invitation to the Palace at Bradbury?   Of course, she wrote me in the most filial spirit.   She had gone there to continue the pursuit of duty.   Verily she was doing her bit in the world.   She considered herself most useful as

the interpreter of Amos to episcopal circles—to say nothing of exercising over him her restraining influence. Beyond asking the gaitered bishop on Sunday morning—he
had arrived at Bradbury late on Saturday night—why he
was going out shooting on the Sabbath, he seemed—
please, this is the Gospel according to Dorothea—to have
made fewer mistakes than might have been expected. He
did tackle Tom on the question of extempore prayer and
reviewed the cathedral services unfavourably in the light
of the Warraranga meetings conducted by his father. He
had also had an altercation with a brawling factory hand
over the latter's right to kick his own dog; and the dispute, though from a physical point of view overwhelm-
ingly in Amos's favour, was only settled by Dorothea,
descending, *dea ex machina* (the episcopal car), on the
scene and deciding that the miner of the dilapidated features should retire with a ten pound note in his pocket
and Amos with the mongrel bull-terrier bitch under his
arm.

Every week came news of Amos. Certainly Dorothea
is a good girl with a highly developed sense of duty. I
did not recognize it when she left me. I thought her
merely selfish and inconsiderate. But on this particular
evening of wind and rain, which I am making all the
bother about, I absolved her from unworthy motives and
credited her with an altruism beyond both her years and
her sex.

I love Dorothea, as perhaps you may be tired of hearing
me tell you. Her swift young presence in the house of
a middle-aged widower is in itself a joy. But to say that
her absence now lay at the root of my discontent would
be such a perversion of truth as even an artist could not
allow himself. No. I did not crave Dorothea.

It was the end of March, as I have said. The flight of

Amos west and Ramon Garcia east had occurred a month ago. The odd thing about the affair—or rather one of the odd things—was that nothing more had been heard of the Ecuadorian. He had disappeared like a superhuman aviator into the blue Italian ether. The few speculations as to his hasty departure were not taken up with extensive eagerness. On this azure coast, gamblers come and live their little meteoric life, and then they go, and the next day the world has forgotten their transient flash across the firmament. Owing to the debauched honesty of the night porter, the secret of Garcia's degradation and loss remained inviolate. As far as I knew, not a soul in Cannes suspected the relation between the disappearances of the two men. Folks asked me, of course—Mrs. Blennerhasset, Madame d'Orbigny, Lady This-that-and-the-other—what had become of my interesting and original nephew. I found a formula.

"The dear fellow has lived all his life in the Bush in Australia and has never been confirmed. He obeyed an urgent summons by telegram from his uncle, the Bishop of Bradbury, to go home at once and submit to the operation."

They appreciated my statement according to their various religious susceptibilities; but, amazing thing! they all believed it like unquestioning little lambs. The only brow-wrinkling person was Mrs. Blennerhasset, who had asked the defecting trio to lunch.

More amazing still—I, the cynical liar, was telling essential truth all the time. For no sooner had Tom got hold of him than he baptized him out of hand, and, the Confirmation season having opened in Bradbury, confirmed him a fortnight afterwards with a batch of a couple of hundred in the cathedral. Such tidings from Muriel, Dorothea and Amos himself. From which it may be gathered that Tom had a swift way with heretics.

And, after this preposterous exordium, you will ask: where was the Princess Nadia Ramiroff all this time? That's what I asked myself. Where? She had disappeared on that extraordinary day of general exodus. The Marchesa della Fontana had lied, over the telephone. Nadia had not gone to Monte Carlo. When I remonstrated later, the Marchesa suavely informed me that Nadia, being called away suddenly, had desired to slip off without undue commotion on the part of her friends. Where was she staying, I asked. The Marchesa spread out vague Russian fingers. On her independent walks abroad Nadia could be written to under care of the American Express Company. Whether she was in Paris or New York or the New Hebrides the Marchesa knew not for certain. I wrote to the Princess at the given address, politely upbraiding her for leaving friends so suddenly in the lurch. Ten days afterwards I received a reply on paper just headed "Rome." She assured me that the only thing that made life tolerable was the knowledge that she had friends like myself. Had I ever heard of a Greek lady called Io who was chased all over the world by a horrid gadfly? She gave me to understand that she was a poor little Io. But as to who or what was the gadfly she gave me no kind of clue.

Of course it might be Ramon Garcia. Had he not taken a first-class ticket to Milan? Milan and Rome are both in Italy—a piece of geographical information which, on second thoughts, it seems superfluous to set down. He was in the neighbour country because he was running away from something; in all probability from the vengeance of the giant Amos, who had constituted himself the champion of the Princess. But why was

Nadia in the same alien land complaining of a gadfly?

It was a puzzle. I don't like such puzzles. They interfere with that hedonistic outlook on men and things which, as I have told you, I have been at such pains to reach.

I answered the letter, contrary to my usual procrastinating habit, almost by return of post. To this had come no reply. I had been worried. But on this coast of Enchantment the sun has the power of dispelling worries like fogs. In the morning when you are awakened and the outer shutters drawn, and from your bed you behold revealed the day's compelling splendour, the cares that may have infested the darkened hours melt away and your heart leaps within you, and, pietist or pagan, you utter some sort of prayer of thanksgiving. Even if you are bent on suicide, resolved to quit an impossible world, you commit the rash act gallantly, with a smiling face, with a good heart, as our soldiers used to say in the war. I don't say you don't do it. According to statistics there are more suicides in fine than in gloomy weather. Whereby my point is illustrated. There is no moroseness, no hole-and-corner business in the matter. You either carry out your resolution or you don't. There is no sordid worry about it. I have known married men on a blue Riviera morning sign, with gay insouciance, frippery cheques which, if presented for signature in fogbound London, would have been mildewed with a wife's impenitential tears. . . . Here you are like a lizard on a sun-baked rock in my garden. If you lose your tail, you take your shoulders as shrugged—the literal action demanding unnecessary effort—and assure yourself that, if it doesn't grow again, a tailless state may, after all, be the more honourable. . . . Even when the Mistral blows, sweeping down the Rhone Valley and howling over the arid vine-clad plains of Provence, with the announced intention of tearing your heart out, you smile, with the indigenous, and say *"Mistral est en colère,"* as though he were really the chartered libertine of winds. And you avoid him as much as possible and get into your house, and through closed windows watch him playing the devil with the dust on the roads and the olive trees and tipping your beautiful blue sea with a myriad angry crests of white. And the sun goes on shining. Mistral tries to blow it out, but he can't. That is why, in Provence, we regard the Mistral with humorous indulgence. The sun winks at us connivantly and engages itself to dispel our worries.

But when Mistral has gone to sleep and the sun perhaps is tired, the north-west winds blow the clouds over the Alps and swamp the coast in miserable rain, and persuade the Mediterranean into the belief that it is a tempestuous ocean, and all is pelting, swishing, roaring black defiance of the coast's birthright, the human soul inevitably reacts. Betrayed by the impotent sun, it is filled with resentment, a culture wherein worry-germs find wriggling joyousness of life.

My body ached with them. My soul was a torment. I felt abandoned by God and man and woman. I rose and took the canvas of the Princess's portrait, stuck it into a practicable gold frame of my own invention and looked at it. The real frame for the Academy Exhibition and the permanent setting of the picture would be the result of the raking of Paris, London and the Infernal Regions, if need be—an Italian Renaissance frame such as enshrines the Isotta da Rimini attributed to Piero della Francesca. Here was another dig of unreasoning irritation. The only work of Francesca—I suppose one ought to call him de Franceschi—I care a hang about is the adorable golden-haired Isotta—and the pedants say that he never painted it. I don't believe it. No more than I believe that Hamlet was written by Bacon to propagate scandals about Queen Elizabeth. You see what was at the back of my mind. There was the same purity of gold and green and pearl in Nadia as in Isotta. The Isotta-esque effect of her had not struck me until I had finished the picture. Then I thanked the God of Painters that by putting her in black I had established an entirely different set of values and so had entered into competition with—if not Francesca—at least some glorious being born to achieve a single masterpiece. . . . Anyhow, the violent difference between the values would not affect the frame, which my memory visualized. And I'm talking about frames but cursively, by the way.

I am also talking about my loneliness and the impulse that made me set up the portrait of Nadia on an easel and gaze upon it in a besotted, middle-aged kind of agony. Bits of Wordsworth and the lady with the murmuring streams reflected in her face passed through my mind. That, I swore, was the true portrait of the Princess. I had dived down deep, and had mirrored on her features the untarnished exquisiteness of her soul.

The thought of her letters to Garcia flitted about me like an obscene bat. I strode to the window and flung it open, an act of unconscious symbolism, for the blazing wood fire had made the room oppressively hot. The damp wind surged into the studio. The bat flew out. I returned to the canvas. I clasped my hands in front of it. "Forgive me, my dear," I cried, "for the moment's desecrating doubt."

The door opened. A hurricane swept the room, over-throwing easel and picture and sending them slithering across the polished floor. I had a momentary impression of two figures in an open space, one François, of a hasty announcement, of a door violently slammed by the tempest, and of the slight, fur-mantled form of the Princess Nadia, standing a few feet from the threshold.

"My God! You, Nadia!" I cried in a foolish way, and rushing to her open-armed, enfolded her in my embrace.

She struggled a bit, and perhaps I, over-sensitive, released her. She cried in French:

"But, my friend, you are mad. What does this signify?"

"It means, my dear," said I, recovering, "that I love you and I can't do without you, and that when you came in I was consoling myself with the companionship of your picture which, as you see, the wind has blown down."

She shivered under her furs.

"It will blow down all kinds of other things if you don't shut that window."

With some impatience and unavoidable noise I obeyed her, for the wind was streaming in, warm and balmy and lung-filling.

"Well?" said I, turning after the final wrench to the window handle.

"Well?" said she.

"I ask you."

"I came to seek a friend in my hour of need——"

"And you find a lover, a man who puts himself and all that is his at your feet."

Her fair Isotta da Rimini face hardened—or the face that would have been Isotta had it not been for the rebellious little nose.

"I have been told that by many men. But what does it mean?"

"Mean?" I cried, puzzled. I suppose we decentmotived Englishmen are regarded as the fools of the earth by Latins, Slavs, Chinese, Abyssinians and Turks. "Mean? I mean that I love you in the common way of men. I mean that I'm about the loneliest thing in God's universe. I've been eating my heart out for the past month. That's what I mean, my dear."

And I did mean it. There she stood in her furs, golden crested, pure profiled, with the light that never was on sea or land in the large and deep sea-green of her eyes. Her pale coral lips disclosed in a smile her young perfect teeth.

I went on:

"You are a Serene Highness. I'm only a Bohemian painter. But my family, the Fontenays, goes back many generations. Any gentleman born may aspire to the hand of a princess."

She came up to me close, warm in her furs, and with a flush on her cheeks, laid a finger-tip touch on my shoulders—but there was a bewildered, scared look on her face.

"My hand—*mon ami*. What are you saying?" she asked in her adorable accent. "Am I right in assuming that you are making me a proposal of marriage?"

I took her hands and flung myself back and looked at her.

"My good child, what the deuce else do you suppose I'm doing?"

She looked at me for a wild moment, flitted to me with the indescribable grace and swiftness of a dragon-fly. I felt the touch of soft lips on the corner of my mouth, and in a fraction of a second of time she had opened the door and fled down the stairs.

I followed her, of course. But there in the hall stood the most perfect of *maîtres d'hôtel,* that infernal François.

CHAPTER XI

"OH to be in April (somewhere else) now that England's here," I murmured, as I landed at Dover in the pitiless misty rain, a rain that chilled all the human kindness I tried to keep warm in my heart, a rain that I knew would go on for ever and ever, all through the summer until it joined up with its autumnal sister Pluviose.

That March day over which I made such a pother was but the final flood of tears of a Southern child. The next morning broke all pouts and dawning smiles which eventually burst into the irresistible laughter of the sun. And sunshine had been mine, even in Paris, until this damp landing, when clouds of depression gathered bleak and heavy around my soul. . . .

I told you how François stood, the model servant in the hall, when the Princess tripped downstairs. Well, this ‘mechanically trained blockhead disregarded my swiftly following appearance, threw open the front door and showed her into the waiting car. I had barely time to murmur a protest and to receive a queer little wave of the hand, when the car—the Marchese's—drove off. And where do you think it drove to? To the railway station. It took her to the Paris train. That I learned half an hour afterwards over the telephone, from the Marchesa. She had arrived that morning from Italy, had stayed at the Villa Miranda just for the few hours necessary to repair the ravages of travel, and then off again to Paris. It was news to the Marchesa that she had called on me. I have never met a human being more

150

barren of interesting information than the Marchesa della Fontana. Nadia's address was always the American Express Company.

Naturally I cursed myself for an elderly, love-sick, impetuous fool. Had I been my cooler self, Nadia would have given me the word of the preposterous enigma. What else had she come for? In her own words, to find a friend in the hour of need. And I had gone and upset all her plans of confidence and hopes of succour by subjecting her to violent, unexpected caresses, followed by a declaration of love and a proposal of marriage. That the shock of outrage impelled her flight downstairs I did not believe. There was the little butterfly touch of her lips on the corner of my mouth which signified, at least, forgiveness. But I realized that what of herself a woman can unburden to a humdrum friend she cannot reveal to a suddenly romantic lover. I had sent my adored little lady off in a scare.

She covered up her tracks as before. I wrote—I will not tell you what I said. If I had the letter here before me I might find some embarrassment in transcribing it. I found that I had loved her from the first day when she had sat for me in her pearl and green and gold beauty set off by the austerity of her unrelieved black corsage; from that first day when I pierced through the veil of worldliness in which she enwrapped herself as in impenetrable armour, and knew, almost as God knew, the integrity of her Russian soul gnawed by unsatisfied longings—not for the barely imaginable exotic, but for the true, sweet and pure things in life. She had been born in a world of decadence, had married in a world of chaos, had been widowed in a world of horror, had emerged, bewildered at her safety, into the peculiar underworld of the Riviera, peopled by the della Fontanas, the Ramon

Garcias, the international gamblers, the crooks, the adventurers, the jewelled ladies skating on the outside edge of reputation, the world of glitter, glamour, ghastliness, the world of rapine.

Into this underworld was she thrown, wistful little snowdrop of the steppes.

You may think me a sentimental fool if you like. But so had I been constrained by a thousand and one indications to regard her; and the first vague intuitions had been bitten in, as it were, like etched impressions, by the extraordinary narrative of my nephew Amos. Then she was, as far as my mind could read the riddle, a poor human soul groping her way through a miasma of impurity.

Of course, that is one side of the question. I want to be honest. That is the spiritual side. But there was also the physical. Now, in the love that man has for woman, what psychological alchemist has ever found the alembic that could rightly precipitate the gross through the immaterial? I yearned to protect the frail spirit wandering lonely and affrighted in an alien land, and, at the same time, all the poor human thing that was I longed for the once-felt soft pressure of her body against mine, the scent of her hair in my nostrils, the touch of her lips and the adorableness of her voice in my ears.

Again you may say I am talking nonsense, bringing in Undine and moonshine so as to cast a glamour over grosser things. But there, too, was the dainty mind, the dancing wit . . . the ever sympathetic companionability. At any rate, there was I, a man in the mid-forties, avowedly, and, I must say, miserably in love with her.

To my letter there had come no reply. When I called in Paris, at the American Express Company, I was politely told that they were not at liberty to give me the

Princess Ramiroff's address, but (as I knew before) they
would forward my letters. I wrote again, with the same
lack of result.

I ransacked Paris to find my frame of which a rumour
had reached me. I tracked it down to a horrible little
shop, in a horrible little street in the Quartier la Villette,
the centre of the butcher industry. There dwelt a horrible old man who seemed to have a horrible passion for
frames which he picked up at underground auctions all
over Latin Europe. Just as a rustic used to grin hor-
ribly through a horse-collar, so did this mildewed and
snuff-vested man scowl hatefully through his upheld
frame. I paid the old villain ten times the price that his
soul would fetch in the open market.

Well, here was I in England again, damp, cold and
miserable. Once, however, in the filial hands of a spry
English porter, my spirits began to revive. The courtli-
ness of the Pullman-car officials introducing me to my
seat as though it were my entry as honoured guest into
a palace cheered me still further. "This is truly the
Land of Freedom," said I, "where everybody guards the
personal liberty of everyone else." To satisfy my physical needs, after a rough crossing, I ordered a pint of champagne. That drunk, I lit a cigar and entered into conversation with my opposite neighbour who, I very soon
learned, was a breeder of fat cattle in Lincolnshire. He
held in delicious scorn the beeves, and the kine of France,
which he had seen on his motor journey from Monte
Carlo to Calais, and ended by inviting me to dine with
him at his place in the country and eat a round of cold
prize ox. Communion with this entertaining and ingenuous gentleman relieved, as the old writers said, the tedium
of the journey. Learning that he would be in London

during the early part of May, I gave him my card and promised to send him an invitation for himself and his wife to the Private View of the Royal Academy. He beamed in his honest English way.

"The only return I can make, Mr. Fontenay, is to ask you down and offer you an ox roasted whole."

The quiet, courtly English humour—there is nothing like it in the world!

I was almost dismayed when the train slowed down in the pale half-light of Victoria Station. Firm friends, we parted hurriedly, for, on the platform, a comfortable lady threw herself into his arms, and Dorothea took me into hers. The latter introduced me to a Mr. Veale, a sketchy young man, who apparently swept the floor and added up the figures of the rag and bone shop and kept guard over its contents of nights with a loaded pistol. To him must I surrender keys and responsibilities for registered luggage.

"My dear," said I, "in that van are priceless works of art which represent my precarious means of subsistence for the following year."

She laughed at my remonstrance. Mr. Veale had been the foreman of the Picture Dealers Clearing House—at least so I gathered from her imperfect English—and could be trusted to convey Masters Old and Young from pole to pole. Her tame taxi-cab was waiting, ticking its heart out. She dragged me to it. I entered and we drove away. She had seen that everything was in order at Featherstone's studio, in the Melbury Road, which I had rented for a couple of months, and she had put the fear of God into the modest staff which he had left behind— and there was a carefully ordered little dinner awaiting us, and she had got in some champagne—1911 Krug—wasn't that what I liked?—and a box of Coronas and one of

Massoura cigarettes, and if there wasn't a blazing fire when we got there, she would raise Cain. All this as we sped through the damp and flaring dusk of the April evening.

I cannot conceive that a child of my own could be nearer and dearer to me than Dorothea. She led me by the hand into Featherstone's exquisite little house. He, as you know, is the marine painter. You can almost smell the salt of his waves and hear their tumult. But he had got it into his mad bachelor head that the only waves left worth his painting were those around and about Cape Horn; so thither had he sailed, leaving in my charge his studio, his cook, his unsold pictures and other treasures. On a casual note from me—for I knew that she had returned from Bradbury, the conscience of her partner not being stout enough to bear the whole guilt of their thievery establishment for an indefinite time—on a note from me, as I say: "My dear—I wish you'd look in at the Melbury Road on Tuesday and see that things are ship-shape——" Dorothea had given up rags and bones altogether and had scoured London for delicacies and comforts, and now, as though the place was hers, ushered me into the little house of magic.

We had the pleasantest of dinners in the vast studio, which took up most of the cubic content of the house, at a small round table drawn up near the fire which blazed under a François Premier chimney-piece purchased, in the happy days of long ago, by an impecunious Featherstone, and subjected to all sorts of undignified white elephant adventures for many years, until tardily smiling fortune took it from God knows where and placed it as a Thing of Delight in the studio of the Melbury Road.

Said Dorothea:

"I'm a child of my age, I suppose. I love dancing and

gaiety and good food and restaurants and nice clothes and other pretty things on me which nobody sees. But now and then I'm pulled up short by what's real. Do you know what I mean?"

I smiled. "I think I do."

"I wonder." She wrinkled her brow. "This, for instance, is real. All the longing and aspiration and love and thought that has been expended in the making of this room. Here you've a proper setting, my dear Daddums. Fancy Uncle Tom and Aunt Muriel in it!"

I laughed. Perhaps it was not the setting for a democratic bishop and a wife scrupulously episcopal yet socially ambitious. There were some riotous masterly nudes about the walls which Featherstone had taken over, for more than he could afford, from the widow of poor young Blenkow who had died unbought and broken-hearted. There was also a sort of sunset colour scheme which could not harmonize with the Bradbury spiritual environment.

"This is real," she repeated, with a certain vehemence, "and you're real. You do things. You create things. Beautiful things like these"—she waved a hand— "which have meaning and endurance. But these other people——"

"Which other people?" I asked indulgently. For by her manner she might have been wiping out all the human race save myself alone.

"Oh—the Bradbury people."

"My dear," said I, "your artistic embroidery swindle is destroying your sense of proportion. 'Art is real, art is earnest,' as the poet ought to have said. But it isn't life. It must have life to feed on"—and here Featherstone's handy man set before me an exquisitely browned leg of baby lamb.—"Your Uncle Tom is in the thick of life. He's as real a person as you would wish to meet in a day's march."

"H'm," remarked Dorothea doubtfully.

The carving, helping, serving and preliminary grateful degustation of the lamb interrupted for the moment the fine flow of conversation.

"My dear," I asked at last, "why did you say 'h'm'?"

"Because I meant it."

"But what has the Bishop been doing to you?"

"Nothing. He has common sense and good manners. But he wants to turn Amos into a parson."

"Good God!" I cried aghast, all the ecclesiastical atmosphere of my childhood surging round about me.

"I quite agree with you," said Dorothea.

"Isn't it astonishing how people can't think outside their environment? For the cobbler, nothing like leather. For the churchman, nothing like church."

"All the same," said Dorothea, "haven't you often told me that it was Uncle Tom who saved you from Holy Orders?"

For the moment I had forgotten. I did not admit the fact. Open admission is not good for the souls of the young. I pish'ed and pshaw'ed instead. My case was quite different. I had chosen my vocation. I could not be compared to Amos. Dorothea demurely let me have my way. I burst out:

"But why? The poor boy is as ignorant as a fish. He doesn't know the difference between the Decalogue and the Decameron."

"Uncle Tom says that won't make much difference."

"He'll have to go to school for six years before he's fit to pass the Bishop's examination."

"That's what Uncle Tom puts it at. First a private tutor and then a theological college. After that a curacy in Bradbury. He's the muscular sort of fellow they want there. He'll learn his trade and, as he's got plenty of money to live on, he'll be able to accept preferment, which most parsons these days can't possibly afford."

Again I waxed profane. Amos in gaiters as Archdeacon, Dean, Bishop. . . . The vision was preposterous.

"I think it rotten, don't you?" said Dorothea. "Just when the poor lamb is beginning to find his feet in the world—to carry him off and stuff him with half-baked theology and then stick a white dog-collar round his neck and tie him up to a bench in a horrid little church in a horrid slum in that disgusting place." Again she added: "It's rotten."

I cast on her a quick elderly glance and noted her flushed cheeks and a light like that of battle in her eyes. I smiled paternally.

"The Church of England would be a far more vital force if it had in it more men of the calibre of the Bishop of Bradbury. He's a great man. Just as one says the Great Soldier, the Great Physician, so without disrespect would I call him the Great Parson."

"I know all that," cried Dorothea impatiently. "I'm not crabbing either Uncle Tom or the Christian religion—"

"And you must remember," I interrupted, "that a pious young man in spectacles wouldn't have much influence in the slum parish which you describe."

She regarded me with angry amazement.

"Well! For shifting of ground I've never met your equal."

"I'm only trying to hold a balance," said I.

"Balance! No thank you."

The last three words accompanied a gesture which waved away my hand holding the champagne bottle.

I smiled again, shook my head, and filled her glass.

"My child," said I, "I only want to get to the real root of this furious indignation."

She flushed again. "Amos is no more made to be a parson than you were. He's made for the big world and the big things and the big way of doing things. It's an infernal shame to tie him up, as I said, and condemn him to the little things. Uncle Tom and I almost had a row about it. He said: 'Do you call training sullen operatives and their wives to wash and respect each other' —I don't mean to wash each other—'and bring up their children decently and, incidentally, to believe in God rather than in Trotsky a little thing?' He thought he had me cornered. Oh! Bishops make me tired!"

She spoke as though it were her lot to go to tea with the whole bench once a week.

"Well?" I asked.

I said "No. Nothing so silly. But you want a zealot more or less burning to do it. Someone who's going to focus his light on this little world. And that's not Amos!"

"And then?"

"He patted my hand and laughed. I hate people to pat my hand and laugh—although they may be Right Reverend Lord Bishops who can whizz about alone in their little two-seaters and do their own running repairs. As if I had no common sense!"

Dorothea threw up her hand and attacked her dinner. After a while:

"I don't believe in all this up-to-date, broad-minded ecclesiasticism of Uncle Tom. Right down in the depth of his soul burns the intolerant fire of Torquemada."

This threw a new light on the character of my very dear brother-in-law. I smiled inwardly, though preserving a grave face; and for nothing in the world would I have patted her hand. As to Amos's unsuitability for a clerical career I had no doubt. Had I not, in fact, sounded the first note of alarmed protest? But the lady had protested inordinately; too much from the point of view of an uninterested spectator. In spite of my own disquietude, I could not but catch a thrill of amusement from her vehemence.

Was it possible that Dorothea, the level-headed, the remorseless-hearted, subtle-brained commanding spirit of the South Molton Street embroidered-bag shop, Dorothea, who had waded through dancing floors strewn with men, had looked upon my ungainly Amos and found him beautiful, the hero of her dreams? Most difficult to determine. She was not wasting away. On the contrary she was the brown-haired, brown-eyed, red-cheeked emblem of health, a Romney picture of youth in its comfortable riot. And she was eating some sort of chocolate mess with serene enjoyment. We laid down spoons at the same moment. I made her my little compliment; for was not she the ordainer of the feast?

"Perfect," said I.

She acquiesced, informed me that by taking over Featherstone's studio and cook I had hit on a lucky streak. I lit a cigar, she a cigarette.

"And Amos? What does he think of it all?"

She shrugged her ignorance.

"How does he put in his time?" I asked.

"That's another thing that worries me. When he can escape from Aunt Muriel, he sits about in public-houses and attends socialistic meetings."

"And the Bishop?"

"He laughs and says it's a good training."

I sighed. "I must run down to the wretched place and see for myself."

We finished the evening happily. I saw Dorothea into a flat-bound taxi, and went to bed. Two or three days afterwards I took train to Bradbury.

The Palace, a vast early Victorian house, lay about a couple of miles out of the grim manufacturing town, its park surrounded by the villas of the local opulent. It was depressingly furnished with a mixture of the heavy sideboards and couches and plush ball-fringed curtains of the fifties and the bamboo flimsiness of the eighties, and all the most melancholy of the crucifixions and pietàs out of the Arundel collection of reprints adorned the walls. I arrived in time for tea, which was served before a little fire in the big drawing-room. Draughts from the blustering April wind swept beneath every door in the place. Nobody except myself heeded them. Muriel, stout, serene and sisterly, was too much occupied in hospitable attentions and in improving her knowledge, at second hand, of the fashionable world as intimately known at Cannes; the Bishop, brisk, hearty, with a meeting before dinner in front of him, was too busy; and Amos was too much taken up both with the pleasures of the table—indeed there were two or three, each piled up with farinaceous sustenance—and with the undisguised pleasure of seeing me again.

When the meal was over, the Bishop rose, lit a bright black pipe—he boasted that he was the last man left in England who had the art of colouring meerschaums—threw the match into the fire and slapped Amos on the back.

"You did quite right to send him here, David. This rugged North's a man's country."

"So I gather," said I, "was Warraranga, where he came from."

Muriel sighed. "I wish I could call it a gentleman's country. If only Tom would let himself be translated. He had the chance of Oxford."

The Bishop laughed. "Oh, I've given up theological scholarship for real work." He drew picturesque parallels of the academic and the practical side of the episcopal career. He had been a scholar in his day, a liturgical authority. Now in the sanctity of his own home he confessed to not caring a hang for outer forms.

"In the years gone by Muriel and I found common ground in a projected Treatise on Vestments. Now the only Vestments I care a hang about are those in which she's pleased to adorn herself."

He made her a little bow. Muriel simpered serenely. She had developed into a fine Juno-esque figure of a woman which she knew repaid thoughtful adornment.

Amos, having fed himself adequately, drew his chair nearer to the little fire and stretched out his feet on the fender cushion.

"My dear," cried Muriel, "your boots are all caked in mud."

They were. Hunks of moist clay fell on the cushion. He regarded them penitently.

"The last time I put on my slippers, Aunt, you said I wasn't to wear 'em in the drawing-room."

The same old Amos. But why had he not been corrected for this solecism in Cannes? And then I reflected that in clean and sunny Cannes there is no mud.

"You should change into shoes," said Muriel.

Docile as ever, Amos rose and shambled with his bear-like gait, out of the room.

"Such a dear," remarked Muriel. "As gentle as a lamb. And he improves every day."

"Wonderful raw material for anyone to work on," said the Bishop.

"Dorothea tells me you're thinking of moulding him into a parson."

"What the soldier said isn't evidence," he smiled. "But suppose I am—what have you to say against it?"

I began my argument. Dorcas had sent him to me so that he could see the world. Tom, by way of counter, smilingly retorted that she hadn't meant me to introduce him to the World's two friends—the Flesh and the Devil. Did I really consider Cannes an ideal school?

"Ideal," said I. "He is up against the World in its complexity, the Flesh in its crudity, and as for the Devil —on his first encounter he tied him up with rope and left him on his own bedroom floor. As it has turned out, I needn't have sent him away from Cannes after all."

The Bishop made courteous admissions. Of course he had heard the story, both from Amos and from Dorothea. But who was the blackmailed lady to whom he had constituted himself knight-errant? Irritated by an un-episcopal twinkle in his eye, I answered heatedly. If he did not grasp all the wonder of Nadia it was not my fault. When I had finished and thrown with some impatience the butt of my cigar into the fire—it had gone out during my speech—he said in that confounded, dry, humorous way of his:

"I can see your princess and can appreciate Amos's infatuation. But still, when a Serene Highness is willing to pay a large sum of money to an unprincipled adven-

turer for letters which she has written to him, one is
forced to speculate on the compromising nature of those
letters. I'm speaking as a man of the World."

"And of the Flesh and the Devil," I cried.

It is only relations that can get home on bishops like
that. I laughed in exultation; but not so loud as to drown
in my ears a gasp from Muriel. I turned and found her
looking at me as though I had gone into the cathedral
with a gun and started to snipe choir boys. But Tom
only laughed.

A clock on the mantlepiece chimed a quarter. He took
out a watch which gave confirmatory evidence.

"Good gracious, I must be going. I'm in the chair."

"What committee is it to-day, dear?" asked Muriel.

His eyes twinkled through his round tortoiseshell
spectacles.

"It's the Diocesan meeting of the Sabbath League for
the Promotion of Cruelty to Christians. I'm going to
smite the Philistines hip and thigh, and I hope I'll be able
to bust up the whole darned show altogether."

"What do you mean?" I asked.

"I mean," said he, "to put my foot down on narrow
Sabbatarianism. 'Remember the seventh day and keep it
jolly.' In the true sense of the word. That's my motto.
The day of rest should be a day of happiness."

"But, my dear Tom," said I, "if you make Sundays
so jolly, people won't go to church."

Said he: "I don't care whether they go to church or
not. I don't want people to go to church because they're
bored so stiff that there's nowhere else to go."

"But what's the good of empty churches?"

"They're empty now. That's what I'm up against.
You've got to find a God before you're happy in a
church."

"And how are you going to make people find God?"
He touched my sleeve with one hand and held up the forefinger of the other.

"My dear boy, that's our business. We clergy haven't been in existence for nearly two thousand years for nothing."

He looked at his watch again, uttered a crisp exclamation of dismay and rushed out. I poked the little fire and made a blaze and also added a few coals. Muriel thanked me. I sat down near her.

"Tom's a marvel," said I.

"If only he had taken Oxford," she replied plaintively. "I'm sure his next step would have been Canterbury."

"But he's utterly happy here. Doing famous work. He's in his element."

"But it's such a horrid element, David. If you only knew what the people were like!"

And I thought, but did not say: "If only you, Muriel, knew what Tom was like!"

CHAPTER XII

THE Bishop had gone off to his study, Muriel to bed, and Amos and I were left alone. Said Amos: "Things ain't any more right in this town than they are in Cannes."

I invited an explanation. He wagged his great head.

"They ain't real. Here's Uncle Tom going about with his gospel of saving men's minds and bodies before he can save their souls, and there's the whole lot of working men who say it's damned cheek of him. They don't want their minds and bodies saved. They've got good enough minds of their own and they're quite satisfied with their bodies. As for souls, they don't believe in 'em. Strikes me that the first thing you've got to do in converting a feller is to make him believe in his immortal soul. Uncle's got hold of the wrong end of the stick."

"I don't see where the unreality comes in."

"Why, everybody, as Scripture says, seems to be imagining a vain thing. At Cannes they think they're getting happiness out of heathen dances and gambling over cards, and they don't; and here they're all running after shadows, just the same, only different." He sucked his pipe and scratched his head. "There's a darned sight too many symbols about."

On enquiring as to the meaning of this cryptic statement, I discovered that the symbolism of his christening and confirmation had left his mind somewhat confused. He continued: "Uncle says the Cross is a symbol— perhaps it is—but mother said it was popish. The fellers

166

I go about among say the Red Flag is a symbol. I ask
'em what of. They say the Federated Labour of the
World. But it seems to me to be a symbol of not wanting
to do any labour at all and be clothed and fed in luxury
for not doing it. They ask me: 'Why should his blooming Lordship have a palace and five thousand a year for
doing nothing, while we toil and slave in a hovel for a
couple of pounds a week?' And I make answer: 'If
you poor fools weren't slaves to your trades unions and
worked sixteen hours a day, year in and year out like
the Bishop, and put the same guts into it, you might be
worth paying for.' "

"And what retort do your friends make?" I asked.

"Retort?"

"Answer—reply."

Amos grinned and knocked the ashes out of his pipe.
"Oh, they replied this afternoon. A great hulking chap
said: 'It's all very well for you to talk, you're the nephew
of the blinking Bishop, and you've never done a stroke
of work in your life.' 'Ain't I?' I says. 'You bring a
sheep here and see which of you blighters can shear it.'
Seems they know nothing about sheep hereabouts. They
laughed at me. I took a glass beer mug and smashed it
on the floor. That's the sort of way to get silence and
make yourself heard. It strikes them sudden-like. I've
seen it done before in Warraranga. I said: 'The first
man who laughs now had better say his prayers.' Well,
the big chap and another feller said something and we
had a scrap and I laid 'em both flat, and then the land-
lord and the barman took a hand and I was chucked out,
and not wanting to make a row in the place, I came home
to tea."

He rubbed his big hands together and regarded me
amiably.

"And this," said I, "you consider to be the end of a perfect day."

"It's been none too bad," said Amos.

After a while I asked him point blank:

"What's all this talk of your taking Holy Orders?"

He stared into the fire for a time and then replied, looking not at me, but into the red glow, the heavy lines of perplexity on his young brow.

"I don't see how leading all these misguided blokes into the light isn't a man's work, as Uncle, the Bishop, says; but whether I'm the man to do the work is another question. I'm up against the stumbling-block and offence of all my life which Mother used to say would prevent me from having full Grace. I'm not meek enough."

It took me a few minutes to attune myself to the workings of his mind. At last I said, as gently as I could:

"From what you have told me I don't think meekness was the prevailing characteristic of your dear mother."

He wagged his head to and fro, still looking in the fire, and replied in all seriousness:

"She prayed for it daily, but, as she said, the Lord in His wisdom never thought it fit to give it her. P'r'aps He felt she was doing His work as well as she could; for, how the blazes a meek woman could have run the station at Warraranga, I'm blest if I know." He ruminated again, and went on: "But with a Minister of God's Word it's different, ain't it? He can't go round punching people on the jaw because they don't agree with him. At any rate, I guess he oughtn't to find the delight of the unregenerate in doing it."

"The delight of the unregenerate!" The classical phrase sounded so odd as it came from the lips of Amos. But a Puritan upbringing had given him acquaintance with odd, half-forgotten formulas of phraseology.

"You really like it?" said I.

He turned to me and nodded.

"If all you feel worth living for is to hunt around the world till you can find a feller and pound his face into a jelly and make his bones all pulp, that's not the kind of spirit a man ought to take with him into the ministry. No, Uncle, I'm afraid I'm not meek enough."

"And who," I asked, though I guessed, "is the fellow in question?"

"Ramon Garcia, of course."

"I agree," said I, "that your impulse can hardly be described as Christian like."

"It ain't. And that's what's knocking me silly."

"Still," said I, remembering the Bishop's allusion to his Sabbatarian opponents, "you have the 'smiting hip and thigh' sanction of the Old Testament."

"I should have to go in under the New Dispensation," said Amos. "I don't think father and mother ever made enough of that. Moses and Joshua and David were all very well in their way—but Jesus Christ's better. And as long as I can't forgive my enemies, I don't see how I can preach the Gospel."

Again I indicated my entire agreement with his point of view.

"If your one aim in life is to make *pâté de foie gras* of the body of Ramon Garcia, you're not in a position to take Orders in a Christian Church."

"That's it, Uncle," said he. "I can go on my knees and pray for lots of things. But I can't pray for Grace to forgive that blackguard. It's no use. I guess that to make yourself a hypocrite before God is the biggest sin on earth. And it's so darned foolish. Like most sin, isn't it?"

My worldliness was silenced. Could greater truth be more simply uttered?

I rose, poured out a mild brandy and soda and lit a cigarette. Amos helped himself from a cut-glass jug to a jorum of barley water.

"No," said he, "I ain't meek enough." The formula was becoming tiresome. "Besides," he continued after a huge draught of the uninspiring fluid, "she couldn't live here."

I started round on him glass in hand.

"She? Who? Dorothea?"

"No, no," said he, "Nadia. The Princess."

I dashed my untasted drink on the tray and, in a sudden whirl of I know not what, gripped him by the collar.

"What do you mean?"

"As soon as I see her again, I'm going to ask her to marry me."

"The devil you are," said I.

"I don't see where the devil comes in, Uncle," said he.

Perhaps our common blood spoke, for, like Amos, I felt at that moment the most unmeek person in the universe. If I could have floored him and kicked him and thrown him out of the window for his colossal impudence I should have done it. A silly calf infatuation for a fascinating woman—that I understood; but the calm assumption of marriage with her as one of the factors in his choice of a profession made me as angry as ever I have been in my life. I walked up and down the long drawing-room, not trusting myself to speak. I have old-fashioned notions of personal dignity. Speech, I knew, would have been to betray, even, to this simpleton, the monstrous situation.

He stood patiently, with his long tumbler of barley water in his hand, watching my angry pacing.

"I don't see why you should be so mad about it, Uncle," said he. "It's my business. After all, she's only a woman, and she's the woman I want."

At last I controlled myself and halted in front of him. "Look here, young man. You talk in a glib way of asking a Princess to marry you. But supposing—which is preposterous—but, at any rate, supposing she's inclined to listen to you, what would you propose to give her?"

"Give her?" he asked, uncomprehending. "You don't mean money, do you?"

"Of course not, you young idiot," said I. "She has exalted birth, position, education, the finest culture of the pre-war world, fascination, wit, beauty, every grace you can think of in woman—what are you qualified to give her in exchange for all this?"

"I dunno," said Amos. He paused for a dubious moment and then brightened up. "Leastways, I could protect her. It'd be a particular kind of fool who'd try to hurt her while I was around. I don't want to put on dog, but the Lord didn't give me physical strength for nothing. And if she wanted me to learn all about painting and music and poetry, I'd do it for her sake. I ain't a fool. And I'm young."

"Yes," said I, "confound you, you're young." But I covered up my bitterness by adding: "And that's why you're a silly ass, falling in love with princesses. If you want to marry, why don't you think of some decent girl in your own sphere of life?"

"You mean Dorothea?"

"I don't," I cried with assumed indignation. "Why drag in Dorothea?"

"She's a very nice girl, Uncle." This in a tone of injured remonstrance.

"I know she is," said I.   "The most charming, delightful, accomplished girl I know.   And that's why I
think your suggesting her name infernal cheek on your
part."

"Well, Uncle," he replied in his disarming, gentle way,
"I didn't say as how I wanted to marry her, did I?"

I looked at my watch.   For me the conversation was
wandering into the realms of the grotesquely impossible.
My suggestion of bed he eagerly grasped.   He confessed
to certain aches in the region of stomach and reins
resulting from the unscientific methods whereby he had
been thrown out of the public-house.   I turned off the
lights, as Tom had invited me to do, and we parted on
the first landing—Amos to seek, no doubt, profound and
stertorous repose; I, to stay awake half the night.

"I am young."

That was the clarion cry before which I fled defence-
less.   Youth rejoicing in its strength, in the superbness
of its actuality and its promise.   And Amos was not
merely the vast, lusty human beast.   Beneath this im-
mensity of brawn, this indisputable certainty of Her-
culean strength, always, from the most deeply rooted
sexual instincts, a man's asset in woman's eyes, there
lay, as guessed by woman's intuition, an undiscovered
country of ignorances, simplicities and chivalries, a virgin
soil which, in loyal exchange for things physical, the gift
assured to her by all the tendrils of her being, she could
plant with all the sweetness that women love and whereof
they reap the full harvest.

That is the only way I could account for Dorothea
falling in love with him; for in love with him she un-
doubtedly was.   Swept off her feet by the physical, she
exulted in the prospect of ultimate spiritual victory.
The eternal conflict is as old as the Stone Age.

Oh! I could understand Dorothea. If they had come to me for my consent to their union I should have given them my paternal and avuncular benediction and sent them forth in full assurance of their happiness. But Amos did not want Dorothea. He wanted Nadia.

Now, as young women in their early twenties, what essential difference, in that never-to-be-defined woman's wonderland of interdiffused sexuality and spirituality, existed between them? Please remember they were not separated by the vast chasm that divides the Princess from the Beggar Maid. In the ordinary way of life, she and Nadia met on the same social plane. Dorothea, on both sides of *her family*, was a lady of proud descent. Both were fine flowers of modern civilization. They existed side by side in that same wonderland. So, if Dorothea had fallen head over ears in love with Amos, why, impelled by identical impulse, should not Nadia have done the same?

"I am young."

The unconscious gloriosity of it!

The next day before lunch I had the chance of a few minutes quiet talk with my brother-in-law. He—I don't remember if I've told you—is a brisk, little, keen-faced bright-eyed man in round spectacles. He gives you the impression of taking this life as a great joke and the life to come as a greater; and yet he makes you understand that the jokes are very sacred and that the pure ineffable laughter thereat dare only be heard in the Holy of Holies of a man's soul.

He had heard, of course, of yesterday's bout of fisti-cuffs. He deplored the incident.

"I'm with Kingsley," said he, "in his plea for muscular Christianity; but—I think the Church ought to assign a limit to the assertion of muscle."

"Besides," said I, "a curate is not best introduced to a parish by being first thrown into it out of a public-house."

"The proposition, as far as it goes," said Tom, "is incontrovertible. The only point is that I wouldn't have him less muscular, and I don't see how he could be more Christian."

"But," said I, "you were just talking of the Church assigning limits."

"My dear fellow," said he, "you're coming into the area of all the heresies of all the ages. Very few people have been able to realize a Church and Christianity as two distinct conceptions."

"I have a glimmer of what you mean," said I, drawing a bow at a venture, for I was somewhat befogged, "and it confirms my opinion that Amos would fight the battle of Christianity better as a free-lance, a *franc-tireur*, than he would by holding a commission in the Church."

"I perfectly agree with you," said he.

"Well then——?" said I.

"Take him away. Educate him. If he wants to join us in after years he can always do so. I thought I'd put the proposition before him. It's a man's job, if, having the Faith, as Amos has, he can take it seriously. But I fully realize that, after a good many years of necessarily narrow training, he wouldn't be the man he is now. Dorothea, who has an unfortunate distaste for curates, has given you a wrong impression."

"I'm glad to hear it," said I. "But why did you leave me with a wrong impression yesterday?"

"When people put pistols to my head, I regard them with the most unchristianlike malice. My dear fellow," he went on, his humorous eyes twinkling, "you sent me a curious creature: a hulking mass of sheer goodness, lit by a shrewd brain, and vitalized by potentially enormous physical passions. What was I to do with him? I experimented. I got the wrong reaction. That's all there is to it. On the other hand, his time here hasn't been wasted. He has come into contact with the raw humanity whose control is slipping out of the hands of the Church and, in the future, can only be safe in the hands of men like Amos."

"You're a bewildering Bishop, Tom," said I. "What do you mean?"

He tapped his breast. "We'll have the last word. Of that you may be sure. Meanwhile, *au bon entendeur salut!*"

And that is all he would say.

The result of this was my carrying off to London an unresisting Amos and housing him in a little spare room in the Melbury Road. Then, busy, with final touches to my Academy pictures, and with the delightful annual picking up of threads in the Art world, I propounded to myself and to Dorothea Tom's question: "What the deuce are we going to do with him?" Amos, in his gentle way, was perfectly happy prowling about the streets of London, turning up regularly at meals, and, as far as I could make out, sleeping contentedly when there was nothing else to do. Now and then Dorothea carried him off to a theatre. With a little touch of irony, I said:

"It's very good of you, dear, to take so much trouble about him."

"It's only my duty to you. If I didn't think you'd understand, I should hate you. Duty is the rottenest proposition in the wide world."

"Unlike Virtue in the abstract, my dear, it's always somebody else's reward."

Our eyes met for a magnetic moment.

"Daddums," said she, "you're a pet lamb."

It was through Cardew, a dear, silly brother artist, who passes his life in painting goats, that Bendyke Hamilton, like the new planet in the poem, swam into our ken. This was his brother-in-law, a gallant, scholarly soldier of fortune, with an M.A. degree, a D.S.O. and one eye, who was now at a loose end. With regard to him Dorothea, Amos and I held counsel together, with the result that we appointed him Amos's temporary guide, philosopher and friend: tutor, Mentor and bear-leader. Amos submitted himself wholeheartedly to a mapped-out course of instruction, which included the cultivation of a pure English speech, the history of painting and architecture, modern world politics, rowing, boxing and intelligent attendance at race meetings and police courts. Dorothea kept an occasional eye on finger-nails and neckwear, while I maintained general supervision. In this manner all of us began to lead fairly contented lives.

The Royal Academy opened. My few pictures, other than commissioned portraits, sold fairly well. My success, however, was the portrait of the Princess Nadia. Even certain critics who complained of the sterility of my work—whatever that meant—praised the Princess. At the Private View there was a flattering little continuous crowd around it. The Arch-Flouter of the Academy and all its works buttonholed me and asked me why on earth I had not sent it into his own New Horror Exhibition, just open a few hundred yards away. Urbanely I said: "What further praise is there for me to covet?" "Of course," he replied, "it's a bit niggly—you poor fellows daren't escape it; but still"—he waved a curved thumb in the air—"there's breadth and intelligence—you'd better come over to us."

Well, I am what I am, and I'm not going over to anyone; least of all to a set of folk who put a woman's ears between her toes and her eyes in the middle of her back. On the wall hung the picture of Nadia looking as Nadia looked, with something of her soul shimmering over her.

We drew near the close of a fretful May. I longed for my beloved Azure Coast and its mad carnival riot of flowers; its June sunshine and sea breeze; its warm blue water in which one could bathe for ever, and its hot and comforting sands. Also its sweet companionable solitude: in June and July I can achieve my ideal. I can be left alone. There's no one to worry me.

Now there came a day when, having to lunch in the West End, and not having seen Dorothea for some little time, I had given her a luncheon appointment at the Berkeley. I found her there with young Claude Worthington. He had looked in at the South Molton Street shop and she had brought him along. In spite of the stupendous success of his Dutroyen cars, he was always ready for a free meal. So, resplendent in health and raiment, did he frankly declare. Dorothea, in her wide way, informed me that, over the telephone, she had summoned Amos and Bendyke Hamilton to join the party. Presently they arrived. I cannot deny that we had a pleasant luncheon. Amos and Claude had buried old hatchets. Dorothea responded outrageously to Claude's advances, while Amos grinned a cousinly benediction. If Dorothea's heart were full of wrath against Amos, it was not my concern. Bendyke Hamilton, an admirable fellow, kept his one tactful eye (the other, poor chap, was somewhere in the dust of Flanders) on the situation and set the young talk going. At the end of the meal Claude sang out:

"I say, Uncle David, have you any pictures in the Royal Academy?"

"Has he pictures? Hoo—hoo—hoo!" roared Amos.

"What do you think, you silly ass?" cried Dorothea.

The blush of confusion overspread the young man's features.

"No, but I say, Uncle David—I'm sorry. I didn't know. Nobody told me. Besides, I've been selling these beastly cars in Bilston and Dudley and Huddersfield and all sorts of places where there's nothing but money and tramways and fleas—the sort of things that don't educate you a little bit. I've had an awful time. How should I know?"

"You should study *The Studio* and *The Connoisseur* and read all the Art criticisms in *The Times* and *The Daily Telegraph*," said I.

"I think you had better throw me out and be done with it," said Claude.

We did not throw him out. Dorothea condemned him to an immediate visit to the Royal Academy close by. Also included in her sentence Amos and Bendyke Hamilton. After I had paid the bill, it dawned upon me that she had ordained me as cicerone to the party. We walked joyously up Piccadilly. There are times when a middle-aged man is intoxicated by the ebullience of companionable youth. Though the afternoon was unsettled, there was a fragrance of spring in the air and the pavements were dry. The pageant of London swept along the crowded roadway. We tried to walk five abreast and laughed foolishly at our jostlings and interruptions and changes of partners. At the corner of Down Street Amos bought from a flower-seller a huge bunch of Parma violets which, rushing on ahead, he thrust into Dorothea's hand. She thanked him prettily, and I then saw her make a grimace at Claude by her side, as who should say: "Why didn't you think of that?"

We reached the gates of Burlington House and walked across the flagged courtyard already furnished with the decorous row of waiting motor-cars. We entered by the centre doors and ascended the majestic flight of stairs.

"Dorothea has been telling me," said Claude, "that the stunningest thing in the whole show is your portrait of the Princess Ramiroff of Cannes."

I took him, the rest following, through the first three galleries into Gallery IV, and turned through the door to the right. It was too soon after lunch for the room to be crowded. In the contagious enthusiasm of youth, I led them towards the centre of the wall where the picture was hung.

And there, standing in front of it, was one solitary and familiar figure.

CHAPTER XIII

IT was Amos who first identified him, and his slithering rush across the polished floor that compelled our attention. Señor Ramon Garcia gave a little gasp of astonishment, and quick alarm sprang into his eyes. Amos bulked over and about him.

"How d'ye do?" said he.

Said Garcia: "I have not the pleasure of knowing you, sir," and with a·half bow turned away.

Amos clapped a hand on his shoulder and the other wrenched himself free. Already the slight scuffle had attracted the notice of the score or so of early visitors in the room. I nodded to Claude and Bendyke Hamilton and we swiftly interposed ourselves between the two men. As a member of the Royal Academy I could scarcely permit a free fight in my own gallery. Dorothea, coming to my aid, hung tight on to Amos's arm. I advanced with what politeness I could command.

"Señor Garcia," said I, "Mr. Burden's last interview with you terminated somewhat abruptly. Don't you think that explanations on both sides might be desirable?"

"You mistake yourself, sir," said he in the crude accent and halting English of the familiar Ramon. "My name is not Garcia, and you are a stranger to me as much as this gentleman."

"And also to a lady signing herself 'Luisa' whose letters have, by an unfortunate accident, come into my possession?"

The scoundrel's eyelids never flickered. "You mistake

me for another," he replied. "I do not know a lady of that name."

Amos, in the grip of Dorothea, shoved himself forward and pointed to the portrait.

"You know that lady, at any rate, don't you?"

"No," said he.

"Then why have you been staring at her?"

Ramon shrugged his shoulders. "It is the portrait of a woman who I think must be beautiful; but it is so execrably painted that one cannot judge."

He took off his hat and swaggered off, leaving an Amos, almost foaming at the mouth, in the grip of the four of us. If he had exerted his strength he would have sent us all flying like clustering infants at a children's party: yet had we not restrained him, he would have made a dreadful scandal, sanguinary in the literal sense, in those decorous halls. He stood among us glaring and panting and in tones modulated according to Dorothea's insistent commands, likened his enemy to everything unclean under the sun. At last he said:

"Let me go. I understand you don't want me to make a scene. But once I get him outside, God help him. And"—he jerked a thumb towards the picture—"I'll give him an extra welt, Uncle, for your sake."

Already there was a little ring of bystanders ostensibly regarding the portrait, but really with ears pricked to catch the flutter of a sensation. Claude Worthington grinned.

"Better slip the leash. We've given the hare a sporting chance."

There was nothing else to be done. Amos, freed, marched away, followed by Bendyke Hamilton, most conscientious of governors. The remaining three of us sank on the nearest leather-upholstered settee.

"Did you ever come across such damned cheek?" said Claude. "Of course I remember the blighter at Cannes. But what I can't understand is—why has Amos got his knife into him or why he denied his identity?"

"There are things in Heaven and Earth, Horatio, etcetera, etcetera," said Dorothea.

"Give it up," said Claude, whose Shakespearian studies had apparently been interrupted by the war. "I never answered to the name of Horatio in my life." Then he burst into a boyish guffaw and clamped my knee in a friendly grip. "But the swine got home on you, anyhow, Uncle David, didn't he?"

If one cannot laugh with youth, one's place is among ghosts in tombs.

Now, I have to record that Amos, once out of my sight, ran through the three first galleries, followed also at a run by Hamilton, thereby giving the quickly assembling after-lunch visitors to the Academy the impression of pickpocket and pursuant, down the stairs into the courtyard, just in time to see Ramon Garcia in the Piccadilly distance, leap into a taxi-cab and whirl away. They hurled themselves into another taxi-cab and, after the manner of the detective stories, sought to give chase. But the May afternoon traffic of Piccadilly is thick, and one taxi-cab resembles its fellows as does one pea its brethren in a peck.

Amos turned up at the studio disconsolate.

"If I'd only been meeker," said he, "I'd have accepted the beggar's lies and just followed him quietly until I had him alone. Until I get those letters out of him, I'll never rest."

I lay back in my chair, my finger-tips joined together, outwardly presenting, for the sake of decency, a placid demeanour, but inwardly feeling the most miserable dog unhung. Those compromising letters were still in the blackmailer's possession. Nadia's flight, her meteoric passage through Cannes, her disappearance, all had to do with some miserable, though I was convinced innocent, episode in which Garcia was a protagonist. And, having him in my hands, I had let him go free, just for the sake of social convention. Yet what could I have done? Like a meeker Amos, I could have played amateur sleuth-hound, and tracked him down to his hotel or lodging and learned the name under which he went; then I could have employed a private detective, who would have given me full particulars of his activities. But after that? I had nothing tangible wherewith to lay a charge of blackmail against him. To do so without the Princess's knowledge would have been an outrage of unimaginable monstrosity. Yet the rascal was beaten already: obviously in blue terror of Amos; his claws cut. Only his Latin American suppleness of brain and nerve had enabled him to carry off the situation. The malicious shaft of criticism rankled not in the soul of the painter—but in the heart of the man. He had got home on me, according to Claude's vernacular; wherefrom he had derived unholy joy; and no man alive delights in providing his enemy with such entertainment. But I let that pass. I had missed an opportunity. What could I do now? New Scotland Yard? Why not? I could easily get an introduction to one of the chiefs. Without bringing any definite accusation, I could tell him my story in confidence, and thus put him on the track of an international malefactor.

I was at this point of my reflections, after a fairly long spell of silence during which Amos sucked at his pipe, when he spoke again.

"I'd like to find that chap and have it out with him once and for all. He's afraid of me. I saw it in his eyes. Only his bluff saved him." The perspicacious young man voiced my thoughts—"He's going to do a bolt, just as he did at Cannes. I'd go round the world to find him!"

Judge me as you will. Here shimmered before my eyes a Heaven-sent opportunity of disposing of Amos.

What aim in life had I been capable of putting before him these last five months? In Cannes, save that of learning superficial manners, there was none. The aim suggested by my excellent brother-in-law he had rejected. His present life in London was entirely aimless. I felt the responsibility of the guardianship imposed on me by my sister Dorcas. Now, here indeed was the aim revealed. An aim, at any rate, absorbing enough for a year or two, during which period, under the mentorship of that excellent young man, Bendyke Hamilton, he would have an incomparable chance of education.

"My boy," said I, "that's a famous idea."

How famous I did not learn till a while later, when, after having told my story frankly to the courteous gentleman at New Scotland Yard, to whom I had obtained an introduction, I was rung up by him on the telephone the next day. My suspicions, I learned, were justified. The man whom I knew by the name of Ramon Garcia had been under the surveillance of the police at the request of one or two foreign governments; but as nothing definite was charged against him, they could not interfere with his personal liberty. He had been staying at the Charing Cross Hotel under the name of Don Miguel Vargas y Uriostos. He had sailed for Buenos Aires yesterday morning.

"All I can say is," came the voice over the wires, "thank God you have got rid of a knave."

I did with the devoutness of a Dogberry. I also thanked Heaven for the miraculous opportunity offered to Amos for pursuing the Aim.

Before talking to Amos I put the proposition before Bendyke Hamilton, that rugged-faced, one-eyed, trustworthy young man. Would he go to the Argentine?

"Would I not?" said he.

"Do you know any Spanish?"

"I speak seven languages, and Spanish is one."

"Seven? How did you manage to learn them?"

"Some in very soft places"—he smiled—"some in hard. Spanish was in one of the hard. I'll take Amos anywhere he wants; but I'd rather not go to Mexico. I was backing the wrong side," he added, after a pause, "and they stuck me in prison. When war broke out, I managed to escape. I don't think I'm popular with Alvaro Obregon. But all that's another story. Anyhow, it would be a long hunt from Buenos Aires to the Mexican border."

I laughed. "But suppose the chase did take you to Mexico?"

"My job's my job," said he, "and I go wherever it takes me."

Here was the true gentleman adventurer, selling his sword to anybody; but, once that sword sold, faithful to death. An early Renaissance Condottiere born five or six centuries too late. No wonder, as Cardew said, he was out of a job in this war-weary world. Anyhow, he was the ideal companion for Amos.

We came to the question of extra fees. He suggested a figure.

"You're a crazy lunatic," said I.

He drew himself up. "I don't think it's exorbitant."

"You're crazier than ever," I retorted. "This is a commercial age and you have a commercial value which you don't seem to appreciate. Take up your pen and write twice the sum and we'll begin to meet on the plane of sanity."

"I'm in your hands," he said, lifting his broad shoulders. "Whatever you say goes. It's nothing to do with me."

At first I thought him a fool. But then I reflected. What standard of values can there be whereby shall be appraised the soul of an artist or the honour of a soldier?

The upshot of the whole matter was that Amos, Bendyke *duce* and *auspice* Hamilton, sailed for Buenos Aires a fortnight later. My new friend at Scotland Yard had provided Bendyke Hamilton with an introduction to the police authorities in the Argentine Republic, and Dorothea had selected a kit for Amos which should suffice him for every zone of latitude from the equator to the North Pole. The amount he had to pay for excess luggage was fantastic. Amos, always meek before Dorothea, submitted gracefully. Trust a woman to know what was best for a man, said he. Triple ass, I thought, why don't you see that it's best for you to rub off your superficial uncouthness, get your alert mind into training and marry Dorothea, who is seriously in love with you, after the silly way of young women of all the centuries? But these things can't be said. We saw him off at Southampton, where he took grateful and grinning leave of us. He was convinced that once in Buenos Aires—where and what it was he had but a foggy idea—he would meet his enemy and, in that wild and lawless land, he would catch him by the neck and squeeze the Princess Nadia's letters out of his throat. Of our Machiavellian scheme of incidental education he suspected nothing. His boyish heart beat with the sense of great adventure. The cosmopolitan crowd on the restless decks, the dark melting eyes of the South American women, the soft, slithering Spanish talk heard on all sides, the swell of the sea-going ship, the multitudinous confusion of luggage-laden porters, the little band of horizon beyond Southampton Waters, which he would cross into unknown seas—all stirred his young blood and caused him to laugh foolishly and wring our hands. Only once did he freeze into seriousness, and that was when Dorothea asked him:

"When you do bring home Ramon Garcia's head on a charger, what are you going to do with it?"

"I don't want to kill the feller," said he. "God forbid."

Dorothea began to laugh, then she began to choke, and then she began to cry, and swiftly she rushed to the taffrail and buried her face in her arms. To compassionate passers-by she was the picture of woman parting from sweetheart or husband. Amos stared at her agape. I stepped aside and put my arm round her shoulders and counselled her to pull herself together. In the process of so doing she swallowed all kinds of imaginary things.

"Oh, Daddums," she said at last, "if only he had a sense of humour he wouldn't be going on this wild goose chase."

"My dear," I murmured, "this is the best thing that could happen to him. When he comes back he'll be full of the fun of the Universe."

Now, for a season, as far as I was concerned, that was the end of Amos. Soon afterwards I returned to Cannes to spend there the two most idyllic months of the year,

June and July, while Dorothea devoted herself to commercial pursuits in South Molton Street.

The heedless folk whom fashion brings to the Riviera during the worst months of the year, February and March, have never seen a leaf on a tree and have no idea of the sensuous beauty of the summer coast. They are ignorant of its profundities of colour, of its intensity of scent, of its unimaginable greenery. The roads, familiar to them in winter as sentinelled by the stark polled plane trees, are endless embowered avenues; all the flowers that ever blow according to their season, in the North, burst out into simultaneous riot. Tall pines are hidden from stem to summit by the lilac of wistaria: bougainvillea covers houses like weed; convolvulus climbs the wayside rocks. There is a mimosa too which blooms. Heliotrope in bushes scents the air. Pink flowers deck the misembryanthemum which straggles downwards over roadside walls. In the gardens are gladioli, poinsettias, and great purple pansies and marguerites and sunflowers and the last mad bacchanal of roses. . . . And there is always the breeze, the contented sigh of the sea, sweeping over the sun-baked land.

The great hotels are shut and all the Houses of Vanity. A heavenly calm descends on the place. Bathers in *peignoirs* lounge through fashionable thoroughfares to the picturesque establishments, and against the golden sands are a hundred flashes of white limbs.

There without fear of rain or mistral one can take a boat and go to the Islands—Saint-Marguerite, where the Man in the Iron Mask was imprisoned for seventeen years—and Saint-Honorat, with its monastery of thirteen hundred years continuous existence—even now its eighth century cloisters remain; or westwards down the coast, La Napoule, Théoule, Trayas, Agay, a coast of romantic mountain-sheltered creeks, called here *calangues,* where one can land and sit and dream and paint, while your blue-jean vested boatman sleeps beneath his awning awaiting your will. And a few appreciators of an earthly Paradise stay on in their villas and now and then, for the sake of sounding the human note, meet lazily together.

If only I had known what had become of the Princess I should have been as happy as I had been all the summers since the war. For a painter need never be lonely; especially a portrait painter released from the turpentiny stuffiness of a studio and chased into the open air to paint whatsoever his whim dictates or his soul desires. But the old, unclouded happiness was mine no longer. Heaven had, as usual, at this time of year, answered my constant prayer to be left alone. Yet sometimes, in its well-meaning, Heaven is too literal. I wanted Nadia; I thirsted for the sight of her; I hungered for the fulfilling warmth of her presence.

I have a silly sailing boat. With hand on tiller and sheet, in blue weather, I would sometimes go off in a day-dream, imaging her beside me and be awakened by the rude and perplexed interposition of my boatman. And then I wondered whether she would really like it. I knew so little of her tastes.

And never a word or sign of her or about her. The Fontanas had left Cannes with the croupiers and the jewellers and the dressmakers, and their villa had been let to some wise Americans for the summer. Never a word since her enigmatic bolt into the waiting car, two or three months ago. I could not hear of her. I went so far in fatuity as to instruct my press-cutting agency to send me all newspaper references to the Princess Ramiroff. None came. I know that there are many

Serene Highnesses *de par le monde,* but the great majority of them are bottled up, thank goodness, in Germany, and their doings no longer interest civilized society. *Mais il y a des fagots et des fagots.* There are Serene Highnesses and Serene Highnesses—and while she was at Cannes, my own particular little Russian Serene Highness's name and photograph were commonplaces in every social column and journal. Now she had apparently vanished from the social world. In what remote corner of the earth had she so effectually hidden herself? And what was the reason of this concealment? I lost myself in speculation.

June and July passed. August I spent with friends in Scotland, and ate the grouse which they laboriously shot for me, and gave them in return what harvest there was of my philosophy. In September I painted a portrait or two in England. October saw me back in Cannes. In November the great hotels opened and the vanity shops along the Croisette; and in December the gamblers began to gather round the tables in the Casino and youth to dance to the dismal cacophony that it loves. My own life went on in its accustomed way. Dorothea came to me for Christmas. Claude Worthington, cock-a-hoop at having invented some kind of Dutroyen gadget and thereby established himself as an affluent hanger-on of the firm, turned up for the *réveillon* of New Year's Eve (having dutifully received his father's Christmas benediction) and, I believe, laid himself and his new fortunes at Dorothea's feet. His heart and purse both spurned, apparently, he went off to Monte Carlo, in reckless mood, won an inordinate amount of money for one so young, and again made the prostrate offering, with the promise of a Rolls-Royce car thrown in. The only result of this was the total loss (as far as his brain could understand it) of his winnings which Dorothea insisted on his investing in gilt-edged securities. In the meanwhile he ate well, golfed cheerfully and thundered up and down the Croisette in a vast, vermilion, million horse-power torpedo car.

"The funny part of the matter," said I, one day to Dorothea, "is that your Uncle Tom and Aunt Muriel adore him."

"When I'm a mother, I suppose I too will adore my offspring."

"But not being Claude's mother——?"

"My use for him," she said, "is strictly limited."

When he informed us that he had sudden orders to scuttle about Italy in Dutroyen interests, but would look in on us, on his way back, and Dorothea replied that she would be at the receipt of custom in South Molton Street long before that, his face fell.

"Some fellows have all the luck," he said.

We accompanied him to the waiting car, in which now sat a smartly attired Dutroyen chauffeur (Dorothea called him the Dutroying Angel), I would have hung back, to give the poor fellow his last chance, but Dorothea clung on to my arm. Claude squeezed both her hands.

"Good-bye, old girl. I'll worry round your funny old emporium as soon as I get back to London."

He stepped into the car and taking the wheel, drove at break-neck speed down the tram-lined hill. Dorothea and I mounted the steps.

"Daddums," she said, "I'm beginning to think that the Troubadours had their distinct points after all."

As for Amos, he seemed to be having rich experiences. He wrote dutifully, somewhat after the manner of the schoolboy, who informs parents anxious for psychological indications, that his house beat another house by three goals to one and that he has broken his wrist-watch while leaning against a wall. I judged from his bald accounts that Ramon Garcia, the ostensible objective of their travels, was as elusive as the famous Pimpernel. Though he had no reason to suspect pursuit, he had been tracked from Buenos Aires to Valparaiso, from Valparaiso to San Francisco and from San Francisco to New York, where now he was hopelessly lost. Meanwhile Bendyke Hamilton, in admirable dispatches, reported educational progress on a Brooklands racing scale. He had made Spanish, of which Amos had picked up the vernacular in an amazingly short time, the vehicle of instruction in the principles of grammar. Whereupon I noted a change in Amos's epistolary style.

The end of January found them in Egypt.

"As the lost Garcia's aim in life," wrote Bendyke Hamilton, "seemed to be the spoliation of all whom he came across, why shouldn't he, said I, take up the old game of spoiling the Egyptians? The argument appealing to Amos as a sound one, we booked passages on a round trip, and having landed at Alexandria, here we are at the Semiramis Hotel in Cairo. This morning we visited Pyramids and Sphinx. He said very little. During lunch, however, at Mena House, he broke one of his significant silences.

" 'I've spent the whole of a very wonderful year trying to come to a conclusion. And I've come to it. I've decided that the old world wants looking after by the young world. The young world, by which I principally mean Australia, is strong enough to look after itself. These hoary antiquities seem to tell me I've got to do something to put the old world right. Warraranga's a wash-out.'

"If it were but a sudden appreciation of contrast, I should concern myself but casually with his remark; but his pronouncement has, I am sure, a far more subtle origin.   Amos is a man of curious intelligence.   Between Warraranga and the Sphinx there has been a whole year's concatenation of thought."

Doubtless Bendyke Hamilton was right.   He is the last man in the world to talk, as the phrase goes, through his hat.   But why the contemplation of the Sphinx should compel an untutored Antipodean to redress the balance of the old world rather perplexed my muddled mind.

CHAPTER XIV

IT was the noon of a March day wind-swept of cloud and moisture, and the wind had fallen to the lightest breeze; so that, in the magical translucency of the air, the old town and the hill villages and the Esterel and the exquisitely curving sails of a score of racing yachts gleamed in sharp, near outline.

When I can escape from my dreadful trade, I love to walk on the Croisette. There I meet only the judicious. For most of the visitors are either sleeping off the effects of a five in the morning return from the Casino gaming tables, or are knocking balls over a net or about an uninteresting series of fields. As I say, only the judicious, who have a sense of beauty as a vital principle, are to be seen appreciatively taking the air. One walks therefore in a sweet spaciousness, yet not so sparsely peopled as to be desolate.

I was returning homewards, thanking God, in my heart, for this gift of light, when, suddenly, my eyes were arrested by a familiar, clear-cut, dainty figure in sea-green, some thirty yards away. She was coming towards me. I hastened my steps, and almost before she was aware of me, I think, I was upon her, with both my arms outstretched. I seized her hands and laughed foolishly. Her face flushed and her glance met mine in some shyness.

"Yes, it's me," she said with a laugh. "I have come back. Every one comes back to Cannes."

"But where have you been?"

"Oh, that is a long story."

"I wrote you letters. Hundreds of letters. And never a word from you."

"I believe so," she said. "You must forgive me. You who are so sympathetic. *Tout comprendre c'est tout pardonner*."

"The devil of it," said I, "is that I don't comprehend one little bit. But I am going——" I laughed aloud in my joy at seeing her once more. "I am going to make the greater gesture. I pardon without comprehending."

She made one of her funny little Tartar grimaces— in which her funny little nose took part, that funny adorable little nose whose modelling, if you remember, drove me to distraction until I sought inspiration in the Pekinese, Chouchou.

"And so you're here again," said I, after the brilliant way of men.

"I have already told you so."

"I don't think it's exactly you," said I. "It's some one even more beautiful."

I had been looking at her with the eyes of the artist, the lover and the critic. I was right. She had gained a year's bloom of womanhood. Contours had softened; colour had ripened; no, that is too crude a way of putting it. Say that there was something exquisitely undefinable in her development. . . . All the old qualities remained; the wonder of mother-of-pearl and peach of her skin, the mutinous mouth, the alternating irony and tenderness in the ever-shifting green-grey-blue of her eyes beneath the bronze-gold lashes. But her mien was more brave and her voice more firm.

"It is pleasant," she replied, "to hear a compliment again."

"That's a queer remark," said I.

"How?"

"Since when have you ceased to receive the compliments of men? Not that mine was a compliment, for it came from feelings far too deep"—I had to distinguish myself from the common herd—"But wherever you go, you have tributes of some kind—Where have you been?"

"Let us say beyond the region of compliments."

I made a little bow. "It pleases you to be enigmatic."

"It's one of the few pleasures that remain to me." She burst out laughing at my betrayal of discomfiture. "My dear friend, don't you know there is nothing more exhausting than a conversation between two people rooted to the same spot?"

I realized that we had been standing all the time opsite each other on the pavement of the Croisette.

"My dear Nadia," said I, "as far as I can command every seat in Cannes is at your disposal."

"Then there may be one at a luncheon table for a hungry woman?"

An open victoria went sauntering by. I hailed it. "To the Villa," I commanded, and we drove off.

"This is a bit out of a fairy tale," said I. "In ordinary life beautiful ladies don't drop down from heaven suddenly in front of bewildered mortals. Where have you come from? When did you come? Why have you come? And where are you staying?"

I ought to have mentioned before that the Marchese and Marchesa della Fontana had not returned to Cannes this season, the wise Americans having extended more or less indefinitely their lease of the Villa Miranda. The Fontanas, I had learned, were at Biarritz, conducting their little private gambling hell for a new set of clients.

Nadia laughed at my questions. It was like filling up a passport or a card of identity.

"Anyhow—if you wish to know—I am staying at the Mont-Fleuri with my maid and Chouchou. I arrived yesterday evening. I am here because I know I shall meet many friends—and," she gave me a sidelong glance —"I come straight out of a convent."

"A convent?" I cried, incredulously.

"Why not?"

"Once in a convent," said I, "they make you take embarrassing vows, and they shave your head and don't let you run loose about the world like the incarnation of a spring morning."

"*Voilà.* Another compliment. But you have the reason why it is so pleasant for me to hear one again. I have given you the word of the enigma."

I reminded her that she had not answered my implied question.

"In my convent I didn't take vows and I didn't have my head shaved and the gate was open for me whenever I chose to walk out. And now,"—she touched my knee —"it's lovely to be back in Cannes. This feast of light! This sense of joyousness!"

We were just passing the Casino.

"Would you care to lunch at the Ambassadeurs, and see the old gay world again?"

She shook her head. "You knew and I knew, when we entered the cab, that we were going to the Villa— Unless, of course, you wish——"

"God forbid," I cried, casting a malevolent eye on the place. "I can give you a better view and as good a cuisine, I won't deafen your ears with raucous music, and I'll have your adorableness all to my selfish self."

It pleased her to be gay. "I'm feeling better and better every minute," she quoted.

"Bonjour, François, ça va toujours bien?"
The excellent François smiled discreet welcome devoid of astonishment. It might have been a year ago when he admitted her to the daily sittings.
"Toujours, merci, Altesse."
He threw open the drawing-room door. I have told you that from this room you can see nothing but sea and sky and the Esterel. She caught her breath.

"I wonder if it's as ravishing to you as it is to me. You live here always. I have come from a little cold garden in which nothing grew, with cold high stone walls all around it, and only grey sky above me."

"Where was that?"

"In Lincolnshire."

"Lincolnshire? What in the world were you doing there?"

I must have presented the most puzzled of faces, for she laughed again.

"I am exhausting myself in telling you that I have been in a convent."

My brain began to grasp the astounding fact. All I could say was: "My dear, you must have had a dreadful time."

"Oh, no. The good sisters were most kind to me. They used to show me their chilblains, poor darlings, but I never had any. They gave me fires and hot baths and flowers in my room—and don't you think I talk much better English?"

As a matter of fact, she did, more free and idiomatic. I made her my belated compliment.

"There was one, Sister Agatha, a perfect dear, who

gave me what she called finishing lessons in English—
and I tried to teach her Russian. But what good Russian is to a nun who cannot have any opportunity of
speaking it or reading it until the World to Come,
when I expect they'll all talk Heavenese, I don't know."

We chatted on the verandah. In the pure light, the
sails of the racing yachts flashed their white intensity
against the cobalt, and the lower slopes of the Esterel
picked themselves out in startling olive. And to all
this wonder was Nadia radiantly alive.

The dining-room leading out from the drawing-room
had the same view from its windows. What Amélie
had prepared for my lonely meal, I knew not; I had no
opportunity of knowing; but I know, or rather, I
remember—for it was a strange day of days in my life,
whose most trivial incidents stand out clear in my mind,
as the physical things stood out clear in that day's
translucent atmosphere—I remember that she sent up
a meal of unsurpassable daintiness. Verily a meal for
a princess of fairy tale. Pink prawns hanging by their
beards over the side of the glass, their bodies immersed
in crushed ice; cold duckling and salad; ivory asparagus with bottle-green ends; a foolish ice-cream of fresh
strawberries and a dish of fruit, golden and yellow. We
talked of many things. Much of her picture. She was
childishly delighted to hear of its success. But, I asked,
hadn't she read the newspapers, the weeklies wherein
the portrait had been much reproduced? She replied
that people didn't read wicked newspapers in convents.
Where was the picture now? I pointed upstairs. Here,
awaiting her good pleasure.

"But you could have sold it and made much money?"

"How could I sell what wasn't mine?"

"That's true."

She reflected for a moment and then stretched out her hand and touched the back of mine in a fleeting gesture. "It's a very happy bond between us, that portrait."

I did not take the obvious advantage of the remark, the moment being too sweet and delicate. The talk shifted. And Mr. Amos?

I gave her casual news. In charge of Mentor, he was going about the world in the pursuit of wisdom. He was seeking it now in the tombs of Egyptian kings.

"I have a very soft place in my heart for your great bear," she said.

Mind you, at the time I could not tell whether she was aware of my knowledge of the scene between Amos and herself at the Villa Miranda; neither could I tell whether she knew of the tying up of Garcia and the abstraction of the lady Luisa's correspondence. In the few letters I had written to her, I may have made reference to Ramon's flight; but I certainly did not narrate Amos's mad exploit. Also whether Amos had written to her or not I did not know. The grotesqueness of our mutual position had prevented me from seeking his confidence; to what he had had to say I listened, but I asked no questions.

I replied to her last remark:

"When he's tame he'll be a very fine fellow."

"I don't want him tame. It would spoil his generosity, his chivalry."

"What do you know about his chivalry?" I asked with an assumption of idleness.

"That is my own knowledge, my dear David Fontenay. I liked him from the first moment he came into the dining-room, over a year ago, with his great honest face and his funny old bag, and stared at us as if we were very shocking people from another planet. I must have looked shocking in that *décolletée* evening dress in the broad sunshine."

She laughed; we reverted to the portrait. She began to talk chiffons. I responded with the facts that every portrait painter ought to know. She confessed herself hopelessly out of date. I pointed to her sea-green dress. Oh, that? She had stepped into a model in Paris on her way down. It was because it went so well with the complexion of Chouchou whom she had redeemed from friends in Paris, that she had bought it. In Cannes she was going to have an orgy of clothes. Presently she returned to Amos.

"I am disappointed he is not here. I counted on meeting him. The last time I saw him he did me a great service—the service of a knight errant. I shall never forget."

This was the first time that the shadow of Ramon Garcia fell across the meal. And luckily—for meals with gloomy shadows all over the table are an abomination —the meal was over. François announced the serving of coffee in the drawing-room. We rose and passed through the folding doors. On the way she repeated:

"Yes, my friend, a knight errant rescuing an authentic princess."

I had a momentary and entirely unworthy struggle with conscience. I am pleased to record that conscience won.

"Perhaps it would interest you to know," said I, "that the good Amos is in literal sense a knight errant, since he is wandering over the earth in search of a scaly dragon whose name you may guess."

She clapped her hands to her bosom and looked at me with scare in her eyes.

"Ramon Garcia?"

"Who else?"

We sat down in the sunshine of the open window. I helped her to a cigarette and coffee. She smoked and sipped mechanically. The delight had faded from her face.

"I really came to Cannes to tell you about Ramon Garcia."

I said gently: "As you came here that last day when you left for Paris—and I thought all the time about myself and not about you, and frightened you away."

She turned her head aside. "You did not frighten me. I was frightened of myself."

My pulses beat quickly. What other significance than avowal lay in her words?

"Then you weren't angry or indignant with me?"

There came a murmur. "You ought to know. I think I kissed you."

I drew my chair a bit nearer. "Then, my dear, you were frightened of yourself for caring for me just a little?"

I admit the fatuity of the question. Let the man in love who has not been guilty of it cast the first stone.

"I could not listen to you as I was, as I felt myself to be," she said. She turned and looked me in the face. "I had been soiled with horrid things for a long time. And I was a thief on my own account."

I smiled. "A thief? My dear Nadia——"

"Yes. A thief. That night—the night before I went to Rome—Amos took me from the Casino to the Villa Miranda. He played cards, against his will and his conscience—and he won a great deal of money. And he gave it to me for the poor Russians on the Riviera. . . . And I had great debts to pay, and I had lost at

Monte Carlo trying to win enough to pay them and I lost all I had . . . and my uncle and aunt would give me nothing—they even wanted to 'administer,' as they called it, Amos's money for the poor—and I was desperate —and I did not give the money to the Russians. I kept it. When an honourable gentleman asks a woman to be his wife, a thief of a woman cannot listen unless she is —*canaille*."

As she talked, she gave me to understand that also, in those peculiar circumstances, a woman could not ask a man for advice on very intimate matters. Speedy flight downstairs had been the only solution. I adjured her to let us have everything now clear and above board. My friendship, I urged, would have flattened out any obstacle in her path; my love would have removed mountains.

"But you see—when I felt myself a thief——" she began.

I hastily interrupted. Of course I appreciated her point of view. But why had she been a thief, as she called it? Amos's winnings could not have been so enormous. She was not without realizable capital.

"But it takes time to realize capital, my friend. I had lost all the ready money I had. I must go to Rome to raise money to live on—and to pay what I owed— and must go to Paris with my capital—a few jewels—to sell them. When I sold them, I sent my cheque to the Grand Duchess and redeemed my debt to the poor Russians. But when I saw you I did not have my hands clean."

She regarded her slim fingers with a little grimace of disgust. I smiled, said something about an over-sensitive conscience. She waved her hand.

"Perhaps the last straw on it, *mon ami.*"

Emboldened to seek her confidence, I asked her why she went to Rome, of all places, to raise money.

"Because my pearls and other few good jewels are in the Banca Romana."

I frowned, perplexed. "But you wear your pearls every night of your life."

Again the characteristic wave of her hand, palm outwards, at the end of her outstretched arm.

"If I had worn the real ones I should have been robbed or murdered long ago. It was my aunt, the Marchesa, who put me up to the trick. She did it herself. And that is where all the trouble came in. All the trouble." She looked at me mysteriously. "No wonder you didn't want to paint them."

"Very possibly I should have found out."

"No. They are too good. No one has yet found out. But you would have been angry if you had spent weeks over them and then discovered they were not real. Has not that thought just crossed your mind?"

"You're a witch," said I. "A golden-haired, bronze-eyebrowed, hazel-eyed, mocking-mouthed sorceress. In your pale green wisps of drapery you're a disguised syren from the sea, and if you keep on looking so adorable, I'll carry you off forcibly to my studio and paint you."

She rose and walked a few steps about the room, laughing, making her pretty gestures.

"Ah no, ah no, ah no! *Voyons.* I thought I was talking to a man who says he loves me. I find only the artist who looks on me as a fisher-girl or a green cow or a bit of cloud in the sky. Just something to paint. Ah no!"

I sprang up and imprisoned her hands, and she stood before me small, but not fragile, in all the plenitude of her ripe womanhood, temptation incarnate.

"My dear," said I, with not a little self-control, "thank God for the artist who stands between a man and—and——"

"And what?"

"Yes, and what?" said I, and I dropped her hands and turned away brusquely.   After a pace or two I halted before her.   A sudden colour had arisen in her cheeks. Of course I was a fool.   I should have swept her up then and there, when she was in the mood of expectation. But I had already outraged her sensitiveness in this same house of mine.   Repetition would have been monstrous, so I thought.   I read in her eyes a touch of her sex's haughty resentment.   I gathered together my English wits.

"Nadia," said I.   "Behind the artist who knows you to be the most beautiful thing God ever made, there's the man who loves you beyond anything God ever made. Will you marry him?"

She turned her head and looked from side to side about the room, and her shoulders twitched as her hands made little helpless movements.   Then she swerved away, shivering, as though with cold, and sat on a chair near the chimney-piece.   Thinking that the mistral might have re-arisen, I closed the French windows and went across to her and laid my hand on her shoulder.   She had her head buried in her arms.

What was the meaning of this lightning change?   A couple of minutes ago she was mocking at my refusal to paint her pearls.   I had lost my head, translating my adoration into the terms of the artist.   She had, in a flash, claimed the terms of a lover. I had responded instantly in the terms only known to an honourable man. And she had broken down. Why?

I hovered over her after the foolish way of men, worrying her with my solicitude and irritating her with my touch, until, all of a sudden, she sprang up and whirled behind the chair and looked at me like a creature at bay. She presented the most pathetic, tragic mask I have ever beheld, her face ivory white, her lips pale, her nostrils distended.

"Why do you want so much to marry me?"

"That's very simple," said I. "Because you're the woman I love."

"Will nothing less content you?"

The question hit me between the eyes. Of anything less I had never thought. And I swear that, as I stood before her, I did not want less. I knew that I could not take less. Whether all the parsonry and canonry and archdeaconry in my blood spoke, I don't know. Possibly it did. But I don't think so. I wanted the exquisiteness and wonder of her all in all or not at all. I had the swift consciousness of the years—the twenty years that separated us. As a wife, to become in the course of vague time the object of an old man's adoration, every chord in my being clamoured for her. To take her otherwise, in her present surrender of despair, would have been ignoble. Twenty years ago—yes—on any terms. Youth to youth, and damn the fool puritanism of the world. But now, no.

I held myself in check and said quietly:

"My dear, what is it? Would you lose so much if you married me?"

She clasped her head, her elbows resting on the back of the chair, and cried almost hysterically:

"Lose? I should gain the whole world. But I can't. Don't you see I can't?"

"But why?"

She stood up and faced me with her arms stiff by her sides:

"I'm already married to Ramon Garcia."

I must have uttered some animal cry of pain, for she rushed from behind the chair and clasped her arms around me and laid her head against my heart.

"Oh, don't, don't. Perhaps all is not as you think. You must listen to what I say before you judge."

She freed herself as soon as she might.

"You sit there and I will sit here, and I will tell you."

CHAPTER XV

WAS there ever a more absurd, damnable and pitiful story? I must tell it to you as best I can.

Two seasons before, the brilliant young Ecuadorian had appeared, a new star, on the Cannes social firmament, one of the discoveries of Lady Verinder. Now Lady Verinder was a great lady who owned a great property in the neighbourhood which, together with unimpeachable social prestige, ensured her the homage and respect of residential Cannes. For myself, I considered her the most intolerable old niggardly bore that ever gave a weak-tea-party. But then, I am but an artistic waif on the surf of things, and my private opinion of influential ladies is as important on the Côte d'Azur as my considered judgment on the smaller English masters of the eighteenth century. Cornelia, Lady Verinder, Dowager Countess, however, chose to nominate herself Lady Paramount, and folk in the vague, idle fashion of folk, vaguely and idly took her at her own valuation. At any rate, her introduction set the hall-mark of good repute on any young man. Such a hall-mark had she set on Señor Ramon Garcia of Ecuador.

It was not Nadia who told me of her imprudence, but old Sir Anthony Bullivant. Having lent Garcia some ten thousand francs a few days before his flight, and naturally not having been paid, he scented a scoundrel and went up in apoplectic indignation to his crony, Cornelia. Whereupon Lady Verinder had confessed, under seal of confidence; which seal Sir Anthony vowed had been

broken for one single instant to myself alone. Probably
the old gossip spoke the truth; for no whisper of the
affair had ever reached me from any other quarter of
the social horizon. It was nothing of an affair, after all.
The silly old woman had made Garcia's acquaintance at
Aix-les-Bains during the previous summer; first at a
gaming-table, where they sat side by side and, with a
joint bank, gained fat profits; then at the Hôtel Ber-
nascon, where they both happened to be staying, and
where it was his good fortune to render her various little
services. He had rescued, for instance, her adipose and
unhealthy Pomeranian from the jaws of a playful wolf-
puppy with an uncultivated taste in perfume. He had
sent her flowers while she lay prostrate from the severe
Aix treatment for which she had no need. He had taken
off her hands, for teas and dances, her elderly companion
on whose nerves social repression occasionally reacted,
rendering her companionably impossible, and restored
her to Cornelia, the contented and humble friend of
twenty years. Lady Verinder desiring a new hat for a
new costume, he took her to the one shop in Aix where
there was one hat towards which climax the costume
was inevitably designed. Said she: "I've never paid
so much for a hat in my life." "On the other hand,"
said he, with, I am sure, a glance at the milliner, "never
in your life have you had such a hat!"

Well, I don't wish to judge the silly old lady too harshly.
Here she found the perfect *cavaliere servente* in all pro-
priety and honour. He was handsome, after his Latin-
American way, impeccably clothed; his manners were
coloured by the floridness one would expect from
Ecuador; he gave the air of careless opulence; he spoke
in the assured rich man's casual way of vast estates,
cattle, horses, wheat. . . . Eventually came the great

lady's gracious invitation. Should he come to Cannes he must call at the Villa Splendida. It would have been a fool of an adventurer who, having such a social opportunity, did not come and call. Ramon Garcia came and called and, pretending to share the olfactory tastes of the wolf-puppy above mentioned, clasped the Pomeranian to his bosom. It was the final act of devotion which Lady Verinder repaid.

Although she seldom entered the Casino, yet they walked together in the House of Mammon as old friends. She conveyed the impression to Cannes that she had loved him from his babyhood. Ramon Garcia was launched.

Forgive me if I mix up my chronology. I am trying to tell the story as best I can. I learned this from Sir Anthony Bullivant in December. What I knew of Garcia both from Scotland Yard and from the administration of the Casino I refrained from telling him. The open ear and the shut mouth are two elementary principles of unruffled existence—especially on the Côte d'Azur. I had made up my mind, however, that so soon as Lady Verinder should come to the Villa Splendida I would urbanely seek interview. But just after Christmas the poor, foolish old dear died in London and was gathered to her fathers, who, accustomed in their time to unquestioned homage, must have given her a problematical reception.

It was, however, in the first heyday of his launch on these azure seas that my Nadia met him. For me, occupied with my own pursuits and desiring to be left alone, the whole of that season passed without my running across either of them. When my story opens, at the painting of the Princess, I had known her but a bare two months.

Of course I had heard vaguely of both. In fact I had

seen them—each in a particular and separate sphere be it understood, for no gossip ever connected their names. But in speaking of them I must use both present and retrospective knowledge.

Ramon Garcia, as I have said, was received by Cannes on Lady Verinder's certificate. His behaviour was exemplary, wherein he exhibited unwonted shrewdness. The rich Latin-American bachelor, the *rastaquouère,* is millions of miles away from the social life of the Riviera. He engages princely suites in palaces of hotels; he makes the air (and all that therein is) sick with the speed of his automobile; the flash of his diamonds can be caught from Saint-Raphael to Mentone; he commands the high places in all the restaurants and sets champagne flowing at the literal rate of liquid gold; but in not one private house does he set his foot. Unless chance brings him into contact with acquaintances from Patagonia or Bolivia, he knows not a soul. He is driven (without overmuch application of whip) to the society of the little ladies who stand with open arms and open purses offering their charming companionship. We residents do not hold up hands in horror at the poor opulent Patagonians; but still, if they run round with little ladies, we do not seek them out and introduce them to our womenfolk. Now, this is to the credit of the astuteness of Ramon Garcia. Whatever he may have done in the darker obscurities of the coast, I don't know. To suppose him a plaster of Paris saint were impossible. From odds and ends of gossip lately gathered, I believe he was one of the most deboshed fish that the Mediterranean could at any moment produce. But that is by the way. Outwardly and socially he exhibited a more puritanical correctitude of demeanour than that of various British cabinet ministers of my acquaintance. I must give the devil his outward due. For my part, as perhaps you may remember, I loathed the fellow from the first moment I set eyes on him. Perhaps I have the Englishman's instinctive dislike of the oiled, curled and perfumed exotic male.

The Fontanas, in spite of speckled reputation, mixed in the highest circles of Cannes. The birth and position of both husband and wife were beyond question. To be admitted to the gambling-hell of the Villa Miranda was a widely-sought privilege. Against *rastaquouères* and little ladies, reeking respectively of opulence and seduction, the doors were closed, much to the regret of the Marchese, who would have brought into his net any fat pigeon, white, yellow or black, who could be plucked. It was the Marchesa who insisted on the social standard. If low-born people were to be cheated, it must be done in their shops and offices and not in her own house.

The well-accredited Ramon Garcia, however, found easy admittance. His reputed wealth made him a welcome guest. At first he lost gracefully. Then he began to win, with equal grace. The Marchese beheld in him a plucker of pigeons as debonair as himself. After a while, I suspect, they came to some private understanding. Be that as it may, it was here, under her aunt's protecting roof, that Nadia and Ramon Garcia met. The scamp who recognized in the Marchese a scamp and a brother, had the wit to recognize the innocence of the Princess Ramiroff. He did more. He fell a dupe to that very innocence. His eyes were dazzled by her rank, by the homage she received from all in Cannes, by her strange beauty and charm, and especially by the apparent king's ransom of jewellery that she was reputed to possess. Now, temporary possession of the lady and permanent possession of her wealth have been the rogue's scheme from time immemorial. That is the worst of rogues;

they would be much more interesting if they exhibited more variety. There is no reason to doubt that Ramon Garcia followed the consecrated track of his predecessors. At any rate, he made love to her; love now romantic, now furious. Carried away, half frightened, she responded. You must remember the Tartar blood in her reacting to the brute. There was also the temptation of the boundless fortune which would restore to her all the things which from childhood she had regarded as essential to existence. She was two-and-twenty. She had every excuse in the world.

Aristocratic, she insisted on discretion in their outward relations. Garcia was one of half a dozen men with whom she danced and dined and motored. Evil tongues had to base their slanders on generalities rather than on particulars. Even when she promised to marry him, she made it a condition that their engagement should remain secret till the end of the season. She shrank from the publicity of the announcement; the eyes of Cannes upon her; the gush of friends; the interviews, the photographs, the hideous head-lines in the social columns of newspapers. She also contemplated, with a timorous gasp, the gulf that lay between a descendant of the Romanoffs and a genealogical-tree-less, no matter how rich and agreeable, native of Ecuador. Serene Highnesses may be forgiven some natural pride of race. Also a woman may be pardoned for vague hesitations, uncertainties and doubts. . . . The romantic, too, had its voice in the matter. Let no one know till April. Let no one know even then. Let them get married quietly in Paris, and take steamer at once away to the fairy lands of Ecuador.

The young man, wise in the psychology of woman, gave ready assent. A couple of months more or less of waiting, what did it matter? King's ransoms of jewellery, like most other things in the world, had to be worked for. Exemplary patience was the hard work of Ramon Garcia.

He showed himself the model lover, discreet, devoted, passionate. There were times when Nadia suffered agony of remorse. Why condemn to obscurity so gallant a betrothed? Why deny him the pride of flaunting her on his arm? For the matter of that, why deny herself the thrill that every woman feels in public exhibition of capture? Of course, he pleaded for relaxation of conditions. What lover would not? But with a delicacy curiously alien to his Latin-American blood. Otherwise, she might have relented.

Yet all might have gone as she had decreed had it not been for the Marchese della Fontana.

There had been a tremendous sitting at the Villa Miranda, a congregation, half chance, half design, of the great international gambling asses who found themselves on the Riviera. Play was high. At first the eternal, idiotic, *chemin de fer*. Then, classical baccarat, with the Marchese, apparently in funds, holding *banque ouverte*. You must bear with me, for a few moments, in my allusion to this imbecile pursuit, but it is the *fons et origo* of all the dramas, comedies and tragedies which are enacted in this paradise of blue and gold. I will spare you details. Just imagine a dozen apparently respectable men and women, mostly men, sitting round a green-baize table at which nothing was admitted as stakes but round mother-of-pearl counters representing a thousand francs, great oblong mother-of-pearl counters representing ten thousand francs and of course thousand franc banknotes by the stack. The counters were issued and redeemable by the Marchese della Fontana.

The party broke up at six in the morning. Nadia, I

may say, having gone to the opera with friends, had retired to bed on reaching home. The story, therefore, of Ramon Garcia's immense gains from the Marchese was only known to her the day after.

Garcia won enormously. The Marchese lost. Ashen grey, he redeemed the international gamblers' counters in notes and cheques. He signed to Garcia to remain after the others had departed. So only the three of them remained in the close-smelling, deserted drawing-room, Garcia still sitting at the green table with a mountain of mother-of-pearl in front of him, the little Marchese plucking nervously at his white moustache, the Marchesa, gaunt and expressionless as a wooden horse, fingering the pearls around her neck. Garcia methodically distributed his mountain into mathematical blocks.

"That is what you owe me, Marchese."

The little man nodded. "Yes. I see. But the black luck I have had to-night! Can there be no arrangement?"

Garcia expostulated with Latin gesture: "But my dear friend——"

"You insist on being paid to-night, or rather, this morning?"

"It is customary. Your cheque——"

The wizened Marchese spread out both his hands.

"Alas!——"

"Eh bien?" cried Garcia, rising from the table and pointing to his winnings. "And that?"

"Be reassured, my dear Ramon," said the Marchese, in the grand manner of the old Italian nobility. "There is always this necklace of my wife."

At a sign from him she unhooked the pearl necklace, in her wooden, unemotional way and laid it on the table.

"It's a *beau geste,* the act of a gentleman, but how am I to know how much it is worth? Far more"—he smiled—"than my poor winnings."

"For one instant—excuse me——" said the Marchese.

He went out of the room, leaving the two together standing on opposite sides of the green table. And they said never a word, for never a word had they to say. In a few minutes the Marchese returned with a paper in his hand.

"This, my friend, is the receipt of Lautier Frères, the Paris jewellers, for the necklace of the Marchesa. You will notice it is almost a catalogue *raisonné*. I insisted, so that there should be no mistake. I gave it to my wife at a time when fortune favoured me. Now, alas! fortune must withdraw it from her hands. If you will take the necklace, which will always command its price, and pay me the difference between this and this"—he tapped with his finger the receipt and a spot on the table in front of Garcia's counters—"all will be regulated between men of honour."

After a pencilled calculation, Garcia, who had been winning extravagantly of late, produced the difference in notes and took possession of the necklace, and, prudent man, the certificated receipt.

For the moment all was for the best in the best of all possible worlds. Ramon Garcia having no particular use for pearls—to present them to his fiancée would be carrying jewels to Golconda—took train to Paris. There he sat himself down at a table in Lautier's discreet and elegant establishment in the rue de la Paix. A discreet and elegantly attired gentleman took his place on the other side of the table. Yes, he remembered the necklace well. He had sold it to the Marchese della Fontana some years ago. He waved away the receipt as a superfluous document. The price of pearls, he argued, had risen since the war. His eyes travelled narrowly over the glittering row and then, with a little frown, he rose. Would Monsieur excuse him an instant? He disappeared. Presently he returned with a long face, accompanied by another elegant gentleman.

"I regret to inform you, sir," said he, "that this is not the necklace I sold to the Marchese della Fontana. That was one of real pearls, as you can see by the receipt. These are imitations. Beautiful imitations. May I ask you, sir, how they came into your possession?"

Garcia, dazed and sick, could only reply that he had bought them two days ago from the Marchese himself. The salesman and the summoned expert shrugged helpless shoulders. Garcia reeled out of the shop, took the first train to Cannes and drove straight to the Villa Miranda. If he had shot the rascally old Marchese there and then I might have respected him. But he didn't. He sought audience first with the Princess.

This was the first she had heard of the transaction. She listened in frozen horror, for she knew that Lautier Frères were right and that the necklace which Garcia threw dramatically on the table was false. That it was false was known to only four people in the world: herself, the Marchese and the Marchesa and the Dutchman who had made it. The same Dutchman had made the copy of her own pearls now lying in the strong room of the Banca Romana.

The real necklace had been sold, just after the war, to an American lady from Missouri. By chance the Marchesa had been wearing it one evening at Monte Carlo, and the American lady, casting upon it covetous eyes, and learning that the Marchesa was a Russian of noble family, concluded that, like all exiled Russians, she would be disposed to consider a generous offer for her gems. To Nadia's knowledge the necklace had been sold. The fact had been a close secret between the three of the Villa Miranda household.

Her uncle had passed on to Garcia the false for the real. It was incredible. She knew him to be a professional gambler; but never had she suspected him of crooked dealings. The monstrosity of the trick appalled her, as she sat wringing her hands, while Garcia, in, I must say, righteous indignation, denounced the Marchese as a most unconscionable scoundrel that ever lured an honourable gentleman into his house. She could only wail that there must be some mistake. What else could she say? To confess her knowledge would have been to betray the noble blood of Italy and the Imperial blood of Russia. It was for her relatives to defend themselves. . . . But as she listened to Garcia's invectives, couched in vulgar words of insult; as she glanced, every now and then, out of the tail of her eye, at the common handsome face convulsed with passion, a shiver of horrible repulsion shook her body and her soul. And presently she rose and faced him. You can see her little face all strained, the green eyes cold as bits of glacier.

"Monsieur Garcia," she said, "why have you come to me, instead of my uncle?"

"Are you not my *fiancée?* I naturally came to you first for an explanation."

"I did you the honour to think that you loved me."

He flung an angry gesture.

"This is no time for love."

"I should have thought," said Nadia, "it was the one and only time for it, up to now, in our lives."

She moved to the chimneypiece and pressed the electric bell-push.

"What are you doing?"

"I am summoning the Marchese della Fontana. The dispute is between you and him."

"It is," said he. "This house is but a gambling-hell and you are the decoy."

She flushed under the insult, but waited till the servant came.

"Tell the Marchese that I desire to see him at once."

"You remain?"

"I remain."

After a long space of silence, he said: "Do you think, Madame la Princesse, that this will interfere with our marriage?"

"I think," said Nadia, "that it reduces the question to an impossibility."

"Not I," said Garcia.

Then came in the Marchese, trim, smiling, elderly, debonair.

"Ah, my dear Ramon——"

Garcia disregarded the offered hand and plunged at once into what, I must repeat, was his most legitimate grievance.

The Marchese listened, at first with an air of puzzlement, as one who hears a fantastic tale, then like a man dumbfounded. When he found chance to speak, he smote his breast and flashed his dark eyes.

"Monsieur, is it I whom you accuse of such turpitude? I sold you the necklace as it was delivered by Messieurs Lautier Frères with their certificate. If the pearls are false, it is their affair, not mine. I pray you to regulate the matter with them, and not come here to impugn not only my honour as a gentleman, but my common honesty as a man."

And Nadia stood there, in a corner of the room,

listening incredulously to this supreme rodomontade of mendacity.

Garcia threw the case containing the gems on the table.

"Pay me what you owe me, *vieil escroc*."

With a noble gesture the Marchese threw open the door.

"*Sortez,* Monsieur."

"I go," said Garcia. "I go to the Commissaire de Police."

"Take your property, Monsieur," said the Marchese, handing him the case.

Nadia rushed wildly down the room.

"Ah, no, no, no. Ramon. I beseech you——"

Garcia turned on the threshold.

"You are suffering from a *crise des nerfs*, Madame. I will hold my hand for twenty-four hours. By then the crisis will have passed, and I hope to find you in a serener disposition."

He bowed and went out. Nadia clung to the old man's coat-lapels.

"What have you done? It is prison for you and ruin for us all."

The Marchese freed himself and held up protesting hands.

"Prison, ruin—what folly! If there is a prison for anybody it is for Lautier Frères who sold me this naughty necklace."

She expostulated. But the real necklace which he had sold to Mrs.—Mrs.——? She had forgotten the name.

"I too," said the Marchese. "Civilization has forgotten her. She belongs to the opulent underworld of the Middle West. To no other type would I have sold

traceable pearls.   When she came to discuss prices she
had cables of them round her neck.   Her ultimate
ambition was to have a *maillot* of them, covering her
bust, so that she shall need no corsage.   She explained,
I must confess, to my cynical amusement, that when
she got back to Hellsburg, Missouri—I think it is the
name of her infernal town—she would have the whole
of her myriad dollar collection re-sorted and re-arranged.
I have not the faintest doubt that she has done it.   The
pearls of our necklace are now mingled, without any
chance of identification, in the lady's suit of pearl chain
armour.   You behold, my child, a man who has based
a long and not wholly unsuccessful life on the philosophy
of fact.   Had it not been for this law-devastating fact,
I should never have sold the pearls to Garcia.   No, no,
my dear Nadia.   Be reassured.   Madame—Madame of
the forgotten name and the necklace have vanished
into space.   There is no existing document concerning
the transaction.   Not even a cheque.   In her apartment
at the Hôtel de Paris at Monte Carlo, she paid me, as
I had exacted, the purchase money, thrice, I am glad
to say, the original cost, in solid bundles of notes.   There
only exists our friend Van Rooden of Amsterdam.
Hermetically sealed secrecy is the secret of his fortune.
Obviously he is out of court.   I repeat it, it is for Messieurs Lautier Frères of the rue de la Paix to explain
their extraordinary conduct in selling me a fraudulent
pearl necklace."

He lit a cigarette with fingers that did not tremble.
Apparently he no more foresaw danger from the police
than he felt remorse for scoundrelly conduct.

Her aunt, to whom she went distracted, gave her no
comfort.   She lifted tired shoulders.

"What can I do?   I am in the hands of my husband.

Besides, I have no doubt that Garcia cheated that evening. He does when he gets a chance. So your uncle only paid him back in his own coin."

Yet, in spite of her calmness, it was she who persuaded her husband that a trip across the Italian Frontier might be an act of prudence. She wrote little notes cancelling engagements, and giving out that the sudden death of a near relative summoned them at once to Genoa. To one intimate and indiscreet friend she spoke vaguely of a large inheritance. The credit-saving rumour soon spread over Cannes, and tradesmen forbore to send in bills. The next day they took train, leaving Nadia alone in the Villa Miranda. They urged her, indeed, to accompany them; but at that time of cataclysm she regarded them with peculiar fear.

After they had gone, came Garcia, loud in his threats. Italy was no sure refuge. Between civilized countries there were extradition treaties. Also before the law could be set in action, he would make the Marchese's name a byword of infamy on the Coast.

Is it to be wondered at that the lonely Princess should be at her wit's end? The Fontanas, for all their callous villainy, were still dear to her. They had welcomed her as a daughter when she had arrived half crazed from Russia, and, with all the regard due to her rank, they had given her their love. They were the only relatives she had left in the world. Their disgrace and ruin were hers. And the man who stormed and threatened had indubitably suffered a great wrong. On her knees she implored his mercy. Even as I write my gorge rises in imagining the ghastly scene. . . . He pulled her to her feet.

"The day you marry me," said he, "I will give you

the pearls and Lautier's receipt.   It shall be your wedding present."

Well?   Were they not engaged?   It is true that his coarseness had revolted her the day before—sending what barbaric love for him that she had shuddering away.   But still—she had known violent men whom she had loved.   Her father, it appeared, would occasionally throw her mother across the room; the act being followed by such penitential devotion that it was possibly not altogether unwelcome to the accustomed lady.   Her young husband, also, had no mean temper.   Possibly it was only the Latin-American blood in Ramon that was so swift to boil.

It was the one way out.   She was young, over-emotional.   Her aunt's insinuation of his dishonesty she spurned.   She trusted him and she consented to a speedy marriage.   It was all mad, silly, melodramatic, what you will.   But you must take into account the state of the woman's mind.   And at her consent, the lover reappeared.   They would go to Paris, there to be married in as short a delay as the law allowed.

"But will you not give me the necklace and receipt now?" she asked.   "My word is my bond."

"They shall be your wedding present," said he.   "A little punishment is good for the excellent Marchese."

It was at this point that my little Princess began to hesitate in some confusion.   Hitherto she had told her story animatedly, with a sense of values, also with logical sequence.   During the narration I scarcely spoke, save to interject a word of sympathy or to put a question on some point that needed elucidation.   As she proceeded with the sordid drama, I could only see a lily of the valley thrown upon a heap of unutterable ordure.   And all the time, at the back of my head, clanged the horrible fact that she was married to Garcia.

The room grew dark with the dusk of the late sunset. We had both forgotten time. The fire was burning low. I sprang to my feet and threw on logs. She was tired. She needed tea. I rang for François, who closed the shutters and gave an expert touch to the fire which broke into sudden and comfortable flame. I smiled, with a brave effort to hide my misery.

"An interval for refreshment," said I.

CHAPTER XVI

"WHAT I have to tell you," she said, after the interval, "is perhaps still more strange."

"You married Garcia. Could anything be more strange than that?"

"Yes, my friend. You will hear."

She went to Paris. Garcia, on the pretext of business connected with his Ecuadorian estates, to London. Parenthetically, I may state that his desire for the publicity of their marriage was no stronger than hers. She made the necessary arrangements with the Mairie of the arrondissement in which her hotel was situated and, without too great strain of patience, awaited his arrival.

In the meantime, one morning there came a cheque drawn by her aunt, the Marchesa, on the Crédit Lyonnais, payable to Ramon Garcia, for the amount of the difference between pearls and debt which Ramon had paid to the Marchese. The poor lady had sold heaven knows what in order to raise the considerable sum. I have no doubt that the Marchese, when he came to know of it, would have beaten her had she not been twice his weight and stature. This, however, is but conjecture. Her letter bade Nadia give the cheque to Ramon Garcia, with what excuses she could frame. Nadia wept tears of relief and joy, under the wild impulse of which she wrote at fervent length to her betrothed, admitting her knowledge of the abominable trick, begging him to have mercy on her uncle for a sudden act of despair, and to return the pearls on the assurance that the original gambling debt would be eventually paid. Of course you will say it was an idiotic thing to do; but women with their soul upside down have been known to do things far more lunatic. Consider the immense revulsion of feeling. Whatever might be the moral code of the Marchese, at any rate the Marchesa, her only living blood relation, of birth as imperial as hers, had freed herself, to the utmost of her power, from participation in the fraud. Indeed, was not the cheque in itself a confession? You must also bear in mind the baffling Russian psychology.

Ramon acknowledged the cheque in lover-like terms. It was unexpected; but at least his due. For love of her he had been willing to sacrifice the money. There was still, however, the original gambling debt to be paid, for which he held as guarantee the false pearls and the Lautier receipt. These he reassured her would be put into her hands on her wedding-day. Again she wrote a compromising appeal to his generosity, to which she received a playful answer. Poor little bit of jetsam of a wrecked aristocracy, what knowledge had she of the world? She had no doubt of the man's integrity. In a few days the honour of her family would be secure again. Also, as I have said before, her precarious future. Furthermore there was the glamour of the handsome male.

It was to be a civil marriage, first of all, like all marriages in France; for French law takes no count of religious ceremony. Afterwards, when the time should come for public display, there should be the grand marriage in the Russian church, with all the Grand Dukes and Grand Duchesses available, in attendance.

On the night before the marriage they dined together at the Café de Paris. When he chose, Ramon Garcia could be a most charming and entertaining companion. His attitude as next day's husband was impeccable.

The dinner was exquisitely chosen, cooked and served, and my little Princess, like all Russian women of the old aristocracy, loved the good food to which she had been born and trained. The champagne bubbles melted deliciously on her palate. The golden upholstered room hummed with the talk of happy people. And Nadia, the horrible weight lifted from her conscience, was happy too. The elderly may react to the joy of life as to an allusion, conscious that it is but an illusion. But twenty reacts to it as to a reality. Otherwise, great Heavens! let us all be born old with the grasshopper an eternal burden, and desire failing before manifestation.

How can I know what he said to her, and by what means he kept her attuned to laughter in the gay environment? I can only interpret to you the impression made on me by her eager narrative.

Suddenly she became aware of a man standing in front of her table, tall, swarthy, smiling—she and Ramon, you must understand, sat side by side on the gold-covered banquette by the wall—and waving away, with an impatient gesture, the attendant waiting near with hat and coat.

"Princess! How delightful to see you."

She stretched a happy hand across the table. "Monsieur Alvarez! But it is old times—Petrograd——"

"And now I am appointed Minister in Brussels. I am passing through Paris on my way from Rio de Janeiro. Ah! *quelle bonne chance.*"

"We must meet and talk of the old times when you came to the palace."

"*Mon Dieu!* What has happened since then? Where are you staying, Altesse, that, with your permission, I can present to you my homage?"

She named her hotel; but blushing: "I leave to-morrow afternoon." Then she said hurriedly: "May I present my friend Señor Garcia—Senhor Alvarez was Secretary of the Brazilian Legation at Petrograd when I was a girl."

The two men bowed formally, and it seemed to Nadia an unconscionable time before they took their eyes off each other. And somehow the upward twisted moustache of the Brazilian seemed to stiffen like porcupine quills. But he turned to her with a smile and kissed her hand across the table.

"Au revoir, Princesse. To-morrow you are at the Hôtel Miramare; and I am at the Ritz, and after to-morrow at the Legation in Brussels. It will be a tragedy for me, if sometime soon, we do not meet again."

"He's a dear," said Nadia, when he had gone. "He knew me as a child and was present at my wedding."

"All the same, he's a Brazilian, and Brazilians think themselves *les petits bons dieux* of South America."

She opened wide eyes.

"You are not angry?"

"I am a Spaniard and he is a Portuguese—I hate Portuguese."

To her surprise, she saw him, an abstemious man, fill his glass from the bottle of liqueur brandy and drink it off at once. At her glance he laughed somewhat boisterously.

"It is not every night that one bids farewell to the life of a bachelor and not every day that one marries the most beautiful woman in the world."

His temporary ill-humour vanished. When the centre of the restaurant was cleared, they danced twice or thrice together. Perhaps it was the perfection of his rhythm that had originally attracted her towards the man. In her defence, I must grant him some qualities. A while later he carried her to the Hôtel Miramare in the private car which he had hired, and, after gallant adieux, drove off.

"And in my hotel bedroom," said Nadia, "I felt very lonely, and all the effervescence of the evening died—and I was depressed so that I did not sleep all night. I tried to tell myself that happiness lay before me; but I could not be certain. I did not like the mere civil ceremony, and could not fix the reasons for postponing the religious marriage. When I rose in the morning, I was a faded little ghost, and you would not at all have wanted to paint me."

Then things seem to have happened fairly quickly. She had just finished dressing when a *petit-bleu*—a letter sent by pneumatic post, was delivered. It was from Alvarez. He deplored the urgency of business that prevented him from calling before his departure for Brussels. The little line had a further purpose, he explained, in that it was to urge her to be prudent in her relations with Señor Garcia, whose acquaintance the best society in South America did not consider desirable. One so young and beautiful as herself must pardon the old and devoted friend.

She strove to think of the missive's significance; but it was too late. Her room telephone rang. It was Ramon downstairs awaiting her.

Of the marriage in the bleak marriage-hall of the Mairie, she remembered little. Apparently her attention had been concentrated on the tricolour sash around the vast middle of the portly Mayor. It was a ceremony as unimpressive as that of registering a death. The functionary's conventional words of congratulation sounded dull in her ears. Had he known that it was a Serene Highness whom he was marrying, possibly he might have seasoned his part with more unctuousness; but to him, she was merely one Nadia Ramiroff, an attractive young Russian of no particular account who was taking as a husband a young South American of high external polish.

They went out of the building into the damp street, fear and depression heavy on her heart. A melancholy drizzle fell tiredly from a leaden sky. The hired chauffeur, across the pavement, dozed by his wheel. Ramon awakened him with a call and opened the car door for Nadia. But before he could step in himself, a pair of decently dressed men, with courteously uplifted hats demanded his attention.

"Pardon, Monsieur——"

"If you're damned reporters, I have nothing to do with you," cried Ramon.

"We are not of the Press, Monsieur," one of them explained in a low voice. "We are agents of the police, and we must ask you to accompany us."

The uninterested chauffeur cranked up a sulky engine. As Ramon began to protest indignantly, the agent raised an arresting hand.

"At least, Monsieur, follow our example of perfect discretion."

Said Ramon. "I am an innocent man. It is monstrous. I have just married this lady."

"Madame," said the agent, crossing to the car, "I regret infinitely having to cause you this unpleasantness. But it is, unfortunately, a formality which must be observed. Monsieur, I hope, will be returned to you within an hour."

She stared wide of him at her husband who stood a foot or two away, white and nervous.

"Ramon, what does this mean?"

"Heaven knows," said he, "These fools have mistaken me for somebody else."

The engine of the car set going, the chauffeur climbed into his seat.

"We have a taxi waiting, Monsieur," said the agent.

Ramon shrugged his shoulders and went off with the men. Receiving no orders, the chauffeur again descended and put his head through the open door.

"Where to, Madame?"

"I don't know, I don't know," said Nadia.

"Back to the hotel?"

"Yes, to the hotel."

So back she went in forlorn agony. On her dressing-table she found lying open the note she had received from Alvarez—"whose acquaintance the best society in South America did not consider desirable." Had delicacy of warning ever been so futile? She sat on her bed and regarded the half-packed trunks on the floor. If only she had her maid! Some human being. But she had left the girl in Cannes; for maids, even the most devoted, talk foolishly. No. She thanked Heaven she had not brought the maid. The arrangements had been that they should go, in the late afternoon, to a hotel in Saint-Cloud, where the English and Americans of their world did not congregrate, and that during the few days they should spend there, they should draw up the program for the future.

She sat on the bed, benumbed, unable to reason. The hours passed. The telephone whirred suddenly. It was Alvarez below. Yes, let him be shown up. In a few minutes he entered.

"If I had known, even suspected, I should have been more frank. But what could I do? . . . I was at our Legation here in Paris when I was rung up by the police.

The gentleman against whom I had laid information had been arrested on coming from the Mairie where he had been married to a certain Madame Nadia Ramiroff. My presence was urgently requested. So I planted them all there—and came here, where, thank God, I've found you!"

Such was the burden of his distressful speech. Her courage returned now that she faced the concrete.

"You gave information to the police? On what grounds?"

"He is a Bolivian——"

"No. From Ecuador."

"From Bolivia. His name is Antonio Perez. I knew him well in Rio de Janeiro. Too well. He conducted himself badly towards a friend of mine, a lady, and ran off with a couple of hundred thousand dollars of her money. For that he was condemned, by default, to prison by our Brazilian Courts. Between France and Brazil there are extradition laws."

"Are you sure that you recognized Antonio Perez?" she asked.

"As sure as I am that he recognized me."

And then she remembered the long mutual stare of the two men; remembered too the unwonted gulp of the glassful of liqueur brandy. She sat on the bed again, clasping her head in her hands. It was true. Hideously true. What did she know of Ramon save the tales that he himself had told her? Why, to test them, had she not gone to any chancery of Ecuador?

Alvarez touched her shoulder.

"Princess, what can I do to help you?"

She raised her agonized face and rested her arm on the bed behind her.

"You have made a mistake, Senhor Alvarez. You will

acknowledge it, with apologies, when you go to the Commissariat de Police to identify my husband."

"It is difficult," said he.

"I know. And it is easy to allow the name of the Princess Ramiroff to be dragged through the mire of Europe."

He smiled tenderly and bowed.

"Princess, I have made the greatest blunder of my life. Your husband is an innocent Ecuadorian gentleman of the authentic name of Ramon Garcia. But *après?* Yourself?"

"You can leave me to deal with Antonio Perez," she said.

An hour or two later, Garcia, claiming husband's privilege, burst into her room without previous announcement. His dark face was purple with anger. He raved at the French police, heaped hideous curses on the head of the imbecile Alvarez and behaved himself like a passionate but righteous man subjected to grave indignity. She listened rigidly with the ice behind her green eyes, until he had finished.

"Senhor Alvarez was right in denouncing you as Antonio Perez."

He started. "How do you know the name under which the bungling fools arrested me?"

"Senhor Alvarez was here to-day. He lied for my sake at the Commissariat de Police." She threw open wide the door to which she had edged: "And now go, and may I never see you again."

And he went out slamming the door.

"*Voilà!*" said Nadia to me. "That was the beginning and end of our marriage."

I took out my handkerchief and wiped a moist brow.

You may imagine my previous state of horrible dubiety. From the beginning of her narrative I had been hag-ridden by the all-important question which I dared not put. And she, save for her first cry: "Perhaps all is not as you think," had given me no key to the riddle. She was all for telling me, in her swift way, the salient facts of the wretched melodrama; for melodrama it was, crude and incredible. Looking on it now, as I write, it might be the archaic plot that delighted our theatre-going fathers. The only factors missing were the hero and the comedy relief. Of psychological values she gave me little. She confined herself to facts. Her story was almost as non-analytical as my attempted reproduction of it. Scene followed scene presented with picturesque vividness; I had glimpses of elementary emotions; sexual attraction, fear, horror, despair, wrath, revolt—what you will; but of the complex workings of her soul she gave me no clue. My efforts to explain them to you must be but blundering. I can only tell you the facts such as she told them to me. Well——

"*Voilà!*" she said, "and that was the beginning and end of our marriage."

I walked about the room, a prey, like the pious Æneas of our boyhood, to conflicting emotions.

"If that is so," said I at last, "why on earth don't you divorce him? Divorce is the only easy and debonair thing provided for in the Code Civil."

Indeed, cynical folks have told me that they are domiciled in France solely on account of the pleasant luxury of its divorce laws.

"That is true," she replied, "but even in France it takes two to make a divorce. He will bring no action against me. For good reasons. I can bring no action against him, because in the eyes of French law he has done me no wrong. He is the injured party, because he protests his desire to live with me. Of course, I can use the detectives and the police and I know not what, and with difficulty prove him to be Antonio Perez, and free myself; but then the whole story would come out, and my uncle and aunt and myself would be overwhelmed in a deluge of infamy. Ah, no, no, my dear friend, that cannot be done."

For the moment, I confess, it seemed a blind alley. My head was a-whirl with her extravagant tale. We had got to the practical end of the marriage, yes; but to the end of the story, no. Why, when I first made their acquaintance they were nominally man and wife!

"My dear," said I, after much talk of little account, "didn't you claim your wedding present?"

"There were implied conditions."

I damned the man loudly and sincerely. She shrugged her shoulders. Technically, perhaps, he was acting within his rights. Anyhow, he had kept necklace and the certificate receipt from Lautier Frères; also the letters which she had written on the subject both before and after their parting at the Hôtel Miramare.

What purpose can it serve to trace in detail the progress of the inevitable blackmail? The Fontanas return to Cannes, where the Marchesa implores her to join them. They stay long into the summer. Nadia visits friends in England. At the beginning of the next season, Cannes once more.

It was then that I met her and fell into a painter's love with her mysterious beauty. It was then that Ramon Garcia, who in the meanwhile had gone, God knows whither, reappeared in the social world of Cannes; and it was then, too, that the blackmailing of the unhappy lady, already tentatively begun, was carried on with remorseless system. As for the Marchese, he snapped cynical fingers below Ramon Garcia's nose. He advised his niece to do the same.

"No fugitive from the justice of a civilized country ever brings a criminal action against another man. It is but walking into prison."

He restated his hardened philosophy of facts. But to how many women born does that philosophy appeal? Can you fancy my little imaginative Tartar princess accepting it?

I think I told you, towards the beginning of this rambling narrative, how I had seen her freeze the brute with the glaciers of her eyes. I also showed her to you, dancing absorbedly with him, when Amos flared indignant. I asked her for the reason.

"*Mon Dieu,*" she replied. "He had begged my forgiveness. He had promised to bring me every scrap of compromising evidence. Only let me be seen with him. Only let me dance with him. Ah—it was a promise and a threat. You are an aristocratic Englishman, and do not know how men work on women. And he is the most perfect dancer in the world. I remember the day. I lost myself. But the dance finished, that was the end.

"He claimed more than dances. It was unimaginable. He continued his persecution. It was in order to satisfy him that I gambled.

"You have thought, although you love me, that I am like all the Russians—a gambler—with gambling in my blood. *Mais non! mais non je vous le jure!*"—She broke away into her more familiar French.—"I hate it. I abhor it. For amusement, yes, perhaps, I might stake the few louis that I can afford—but to regard those horrible counters and notes as gain, as something essential

to my position in the world, my security, my happiness—
ah! I feel that I have my hands unclean, and from the
hands the soil goes to my soul.

"It was to pay him that I played. I began to impoverish myself. Don't you see? He had the false
pearls, the certificate, my letters, the proof of our marriage. It was threatening, threatening, every day."

"My dear," I groaned, "why didn't you take some
honest gentleman—myself, for want of a better—into
your confidence?"

"I suppose we Russians love to be lonely. It's a form
of vanity. We are the only European people who can
sympathize with the imbecile Spartan boy and his fox.
Besides, you all cry out against a false analogy. 'Why
attach such value to the vermin of a fox?' Only the
Russian can understand. But no matter. You saw, *cher
maître*, without understanding."

"I saw, my dear," said I, "the haunting tragedy of
the past in your face and I did all I could to interpret it
—but that actual gnawing at your vitals. Oh, my God!
And you, all smiles and charm! What kind of a steel-
nerved wisp of a woman are you?"

She laughed as she resettled herself more comfortably
in the easy chair.

"I suppose I'm just atavistic Russian, with all kinds
of prides and weaknesses and barbarities in the making
of me; just superficially civilized. I've heard lots of
intelligent Englishmen—really intelligent men—not the
stupid little sect who call themselves intellectuals, and
have societies at what place do you call it? Hampstead?
and never produce anything intellectual, but are only
shams and charlatans—I mean intelligent men like yourself, dear friend, who have said to me that they cannot
read Dostoievsky with pleasure, because he seems to be

a madman writing about madmen. I have lived among you, in your western civilization, and I can understand your point of view. We must all seem to you mad. But neither Dostoievsky nor his characters were mad. They were just Russians, like me."

I replied with a smile that I had read, with somewhat of a whirling brain, the works of the great genius to whom she had referred, but that never among them had I met my Nadia.

"You must take a composite photograph of all his women and your Nadia will bow to you."

Well, this was by the way. The whole of our talk, as you may well conceive, was interspersed with such excursions from the main line of narrative. Even the crisp, calculated dialogue of the theatre takes some hours to effect its narrative purpose. In a court of law, where the irrelevant is ruled out, days may be spent in the unfolding of a drama. It can be no subject for wonder, therefore, that when I looked at my watch it was nearly eight o'clock.

"We must dine, my dear," said I, "and get the whole thing straightened out to-night."

She came down from Dorothea's room without her hat, crowned by the glory of her golden hair. During dinner we talked of heaven knows what, for there was François, ministering angel, hovering round us, and like most ministering angels (terrestrial, of course) a confounded nuisance.

She waved a hand around the room.

"I wonder if you can realize what all this means to me. Peace and security and beauty."

"Nothing else?"

"We mustn't speak of the 'else's.' Taboo. They are implied."

Again my elderly heart beat more quickly.

"That is enough for me for the present. More than enough, my dear. To-morrow, as soon as we have everything clear, I will see about the future."

The evening session completed the story up to date. We must go back to the scene at the Casino, when Amos dragged her from the escort of Ramon Garcia. You may remember they were in earnest conversation at the far table under the lee of the bar. He had made the most exorbitant of his blackmailing demands—a hundred thousand francs. This was to be the last payment in full for all compromising documents. In all truth had she likened herself to the Greek lady, Io, driven by a gadfly. The gadfly had driven her to Monte Carlo to try to win a part of the preposterous sum. She had returned, a tortured loser. She appealed in vain to his pity. Would he not wait? He held up before her impossibility like a blank wall. But he must wait. At the moment she was penniless. The remains of her fortune lay in Rome. Then to Rome, said he, must she go, next day, by the Cannes-Rome Express.

At that moment, hulking knight errant, came up Amos. The history of the next twelve hours or so I have already told you. How Amos had accompanied her to the Villa Miranda, played against his will, and won, and given her the money for the Russian poor; how she had given him, in her woman's way, half her secret, to wit, her own compromising letters; and how he had committed burglary with violence in the room of Ramon Garcia. I have told you, also, how the latter fled without drum or trumpet, to Italy, and how the Princess went to Rome. But why, I must tell you now. It was very simple. The Princess went to withdraw some jewels from the Banca Romana;

Ramon to be on the spot to receive them. He knew her address, that of a sister of the Marchese, with whom she was on affectionate terms. She paid him and claimed the documents. All were in a packet, said he, in the hotel safe in Cannes. He wrote and signed an authorization for her to claim it. She returned to Cannes exulting in the new sense of freedom. Except for his nominal husbandship he had power over her no longer. At the Cannes hotel the manager raised surprised eyebrows. There must be some mistake. Monsieur Garcia withdrew the only packet in their keeping on the morning of his departure.

When she arrived at this point of the narrative I lost my temper and stamped about the room and swore, and piled mountains of choice invective on the head of the unutterable blackguard who had tricked her once again.

She shrugged fatalist shoulders. *Nitchevo.* What did it matter?

She had some other jewels to sell, in order to live. Paris was the market. So to Paris was she bound. But on the way she had sought me and my solid Englishman's counsel. And, as I have told you, and explained the reason, I had frightened her away.

In Paris she broke down. Her physician prescribed a period of rest. An English friend recommended the Lincolnshire convent. And to the convent she went, having signed a letter, on her doctor's instructions, to the American Express Company in Paris to forward no correspondence. It was as simple as all that.

"So you see, *mon cher ami,* why I did not write to you."

We discussed the matter for a while. Then I asked:

"But now you've come out of the chrysalis stage and fluttered into the butterfly world again, what about all the mass of letters that must have awaited you in Paris?"

"If I tell you, you will only think me a mad Russian."

"No matter what I think," said I. "Tell me."

She regarded me ironically for a few seconds. Then—

"Of course I went to the American Express. They poured out stacks and stacks upon the table. There were letters many months old. I told the clerk to make a package of them. I took the package to the hotel. What could I do with all those old letters? *Mon Dieu!* I could not read them. So I looked about the bedroom for something heavy, and all I could find was one of the fire-dogs in the chimneypiece. I tied it up with the string of the package and at night went out and took a taxi to the corner of the Pont des Arts. I walked along the bridge and when no one was looking—plop!—I dropped it into the river. So it all lies now at the bottom of the Seine."

"It never struck you," said I, "that in the package there might be some quite pleasant communications from your humble servant?"

"It did, *cher ami*," she replied earnestly. "And that's why I've come to Cannes. And the pleasantness, to-day, of my humble servant," she added, rising, "eclipses all that he can possibly have written."

I acknowledged the tribute—I hope adequately. "But," I remonstrated, "there may have been letters there of supreme importance."

"*Nitchevo,*" she said again. "At any rate, I begin life afresh."

She went upstairs to put on her hat. It was late. François and Amélie between them found a wrap belonging to Dorothea which I hung about her before she should descend the steps to the car which would take her to the Hôtel Mont Fleuri. We were alone in the vestibule.

"I'll take you to the hotel."

"No," she said. "I prefer to leave you here. Break off for the night, suddenly, like this."

She came close to me, with her upturned adorable face. I threw my arms around her and kissed her; the world stood still, until I became conscious of a little sinuous movement and a little laugh and then of a little elusive shape in some kind of mantle fumbling with the door-knob.

Sanity returning, I opened the door and accompanied her to the car. As it drove off she kissed her hand.

"A demain."

CHAPTER XVII

IT goes without saying that during the course of our long day's conversation I had described Amos's peculiar adventure of which she heard now for the first time. I had shown her the packet of Luisa letters at which she upturned an aristocratic nose of distaste. She tossed them back to me, after scarce a glance, as though they had soiled her fingers. The fulfilment of Amos's chivalry had appealed to her far more strongly. The picture of Garcia bound with ropes on the floor while Amos rifled the despatch case tickled the barbaric in her; she rose and clapped her hands and almost danced. If only she had known! I could only reply that had she not fled that day so precipitately downstairs, she probably would have been informed.

"I have a warmer place than ever in my heart for Amos," she declared.

After that, we discussed the possible reasons for his non-pursuit of Amos and the bribing of the conducteur to keep secret his humiliating plight. It was then that a luminous idea struck me. He was flying from French justice. His outrageous demand of a hundred thousand francs was the act of a desperate man, and his journey to Italy had a double purpose. Now, he had played very high at the Casino, and like all high players, with undoubted credentials, he could draw cheques for what amount he pleased at the Casino desk. What if a cheque or a series of cheques so cashed had no possibility of being honoured unless he paid the corresponding sum immediately into his bank?

I could not rest the next day until I had obtained interview with one of the chiefs of the Casino. When I asked him whether they were particularly interested in Ramon Garcia, at first he exhibited a polite indifference. When I informed him that I was personally interested in the aforesaid gentleman, and that I could put them in the way of obtaining his international police record, he grew more alert.

"*Mon cher ami*," said I, "you know me as one of the most discreet of the Foreign Colony in Cannes. The secrecy of what you choose to tell me will be inviolate."

And eventually after a little elegant fencing on both sides, the Casino authority confessed. I was right in my surmise. Monsieur Ramon Garcia's cheque for a large amount had been returned from the Paris bank on which it had been drawn. It was the first time that such a thing had happened—in the case of Monsieur Garcia, *bien entendu*. They thought it was a mere matter of negligence on the part of Monsieur Garcia. They had written but received no reply. They could only then think that he was a vulgar *escroc*.

"But knowing him to be a crook," I cried, "why didn't you put the police on his track?"

"Monsieur Fontenay," said the diplomatist, "we are the administration of a Palace of Pleasure. Nothing spoils pleasure more than police. Monsieur Garcia was the intimate of our most influential and wealthy patrons. To have instituted police proceedings, invoking extradition laws and arousing a world-wide publicity would have caused a scandal most humiliating to those same patrons. Again, we are not duped very often. But when we are such fools as to be duped, generally it is to our advantage not to let the fact be known. The percentage on the tables which we take—unfortunately most of it goes to the State and the Municipality—comes to twelve, thirteen million francs in the season. The loss on Monsieur Garcia's cheques is insignificant."

I strode out into the sunshine, more or less a happy man. Now I had the whole story from beginning to end. Suddenly I stopped short. No. All except that which might be told in the Luisa letters. Hitherto I had not examined them. Not only was my Spanish weak, but my sense of delicacy was strong. It had seemed monstrous to read the intimate outpourings of a love-stricken woman. But now, considering that Nadia was the nominal wife of the wretch, it was my duty to acquaint myself with the contents of the letters. A hope thrilled through me. What if they proved that Garcia was married already? In this hurly-burly of melodrama, nothing could be impossible.

Now there happened to be passing through Cannes a fellow student of mine at the Beaux-Arts, one Waterson, who, having proved himself to his own satisfaction to be an execrable painter, had gone to Venezuela, where, after many years, he had made a fortune out of dried beef. He should talk Spanish as fluently as Luisa herself.

I retraced the few steps I had taken and re-entered the Casino, whence I telephoned to Waterson at his hotel. His voice came through. He would be delighted to lunch with me and translate as much Spanish as I liked.

So Waterson, a plump, bald, florid and smiling man, came and lunched and translated. I made up some kind of fairy tale in explanation. A novelist friend, into whose hands the letters had come, desired to know whether they contained any form of romance.

There was romance enough, if such can be called a crazy woman's passion for a cold-hearted scoundrel.

Often Waterson paused and took a gulp of whisky and soda, and declared that the sensuous muck made him sick. The lady recognized no bounds of reticence. It was the history of as vulgar an amour as you please. The only concrete facts one could gather was that she lived in Buenos Aires, that she had forsaken all other men for Ramon Garcia, that he was the father of her two children and that, without his inspiring presence she did not see how she could bring them up to adore him with her own passionate worship. Of the children being born in wedlock, not a hint. All very much indeed to the contrary. There were naive references to financial help in the past, for it seemed that the lady had large possessions; then, eventually, vehement refusal to finance the faithless one any more. Her husband, it seemed, had taken vows of religion and entered a monastery before Ramon dawned on her horizon. He could not sue for a divorce, on religious grounds. Marriage was impossible. The miserable Luisa could only appeal to the chivalry of Ramon. She might as well "use question to the wolf," thought I.

Except that they threw a sidelight on Ramon's general infamy, they gave me no help whatever. Amos might just as well have stolen his socks. The only clue they gave me was his possible motive for sailing to Buenos Aires, which was a matter of infinitesimal importance.

I dismissed Waterson with my blessing and a Corona Larga as a reward for valiant service, and sat down to survey the situation. I tabulated the facts.

Ramon Garcia and Nadia were legally man and wife. They had separated, as the phrase goes, at the church, or rather the registry door.

He still retained the instruments of blackmail. The

false pearls, the Lautier Frères receipt, and her few compromising letters.

He may have bombarded her with demands and threats for the past year. But of these she knew nothing, for nearly a year's mail had she nonchalantly cast, secured by a heavy fire-dog, into the Seine.

Ramon Garcia himself had disappeared from civilized ken.

In the meanwhile, were it not for the villain's mere encumbrance on the earth, I had every delicious reason to believe that she would marry me to-morrow.

Incidentally I may mention that here were two days' work irretrievably lost. I was painting, on commission, a portrait of Sir Floodeley Pirrington, who owns all kinds of funny newspapers and magazines, which I never read, and thereby controls the political ideas of millions of foolish people in England. Two sittings had I airily postponed; and he was leaving Cannes at the end of the week. It was irritating, for he had a fine, brutal, fascinating face: supremely paintable.

"Look here, my dear fellow," so rang his voice over the telephone, "I'm sorry for your troubles"—I had, of course, invented troubles—"but I'm sorry for my own too. I can only give you a couple more sittings. Six to-morrow and the next day."

"How can I paint you in the evening?"

"Evening? I mean six o'clock in the morning."

"Good heavens," said I, "is there such an hour?"

I heard a laugh at the other end of the wire. "Call it seven then."

"Eight."

"Half past seven at the latest, or the deal's off."

I groaned and yielded. But what a dreadful fellow to call the painting of his portrait a deal!

I made a most successful picture of him with deals lurking in every feature of his face, which was my revenge on him for dragging me out of bed at untimely hours.

Nadia found in Cannes many welcoming friends, among whom apparently the word had gone round that we had peculiar pleasure in each other's society. So I saw much of her, now and then at restaurant dinners, but more often in private houses. Her gambling days, she avowed, were over; so the rooms in the Casino saw her no more. Sometimes I accompanied her to the opera, and, during the intervals, sat out with her in a corner of the vast hall, or aided her to play a childish game of boule. Sometimes she dined and spent the evening at the Villa. The days passed suavely in a kind of autumnal idyll. I made elderly love to her, to which she responded with young fragrance. It was an affair of laughter and tenderness with her, and there was a touch of poignancy. The question of divorce was not overlooked. We consulted lawyers. The difficulty was that there was no husband or husband's representative to put in an appearance. There would be no means of letting him know that he was divorced. One attorney suggested with a smile that he could always bring forward a man of straw to impersonate Monsieur Garcia, and once the decree pronounced, the matter would be ended for ever. Apart, however, from the inherent non-morality of the proceeding, I did not think it fair to a man of straw, to allow him to proclaim himself, against his knowledge, a fugitive from justice.

"We will find a means," the lawyer reassured us, "the law of divorce in France is not so formal as all that."

March came to an end. Easter approached. Dorothea flashed from South Molton Street, which, as far as I could gather from her tale, was overwhelmed by meteorological and financial depression. Another woman, supported by a chorus of duchesses, had opened another embroidered-bag shop at the other end of that exclusive thoroughfare, and the rival establishments were engaged in the non-lucrative pursuit of cutting each other's throats. Thank God, said Dorothea, her partner loved work and battle and the struggle for—life. She, herself, was fed-up. She craved the calm of Cannes in order to map out a plan of campaign and to think of some line of novelty that would turn the interloper green.

She had the spacious impudence to propose that I should paint and sign little pictures on vellum which she could work into the sides of her bags. When I asked her how much she would pay me, she assumed a hurt expression. Of course, if I had sordid ideas like that, no doubt the firm would pay me a commission, say five per cent, on the sales.

"And what about the dealers and my market-prices?" I asked.

Of course, she knew nothing about that. Neither did Nadia, with whom she had conspired.

"Ah, David dear," said the latter, "it is not like you to be so ungenerous. Such a little thing. Just a graceful copy or so of one or two of them"—a wave of her arm indicated studies and sketches and unsold pictures, such as every painter has, around the studio walls—"*Voyons*, paint one for me and I will give it to Dorothea."

Could I, being in love, resist her? In an absurd Lancret inspiration, I painted two artificial eighteenth century things, four inches by three, with Nadia as my model. I had the devil's own business in getting a white wig from Paris that would suit her; but when the right one came, she looked so adorable and dainty in it, to say nothing of the V-necked, flowered silk dress that I lost my heart to her all over again, and painted her, forgetful of the fact that my little masterpieces would be exposed for sale in Dorothea's fraudulent emporium in South Molton Street.

To anticipate history, I may say that the opposition lady having soon afterwards eloped with the most favoured young man of one of the duchesses, the shop shut itself up of its own accord, leaving the field once more open to the old firm; whereupon Dorothea, woman of business, and entirely free from moral scruples, took the tiny pictures to a dealer whom she knew to be favourably inclined to my work, and sold them for a far higher sum than any woman in her senses would have given for them if they had been stuck on the sides of embroidered bags.

But at the time when I handed them over, finally to Nadia, to deliver to Dorothea, I gathered my wits together and sighed at the thought of the vain purpose to which they would be put.

This was not the only dark intrigue that was woven in Dorothea's brain. You may imagine that the arrival of a grown-up step-daughter in the house might have given a jar, no matter how momentary, to the course of the idyll. Not a bit. The interested young woman went out of her way to enhance its charm and its grace. From polite acquaintances they developed into fervent friends. God knows what they said in confidence or conspiracy, one with the other; but in Nadia's presence, I felt that we were enveloped in a new atmosphere, very sweet and tender and understanding.

"You know, darling," Dorothea said to me one day when we were alone, "I didn't much care for the Princess a year or so ago. You've got to know people. Besides, all those months of retreat and purification in the convent—she has told me all about it—must have had an enormous influence on her. I think she's the most exquisite flower of a woman on the earth."

"And if I happened to be of the same opinion, my dear," said I, "what would you say?"

It was the first time that the natural delicacy of our mutual relation had allowed us to come to grips with things. I love Dorothea's frank brown eyes. There is always a smile in them.

"I should say, my dear Daddums, that if I were you, I would take Nadia all over the civilized world until I could find a country in which she could get a divorce."

"Would it please you," said I, "if——?"

"It would give me all the happiness in the world."

"All?"

Our eyes met. She read in mine the implied question. A flush mounted to her cheeks.

"You are an artist," she said. "You ought to make allowances for exaggeration." She swung away for a moment and then returned. "What has it got to do with me? I'm only thinking of you and Nadia. Of course, mostly of you. It's just damnable, isn't it?"

"Utterly," said I.

"Why don't you run away with her, and let Society go and boil itself? She wouldn't mind."

I laughed. What else could I do? In its far-reaching, cold immorality, modern youth leaves the Renaissance chaste and innocent.

I asked her for news of Claude Worthington. It was odd not to have his Dutroyen scuttering all over the place when she was in Cannes.

"He thinks I'm in Scotland," she answered calmly, "with the McCallums in Ross."

"The——?" I questioned, for the name was new to me.

"The McCallums. He doesn't know their address. Neither do I, for the matter of that. Anyhow, it'll keep him quiet."

"On the contrary," said I, "as bits of Ross are scattered all over Cromarty—or the other way about, I forget which—and as the folks you speak of exist only in your imagination, you'll keep him exceedingly busy."

"It'll keep me quiet, at any rate," she laughed.

From these and subsequent remarks I deduced that the suit of my young nephew was not progressing.

Presently, into the midst of the idyll, dropped Amos and Bendyke Hamilton; this time not wholly unexpected, for I had heard of them doing the grand tour in Italy. This time too, instead of the shambling, uncouth giant in the dreadful billycock hat who had entered my dining-room, over a year ago, with his ancient Gladstone-bag, there appeared a very trim, though no less brawny gentleman, who wrung my hand, and, in the politest way in the world, expressed his pleasure at seeing me again. When I gently upbraided him for not having given me notice of his coming, so that I should have had his room swept and garnished, he begged me not to be in any way distressed. Bendyke and he had already engaged rooms at the Beau Rivage.

You see, he just walked in one April afternoon, and was shown up to the studio where I was laboriously painting Sir Floodeley Pirrington's nether garments from the lay-figure. There had been talk of his coming to Cannes; but no date had been fixed.

"You're looking exceedingly well," said I.

"Well?" He grinned in his old pleasant way, and threw up his chest and braced his arms. "I could knock down an ox with one hand and take him up and eat him with the other."

"Travel agrees with you," said I.

"There's nothing like it. I was grateful to you before, Uncle, for all your kindness; but I'm more grateful to you still for sending me off on this wild-goose chase. I've got some idea which I hadn't before, of the size of the world, and the countless variety of ways in which different nations and different folks look at the same old thing."

"What same old thing?" I asked, amused.

"Why the same old principles of human life—food, sleep, love, marriage, self-protection, law, order, the primitive essentials. Every section of society I've come across wants to be happy, just to enjoy these elementary sanctions. And yet every section seems to get at them in the most roundabout ways. And it would be a very wise man who could say that one is right and another is wrong. If anybody had told me in Warraranga that the earth was so chockful of interest, I shouldn't have understood what they were talking about."

"And now?"

"Now?" He lit a cigarette extracted from a gold cigarette case—he who once found no comfort but in pipes and reduced the mouth-end of a cigar to the horror of a sucked stick of asparagus—"Now?" He grinned again. "Now, I do understand. I'm beginning to be educated. I appreciate what education means, and by Jove, I'm going on with it!"

I could not but admire the honesty and simplicity of the man; he held me by the luminous purpose in his blue eyes. During the year he had gone far; his spirit many thousands of leagues farther than his body. The native intelligence I had divined at our first meeting, then clogged with prejudice and working darkly, had developed, in conditions of clearance, and was in process of swift reaction to the multitudinous phenomena of existence.

Outwardly, too, he had changed. He had almost lost his Australian twang, and his accent was that of the cultivated Englishman. His manners were softened. He seemed to be able, instinctively, to control the old ungainly movements of his huge frame. He had lost his bear's shambling gait. He was brisk, free and frank in his movements. As he lounged in chair or stood, talking, he had all the ways of a simple gentleman.

To go back to his excursus into education, I asked him for his theory on the subject.

"I naturally have my own ideas; but I should like to hear yours."

Of course, he fenced a bit—I admit my question was somewhat vague—and I appreciated the shrewdness of his fencing. At last I thrust brutally:

"What do you actually mean by the term 'education'?"

He riposted pat: "To get that universal knowledge of human things which gives you a perfect sense of values."

As far as my philosophy goes, his definition was unassailable. Yet how did he acquire the mental equipment to formulate it?

Of course, Dorothea, Nadia, I myself, in our respective small ways had begun and carried to a certain point the development of Amos from the Warrarangan demi-savage to the outer semblance of civilized man. Any willing dullard we could so have trained. But here was an Amos beyond my ken, talking of abstract ideas, not in his former groping, half-articulate fashion, with the worried lines on his brow of a dog trying to express itself, but in easy crisp English, as devoid of confusion as of priggishness. How, I said, had the miracle been accomplished?

He answered my unspoken query.

"Bendyke Hamilton's the most wonderful man I've ever met," he said, suddenly. "He knows everything, from the way to treat foot-and-mouth disease to the hang of the Einstein Theory. And he throws his knowledge at you broadcast, just as he throws his time and his physical powers and his courage and his ordinary experience. Why the deuce isn't he Prime Minister somewhere?"

Said I, guardedly: "You've found your year with him useful, I hope?"

He almost roared. "Useful! He has been a kind of daily revelation to me. He has opened my eyes. He has made me read. He has crammed my thick old skull"—he rapped it with the knuckles of both hands—"with all sorts of things. Useful!" He caught a quiet smile in my eyes and then he grinned. "I don't think he's quite taught me yet to know, Uncle David, when people like you are pulling my leg."

At this juncture Dorothea burst into the studio with a conventional "Can I come in?" and stood for a second amazed at the sight of the unexpected Amos.

"Hullo! You? You've turned up at last?"

He advanced, smiled, took her hand and bent over it in a most courtly manner.

"Yes, Dorothea, I've turned up."

She stared at him, conscious of subtle change; and for the moment, all she could say was:

"Oh!"

CHAPTER XVIII

AFTER a while Bendyke Hamilton joined us, quiet, unassuming, capable. As I looked at him and thought of Amos's ingenuous tribute, I smiled sadly. Thousands of his type have been building up the Empire for the past hundred years, either at the outposts, ruling our wild territories, or, confined in the narrow limits of our great public schools, teaching others how to rule. Men of great attainment, lofty character and infinite patience, they remain, to the wonder of the injudicious, in perpetual obscurity. What element of success is it that they lack? Why, cried Amos, should not Bendyke Hamilton be Prime Minister? Why should not So-and-so, any old public schoolboy can cry, casting his mind back to some heroic humourist who taught him Latin Prose and the philosophy of honour and all sorts of other things that he only half understood at the time—why should not So-and-so have emerged resplendent as a great National Figure? The answer is that the type lacks ambition in the nobler sense, and in its coarser and blatant sense holds it in sensitive scorn. Their consciences' approval of the day's work perfectly accomplished is the only reward they crave.

There sat Bendyke Hamilton, lean, fine-featured yet ruggedly lined, the tones of his bronzed face melting into the brown of his close-cropped hair, the black patch over one missing eye, the other alive with purpose and authority. Wanting a little speech with him alone, I had unceremoniously sent Amos and Dorothea out to take the air. I thanked him warmly for what he had

done for Amos.   In his English way he repudiated claims
on my gratitude.

"Anybody can fill up a sponge, provided he has water
enough.   The   only   difficulty   is   the   water-supply,
especially when the sponge is the size of Amos."

I laughed.   "To begin with, it's something to be able
to diagnose receptive powers.   I don't think I did myself
and I'm quite sure his other uncle, the Bishop of Bradbury, didn't."

"You've got to live with a shy man before you know
him," said Hamilton.   "After that it's easy.   It's I,
Mr. Fontenay, who am grateful to you, for giving me
the job—one of the most interesting I've ever had.   All
the time it has been like a psychological process revealed
on the cinema."

I invited him to explain.   He relit his pipe and began
to talk frankly about Amos.   How the primary object
of his Odyssey had been the tracking down of the elusive
Garcia; how the imperious craving to realize subjectively
the significance of the new phenomena that presented
themselves objectively before his eyes and his mind
had gradually reduced the Aim to a secondary purpose;
how the psychological process before mentioned had
started and continued.   Diverging here and there into
detail, how Amos, who once had found the mechanical
act of reading a difficult matter, had leaped, as a child
leaps, with a flash, into sudden reading of the clock,
into the faculty of taking in a printed line at a glance,
instead of painfully weighing every word; how, there-
after, he had been greatly put to it to satisfy Amos's
omnivoracity; how he had learned Spanish in a few
months.   How he had sought with childlike eagerness
to understand the civilizations of the various countries
through which he had passed, the South American

Republics, the United States, Canada, Egypt, Italy.

"Amos is a great chap," said he.

Than that, the type of Bendyke Hamilton could pronounce no higher encomium.

After a while:

"And the unspeakable Garcia," I asked, "what of him? I understood you lost track of him in New York."

Hamilton rubbed the mouthpiece of his pipe over his eyebrow—it's a queer habit I have noticed in the case of a few other men, all of them bachelors—and looked at me quizzically.

"May I plead guilty to a pious fraud? I think the end has justified the means. If you will call to mind my periodical reports, you will see that they were all to do with Amos and nothing with Ramon Garcia."

I reflected. He was right. All the news of the hunting of Garcia had come from Amos.

"We never got on to the track of the beggar," said Bendyke Hamilton. "I presented our letter of introduction to the head of the Buenos Aires Police, and explained our business. He was immensely civil. He knew all the misdeeds which Ramon Garcia had committed since his tender infancy. The Police Force of the Argentine Republic was at our entire disposal. As soon as he had any news of the man, he would let us know. He bowed us out most politely. Amos, to whom I had interpreted, was tremendously bucked. We stayed a long time in Buenos Aires and I saw the beginnings of the process I've tried to describe to you. Meanwhile no news of Garcia. I went, by myself, to the police, having my suspicions. The official upbraided me for my pertinacity, while praising my Spanish. Had I not lived long enough among them to appreciate mere courtesy? How could they entrust police secrets to an amateur? I absent-mindedly took out of a waistcoat pocket a crumpled thousand-peso note and smoothed it on my knee. He looked at it hungrily. I smiled. 'Señor,' said he, 'I am an honest man.' From the other waistcoat pocket I drew out another. I thought I might legitimately charge them up to expenses."

"Why, of course," said I.

"The poor chap nearly cried. With a sob in his voice he repeated that he was an honest man. If he could be of service to me, his soul would be at my disposition; but—and it then dawned on me that the honest man had no more knowledge of Ramon Garcia than of the Man in the Moon. I put the notes back in my pocket. But I tried to get home a hit with Scotland Yard. They had cabled about Garcia. I gave him the approximate date. He sent for a myrmidon and they looked up files. The only cable they had received related to one Don Miguel Vargas y Uriostos alias Antonio Perez. 'That's the man,' I cried. 'He was known by the first name in London.' "

"And by the second in Brazil," said I, remembering Nadia's story.

"Anyhow," Bendyke Hamilton continued, "the police assured me that he had not landed in the Argentine. When he did land they would not fail to let me know. Sincerity rang in every sorrowing tone of the honest man's voice."

"But where does the pious fraud come in?" I asked.

"I'm afraid I invented a kind of drag-hunt. It kept Amos going for months, right away from Buenos Aires to the Canadian Pacific border. When we got to New York, I thought it best to lose the scent. In the meanwhile he had got bitten with the love of travel for its own sake. You'll remember you told me that the chase was only a pretext. Still, I must make my apologies."

I accepted them readily and laughed over certain of his reminiscences, for Amos had not been an easy man to fool, especially at last, when he had picked up enough Spanish to carry on with.

Presently Dorothea and Amos returned from their stroll. We had tea. Amos talked of the wonders of far countries. Eventually I asked him what he proposed to do in Cannes.

"I don't propose to do anything, Uncle David. Unless you can tell me what there is to be done—or unless you think I ought to carry out mother's instructions and stay with you."

I was unable to suggest any possible form of useful activity, and I reasoned that as long as he kept in respectful touch with me he would be spiritually obedient to his mother's wishes. In the meanwhile what were his plans?

"We're starting homewards to-morrow. I only looked in here to report."

Here I must mention that they had run across Claude Worthington in Rome, who with his alien Dutroyens was waging fierce war against Italas and Fiats, and gaining not inconsiderable victories, in spite of the adverse exchange. To sell a small touring car to Amos wearied of the confinement of trains and boats had been an easy matter. In this car had the pair arrived in Cannes, and in it they proposed to start for Paris on the morrow.

I deplored the shortness of his stay, but commended his desire not to linger in this land of idleness.

"It's the best thing you can do, my boy," said I, with (according to Dorothea) the detestable superiority of middle-age. "Go to London and mix in Society."

"I rather want to see what things are like in the East End," said Amos.

"But don't neglect the West," I counselled. "Things are quite as funny and as worth studying as in the East. Don't forget that a well-bred baronet is as much God's creature as a hearty drunkard on the Ratcliffe Highway. If you want raw materials go down again to Bradbury and study social conditions there in the light of new knowledge."

"I'm going," said Amos. "Besides, I'd like old Bendyke, before he cuts himself adrift from me, to know Uncle Tom. They'd get on well together." He turned to me, confidentially. "I'd like to hear them arguing, you know. They'd go hammer and tongs at each other, and I reckon I'd learn a lot. You see," he went on, after a stride to the tea table, whence he returned with a mighty wedge of sticky cake, "there's something darned wrong with the world, and I don't know what it is, and nobody and no book seem to be able to tell me. It strikes me I've got to find it out for myself. It ought to be such a jolly old world———"

"Why?" I interrupted.

"Well—the sun and the flowers and the kindly fruits of the earth, and art and music and poetry and human beings whom I've generally found inclined to do good rather than harm—I don't see what cause there should be for misery and suffering and hatred and war and murder and starvation. I want to get to the bottom of it."

"Millions of men have spent their lives in trying the same thing. You'll have to be quick if you're going back to Warraranga in three and a half years."

Still holding the wedge of cake, he shook his great head.

"I'm not going back to Warraranga," said he. "Perhaps a visit, to arrange affairs—Bendyke has helped me to see where I stand—but to live there?—No!!"

He grinned and attacked the wedge of cake. Travel had not developed his mind at the expense of his lusty appetite. While he was thus engaged, I remembered one of Bendyke Hamilton's letters, in which this decision had been recorded. When he had finished and dusted the crumbs from his lips with his pocket-handkerchief, instead of the back of his vast hand, a habit of which Dorothea had tried in vain to break him, he asked me cheerfully:

"Do you know the London School of Economics?"

"I've heard of it," said I, "but I can't profess to say that I know it."

I had heard of, and had equally dim ideas concerning, the Eleusinian Mysteries.

"I'm going to study there," said Amos. "Bendyke says it'll give me a foundation to build up on."

I approved sagely. "To carry on the image, what kind of an edifice do you propose to erect?"

"I don't know," he replied, "the important thing now is to get the beginning solid."

Dorothea, who had been talking gaily with Hamilton, burst in:

"You must be in a frenzy of excitement over it, Amos."

He turned to her in his big, gentle way.

"Over what?"

"The London School of Economics. I envy you. It must be quivering with human emotion."

He upreared his great bulk and crossed to her chair and looked down on her.

"Why should you laugh at me, Dorothea?"

She leaned back, her cheeks flushed. "Because you're so stupendously solemn. Like the young school-teacher who has just discovered Karl Marx and Ruskin and Henry George. Isn't he ever flippant, Mr. Hamilton?"

Amos swerved aside after the way of a wounded animal. It was monstrously pathetic. Dorothea leaped up and caught him by his arm.

"Oh, Amos, I'm so sorry, I didn't mean to hurt you."

"But you did," he said simply, smiling into her eyes. "Uncle David only wanted to know what my plans were, and I told him. I must get some education before I'm of use to anybody. You were the first to begin to teach me things."

"I'm a beast," said Dorothea. "Forgive me."

"That's easily done," said he, and took her shoulders in his hands and shook her with reassuring tenderness. "You see, I can't get away yet from my early training, when the idle jest, as they called it, was regarded as a sin and a praying matter. We were darned serious in Warraranga."

"Thank goodness you're not going back," said Dorothea, recovering herself.

"Perhaps that's one of the reasons," said he. "I'd rather like to learn how to laugh. It must be a great help in life to see it humorously."

"But I've seen you laugh," Dorothea declared contritely.

"Oh, yes. When a man sits down on a tin-tack, I can scream. But—wait. Yes!" He held up both arms to command silence, and an expression of delight overspread his broad and rugged features. "I see what was at the back of your mind. The idea of me going to a School of Economics—it was like a bear using a powder-puff!"

He slapped his thighs and roared with laughter, in which, laughter being notoriously contagious, we all joined. Talk flowed in easier channels. When the two men rose to depart, I bade them return to dinner.

"Well!" said I to Dorothea when we were alone, "what do you think of Amos?"

"If you want me to be epigrammatic, I can't. I find him tremendously brushed up both inside and out."

"It's curious," said I, "that he made no allusion to the Princess."

"It isn't really," she replied. "From you, he had nothing more to find out."

Her statement being obscure, I demanded an explanation.

"It was the first thing he asked me for as soon as we got outside—news of Nadia. Apparently he has been writing her hundreds of letters, and of course getting no answers. He's still crazy about her. Oh, I had a very pleasant walk I assure you. I don't mind, of course. But I should have been better pleased if he had fallen in love with a beady-eyed lady in Uruguay. There would have been some sense in it. He would have half forgotten all about her by this time. But Nadia's a sort of maudlin obsession. It's grotesque."

It was. Had I not suffered, or rather had not my vanity suffered, from the grotesqueness of it? His silence had led me to hope that the ardour of the chase of Ramon Garcia having cooled, so had his calf passion for the Princess. I frowned and bit my lip and muttered mild anathema on Amos, more in testiness than in anger.

"But still, my dear, I don't see why he shouldn't have mentioned her to me."

"I told him that we knew nothing at all about her. Just as he had written, so had we all. She had simply disappeared from human ken."

She turned on me an honest face of which every feature shone with conscious virtue. I gasped. Such splendour of mendacity, combined with such reckless disregard of discovery, is granted but rarely to the most gifted of mere men.

I expostulated. Amos would be bound to meet her. Why, she might be running in to-night, it being her charming custom to come and take us unawares.

"You've forgotten," replied Dorothea, in a withering and entirely disrespectful tone, "that she's staying for two or three days with Mrs. Blennerhasset at Cap Ferrat."

"That's true," said I.

"And you don't realize that Amos and his friend are leaving Cannes in the car to-morrow morning."

"That," said I, "is a mental fixture."

"Well," she shrugged, "why are you in such a state of worry? He'll go happily, first to Paris to carry on his education, and then to London and start his career. Men may have a sentimental love for a woman's shadows, but when there's not a trace of a shadow left, they sort of get over it. At least——"

"At least that's your experience, my dear?"

She flounced away, saying that I was hateful, but returned when I put serious propositions before her.

"But suppose Amos comes back to Cannes?"

"He's never coming back. What should he come back for? Your beautiful eyes, Daddums? Mine? He can see mine any day in South Molton Street. If he wanted to fool about the Riviera, why doesn't he do it now, instead of limiting his stay to a few hours?"

I admitted the logic of her reasoning. "But," I added, "there's always the possibility of Nadia and myself marrying—the prospects of divorce are growing rosier and rosier every day. When the wedding is announced, what will Amos say to you and what will you have to say to Amos?"

She bade me not worry. She could look after herself.

"I don't think you've been at all kind, Daddums. Instead of being grateful to me, you're sitting on a silly pinnacle of abstract morality. Suppose Amos knew that Nadia was on the Coast, do you think he'd rush away? No. He'd stay and make himself a damn nuisance to everybody. I have spoken."

She blew me an ironical kiss and bounced victorious out of the room.

The young men returned to dinner. Nothing very much happened. I noticed that Dorothea devoted herself ostentatiously to Bendyke Hamilton, who took obvious pleasure in her society. Most men did. She had wit and knowledge of the world, and in her honest brown-eyed and high-coloured way was by no means unpleasing to look upon. As it was a warm and windless night, she took him out on to the drawing-room terrace to see the effect of the full moon over the sea and the Esterel.

Amos enjoying a cigar, after the fashion of trained Christians, said, with a grin:

"It would be very jolly if those two——"

I could have thrown boots or fire-irons or anything handy at his head; but there was only a futile paper-knife on the table, within reach. Why on earth couldn't the young idiot see that Dorothea, in love with him and ready to marry him, would have devoted her life to him and guided him in all his ambitions and eventually insisted on the King sending for him to make him Prime Minister—instead of Bendyke Hamilton? To say nothing of the warm wealth of herself that she would give him, and the splendid children that would be the joy of his life.

I replied drily: "If Hamilton had wished, he could have found a wife long before this. But an honourable gentleman without a bean in the world doesn't go about asking comfortably-off young women to marry him."

Amos growled. "Society's in a rotten state. If any two are made for each other, it's those two. And it's just a question of money." He reflected for a moment. Then, he added ingenuously: "The simple common-sense things are those that can't be done. I'd willingly share half my money with Bendyke—he's the only brother I've ever had—and then he could marry Dorothea, who's the only sister I've ever had. But he'd think me soft-headed or half-witted if I proposed it; and if he did accept, the world being what it is, I shouldn't have the same respect for him. It's beastly. Everything's upside down, isn't it?"

As I had my private reasons for not wishing to discuss love and marriage with Amos, I went off on a side issue and asked him what were Bendyke Hamilton's immediate plans, now that he had fulfilled his mission. Amos, in his reference to the Bradbury visit, had hinted at their approaching separation. He passed his hand ruefully through his hair and wrinkled his brows.

"He has been offered a job as big-game expert by some scientific expedition that's going to East Africa—or at least some darned region at the back of beyond of East Africa."

"Why don't you go with them?" said I. "All scientific expeditions are short of money. You put up some and they'll take you like a shot—especially a chap of your physique. You'll learn no end of things about

plants and beasts, and when you come back you will
perhaps find the world right side up."

"I don't say that I shouldn't like to go," he replied,
seriously, "but I've mapped out my life differently."

The docile demi-savage had developed into a young
man of independent judgment and purpose. A year ago
his rejection of the parsonical career proposed by his
uncle, the Bishop, had been negative. So would he have
said "no" if invited to a drunken orgy or an old ladies'
tea-party. But now his sacrifice of an alluring adventure
was positive. He had his route traced out. He knew
whither he was going. His bent brows and quiet manner
were easy to read.

François brought in the tray of drinks. I waved a hand
mechanically hospitable. Amos rose and, to my astonishment, helped himself to a mild brandy and soda. Then
I remembered that he had drunk light wine at lunch and
dinner. But still, I cried, with a laugh:

"Hullo—what about the 'wicked stuff,' as you used to
call it?"

He winked as he drank to me. "I said something to-
day about getting a sense of values. I hate intolerance."

I agreed with him and we discussed the matter in
pleasant fashion. Then I brought him back to the East
African suggestion.

"Yes, I've mapped out my life differently," he repeated. "Trees and wild beasts won't teach me what I
want to learn. And then, in East Africa I'm not going
to find that infernal villain Ramon Garcia."

It was the first time he had mentioned the man's
name, and I saw his great fists clench.

"We lost him, as I told you, in New York. But, by
God! If I have to wait twenty years I'll get him some-

how. He hasn't any right to live"—the angry veins stood out on his brow—"he's a cumberer of the earth."

"I'm glad to see," said I, "that your hatred of intolerance isn't absolute."

"There are just a few absolute things in life, Uncle David. The love of God and the hatred of the Devil and all his works. To me, Ramon Garcia's the Devil." He paused, then fetched a deep breath. "I really did think I should come across him in Buenos Aires."

"I fancy," said I, "that if you went to Buenos Aires you'd stand a good chance of finding him now."

"Why?"

"Do you remember the packet of letters you stole? Signed 'Luisa'? I've had them translated. Here's a lady, mother of his two illegitimate children, with apparently lots of money, who was in the habit of supplying his needs. It's obvious that, when he got broke, he should return to her."

In hot excitement he demanded her name and address, as though he would start for the Argentine on the morrow. But alas! I only had the lady's Christian name. Amos sank in his chair, depressed. Presently he brightened.

"That kind of shark always comes back to Europe. That's where the mugs are. At any rate, Bendyke says so."

"What do I say?" cried Hamilton, entering with Dorothea by the French window.

Amos repeated the statement. Hamilton smiled.

"There are three reservations of them. From Hyde Park Corner to the Strand. From the Arc de Triomphe to the Café de la Paix, and from Cannes to Mentone."

"And that's where we'll get Ramon Garcia," Amos declared. "First we're going to Paris. Bendyke tells me there's lots to learn there. Museums and things. Perhaps we may run into him in a picture gallery like in London. We'll stay about a fortnight."

When this conversational theme petered out, I said to Bendyke Hamilton:

"Amos tells me that you're thinking about going big-game shooting in East Africa."

"And I've been telling him," cried Dorothea, "that Amos needs him for at least another six months."

Amos jumped up, delighted. "Have you really, Cousin Dorothea? That's what I've been trying to get into his head all the way up from Rome."

"I should like," I remarked blandly, "to hear Mr. Hamilton's ideas."

His brown hand plucked at his little moustache, and I swear that his one eye flashed for an instant towards Dorothea before he replied.

"I'm not really very keen on East Africa," said he.

CHAPTER XIX

THE two young men left Cannes on the following morning in Amos's newly acquired Dutroyen car. In the afternoon Dorothea received a letter from Claude Worthington telling her of the sale. She showed me part of the letter—the other part was doubtless of a character so idiotic as to be unshowable to the grave and reverend senior that I was in Dorothea's eyes. He would have written before, said he, but a mysterious illness, diphtheria, meningitis or nervous prostration—the doctors could not decide—had laid him low. According to his own opinion he was suffering from the shock of having sold a car to Amos. The latter had taken it like a lamb—the show car which he was driving. Almost taken it out of his mouth, so to speak, and shoved a cheque into his hand. The first time he had appreciated the sacredness of the Family! Wished to heaven he had more family. Couldn't Dorothea and I scrape up a few more millionaire cousins to buy his silly old cars? Amos was got up fit to kill. He had the manner of the Ambassador to Yucatan. "Said he: 'Do you still maintain that the car has a Rolls-Royce engine at Ford price?' 'No, old man,' said I. 'It's an inferior Ford engine at super Rolls-Royce price. Only, to friends and relations I'm empowered to deduct five hundred per cent discount.' And then he laughed like blazes and whanged me on the shoulder, which brought on my illness, and even now I can't crank up a car. I sold him the old bus anyway; but I never realized that selling cars on commission was a dangerous trade. I'll have to take out a new Accident and Life Insurance. If you see him, tell him from me it's a damn good car. Of course if he wants it to jump like a chamois over the Alps, or swim rivers in flood, it'll get sulky and turn round and bite him; but otherwise—as I say—it's a damn good car and I've let him have it cheap and my commission will just buy me a drink—and filthy at that. If you'll wire me how long you'll be in Cannes I'll run up and get the taste out of my mouth with one of François's cocktails. And then, darlingest old girl——"

The page ended. I was about to turn it, when Dorothea, reading over my shoulder, plucked the letter from my hands.

"The rest is silence. The deepest and most awful silence."

"Why?" I asked. "Claude's a very gallant, worthy and entertaining gentleman."

"So are you, Daddums. And I love you to distraction. But even if it were within the range of possibility, I wouldn't marry you for anything under the sun."

I thanked her for her dainty outspokenness—but asked her why.

"You and Claude are North and South Poles asunder. But neither of you are—in French—*mon type.*"

"And may I, your father, under the law of most civilized countries, know what your particular *type* is?"

She took my face in both hands, and, at close quarters, looked into my eyes—for a modern young woman she is remarkably versatile in feminine expedients—and said in a low voice:

"No and no and again no."

She brushed a filial kiss on my forehead and withdrew, laughing.

Now, remember, the relations between my step-daughter and myself were very delicate. To me, very precious. The sweetest, purest, most loyal love that woman can give to man was mine. It was on the tip of my tongue to ask her whether her *type* was Amos. But between us was that imperceptible line of demarcation which our souls, unknown to ourselves, had decided not to cross without mutual consent. Now, her enigmatic and full-hearted negative, like most women's negatives, was such as to give a perspicacious man positive information. I smiled grimly and once more anathematized the insensible Amos on the point of losing substance for shadows.

A day or two later arrived Nadia from her visit to Mrs. Blennerhasset at Cap Ferrat. She commanded me to tea at the Mont Fleuri. The first thing she said was:

"I hear my beloved bear has been here."

"How the deuce did you learn that?" I asked.

"A friend of mine at the Beau Rivage saw him. He was with another man. Why didn't you let me know? I would have telephoned for him to come and see us. Mrs. Blennerhasset would have sent her car."

"He only spent one night here—*en passage*," said I.

"But he would have spent two nights, three nights, a fortnight, two months, if I could have let him know I wanted to speak with him."

I smiled, admiring the imperious poise of her head.

"I suppose," she added coldly, "he made enquiries about me?"

I could not deny it. "I believe," said I, "that many letters from him, as from me, and lots of other people, are now at the bottom of the Seine."

"All the more reason for my seeing him. I don't think it's kind of you, David."

Now, here was the first indication of the impossible

position in which Dorothea had put me. I made lame excuses. Amos was in an inordinate hurry to return to England.

"Who is the lady?" she asked.

"Lady? My dear, Amos's head is too full of all kinds of things to have room for ladies. Besides, if he had a Dulcinea in England, do you think he would have left her for a year in order to look for Ramon Garcia?"

"Then why such hurry?"

I explained the immediate ambition of Amos. Her delicate brow wrinkled incredulously. Then she asked:

"He has given up searching for Ramon?"

"By no means," said I. "But as Ramon has eluded him in the New World, he feels certain he will find him in the Old. Meanwhile he's attending to his own evolution."

"I think you're right," she said, after a pause. "I follow your reasoning. There can be no lady in the case. Except"—she made one of her adorable little grimaces of mockery—"except perhaps me."

"That's absurd," said I.

"I don't find it so at all," she retorted heatedly. "I can see no reason why a romantic young man should not fall in love with me. Can you?"

I had to reply that the wonder was that all mankind were not sighing at her feet.

"Then why not Amos? Have I not told you he was a knight errant? I don't believe knight errants went after dragons just for the love of dragon killing——"

"Why not?" I interrupted. "It was the big-game shooting of the period."

"Bah! When you talk cynical like that I don't like you. They went for dragons out of love for the princess. You yourself have asked why he should go hunting

Ramon if he had a young lady in England. He went after Ramon because he was in love with me."

This was by no means an idyllic conversation. Out of humour, I refused tea and lit a cigarette. She did not realize the monstrous impertinence of Amos in daring to be in love with her. It actually gave her pleasure. With me, as I have told you, it has been a matter of annoyance, humiliating through its grotesqueness, for the past year. She looked at me with wicked yet enchanting irony.

"*Gros Jaloux!* What does it matter to you if a hundred men love me, when I don't love any of them at all? When I only love one man in the world?"

My ill-humour dissolved into mere amorousness.

"And who is the favoured mortal, Madame?"

"Drink your tea, which I have ordered, and I will tell you."

At that absurd moment I would have drunk eisel, like Hamlet, had she bidden me, or camomile or sparkling burgundy or carbolic acid. There was an interval for idiotic refreshment. A grim French lady crocheting in a far corner of the lounge regarded us disapprovingly, her mind being assured of the worst.

When I rose to go, Nadia returned to the wretched Amos.

"Now that you know that the stupid *grand artiste* has my whole foolish heart, will you tell me where I can write to the poor dear bear?"

"The Palace, Bradbury, will find him."

She opened astonished eyes.

"A Palace? Then he must be a Prince, like the poor bear in 'Beauty and the Beast.' "

I had to explain Tom and the hyperbolical designation of his episcopal and draughty house.

"When you do write," said I, "you might perhaps let

him suppose that you've just turned up in Cannes."

Naturally she asked why.

"He might be hurt at our not telephoning to you at Cap Ferrat."

I did my best to retrieve Dorothea's blunder in tactics; but I don't think I had great success. Nadia sped a puzzled glance at me and I saw the ripple of a shrug pass over her shoulders.

"Perhaps you would rather I did not write at all, *mon ami?*"

"Oh that——" said I, "that would be too insane. Write to the boy as much as you like. For the next fortnight or so he is staying at the Hotel Folkestone in Paris."

I went away a happy lover, placed in undignified position. How could I have taken her at her word and accepted her offer not to communicate with Amos? And yet by not doing so I had betrayed Dorothea.

In this complicated world, no matter what principles of hedonism one sets out to follow, there are always cross-currents which sweep one out of the simple course; cross-currents set up by other people, by Dorothea in this instance, by her calm and feminine mendacity. When I reached home I rebuked her. She took my re-criminations calmly.

"Why didn't you say that her silly ass of a friend at the Beau Rivage was mistaken?"

"I'm an old-fashioned man," said I, "brought up in the strictest of ecclesiastical circles——"

"And George Washingtonian ideas."

"Precisely, my dear. If George had said, 'I didn't cut down the cherry tree,' his father would have retorted, 'You did, you little liar,' and would have lammed the life out of him according to the custom of the times. And

George knew it. He was a man of genius. He realized, at a tender age, with Macchiavellian astuteness, that in certain crises there's nothing like Truth for the simplification of life."

"I'll go up to Nadia and tell her the Macchiavellian truth," said Dorothea.

"Well, my dear," said I, "it's your funeral, not mine."

The next morning all these trumpery trifles were knocked out of my head. There came a telephone message from the Chief of the Casino. Would it be convenient for me to see him in his office at half-past eleven? Or would I do him the honour of appointing an hour at which I could receive him at the Villa?

Now, it happened that in the course of a semi-professional talk with a local journalist I had rather severely criticized, from the artistic point of view, certain decorative schemes for the Saturday gala dinners. My criticism had been printed. Thinking that this was the subject of the interview so courteously requested, and loving courtesy for courtesy's sake, I sent word by François that I would call at the Casino at the hour suggested.

I was received by the whole hierarchy.

"Monsieur," said the Chief, "a short while ago you did me the honour of consulting me about a certain gentleman."

"About a swindler," said I.

The little man spread out his hands.

"Monsieur, no one is a swindler until he has proved himself to be one. For a long time I thought, as you, of this gentleman. It was a question of a cheque for a large amount returned from a Paris bank. You said: 'Why -

not take action?' I replied, as you remember. Yesterday this gentleman presents himself at the Casino——"

I leaped from my chair, as if propelled by high explosive.

"Garcia! He is here, in Cannes? That damned scoundrel!"

"Pardon, Monsieur, you have to prove your scoundrel. Listen to me, I beg you. He came yesterday to the Casino. He explained all. He is a South American; perhaps you do not know that he is an explorer——"

"An exploiter," said I.

"*Un explorateur,*" said the Chief, blandly. "He has been away a year exploring the Andes, away from civilization. On his return quite recently he found from his Paris bank that his cheque had been dishonoured. It was the first intimation he had received. It had been a hurried mistake in cheque-books. His big account was in another bank altogether. It was but a careless mistake."

"As a man of the world," I said, "do you believe it?"

"It is *justement* as a man of the world that I believe it," he replied, with an impassive face. "And for the good reason that he repaid the money with interest."

"The devil he did!" I cried.

"It is as I tell you, Monsieur Fontenay. He presented himself yesterday afternoon. He made his explanation. He drew out his cheque-book—we calculated the interest —he invited an official of the Casino to accompany him to the Crédit Lyonnais. The Crédit Lyonnais honoured his cheque by giving our representative their draft in our favour. The incident therefore is closed in all loyalty."

"And you have readmitted this man to the Casino?"

"Why not? He even played last night and won much

money.   There was high play.   But that has nothing to
do with us."

"Except that the higher the play the more percentage
goes into the Cagnotte."

He spread out his hands again.

"Precisely.   What would you have?   Especially when
seventy per cent of it is taken by the State and the
Municipality."

He almost persuaded me that the Casino was a profit-
less institution and was conducted on principles of pure
philanthropy.

I remembered that, at our last interview, he had stated
that, in proportion to their immense profits, Garcia's debt
was but a trifle.

"And where is Monsieur Garcia staying?" I asked.

He mentioned the hotel—the Palace of Cannes on the
Croisette.

I went away in a state of mind both muddled and
excited.   Why had he returned to Cannes?   The repay-
ment of the money could only be the moving of a pawn
in a subtle game.   Knaves don't make *beaux gestes* for
nothing.   Perhaps it was in order to open the doors of
the great summer gambling resorts, Vichy, Biarritz,
Aix-les-Bains and Deauville which, had he not paid,
would have been barred against him.   Perhaps, too, it
was to rehabilitate himself in Cannes, or rather to reas-
sume his old and, up to now, undisputed position and put
pressure on my Princess.   At any rate, it was colossal impudence.   Had I come across him as a literary figure,
like Casanova, for instance, I should have admired him
prodigiously.   As it was, I heaped on him every curse
that an excellent memory and a fair imagination could
suggest.

Whence had he obtained the money to throw away on

his noble act? Whence the means to establish himself at the Palace, an hotel, which, to say the least, does not cater for the indigent? Whence too had he come? That he had gone to Buenos Aires nearly a year ago I knew for certainty. Had he spent the time, as I had suspected, in robbing the infatuated Luisa of the remains of her fortune?

I was revolving these worrying themes in my mind when I found myself outside the Palace, which you will understand is in a contrary direction from the Casino to my villa. My subconscious self must have led me. I entered and was about to enquire at the desk, when I saw him standing alone in the centre of the great hall, perfectly dressed in a blue serge suit and grey waistcoat, and all over pearl tie-pins and diamonds.

He took off his hat and advanced towards me beaming welcome with outstretched hand.

"My dear Monsieur Fontenay. How delightful to see you again."

I disregarded his hand and did not raise my hat.

"The last time we met, you did not express such delight."

"When was that?" he asked in a tone of surprise.

"At the Royal Academy a year ago."

He spread out his hands. "I don't remember to have had the pleasure of seeing you at the Royal Academy; all the more because I never went there."

"You were standing in front of one of my pictures. You chose not to recognize me—or my step-daughter and nephew, who were with me."

"Really," said he with a perfect air of puzzlement, "I don't understand. When was this supposed encounter?"

"About the middle of May."

He laughed indulgently. "My dear sir, it could not have been I, for I was not in London at the time. The whole of the month of May I spent in Brussels."

Again I say that, had I no grudge against him, I should have admired him as the most accomplished liar it had ever been my lot to meet. Said I:

"Can't we find somewhere less public than this?"— I waved a hand around.

"Certainly." All oily courtesy, he led me down the lounge till we found one of the bays deserted. He sat down. He offered me an *apéritif* which I declined. It was the hour—just before lunch, he urged. I refused again.

"What I have to say ought not to take many minutes. In the first place it is no use your lying to me. You were in London under the name of Miguel Vargas y Uriostos. You had your own reasons for not wishing to be recognized—reasons more or less explained to me by the police at New Scotland Yard. You fled, as you fled from Cannes—and took steamer to Buenos Aires."

"My good Monsieur Fontenay," he replied, "your excellent London police have been following a chimera. I never heard of the name—Uriostos—what?—in my life; and I haven't been to Buenos Aires for many years. Not even been to South America."

He pulled out his watch and rose. He must beg me to excuse him. It was later than he thought and he was expecting a friend to lunch. I rose too, very angry.

"Then why did you lie to the Casino people yesterday and tell them that you had been exploring the Andes?"

With a reddening of his dark face his manner changed.

"It seems that you are seeking a quarrel with me, Monsieur Fontenay."

"I don't quarrel with thieves and rogues," said I.

"I am a South American and a bad enemy, Monsieur Fontenay."

"You're a damned bad everything," said I in English, for we had been talking French. *Cartes sur table,* eh? I know all about you. Do you think my nephew didn't tell me of tying you up? Do you think that what I have read of the letters of the unfortunate Señora Luisa hasn't told me what manner of man you are? Do you think that my friends at the head of the London police are fools, Monsieur Antonio Perez?"

His congested face grew livid.

"Mention that name again and, by God, you are a dead man!"

"Do anything to cause me displeasure," said I, "and the French police will put handcuffs on you."

"You'll be dead before they do it," he snarled.

He strode out of the bay down the central gangway of the lounge. I followed him into the hall, sick with horrible foreboding. He was expecting someone to lunch. Nadia, of course. But surely she would have sent me word, or come to me for protection. Yet, on the other hand—and the thought smote me like a blow over the heart—what did I know about that strange Russian soul? I sat down on a couch by the restaurant door and waited, while Garcia paced up and down like a lost soul, every now and then casting at me malevolent glances. Once, losing control, he halted in front of me.

"Are you too waiting for somebody?"

"Of course, Monsieur. Otherwise, why should I be here?"

"That is good. For, listen to me, I have a short way with spies."

I snapped my fingers and called him a windbag, and, in this grand manner, turned my back on him.

It was the most agonizing wait I have ever experienced. The seconds dawdled into minutes. At the sight of every natty feminine figure, with face hidden under the shapeless, hideous modern headgear, entering through the revolving doors, my heart leaped in anticipated terror. Presently my brain cleared a little and I rose. It was essential that I, and not he, should be the first to greet her. I passed through the revolving doors and waited on the pavement, while the cars conveying the hungry crowd of lunchers swept up the semicircular path, stopped for the minute or two of disburdenment and drove empty down the other quadrant.

An open horse-cab drew up, occupied by an elderly white-moustached gentleman. I had a confused sense of familiarity. But it was only when he descended and turned to pay the cabman that I recognized him.

It was the Marchese della Fontana.

His quick eyes pounced on me, and he rushed at me in eager greeting. How did it go with me? And with my most charming daughter? And that interesting young man, my nephew? I responded by asking news of the Marchesa. She was well. He had left her in their villa at Biarritz. He had just arrived that morning in Cannes. Had I seen our good friend Ramon Garcia? He was engaged to lunch with him; a little late. But an old fellow like him must take time to repair the ravages of travel. He looked as clean and as spruce and as much at ease with himself as ever. He was staying, he informed me, at a small hotel near the station, as it were, incognito. Just a little visit on affairs. His villa, et cetera. He hoped we should meet soon. He wrung my hand warmly and entered the hotel.

Not a word of reference to Nadia, from which it seemed

reasonable to conjecture that the two rogues were lunching alone together.

There was only one thing to be done. I took a taxi from the stand in front of the Palace and drove to the Hôtel Mont Fleuri.

The concierge smiled on me. Madame la Princesse had just gone into the salle-à-manger. Yes, she was alone.

I gave up hat and stick and marched into the diningroom. From her table Nadia saw me and smiled and waved a welcoming hand. I approached.

"My dear, what a beautiful surprise! *Garçon, un couvert pour Monsieur.* For you will lunch with me, won't you? I have only just begun."

Her gaiety proclaimed her ignorance of Ramon Garcia's movements. At any rate, I had arrived in time to prepare her for new blackmailings and to defend her from them to the utmost of my powers. I sat down, and, while the preliminaries of my meal were being attended to, we spoke of trivial things. When we were at peace, she regarded me with an air of concern.

"My dear David, you look worried. It was not to have a little feast with me that you came. Something has happened."

I told her. She grew very white. For conversation's sake we made a pretence of eating, and, as soon as we could, escaped from the dining-room and found a quiet spot in the hotel garden. There I related at fuller length the story of my morning. She listened, nervously clasping and unclasping her hands. Her attitude was piteousness itself. Once she cried:

"If only I had remained in the convent!"

"You would have died of grey weariness, my Nadia. It was better to come out into the sunshine and face

things. Besides, am I not here to face them with you?"
She laid a light touch on my knee and smiled sadly.

"Yes, my dear. I know I oughtn't to be afraid. But
I am. Now that he has resumed confidence in his position in France, he will have all the audacities. And why
has he summoned my uncle from Biarritz? There is
some conspiracy between them of which I am the
subject."

I tried to combat the proposition, which I felt was
indisputable. I am a poor liar and I am afraid my words
brought no conviction.

"*Mon pauvre ami,*" she said, "what can a sensitive
artist like you do against them? You must let me
defend myself. If you get in Ramon's way, he will find
some means of stabbing you in the back."

I smiled reassuringly: "My Nadia, my reputation,
thank God, is unassailable—at least my conscience tells
me so. He can stab as much as he likes."

"It is not your reputation," she replied, with fright
in her eyes. "It is your body that he will stab."

Again I laughed. I had not told her of his braggart
threats. A scamp of Garcia's type runs the risk of the
guillotine only when his sexual passions are involved,
or when the lure of a vast fortune blinds reason. In
the present case there were neither of these motives.
And Ramon was as cowardly a dog as ever barked and
ran away as soon as one bent down to pick up a stone.

"I'll take all the risks," said I.

"I don't want you to take them, David."

"But I'm going to." My vanity was pricked by what
seemed to be her lack of confidence in my supermanhood.
"And what I'm going to do now, this minute," I declared,
"is to take you straight from here to the Villa. Your
maid can pack your things and bring them along in the

course of an hour or so. Of course, there's a room for her. Dorothea will stay in Cannes as long as I like, so there'll be no outrage of the proprieties. If Garcia or your uncle desires to see you, they can do so, at my house and in my presence."

She stared in front of her, with parted lips and shook her head slowly.

"No. I can't do that."

"You would, Nadia, if you loved me."

She started up and came within my encircling arm.

"Yes, yes, David. I do love you and I trust you. It is only for your sake."

I smiled into her anxious face and assured her that my sake was her sake and all our sakes. She must be an obedient little princess and do as I told her. I rose and held out my hand. She took it and followed me to the hotel. I saw her into the lift and gave her injunctions to bring Chouchou with her. I went to the telephone and bade Dorothea prepare her room and send Maxime at once with the car. Now and then the high gods bestow upon a man in love a gleam of intelligence. If I had put my proposal before her as a matter for discussion, we should have argued about it for hours. But, guided by this Heaven-sent gleam, I gave her definite orders, with the result that twenty minutes afterwards she came down, the dog in her arms, followed by the maid, a treasure she had told me she discovered in Paris, carrying odds and ends of feminine paraphernalia. Maxime was there. We drove off.

"Now, my dear," said I, as soon as we were safe in the Villa, "now that you are to live beneath my roof, I feel sure that you're my very, very own."

At the drawing-room door appeared Dorothea, who threw her arms about her and drew her into the blue marvel of sea and sky and dreaming promontory. Dorothea burst into fervent assurance of love and comfort and protection. And I, putting a hand on the shoulder of each beloved woman, turned to Dorothea and said, perhaps very absurdly:

> "Neither harm, nor spell, nor charm
> Come our lovely lady nigh."

CHAPTER XX

THERE had I my beautiful Princess under ward and lock, with myself as Governor of the Tower, Dorothea as wardress, and my excellent servants as devoted gaolers. I defied harm to come to her. We drew up the terms of her custody. Within the grounds she was free to walk—round the little rock garden and up and down the declivitous hill-side that ended on the Boulevard du Midi, that is to say, the road by the seashore. The wicket gate at the bottom of the path, for the first time in its history, was locked, and the key hung up in the hall. Should the Princess desire to walk abroad, it was agreed that she should do so only under my escort. Should she desire to go further afield in the car, she would be protected either by myself or Dorothea. Access to her presence should be permitted only after a council held by the three of us.

When we had drafted this protocol, we sat down and awaited events.

We had not long to wait. About six o'clock came a telephone call from the Marchese. Would I have the kindness to spare him a few moments on business of grave importance? I replied that I was at his service. Five minutes or so later he was announced and shown into the studio.

"Mr. Fontenay," said he, "I learn on enquiring at the Mont Fleuri that my niece, the Princess Ramiroff, has left the hotel on a visit to you."

"On a visit to my daughter," I corrected.

"Perhaps the sudden events of to-day have been the motives of your daughter's invitation?"

"I am not aware," I answered truthfully, "of my daughter's motives."

He flicked his white, carefully tended hands.

"After all, it makes no difference. She is under your roof. May I have a short conversation with her in private?"

"If she desires it, most certainly, Marchese; but I don't think she does. I am entirely in her confidence, so what you would say to her, you may say, without compromising anybody, to myself."

Said the Marchese, with the great dignity of a little spick and span, white moustachioed nobleman:

"You arrogate to yourself, Monsieur, rights that I cannot recognize."

"Your inability distresses me," said I.

"I could only recognize this—superficially—on certain grounds."

"The grounds which you have the delicacy to insinuate are non-existent."

"That is easily said."

"If a man younger and less privileged by relationship, Marchese, said that to me," I retorted, trying to keep my temper, "he would find himself very quickly either in the rue Georges Clemenceau or the Mediterranean. It would only depend on which was most handy at the moment."

"Then, again, I ask you, Monsieur," said the unruffled Marchese, "what rights have you over the Princess Ramiroff?"

"The rights of asylum which she has in my house."

"Monsieur Fontenay," said he, "I am sorry to have to use plain speech with you——"

"Of that," said I, "I feel quite certain."

"Monsieur!" He drew himself up indignantly.

"What can I do more," said I blandly, "than agree with your statement?   Pray, proceed."

"It comes to this, that you have no right to give asylum to a woman who is claimed by her husband."

This, I acknowledged, was plain speaking.   "You come then to the Princess as an accredited—I almost said discredited—ambassador from our beautiful friend Ramon Garcia."

"A very much wronged and honourable gentleman."

"My dear Marchese," said I, "do me the credit of recognizing me as an elderly sinner, who knows a crook when he sees him.   Also believe me when I say that I have the police *dossier* of Monsieur Garcia which proves him not to be an honourable gentleman.   But as to his being very much wronged—by you—that I admit frankly.   The history of the false pearls, I cannot regret to say, is not unknown to me."

He jumped up from his chair and thumped the little table by his side.

"Monsieur, I repudiate my responsibility for the pearls.   They were the pearls which Messieurs Lautier Frères sold me."

The discussion was becoming wearisome.   With difficulty I drummed into his head my acquaintance with the authentic story—the sale of the genuine pearls to the lady from Missouri.   At last he put on his grand air.

"I demand to see my niece."

I informed him that only accompanied by the Commissaire de Police, who would require admission in the name of the law, would I even inform the Princess of his visit.

There was a long silence, during which, after offering him various forms of alcohol and tobacco, which he refused, I lit a cigarette and put a log or two on the fire

and pottered around, while he sat, with his sleek white
head buried in his hands. Presently I was aware that
he had broken down, and that tears were trickling between his fingers. I touched his shoulder.

"Marchese——" I began.

He lifted an old, worn face. "Monsieur Fontenay,"
said he, "I am an old man and no longer have the
strength of youth. I have acted wrongly, foolishly, I
confess. Pray bear with me."

My heart went out to the pitiable and crumpled old
man. I was conscious of having won some kind of
victory. But there are victories, even the most legitimate, which leave you remorseful. For a young man—
and my middle age was nothing to his seventy years—
there are few things more poignant than an old head
bowed down before him, in dishonour. I told him that
not only would I bear with him, but would do anything
he liked, provided that he ranged himself openly and
defiantly by the side of the Princess and myself. In
his emotional Italian way he rose and gripped my two
hands, and suddenly freeing himself, pointed at them.

"You are right. Into those, the hands of an English
gentleman, I commit my honour."

I repeat, it was very touching. But I was unaware
of the extent of his commitment.

"It is essential, Marchese," said I, "that you should
speak to me in absolute frankness."

When the Latins keep their heads, they manifest in
argument the succinct speech and the logical development of idea of their literary ancestry. They can be
as close and definite as Tacitus. But when once their
emotions run away with their brains, they throw back
to the unrestrained savage races whence they sprang and
over which Rome spread its veneer of civilization.

The old Marchese abandoned the polite French in which we had been conversing and burst out into a torrent of Italian which I happen to understand, but speak haltingly. It was mostly sound and fury signifying nothing. But there were bits which revealed the situation.

My reading of it was this:

Ramon Garcia, full (I was sure) of ill-gotten money, had reappeared in the social world, confident, and expecting everybody else to be confident, in his integrity. In the insolence of his position, he had summoned the Marchese to this meeting in Cannes. Behind the summons there sounded something more than a hint of blackmail. So long as the Marchese could bluff out the story of the pearls, he was safe. But Ramon Garcia held the Princess's imprudent and wild letters in which she explicitly incriminated her uncle. Hence arose quite a different state of affairs. There was the question of the original card-debt—you will remember that the Marchesa had cancelled the difference between that and the purchase money of the necklace. This the Marchese, having had a streak of luck at Biarritz, offered to pay in return for jewels, certificates and letters. Garcia, at lunch, had waved aside the proposal with the air of a millionaire. A few thousand francs! It meant nothing to him. It would merely keep his new Hispano-Sousa car in petrol for a month or two. Money to him was of little concern. Had he not proved it by his year's silence? A grasping man would not have had such consideration. A far more delicate matter had induced him to seek the interview.

It was then that Garcia had staggered the old man with the announcement of his marriage, the year before, to the Princess. Both men knew from the Paris-English newspapers of her return to Cannes, and her address at the Mont Fleuri. Their type has to read the social news with the same hawk eye as the speculator follows the daily Stock Exchange quotations, or as the earnest and ignorant bride devours the cooking receipts in the weekly journals. Both the Marchese and his wife had written to Nadia and she had replied in colourless terms. Of her marriage, Garcia's spoken word had been the first intimation.

"I don't know who Monsieur Garcia may be, but I do know that his social position cannot qualify him to be the husband of my niece. Her descent—ah!——"

The old man wept again. This time he allowed himself to be comforted by a cocktail and a cigarette. Garcia, said he, had put before him a speciously honourable proposition. Let the Princess, under the Marchese's persuasion, acknowledge the marriage to the social world of Cannes, and take up their position as man and wife, and all compromising articles should be handed over to him. Otherwise Garcia had no option but to take legal proceedings. What could he do? He implored me to help him.

"My dear sir," said I, "why didn't you talk like this to me when you first came in. I feel rather hurt at your —let us say—your depreciation of my intelligence."

He replied apologetically that he had thought to succeed in a policy beyond his powers. He was an old man, he repeated, and his strength had given way. Now he was at my mercy. Also at that of his niece.

"What am I to do to save the honour of myself, my wife and the Princess Ramiroff?"

What the deuce could the poor old rascal do? I am afraid I looked at him rather helplessly.

"I know I have brought it all on myself. But *que*

voulez vous?   My wife and I have to live in the position in which it has pleased God to set us.   I keep a *tripot*—a gambling-hell you call it in English.   But it is a precarious means of livelihood.   The margin of chance, naturally, is in my favour.   But sometimes luck goes against me.   So what can I do but adopt occasional means of correcting Fortune?   Those in whose disfavour I am compelled to correct it, are rich and entirely undeserving of her favours.   Except in this case I do not think I have made a mistake in the whole course of an honourable life.   Who would have expected an adventurer like Garcia—Oh, no, Monsieur Fontenay—I was not deceived by him one minute—I know my world—who would have expected him to go straight to Lautier Frères, instead of disposing of the necklace, as you know I disposed of the original, at an immense profit?   It is heartbreaking."

And so did the immoral old gentleman proceed for a considerable time.   No idea of his mean depravity seemed to have crossed his mind.   He was a bit of flotsam battered about by the waves of evil chance.   God, whom he invoked, had called him to a certain lofty status in life.   If he had not the material means to maintain himself thereon, it was the obvious fault of the Almighty and not of himself.   But, on the other hand, to descend voluntarily from that status would be a sacrilegious flouting of the Deity, which, to him, a pious man, was unthinkable.   So, in order to carry out the divine decree, he cheated wherever he had a perfectly safe opportunity.   For the greater glory of God he appeared before the world as the great gentleman which he was created, and had never allowed the breath of scandal to tarnish his nobility.

I truly believe that this was the faith in which the Marchese della Fontana, with quarterings of half the proud and princely houses of Italy on his coat-of-arms, had lived and would, after the way of mortals, one of these days, die. It would have been a vain matter for me to point out the impropriety of his way of life. It had marked that of forbears, direct and collateral, in mediæval and Renaissance times. He was bound in what Paul Bourget, in a recent novel *La Géôle*, calls, "The prison of heredity." Those ancestors were like children. What they saw they wanted, and what they wanted, if they were strong enough, they took. At a large family luncheon table, at dessert, many years ago, cried a tiny friend of mine, now, I must say, a grown-up and most adorable being: *"If there's any cream, I need it."* Observe, it was not the expression of a mere desire; it was the assertion of a physical right, to which, in the baby mind, the inconsiderable necessities of the whole luncheon party should, without question, be sacrificed.

"If there's any money going about, I need it," said the Marchese della Fontana, with, I am sure, the same self-bound simplicity and lack of *arrière pensée* of my tiny friend.

This digression is not quite so irrelevant as it may seem. Had it not been for Nadia, I should have been impressed by the Marchese's troubles only in so far as they revealed to one curious of the by-ways of human nature the atavistic reversion to a childish moral outlook on life. As the non-moral descendant of those who took what they needed, irrespective of the claims of anyone else, he must get out of the mess he had made in the modern world as best he could. But—and there's the rub—into the middle of the mess had he inextricably dragged the little dainty princess of my heart's desire.

I couldn't say to him: "You wicked old man, you have brought all the trouble upon yourself, so don't ask an honest gentleman to help you." Rhadamanthus himself would have blubbered in sympathy.

I had to stretch out to him the hand of friendship and promise him the limit of my protection from the base-born, non-coat-of-armoured fellow-rascal, who had dared to interfere with his aristocratic and divine right of rapine.

"And now," he said, "what are we going to do, my dear friend?"

"That remains to be thought out. If I were you, I should go straight back to Biarritz and refer Garcia to me."

"Monsieur Fontenay"—his attitude was that of courtliest apology—"when I first came, I brusquely asked you by what right you gave asylum to my niece. May I repeat the question more courteously and from a different point of view?"

"From that different point of view," I answered, smiling, "I will answer your question. The Princess has promised to marry me as soon as the divorce proceedings, which are already initiated, come to a satisfactory end. I presume you have no objection to me as her suitor and prospective husband?"

He replied, with a bow, which should have had the accompaniment of silk stockings and lace ruffles, that nothing would give him more delight.

"But," said he, "you should have obtained the decree months ago. The return of this dreadful man alters everything. She cannot, as far as I know the Code Civil, divorce him when he is anxious to take her as his wife. It is for him to divorce her, which he has his reasons for not wishing to do."

Nadia had said something of the sort. But she referred to the position before their respective disappearances from our ken. The present situation was far more serious than I imagined. I went off on a side issue.

"If he is so keen to have the marriage made public, why doesn't he announce it himself?"

The old Marchese gave explanation, which forced itself on me almost as soon as the words were out of my mouth. As the acknowledged husband of the Princess Ramiroff and thus acquiring her status in international society, he could scarcely prosecute her uncle for a criminal offence.

"That makes things awkward," said I, but I put on my best manner and strove to reassure him. After a while of talk he asked humbly whether now he could see his niece for a few moments, in order to deliver her aunt's affectionate messages. I left him with a second cocktail and a cigarette and went in search of Nadia. I found her in the drawing-room with Dorothea. I sketched the situation hurriedly. She consented to meet him, but in my presence. We returned to the studio. The old gentleman kissed her forehead solemnly, enquired after her health, gave her news of that of the Marchesa, and dwelt on the calmative influences of conventual retreat. Nadia made apposite remarks. It was a graceful little comedy.

"The object of my visit," said he, "was to discuss with you matters that you could not but regard as painful; but our dearest of friends here has relieved me of that more than heavy responsibility. In his hands I placed my honour and my fortune and I am more than content to leave yours in them also. You have all my most earnest wishes for your happiness. Monsieur Fontenay"—he turned to me—"I take my leave with a far lighter heart than when I greeted you this evening."

He again embraced her, in his dignified way, and we

accompanied him to the street door. He swept us a gallant salute and ran down the steps like a young man without a care in the world.

After dinner the three of us held council of war. Nadia was tired and depressed; frightened, too, at Ramon's presence in Cannes, in spite of the guarded fortress in which she found herself. Said Dorothea to me:

"If you two are so keen on each other, why don't you get a price from Garcia for the restoration of everything and consent to the divorce. It'll be rather stiff, but if I were in your place, Daddums, I should think Nadia worth it."

"If the worst comes to the worst, that's exactly what I intend to do," said I.

But Nadia, with a sudden flush in her cheeks and an incomprehensible frostiness in her eyes, would have none of it. No. She loved me, but she was not going to be bought from her husband like a woman of a savage tribe. It was revolting.

"You would always have at the back of your mind, when you paraded me on your arm—'Here is the little lady whom I purchased for a million, two, three million francs, whatever it might be.' Oh, no, no! A thousand times no!"

I felt as though she had struck me in the face. Dorothea anticipated my reply.

"Nadia, you ought to be damn-well ashamed of yourself."

"How would you like to be bought?" Nadia flashed. "You, with your English pride. Do you think Russians have not equal pride to yours? Even greater?"

I stepped in pacifically between them, for here was the beginning of a not very pretty quarrel.

"Nadia, you know that I would impoverish myself for your sake." I smiled and quoted: " 'All for love and the world well lost.'   But——"

She would not listen to the qualification. "I do not wish you to impoverish yourself. I forbid you to spend a penny."

"Listen," said I. "I had not finished. Remember I said: 'If the worst comes to the worst.' But there are other ways. Who in Cannes, for instance, knows of Antonio Perez?"

In her pessimistic mood she shrugged her shoulders.

"And who cares?"

"Ramon does, very much indeed. When I mentioned the name to him to-day, he was really quite cross with me. Although I shall insist on seeing him to-morrow, I doubt whether we are on speaking terms."

Dorothea, understanding, smiled. But Nadia, usually so responsive to shades of expression, made a passionate gesture.

"You turn everything into a jest, you English. Why don't you go and kill him?"

"Perhaps I will," said I, "but I should rather like him to try to kill me first."

She cried: "If only I were a man!"

"You wouldn't be in this position, my dear," said Dorothea.

Nadia turned on her. "Ah you—you have nothing to do with this."

"Yes, I have," replied Dorothea. "I strongly object to my father going out and assassinating Ramon Garcia. It's too silly for words."

"If you both think I'm talking like a foolish woman," said the little Princess, with great dignity, "there is nothing left for me but to retire."

She swept towards the door. I rushed to intercept her.

"My darling Nadia——"

"I am not your darling Nadia," she retorted, with the glacier ice in her green eyes, "You would give money for me. Any rich man can do that. But you will not give your life."

In a flash, she was through the door which she slammed behind her.

Dorothea came up with a friendly hug. "My poor old Daddums, I've afraid we've been and gone and done it."

I asked her if she had ever heard such unreason.

"I've practised it myself for years," she replied. "And so has every woman with whom you've been acquainted."

CHAPTER XXI

I CANNOT say that my interview with Ramon Garcia, supercilious in insolent security, was a success, either of diplomacy or of the owner of the whip-hand. I certainly mentioned the name of Antonio Perez to him, and remained unkilled. That was so much to the good. I should exceedingly dislike to be killed. It would be the final interference with my comfort and would upset all the schemes on which I had set my heart. Neither did I carry out Nadia's Beatrice-like behest and kill Garcia and eat his heart out in the market-place. Had I done so, the French Republic could have got hold of me and kept me in an uncomfortable prison for a couple of years, at the end of which they would have cut off my head. It were preferable that Garcia should assassinate me; for it would have come to the same thing in the end, as far as I was concerned, and I should have been spared the dismal years of waiting.

Of course he repeated his threat, but more vaguely. He did not defy me on a specific count. He had a small suite looking on to the tennis courts, on which the last tournament of the season was being played. I think I annoyed him by going now and then on to the balcony and appearing to take more interest in the nearest match than in his conversation. Hence a counsel I would give to the young: Always keep calm and put your adversary in a vile temper. You can nearly always restrain him from physical violence, but he can't restrain himself immoderation of speech. I flatter myself that my attitude was cool and mordant, while he flew in such

301

red and purple rages that his superficial politeness deserted him entirely. He used beastly language in which he gave himself away as Antonio Perez. He admitted, nay, proclaimed, in his foaming anger, that he had fooled us all and spent months in Buenos Aires.

He declared that his admissions were but to demonstrate what a grass-eating, non-intelligent, inconsiderable beast of the field I was. What could I prove? That my savage of a nephew had taken him unawares while sleeping, in the most dastardly manner, and had stolen his private correspondence. It was only pressure of business affairs and respect for my honourable position in Cannes that had prevented him from proceeding to the utmost rigour of the law. And the letters? What concern were they to any court in France? In what possible way could they be brought before any tribunal? To prove what a *mauvais sujet* he was? Bah! They could only be produced, if he were being tried for a grave offence, and then they would be rejected by the court as irrelevant. In short, he demanded, for what specific act, since I was amiable enough to impute to him the charge of swindling, could he be arrested? For alleged follies with a rich and foolish woman in Rio de Janeiro, under the name of Antonio Perez? Bah! once more! Had not the besotted Senhor Alvarez, the Brazilian minister declared, before a Commissaire de Police in Paris, that he was not Antonio Perez? Would he dare to stultify himself by eating his words? Not he. In his Spanish estimation, a Portuguese was such a stupendous fool that he would rather cut his throat than be proved one. Very much like the English. So that, he declared, snapping his fingers most unpleasantly under my nose, was the end of the matter. Meanwhile he remained a wealthy gentleman from Ecuador. I suggested that

enquiries at the Ecuadorian Legation in Paris would prove
that he was not.   There were two, he declared trium-
phantly, two Ramon Garcias, with great estates, and he
might be either of them.   In detail he countered me on all
points.   As for the divorce, he would not hear of it.
Had she not banished him, two hours after their marriage, on account of this baseless charge, this horrible
suspicion?   Had he not, through motives of supreme
delicacy, left her for a while?   Had he not written her
impassioned letters for nearly a year, to which he had
received no response?   Had he not come to Cannes now,
for the sole purpose of urging her, in the French legal
phrase, to *réintégrer le domicile conjugal?*

"And to get possession of her few trumpery jewels,"
said I, "which, on my word of honour, are of small importance to any crook of such high standing as yourself."

"But I am a man as well as what you choose to call
me."   The veins stood out on his forehead.   "I have
sworn to God that I shall have that woman in my arms."

My laugh must have resembled that of the hyena,
for I felt almost physically sick at the thought of the outrage.   This was one of the occasions when I went to the
window and looked out at the tennis and closed my ears
to revolting words.   Then, at last, when he had evacuated
his store of verbiage, I turned.

"You're a self-confessed impostor and blackmailer.
I am not a rich man, but I have certain capital.   How
much will you take to surrender everything and to give
us your collusion in the divorce?"

He almost spat at me in his impudent triumph.   He
called me all sorts of insulting names.

"What is the use to me, a millionaire, of your mean
two or three hundred thousand francs, which is all you
could afford me?   A millionaire?   Yes, you English

duck. The lady, Luisa, is dead, and she has bequeathed to me her enormous fortune. I could buy you and yours a hundred times over."

For a moment or two I was silenced. Such a possibility had not entered my mind. It was, however, a reasonable explanation of his sudden accession to wealth. Luisa, most certainly, had existed. Her letters gave implicit evidence of her fortune; also explicit evidence of her passionate love for the rascal father of her two children. There was nothing abnormal in the fact of the poor woman dying.

"If you wish to know," said he, "her illness was the cause of my leaving England so suddenly. I remained with her to the last. She made her will, as I say, in my favour."

"What about the inquest?" I asked coldly.

Then again he burst into his Latin-American fury. Was I accusing him of being a murderer?

"I would accuse you of anything," said I.

He sputtered things in his wrath. I was this, that and the other to dare to accuse him. The inquest proved that the lady had died from natural causes.

"So there was an inquest?"

He stared at me for a moment, realizing that he had fallen into the trap of the leading question. He formulated more uncomplimentary indictments of me, while I looked out of the window.

"There's a most interesting game going on here," said I.

He damned both me and the game.

"And the two motherless children?" I asked, after a while.

"If you are so anxious to know my private affairs, I have knocked their heads together until they are dead."

I smiled and stood up before him, my hands in my trousers pockets.

"My dear fellow, why complicate the simple truth you have told me with exaggeration?"

"Because, Monsieur, my affairs are in no way your business."

"On the contrary," said I, "you don't seem to realize that your affairs are the absorbing interest of my existence."

We went on like this for some time longer—backwards and forwards over the ground of our dispute. He claimed the right to visit the Princess. I stated that the Princess was my guest and that on no consideration whatever would I permit him to cross my threshold. I would give instructions that even my telephone would not be at his disposal. Letters—yes—the Princess's correspondence was naturally sacred. If she chose to give him rendezvous outside my gates, I could not restrain her—she was a free agent. But I should strongly advise her to trust to my protection.

"After all," I said, "what can you expect? She regards you with horror as a swindling adventurer and a blackmailer."

At last he made a crisp declaration.

For the charge of blackmail he cared not a centime. Blackmail was a weapon which gentlemen used as a rapier and not as a bludgeon. He, with Hidalgo blood in his veins, could only use the rapier. He would give both the Marchese and the Princess a week to consider the situation. His ambition was to be the declared husband of the Princess Ramiroff. His simple man's passion was to be the effective husband of the glorious woman whom he had married. In her horror, which it was natural for me to invent, he did not believe. Women

were always saying foolish things and repenting of them
even before they were said.

"I, Monsieur, have perhaps more experience than you.
To attract women, young and old, has been my profession
and my pride, even before I reached manhood."

I called him a beast; but he only smiled.

"I only state facts. Discussion is useless. Let us
look to the future."

He developed his plans.   If, after a week, the Princess
and the Marchese proved recalcitrant, the law should
deal with the Marchese, whose conduct in selling him
false pearls he invited me as the flower of English honour
to define.   I reminded him that his out of pocket expenses,
as it were, had been redeemed by the Marchese's cheque.
Only the gambling debt, not recoverable by law, was
due to him.   It pleased him to jeer at the proposition.
He had the advice of the best *avoué* and *avocat* in
Paris.

Again he snapped his fingers and thumb under my
nose.   For the first time I lost my temper and, with a
"Don't do that!" which, to a spectator might have seemed
comic, I dashed my open hand in his face.   He staggered
away.

"Now I shall certainly kill you."

I recovered my balance. 'Why don't you do it?"
I asked.

Furiously he pulled open three or four drawers of a
bureau and at last plucked out a huge Browning.   I
must confess to a certain nervousness.   But even before
I started a rush at him, in self-defence, either a chord
of memory must have sounded in his brain, or it must
have been play-acting, for he dashed the unloaded
weapon on the floor.

"Caraio!" he cried, which is one of the naughtiest things, I believe, one can say in Spanish.

I burst into irrepressible laughter of reaction and made what I think was a dramatic exit. I laughed most of the way down in the lift, to the discreet astonishment of the attendant. When I reached the Croisette I began to put my mind in order.

I had won but a Pyrrhic victory. As I have said, all I had done was to wring from him full admission of his crooked career; also to confirm my theory of his physical cowardice. After I had pushed his face, I expected him to fall upon me tooth and claw—indeed, being a middle-aged man of not the robustest physique, I confess that I passed an anxious second or two—but all he could do to avenge the insult was to try to assassinate me with a pistol which, on mature reflection, I am sure he knew was unloaded. That way lay comedy. On the other hand, he held a very strong position, of which no qualms of honour or conscience would prevent him from taking the fullest advantage. The only legal point in our favour was the Marchesa's cheque—and that might be explained away by the subtlety of the legal mind. I felt myself to be floundering in a hopeless morass. Supposing, thought I, I went to him with my old service revolver— I should have a few cartridges left—and at the point of it demanded his blackmailing outfit? But the irrepressible Comic Spirit prevailed. I saw the scene pictured cinematographically as an episode in some abominably vulgar melodrama. No; it must be a battle of wits. After all, the rogue had given us a week's grace.

I found the Princess awaiting me on the drawing-room

terrace, in her favourite sea-green attire. The orange-tawny Chouchou, inheritor of the subtlety of his Chinese ancestry, welcomed me with arched tail, wriggling body, feathery tramplings of his outspread fore-paws, and proud uplifting of his leonine little head. I caressed him for the second or two that is prescribed for Advantageous Persons in the Book of Ceremonies of the Pekinese, and then he curled himself up in great dignity at his mistress's feet. The ceremony over I advanced to the Princess. I kissed her hand and held it, while she looked at me out of her ironical eyes, with a little mocking smile playing around her lips.

"Dorothea has beaten me. I am black and blue all over. She threatens to turn me out, with my boxes, into the rue Georges Clémenceau to wait for a train, if I do not say that you are the most perfect and most delicate-minded of human beings, with the profoundest knowledge of a woman's soul."

I sat down beside her on the cane settee, still holding her hand, and smiled.

"And do you say it?"

"Oh yes, I say it."

"And you're not angry with me any more?"

"That's not the question."

"It is," said I, "because I adore you——"

I must have gone on with my rhapsody for five minutes by the clock. At the end of it, she was all radiance.

"*Très bien.* That's how a woman likes to be talked to. *Mon David chéri,*" she put her lips invitingly close— "I am angry with you no longer."

After a pleasurable interlude of reconciliation, we came to business.

"And you have not bought me after all?"

I told her Ramon's story of inherited wealth. In

fact, I related—I think picturesquely—my recent interview. When I came to the pushing of Ramon's face,
she laughed her silvery laugh and flung her arms around
my neck.   For the first time in my life I felt a Paladin.

"That's just as good as killing him," she declared.

"I'm afraid it isn't," said I, "for it has made him
more cross and malignant than ever."

She looked pensively at the point of her tiny white-
shod foot.

"If he only were a brave man——"

"What then?" I asked.

She shrugged her shoulders and still contemplated
her shoe.   There was a span of silence.

"What would you have done if a man had pushed
your face?"

Such a question an Englishman can only answer
jestingly. I said that I should have done my best to
mutilate him beyond repair.   She took the reply seriously
and touched the ribbons, Legion of Honour and Croix
de Guerre, which, living in France and out of courtesy
to French custom, I wear in my buttonhole.   To explain
the gauds to you, I may mention that I was acting
liaison officer when I very foolishly and rashly got the
bullet through my lung, which determined my domicile
in Cannes.   For being able to speak French they gave
me the red ribbon, and for my pure and ignorant idiocy
in exposing myself to a Boche bullet they gave me the
Croix de Guerre. The Princess touched the ribbons,
however. I could not go into all the details of depreciation. At the moment, I confess, I had no particular
desire to do so.

"These are proofs of your courage."

"They're nothing of the kind," said I.

She made the funny familiar gesture of waving hands.

"You English are all the same. I once met a V.C.—
that is your greatest honour, the Victoria Cross, isn't
it? I asked him how he won it. He said he was between
the devil and the deep sea, and was, how you call it?"—
she rubbed her finger-tips together—"yes, in a blue
funk; and he thought the devil's side was safer and
he went and they gave him the Victoria Cross. If he
had chosen what he thought was the most dangerous,
he would never have got it, because he would have been
killed. And I laughed, because I know you English.
A Russian or a Frenchman would have been simple
and told me just what he did. But an Englishman—no.
He is more proud than any other man; but he hides his
pride in his soul "

"And he isn't such a bad fellow after all."

"*Voilà!*" she cried, laughing. "Am I not right?
Could such words come out of the mouth of anyone but
an Englishman?"

She was in high good humour, so was I. It seemed
marvellous that she should have got the key to our
queer English psychology. I don't think I ever adored
her more than at this moment.

"All this is very well," said I, "but what on earth
are we going to do?"

"*Nitchevo.* We have a clear week in front of us.
Let us run over to-morrow and lunch at Monte Carlo.
Just you and I. *Veux-tu?*"

I would have *vouloir*-ed anything in the world. I
promised. We spent a happy day. Once more I neglected my work, and while she took her siesta on the
studio divan I made a crayon sketch of her. We went
out for a drive through the cork forests of the Esterel
and returned from Saint-Raphael by the wonderful
Corniche d'Or.

The next day we motored to Monte Carlo. When we surrendered ourselves to the swooning beauty of the Bay of Villefranche, I put my arm around her and held her close and her head rested on my shoulder and the loveliness of the earth entered our souls. It was a day of windless sunshine. At Monte Carlo we sat before the Café de Paris, amid the idle throng grouped at the great umbrella-shaped tables, and sipped our *apéritifs*. The pigeons, iridescent in the sun, circled from the cornices of the long white Casino, terminating in its main rococo building. And up and down the steps, and in and out of the doors, were the never ending ascent and descent of human beings, for all the world like the eternally busy entrance to a hive. And round the circular garden separating the Café from the white Hotel de Paris, known to the coast as the *fromage,* or the Camembert, or the Cheese, wandered the seekers after the gentlest of exercise, or sat the idlers, either unthirsty or woefully careful of their pence. Among us at the Café, white-capped waiters passed with high-held trays of drinks clinking with ice and accompanied by little vases of straws. Drink-disillusioned philosopher that I am, knowing the general abominableness of these apparently enticing beverages, I am still conscious of their appeal to my imagination. As a spectacle I would mourn their suppression in dust and ashes. With some such foolish reflections was I trying to entertain my joyous companion, when suddenly a man rose from a neighbouring table and, bareheaded, approached us. It was Ramon Garcia, more offensively oiled and curled than ever, in a sartorial miracle of a peacock-blue suit and with shirt and hat and shoes in harmony. To me the effect was spoiled by an over-abundance of pearls and diamonds wherever he could stick them.

"Princesse, I could not resist coming over to offer you my devoted homage."

He held out his hand. She proffered hers, which he kissed with a flourish.

"Ah," said she, nonchalantly. *"Comment ça va?"*

"Très bien, merci. Et vous?"

She replied that equally she was in good health. Chouchou, the orange Pekinese who accompanied her, arched a rigid tail over his back and barked furiously at the intruder. Garcia showed his white teeth in a smile.

"My friend Chouchou does not welcome me."

"He speaks his mind in public, Monsieur, which convention does not permit to human beings."

"Tiens," said he, as though he had realized my presence for the first time. "It is Monsieur Fontenay."

"And neither Monsieur Fontenay, nor Madame la Princesse, nor Chouchou desire to have any further conversation with you." I rose, and, in my most affable way, so that no one at the close encircling tables should suspect that we were not on terms of polite acquaintance, I raised my hat and said, in a rather loud voice:

"Au revoir, Monsieur. It was charming of you to come and salute us."

And Nadia bent her head very graciously and said: *"Au revoir,* Monsieur."

So Monsieur, unless he had wanted to make a scene, could only grin horridly, and move away with a florid sweep of parting salutations. Nadia's face flushed delight. She squeezed my arm, and declared that I was *impayable;* which means that the wealth of the earth could not balance my personal equation. It was the only weapon to use against such submerged wretches, the domination of a fearless and distinguished personality.

"All the same," said she, "I should like to have had a little conversation with him, so as to tell him what I think of him. I, too, though you may not think it, *mon David chéri*"—she tossed her head adorably, so that her baffling little nose, of which I have spoken to you very seriously, almost disappeared as a feature— "I too have a dominating personality. I suppose we couldn't ask a waiter to call him back."

"My dear," said I, "the less you see of the brute, the better."

"As you like," she replied. "I am content to follow you blindly."

We lunched, not at Monte Carlo, where we might have met him again at close quarters, but at the Réseve of Beaulieu. Seated at a window table, with the blue sea and sky before us, and eating a *bouillabaisse,* to the making whereof the Mediterranean had entrusted all its treasures, we forgot the shadow of our common enemy, and talked light-heartedly of many things; of our love and the radiant days we should pass together when this spectre of evil should be exorcised.

"The night before last I was so wicked. It is one of the ways of women. If you thought us angels, I should have nothing to do with one so silly. The old people were very wise. In religion there are not any female angels. All are male. There are women saints—yes. But how many of them would my dear poor David wish to have married? Bah!" She sipped her old brandy poured into a vast Baccara glass from a canvas-covered *dame-jeanne,* which, Anglicè, is a demi-john. "If a woman isn't a woman no man wants her. At least, no man in his senses. And he has got to take her with all the secret workings of her mind, which depend on the physical condition of her sex. To say that a woman

can think like a man! It is nonsense. Even a sexless
woman can't. She can only think like a sexless man.
But a true woman and a true man—it is impossible that
they should think alike. It is physiological contradiction in terms. Foolish women imagine they know men.
Feed his lower appetites and he will be the little lamb
that eats out of your hand. No, my friend. I am young
and have not much experience. But I know that man is
as much a mystery to woman, in her secret soul, as
woman, in his brave outspoken way, is to man. And if
it were not like that, there could be no love outside the
physical sphere. It is the mystery of each other, with
eternal, tantalizing shafts of light shooting through it,
that binds a man and woman together. I know."

She nodded her head sagely.

I quite agreed with her as to the material mutual non-
comprehension of the sexes, but maintained a theory that
woman was the less comprehensible. Also that the
poetical young lover—in these days a *rarissima avis*—
who declared that, through her very womanhood, his
sweetheart was an angel, would be paradoxically indignant if asked to apply the same term to his washerwoman.
Indeed, we got on famously and never mentioned the
name of Ramon Garcia. After lunch we drove home,
and, as we neared Cannes, she seemed to grow more and
more light-hearted and more fantastic in her talk.

When at last we emerged on to the Croisette, and the
bay and the old town perched on the Souquet and its
towers, and the Esterel burst into sudden view, she
clapped her hands rapturously and clutched my arm.

"I love it more and more every day. When I'm happy
like this I can even love the Palace which throws the
whole place out of scale."

"Are you so very happy, Nadia?" I asked.

"Yes. I feel that all is going to be well. I feel that God is going to send us a messenger to put all things right."

I laughed, half-convinced by her faith.

We reached the Villa. As soon as François opened the door she rushed across the hall into the drawing-room. I followed her more sedately. And there, I saw her shaking by both hands a grinning Amos, while Dorothea and Bendyke Hamilton looked on benignantly.

To Amos I said: "I'm very glad to see you, but what the devil are you doing here?"

Dorothea came up to me. "He left his pipe behind him, darling, and came to fetch it before he started for England."

Amos's grin grew broader; Nadia laughed as though it were the greatest joke imaginable. Bendyke Hamilton had the tact to look out of the window.

"No, uncle," said the veracious Amos, "I had a telegram from the Princess telling me to come back. And, of course, I came."

I looked at Nadia with a wrinkled brow and questioning eye. I cannot say that I was in any way delighted by this second coming of Amos. She reproved me gaily for my ogreish air.

"And didn't I just tell you I felt sure a messenger would come? The only doubt was that Mr. Amos might have left Paris."

"I'd have come to you from Honolulu," said he.

"You couldn't do less, my friend," I remarked, drily.

"And to think that I've got him at last," cried Amos exultantly. "I knew that the Lord would deliver him into my hands."

"It seems," said I, "that it was rather the Princess."

"The Lord's Agent. His ways are wonderful. It is

not human chance, but a Divine direction that has brought them here, within a couple of days of each other."

"But, my dear friend——" began Nadia.

"What I say is quite true," Dorothea interrupted, with the most obvious collusory stare at the Princess. "You arrived on Monday. Ramon Garcia on Tuesday, and this is Thursday."

"*En effet*," said the Princess unblushingly. "It is exact. Isn't it, David?"

What could I do but yield to the atmosphere of monstrous mendacity with which Dorothea had surrounded us, in order to save her face? So long as I lied and Nadia lied and Dorothea lied, Amos was as happy as a sandboy, which seemed to be the only thing that mattered. How Dorothea had wriggled out of her disgraceful position, I still have no notion. It is a subtle faculty, denied to mere man, which is the Heaven-sent gift of women. Man's excuses are traditionally blatant. "The woman tempted me and I did eat," said Adam, and, of course, he was kicked out of Paradise. But if the Creator, Who, incidentally, knew what He was about, had unwisely tackled Eve, there would have been quite a different story about the apple-eating. And the Ancient of Days would have said to her: "My dear, I never dreamed that things were like that. You and your dear good man can go on eating apples for ever and ever." So would the course of the world have been changed and there would have been no Tutankhamen and no Germans and no dry America and no Bolsheviks to worry us; and we shouldn't be here to be worried. As I say, the Creator was perfectly right, according to His point of view; but according to mine, He might have given the world a Chance.

Dorothea was beautiful in her serenity; so was Nadia, who had read instantly Dorothea's wireless message.

Amos demanded tea, at which meal he ate vastly. Nadia's smiles brooded over him. She loved men with great appetites. She radiated happiness. Why should she be a prisoner any longer? Had she not two—nay, three—she nodded graciously to Bendyke Hamilton—stalwart defenders? Let us all dine at the Palace. It was Thursday, the Gala night dinner.

Although such entertainments are not greatly to my liking, I welcomed the suggestion. By telephone I secured a table and, so as to equalize the sexes, the company of a charming American woman, a painter, whom I wanted to sit for me and who delighted me with the fantastic proposal that she should paint me while I was painting her.

At the appointed hour the young men met us in the hall of the Palace. Amos rushed up to us, regardless of the presence of Mrs. Van Buren.

"The swine's not here. As soon as I left you, I came and asked for him. He's staying in Monte Carlo for a day or two."

I saw the admirable Bendyke adroitly kick the lower part of his calf. Amos stiffened visibly.

"Who's the unworthy pig?" asked Madame Van Buren.

"A gentleman whom my nephew doesn't like," said I. "May I introduce——?"

I made the necessary introductions. We went into dinner. Dorothea, as hostess, placed the guests, Amos between Mrs. Van Buren and herself, and Bendyke Hamilton between herself and the Princess. She has an unquestionable social way of command. Otherwise I would have suggested, through scorn of an undignified

jealousy, the shifting of places of the two young men.
But it was all done before I could utter a word. Mrs.
Van Buren took great interest in Amos, who had refresh-
ing things to say of her country. And I, cocking an ear
now and then, found that he could say them very well.

During the important part of the meal the band dis-
coursed discreet music, so that conversation was possible. Then somewhere about the ice the dancing began. I saw the one eye of Bendyke Hamilton meet the
two eyes of Amos and deliberately wink. To my amazement, Amos turned with a polite invitation to Mrs. Van
Buren and rose with her to take the floor. Dorothea,
who had her back to the dancing square, turned and
looked at him with mouth almost agape, from which position she was rescued by Bendyke Hamilton, who carried
her off. Nadia, her eyes aglow, seized my wrist.

"But look. He dances beautifully, my dear bear."

There was no denying the fact that the once shambling,
hulking fellow moved now quite correctly according to
the rules of the game.

"Your interesting neighbour"—she had been mightily
entertained by Bendyke during the meal—"is the most
marvellous trainer I have ever known."

I conceived a greater admiration than ever for Bendyke Hamilton, for his accomplishment, his tact, his
never-sleeping vigilance. Had I not caught the kick and
the wink? Trivial things, but indexes of nearly a year's
inexhaustible patience and devotion to duty.

Said Nadia: "You have no need of training. Come
along."

We swept into the maze. She danced divinely, giving
herself up to the ecstasy of the rhythm. It was her first
night out after a year's imprisonment. Her body against
mine was warm and yielding, her feet were like gossamer

things that did not count. I gave myself up to the sensuousness of it all. We stood for a second and danced the encore. I had not yet held her in such close embrace. I whispered foolish and passionate words, and her up-turned face smiled response.

The dance over, we returned to the table, with the others.

"Oh, if you only knew how wonderful and beautiful it is!"

Scarcely had we sat down again than the band struck up anew. Amos claimed her. Bendyke carried off Mrs. Van Buren. Dorothea made a wry face at me from the opposite side. Well, I was in for it. It was Nadia's fête. It was curmudgeonly not to throw oneself into it. Dorothea made me the compliment of saying that if I took a few lessons I would make all the young men take back seats. But I know my Dorothea and her tricks and her manners.

"When did you dance last, Daddums?"

"God knows," said I. "Before the war I think."

"When you marry Nadia you'll have to give up the pretence of being an elderly fogey and dance like the devil."

"I'm starting to-night, my dear," said I, feeling extraordinarily young.

It was I, who, when the dancing was over, suggested further orgy at the Casino; but Nadia confessed to fatigue. I learned later that Dorothea, in her motherly way, had whispered something to her of the old shot through the lung, which invalidated me from over-great physical strain. Dorothea and Mrs. Van Buren and the two men went off in Mrs. Van Buren's car to the Casino. Nadia and I went home alone. She, nestled in my arms, cooed her joy.

"Once when it was my life, I hated it. If it was to be my life again I should hate it again. But every now and then, when one feels starved, to abandon oneself to joyousness, oh, David *chéri,* you don't know what it is like."

The sweetest of good nights did she bid me when we reached the villa. She ran upstairs, blew me a kiss at the turn, and disappeared. The happiest of defiant mortals, I watched the last cubic content of space which she had occupied, and then, about to hang up my coat, I noticed a telegram on the hall slab. I opened it casually. But when I read it I received a great shock.

"Mrs. Fontenay dying. Come at once. Brown."

I told you long ago that I had a mother living, a fragile sphinx, in the retirement of the Somersetshire hills. Brown was the name of her companion. Every time I was in England I paid her dutiful visits. But she was so aloof from the world, leading a strange, spiritual life of her own, that my mind had conceived from my boyhood no deeper impression than something delicate and dear. Dorcas's elopement and my father's death seemed to have freed her from fleshly ties. She received me in her fragrant, Virginia-creeper-covered little red brick house with exquisiteness of welcome. But of my life she asked few questions and on it she made no demands. In late years she retained the traces of the Dresden china beauty of her youth. She was always dainty in her surroundings and her dress. Of evenings, even when she was alone with her companion, she wore lavender silk and old lace. She was proud of a collection of the early English water-colourists, and had added to the stock of Missals which Muriel had given over to her shortly after her marriage. She was not a mother who had taken a son, in petty or great trouble, in error and repentance, to her bosom and given him consolation. She was—I speak most reverently—a kind of Lady Without Sorrows. A woman whom to know was to love; yet who gave you back nothing but the unconscious graciousness of her smile and the touch of her delicate hands.

The life-long pictures of her unrolled before my mind as I held the telegram. Then, with a sigh, I went up to my room. It never crossed my mind to question the necessity of my departure by the first train to-morrow. In my material life she played no part; but in my spiritual life, clogged though it might be by material things, she had always been something elusive and precious, even perhaps wondrous, like some rare and incomprehensible creature of sea-foam who had given me birth.

It was only later, when I stared wide awake at the shaft of moonlight coming through my open window, that I started to the realization of the immediate situation in Cannes. I should have to leave Nadia to the mercy of the abominable Garcia. A week's grace had he given her. I should not be here in this critical time to cover her with my protection. And then, with a gust of gratitude and remorse, I remembered Amos.

Nadia was right. God had sent him to be her champion. And, for the first time blessing Amos in my heart, I fell asleep.

CHAPTER XXII

GENTLE rain and mist overspread the Somersetshire hills, soft in their spring green, when I arrived at the little station. The rickety taxi slithered along the red roads. The air quivered with a sigh, as for the youth of things enveloped in the mystery of doubt of future achievement. Semi-voluntary exile though I was, I felt the call of my native soil. I apostrophized it in my heart, bidding it good cheer and a cease to its young and budding melancholy. How many times in my boyhood had I sat beneath the shelter of trees and cursed, after the familiar fashion of boy's anathema, my inability to express with my amateur outfit, technical and material, that same shadowy mist half hiding the modest bosoms of the hills, with here and there a break, stark and triumphant, revealing their tender beauty.

We who live in the land of olive and cypress, in the land of exotic palms and mimosa and bougainvillea, where the seasons' difference is scarce perceived, find it a rare privilege to go north and meet an English spring. We meet what to us, having perpetual fulfilment, is denied, and what the human soul craves for ever, namely, the promise of things to come. For us there is not the inspiration of the awakening of life from its winter sleep. There is no winter, there is no sleep. Only when the exile returns, in spring, does he become reaware of this eternal miracle of things new born, the first green buds, the first shy flowers which, he knew not why, sent long years ago the thrill of hope and of joy through his young

veins. Where in the South could be rolling hillocks so
freshly green? Where such hedges hawthorn-scented?
Where such valleys of yellow daffodils? Where the enchantment of rugged oak and elm, storm-beaten mothers
centuries old, parading, almost incongruously, their new
and infinitely gracious progeny of baby leaves?

In my heart, being old, perhaps, and having lessons of
patience, I did not require the sun; but accepted, as I
had done in my boyhood, the promise: "What ye have
sown in tears ye shall reap in joy."

I was going to a house of death, for news had reached
me during my journey that the fragile lady, my mother,
had passed away. I had left a house of menace, wherein,
though guarded, the exquisite woman whom I loved was
besieged by the spirit of evil; yet, as the ramshackle
motor-car jolted me through the green swelling country in which I was born, through the dear sadness of its
misty pretence of rain, my soul was uplifted by its
eternal promise of the new and fruitful life that was to
come.

Of the house of death, there is nothing to say relevant
to this story. My sister, Muriel, and Tom, the Bishop,
were there. We recalled times long since past. We examined the collection of Missals. Also the MS. of the
Treatise on Vestments (as far as it had gone) which my
mother had preserved bound in morocco leather. They
sentimentalized a bit over the volume. Had not their
hearts run away with those heads occupied over sacred
vestments and suggested marriage garments in their
place?

"What a young ass I must have been in those days!"
laughed the Bishop.

"And I thought that both you and I were tremendously
clever," said Muriel.

"In our souls," said her husband, "lurks the same sneaking opinion."

Tom, in his beautiful sensitive voice, read the burial service over the grave in the primitive village churchyard. The young vicar, shy and nervous in the presence of a bishop, was in secondary officiation. I had never seen Tom in his lawn sleeves before. It struck me how efficient he was in his sacerdotalism. In no matter what branch of human activity, I have always loved to see the expert at work. And there was something more than the perfection of human craftsmanship in Tom's command of the simple ceremony. I beheld a transfiguration of the little brisk man's spectacled face. I bowed my head before it, feeling the least significant of mortals.

A grey-headed solicitor from Yeovil produced my mother's simple will. Tom, being a man of affairs, which, as an irresponsible painter, I could not be in my mother's estimation, was appointed sole executor. Diocesan affairs called him imperiously to Bradbury. Serious tidings by letter and telegram summoned me to Cannes. We left Muriel and the solicitor and Miss Brown to perform the last miserable functions and went our several ways. I arrived in Cannes after exactly a week's absence.

I have often asked myself whether things would have taken a different course had I been on the spot, to exercise my authority and, more or less, my control. I doubt it. *Che sarà sarà.* What has to be, will be. Yet who knows? At any rate, fate ordained that it should be a week blotted out from my effective life.

I have been writing this account of myself at various periods during the last year or two—in a rough way, mainly at first for my own delectation and interest. The

advent of Amos and his meeting with Nadia lunching
with me in her shred of an evening gown, awoke in me
the Comic Spirit.   Well, perhaps, by so saying I depreci-
ate my sense of humour.   Let me say, rather, that it
evoked in my artistic self the desire to catch and express
that same Comic Spirit in an alien medium.   I began.
The habit grew upon me.   And now, what I put before
you is an editing, as far as my powers go, of my memories
of the Comic Years.   I know, from my own professional
point of view, that before you can begin to paint a picture you are bound by all sorts of canons both of tech-
nique and æsthetics, which it would be tedious to enu-
merate.   But of those which regulate the art of story telling I have no notion.   Therefore if, following my own
instinct, I appear to go in and out and round about, I
must crave your indulgence.

Nadia, Dorothea and Bendyke Hamilton met me at
the station.   The rest of the day was entirely taken up
with their various recitals of the things that had happened.   There was also a Colonel Wigram, of whom I
had never heard, summoned to the Villa.   I went to bed
with a splitting headache and a dazed brain.
    I can only co-ordinate their respective accounts, and
my reading of them in the light of subsequent events,
into which I hope is a logical sequence of narrative.
    When I left Cannes, the Villa being in the nature of a
stronghold without a responsible captain, Amos was
elected my deputy.   I had urged him to sleep in my
room; but he took it into his head that it would either be
disrespectful to me or that it would be quarters too syb-
aritic for a captain of the guard.   My two spare rooms
being occupied by Nadia and Dorothea—the Villa, I
must give you to understand, is not a palace—he had a

camp-bed set up in the studio. He and François, as sergeant, defended the place by night. Bendyke Hamilton in humorous spirit accepted the position of lieutenant, and with Maxime, the chauffeur, as corporal, contributed to the defence by day.

Apparently the night defence was at first but a formality, in that the two young women defended were out each night until all sorts of hours in the morning. The sword hung over Nadia's head. What did it matter? Why, until it fell, should she not enjoy herself? For the first three days they enjoyed themselves wholeheartedly. The excellent Maxime drove them all over the coast. They lunched in weird mountain inns. They danced in the afternoons. They dined at restaurants, they went to Casinos and danced and supped with the recklessness of youth. None of them gambled. Amos stuck to his principles; Nadia, free from the blackmailing horror, regarded the tables with aversion; Bendyke Hamilton bluntly called it a mug's game for a poor man; and Dorothea, little gambler though she was, yielded to public opinion and kept away.

Two young men and two young women split inevitably into two definite pairs, especially when each of the young men has formed his very definite choice of partner. Dorothea, soul of loyalty, did her best. She thrust Bendyke almost savagely on Nadia and led Amos away herself. But to the young gods it appeared otherwise. As soon as the first polite opportunity occurred for a confounding of Dorothea's strategy, Amos sped with his grin to the Princess, and Bendyke, like one relieved from honourable duty, rose with an air of relief and took possession of Dorothea. As I say, Dorothea was loyalty itself. Had there been no Bendyke Hamilton to testify by word and action the enormous interest he had sud-

denly found in her, she would have supported Amos's
blatant disregard of her and his absurd assertions of his
passion for another woman, I will not say with pleasure,
but at least with her cool and acerb philosophy. But
after all, there was Bendyke Hamilton, a type new to her
experience. Claude Worthington had laid every blessed
thing, poor fellow, that he could (mostly on wheels) at
her feet. But, as she said—descending for the sake of
metaphor into the ungenteel—she could have taken him
between her fingers and thumb like a chicken-bone and
eaten him. To no woman, except perhaps to an Amazon,
is such an ideal husband. Claude was hopelessly out of
court—the Court of Love. Then Amos. Certainly his
bulk and his strength and his sweet docility had stirred
in her the barbaric feminine. Two months before, had
he come and asked her to marry him, she would have
flung herself in his rough arms with the assurance of being his for ever. But Amos did nothing of the kind.
As soon as he met her after a long absence, he said she
was his sister and demanded news of a Princess of the
Moon. The fool ought to have known that women, unless blood-bound, hate being sisters. Dorothea, with all
her young pride, loathed it. Then, on top of a humili-
ated hour, came Bendyke Hamilton, with immediate consolation. *Que voulez-vous?* What could you expect?
Here was a man as masculine as you please; hardened
by every conceivable virile adventure; a man of universal
knowledge and swift brain; to whom, unlike Amos, she
could teach nothing—nothing save, perhaps, the vague,
unformulated, delicate, man-hidden truths of existence
which are women's fond and precious secret possession.
It is not that she had not met men of intellectual distinc-
tion in her London life. She was a woman of the modern
world; nay more, a fine product of the modern world.

By no means had she only Claude and Amos *pour tout potage*, for sole food for tender fancy. Among aspirants had been a young professor of physics, whose name now, through his discoveries of the little habits of electrons, has suddenly become a household word; a man too, spiritual and sensitive, the scientific poet. I know him for a man of sweet integrity and charm. He offered his heart and soul to Dorothea. But, said she, long ago to me: "My dearest of dears, he's everything a girl could wish for, and I feel a beast in turning him down, but he has got such wet hands!" And he had, poor fellow.

All this, merely to tell you that my beloved Dorothea was not out in the world to gather a husband where she might. She had wide field of choice. But she sought what she called her type. And, all of a sudden, on the moonlit terrace of my villa, did it occur to her that her type was personified in the wise, one-eyed, adventurous gentleman, whose sole interest in the universe seemed to be her warm and comely self.

It would have been against nature had she not eventually let Amos go hang and given herself up to the splendour of a new and very real romance. And, after all, in spite of the education of travel and Bendyke's assiduous social polish, Amos was the same old comfortable bear in whose antics, although very much more refined, Nadia took a childish delight.

All went merrily for three days. Amos, keeping check upon the enemy, learned that he was still at Monte Carlo. As yet Garcia gave no sign of interest in the Princess's affairs. In the opinion of Bendyke Hamilton, admitted into full confidence, he was putting up a magnificent bluff. He set out his arguments. Our best plan was to call it as soon as it was declared.

"With me, what Bendyke says goes," declared Dorothea.

"I have every confidence," smiled Nadia, "in Mr. Hamilton."

Amos growled: "I've only confidence in myself."

"What are you going to do?" asked Dorothea.

"Just let me get at him," replied Amos.

Nadia sat up in her excited way. "And when you do, what's going to happen?"

"He'll be sorrier for himself than ever he was in his life."

What he counted upon doing neither his three companions, then, nor I afterwards, could form the slightest notion. They treated him with affectionate banter.

"You think me a fool," said Amos, "but you'll jolly well see."

Well, *Fortuna favet fatuis*. Fools, or those whose human limitations make us regard as fools, more than often enjoy Fortune's favours.

We come now to the way in which she showered them on Amos.

It was the fourth night of my absence. The quartette had spent the day in a motor-boat picnicking down the coast. They dined and danced after dinner at the Casino; but the two young women, tired after three nights racketing till morning, and after their day on the sea, went home at a comparatively early hour. The men remained. A turn through the rooms, a drink in the bar, and they too would go to bed.

And there, in the rooms, they came upon Colonel Wigram, who, figuratively, fell into the arms of Bendyke Hamilton. They had been together, fate-driven, at school, in Mexico, on the Somme and on the Zambesi, and in the same I Zingari cricket eleven. They were men of the same type of modern gentleman adventurers and everywhere had they been sworn brothers. Wigram was a tall, dark, almost ascetic-looking man, clean shaven, with an ironical, devil-may-care humour in his eyes and at the corners of his lips. He had come to Cannes, he scarce knew why. To escape the wretched weather in England which had brought on his old malaria. He had retired from the service, had married a wife who, after a week's unprincipled orgy in the Paris shops, would join him in Cannes with the smile of an innocent angel on her face. Bendyke must know her. Quite a nice girl, although he said so as shouldn't! Why, now he came to think of it, an invitation to the wedding was sent last year to Bendyke, who had taken no notice of the summons. What the devil did he mean by it? Wasn't the Travellers' Club a good enough address? Bendyke replied that for all he knew the letter might be reposing in some Bolivian post office. Most of last year he had been fooling round the South American continent with his friend Burden. He turned and plucked Amos from his polite contemplation of the game at a neighbouring table, and introduced him. Burden was a wanderer even as they. Said Wigram:

"There is only one thing to be done," and he led the way to the bar. But the little room was packed. It was just that quivering moment of full season before the headlong, senseless flight, as though from a City of Destruction, or like the rush of the Norwegian lemmings into the sea, which every year empties the Riviera within a few days. The air reeked with gin and lemon-juice and cigarettes and perfume and perspiration, and vibrated with the shrill clatter of tongues. The three men lingered for a moment on the threshold.

"How can we talk, my Bendyke," said Wigram, "in this dreadful Zoo?"

"How, indeed?"

"At the Palace where I am staying there is a bar vast and airy, and, at this hour, comparatively unpeopled. I would suggest it to our friend Burden if I felt sure I wasn't dragging him away from other delights."

"I hate this darned place," said Amos.

They took cab to the hotel, passed through the long empty lounge and entered the comfortable saloon. A few scattered couples sat in discreet discourse on the leathern seats by the walls, and one young gentleman, sucking something through straws, sat on the high stool by the bar itself. The three men sank restfully in a corner by the door. The waiter brought their refreshment. Wigram, unlike most of his kind, was a lover of talk. He talked well and picturesquely. He seemed to know every inch of the Western Hemisphere as intimately as Amos knew Warraranga. He seemed to be as familiar with the remainder of the surface of the globe; and though much of the conversation turned, in Othello's words, on most disastrous chances and moving accidents by flood and field which the two adventurers had shared together, they made Amos feel that he too was an interested party, so that he listened in rapt fascination. They exchanged war memories. All the stories began:

"You remember the fellow——?"

One fellow recalled was a Captain in a regiment in a neighbouring trench, who dropped down one foggy evening and was brought into the mess in the horrible candle-lit, reeking dug-out. Befogged, he asked for a drink and a guide back through the trenches. Hospitable hands reached for glass and whisky bottle.

"And then suddenly," said Bendyke, "Wigram shot the blighter dead."

"Lord, why?" asked Amos.

"Well, he saw that the silly fool had forgotten to take off his gold wedding ring, that he had a duelling scar over his eyebrow, and that something bulged beneath his tunic. And that something was a bomb with a time fuse, which he was going to leave behind."

Said Amos: "I wonder how it feels to kill a man like that in cold blood."

"If it's your life against his," said Wigram, "it's the most exquisite sensation in the world; it feels just bully."

And then, after many others, there came a story of one Jenkinson, an Australian, killed, poor chap, at Gallipoli —but in his time a mighty hunter before the Lord. How the three of them were together in the East African Hinterland; how a native guide in whom they trusted, brought them, as he thought into the trap and shinned up a tree; and how Jenkinson had picked him off with his rifle, and left him dangling from the branches.

"It must take a lot of nerve," said Amos.

"Only a cold brain," said Wigram.

At that moment a man with a vast diamond solitaire in his shirt front entered the bar-room, stood for a moment, and then, as one not seeing the companion whom he sought, swaggered out again.

"There! That's him! Do you see?" cried Amos, starting up; but the nervous grip of Hamilton wrenched him down.

"Be quiet, you fool!"

"What's the matter?" asked Wigram, in his quiet way, flicking off his cigarette ash.

"I've been all over the world to try and find that devil," cried Amos, "and now I've got him."

"And now you've got him, what are you going to do with him?"

"That's for him to decide," said Amos.

"Sounds interesting," said Wigram.

Amos put his great hand on Hamilton's shoulder.

"Bendyke, the Lord has delivered him into my hands. I've often told you that He would.   Now is the appointed time.   Now is the day of salvation."

Beads of sweat stood on his rugged forehead.   A dangerous light gleamed in his clear blue eyes.

"What do you think you're going to do, man?" asked Hamilton.

"I'm going to break into his room—I know the number —and have it out with him once and for all."

Bendyke turned to his friend.   "Run like hell down the corridor and see what the blighter's doing."

So Wigram lounged out, and as soon as the door was closed he sped according to Bendyke's commendation and arrived in the vestibule just in time to see Ramon Garcia enter the lift and be carried heavenwards.   He returned to find the pair in earnest consultation, into which he was immediately taken.   The barest skeleton sketch of the situation satisfied his curiosity—if a knowledge of data, so as to render unquestioning assistance, can be so called.   As ever, his services were at Bendyke's unreserved disposal.   Bendyke, a man of resource, laid down the plan of campaign.

Amos sat like a growling bear, swerving from side to side, his great fingers working, both in an unregenerate lust to get at his enemy and in a spiritual ferment to free his Princess from the power of the dragon and listened sullenly to the argument.   He was all for following Garcia to his room.   But he must yield to subtler counsel. He must not expect to do his tying up and burgling trick

twice with impunity.   There would certainly be a scrap
of some kind in Garcia's room.   Why not provide
himself with a possible alibi, if occasion demanded it?
Wigram had a room on the fifth floor of the hotel.   Let
that be their base of operations.   As they developed the
scheme, Amos's lips parted in a grim smile.   These adventurer fellows had wonderful brains!

They left the bar and went to the main lift in the hall.

"Good night, old man," said Bendyke.

"No.   Not yet.   Come up to my room and have one
more.   I have just a little 'pre-war.'"   He turned to the
lift attendant, with a laugh.   *"C'est rare, n'est-ce pas?"*

"Well, just one.   What do you think, Amos?"

Amos made a grimace of acceptance.   The attendant
carried them up.   As soon as the lift began its descent,
Wigram halted.

"Just follow the numbers.   They correspond on all
floors.   There's the main staircase.   You see, from my
room, which is along here, you take that corridor to the
left."

"I see," said Amos.   "I shan't forget."

Wigram unlocked his door and they entered the room.
Amos threw hat and coat over a chair.   He would come
back as soon as he could and tell them all about it.

"I'm coming with you," said Bendyke Hamilton.

Amos objected.   Two to one wasn't sporting.   He
wanted to have the beggar all to himself.

"I'm coming with you to see fair play," said Bendyke.

"And I," said Wigram, "shall smoke a pipe and read
Wordsworth till you return."

Bendyke took command, Amos yielding grudgingly.
First he must go ahead and see that all was clear.   At
Bendyke's arresting hand, he halted; at his beckon he
followed.   They fled swiftly up the carpeted stairs.   The

long corridors, to Amos's responding nerves, were tense
with silence. With swift care they reached Garcia's
door. It was locked. Bendyke rapped softly with his
knuckles. Steps approached and there came a voice:

"Qu'est qu'il y a?"

Bendyke answered in the semi-Italian accent of the
coast. "A telegram for Monsieur, which the concierge
forgot to deliver when Monsieur came in."

An exclamation of annoyance within, and the door was
flung angrily open. Garcia had just time to stare at
his unexpected visitors when Amos rushed upon him and
drove him into the bedroom, while Bendyke quietly shut
the door of the little outer vestibule. Then he entered
the room and shut that door too, and, after a swift glance
around, stood with his back to the bell-push. Garcia,
knowing the physical strength of his enemy, had instinctively retreated into a corner by the window. Amos sat
on the edge of the bed, his hands on his knees.

"You have come to steal letters from me, as you did
before," said Garcia.

"You're right," said Amos. "Now, don't move, or
make a noise, or I'll come and hurt you. I'd like to hurt
you, but I don't want to. Understand? Just stand
there, or sit down on the chair by your side and let us
talk quietly."

"I stand," said Garcia. He was fully dressed, save
for the coat and waistcoat which he had thrown off.
"Tell me exactly what it is that you want."

"I want first the letters that the Princess Ramiroff
wrote to you. Then the pearl necklace. Oh, I'll pay for
it. I know what it cost. Then the certificate and receipt
from the Paris jewellers. And then a letter right now to
the Princess, saying that you don't intend to live with her
as you're going off with another woman to the nearest

place to hell you can think of, so that she can get her divorce—and—well—that's all."

"You have forgotten," said Garcia, ironically, "the two hundred thousand francs I won from the Marchese della Fontana."

"One hundred thousand, you liar," said Amos. "I'll give you a cheque for the difference between that and the cost of the pearls."

"*Vous avez un toupet,* Monsieur—I wish that I knew the English for it."

"You've got the cheek," said Bendyke impassively.

Amos had forgotten him; he turned round instinctively, as though he had heard a voice from another world. Garcia swung the chair near him to the side of the dressing table which stood across the corner of the room, and sat down.

"Yes," said he, "you have got the cheek, Monsieur Burden. And if I do not do all these fine things you tell me, what will happen?"

"Something very nasty," replied Amos. "I was a fool not to have spoilt your beauty for ever the last time. Remember? But, by Gosh! I'll do it now!"

Said Bendyke Hamilton, in French, in the same impassive and disinterested way: "I should advise you to consider very seriously what our friend says. He is a man of his word, I assure you. If you haven't understood his proposals, I'll translate them for you."

Ramon Garcia swung round on him.

"And you, what are you doing here in this blackmailing outrage?"

"I am interpreting, should there be any need, between my friend who speaks little French, and Monsieur Perez the blackmailer, who speaks English with difficulty."

Garcia, glossy-haired, glossy-moustached, handsome, a fine figure of a man as he sat there, the solitaire diamond gleaming against the whiteness of his shirt, looked furtively at the two men and to the open window and passed one hand over his moist forehead and nervously tapped the corner of the dressing table with the other.

"Messieurs," said he in French, "I do not deserve this at your hands. I have done you no wrong. It is the Marchese della Fontana who has wronged me. You call me Perez. I avow that is my name. Have I not already avowed it to Monsieur Fontenay? For all that I can easily defend myself. It has nothing to do with you. . . ." He went on at some length.

"What's the fellow saying?" asked Amos at last.

Bendyke translated the substance.

"Tell him to cut it out," said Amos, "and come down to business."

He reared his great bulk threateningly from the bed.

"I'm about tired of this. What are you going to do?"

Garcia cowered in his chair, ghastly white under his olive skin.

"Monsieur Burden, I cannot do as you ask. In London, having no money, I sold the false pearls for the few pounds that I could get. The receipt of Messrs. Lautier Frères, and my wife's letters, have been torn up long ago."

He covered his face in his hands. Amos looked at Bendyke, still rigid against the wall.

"Did you ever hear of such a swine?"

"Often," said Bendyke.

"Well, it's one thing off our chests, anyhow," said Amos, with a deep breath of relief. "And now what about the letter to the Princess?"

The man looked up, red-veined, ugly, murderous.

"You have won, you damned Englishman. Yes, I'll write it."

He rose, looked around as though to seek writing materials. The eyes of the other two men turned instinctively in search. And there, on a bureau on the other side of the room, near Bendyke Hamilton they lay. Then suddenly from the latter rang a cry:

"Look out."

For Garcia had swiftly opened the drawer of the dressing table and stood at bay with the famous Browning pistol in his hand.

"Sortez, sortez!" he cried and burst into a roll of Spanish anathema. Bendyke and he exchanged a few words in Spanish.

"I think he means it, old chap. We had better clear out and wait for the next innings," said Bendyke.

"I don't care a hang," said Amos, and, with a sudden dive he collared him low around the loins, and held him up close and with the free hand strove for possession of the pistol. Ramon managed to slither down till his feet touched the ground. The man must have felt that he was fighting for his life. Bendyke Hamilton threw himself upon the pair and tried to snatch at the pistol. But Amos, disengaging a huge arm threw him flat, and gasped:

"This is my job. Didn't I tell you?"

So the pair struggled for a few instants. They neared the open window. There was far more nervous strength and agility of movement in the South American than Amos had reckoned upon. At every movement he eluded his bear's grip. The fingers that clutched the pistol were of iron.

Bendyke picked himself up from the floor to which he

had been swept, just in time to see a flash on the balcony, hear a shot, and then be aware of the single figure of Amos standing there, his right hand grasping his left shoulder, and a wild look of horror on his face.

CHAPTER XXIII

BENDYKE realized the immediate peril. He lugged the bewildered Amos into the corridor, shutting the door behind him, and down the yet silent stairs into Wigram's room, which had been left unlocked. Wigram rose from his chair and laid down his book.

"Hullo? Hit?"

Bendyke answered. "Yes. The brute got him. Let us have something to drink—for his sake first, and for all our sakes if anyone should come. We've been here all the time. Understand?"

Amos sat on a couch still holding his shoulder. He was conscious of burning pain, and a horrible warm wetness. The two men hurried and set out travelling flask, glass and mineral water bottle from the bedside, and the two tooth-tumblers from the bathroom. They gave Amos a stiff dose of brandy. He nodded.

"That's better," said he.

"Let us have a look at you," said Wigram, preparing to take off Amos's dinner-jacket.

But Bendyke stopped him. "No mess here, for God's sake. We must cover up our tracks."

"Where's the other fellow?"

"On the pavement, six stories down."

"I don't know how it happened," said Amos. "One moment I was holding a sort of wild cat and the next he wasn't there. That's all there is to it." Then, after a pause: "Funny you fellows should have been talking downstairs of killing men. I guess I've killed one to-night. I didn't mean to. Before God, I didn't."

"We know you didn't, old chap," said Bendyke. "But before men and magistrates it might seem as if you did. We must get out of this, and home as quick as we can."

"Play-act a bit," said Wigram. "Can you stick it?"

Amos set his teeth. Yes, he could hold out. Seeing the blood trickle down his wrists, Wigram whipped from a drawer a grey silk muffler and bound the wet arm tight. With stoical endurance of agony, Amos let them fit him into his overcoat. Wigram looked out into the corridor. All was quiet. Apparently no one had heard or concerned himself about the sharp crack of the pistol. They went to the lift-cage and rang the bell. The machinery quivered. As soon as the lift appeared, Bendyke and Wigram broke into hearty farewells.

"We've kept you up to all hours."

"Not a bit. The night is young. I'll come down and see you safely out."

They descended. Amos said: "That was a jolly good story you told about the war."

The lift attendant, who had the Military Medal ribbon in his buttonhole, smiled. "There are many good stories to be told about the war."

They reached the quiet vestibule. Bendyke noted, with a sigh of relief, that the dead thing, lying crumpled only a few yards away outside, had not yet been found. Luck helped them further. As they reached the door a taxi drove up with a party of tired revellers. Wigram rushed out and secured it and waved farewell to his departing guests, as though they had spent the merriest evening together.

Bendyke helped a stumbling Amos up the steps of the villa and opened the door with the key, which, after our

primitive Southern way, Dorothea had left under the mat.
And then, all of a sudden, Amos swayed and fell in a heap
on the floor of the vestibule.

There was Bendyke in a strange house of which he
only knew the drawing-room, dining-room and studio.
To lift the vast mass of Amos was beyond one man's
powers. He must seek Dorothea at once. He strove
to construct the plan. The studio was at the top of the
house; its roof projecting high. But, as you stood on the
landing, there was a low corridor obviously leading to
servants' quarters. The guest rooms must be on the first
floor. He mounted swiftly, turning on the electric
switches. For some careless reason, the door of my bedroom was ajar. He peered in cautiously. The next
room, he argued, must be Dorothea's. He knocked
sharply. A voice, which he recognized as Nadia's, in
sharp instinctive French asked who was there.

He had argued rightly that Dorothea's room should
be next to mine; it was the big and beautiful room, with
a bay and a balcony; but Dorothea had yielded it to
Nadia and taken the smaller room further along. So it
was Nadia whom he awakened. The voice came again,
querulous, frightened.

All he could lamely reply was: "I'm trying to get at
Dorothea, Princess."

"Wait a minute."

A streak of light appeared beneath the door. There
was a rustle of garments and soon the Princess flung open
the door and stood before him, in indignant accusation.

"What do you want Dorothea for at this hour of the
night?"

"Never mind," said he impatiently. "Where's her
room? Anyhow, will you go and tell her I want her?"

She drew herself up. "I beg your pardon. Something has happened. What is it?"

"If you wake up Dorothea, I'll tell you."

She gave him a frightened glance and sped down the passage. In a few moments, both women appeared in their dressing-gowns. He addressed Dorothea.

"It's Amos. He's been shot through the shoulder by Garcia. Nothing serious. But he has fainted downstairs."

It was Nadia who flew down first. The others followed her and found her already kneeling by his side and wailing foolishly as though he were dead.

François was aroused from his basement chamber. Bendyke and he carried the unconscious Amos into the drawing-room and laid him on a divan. Dorothea, capable woman, caused sheets, blankets, hot water, dressings, towels to appear miraculously. Nadia too recovered and gave efficient aid. By the time the doctor, summoned by telephone, arrived, Amos was comfortably bestowed on the divan, and my Aubusson carpet ruined for ever by his blood-drenched clothes. He also had recovered consciousness and called himself a fool for fainting.

The doctor dressed the wound. It was clean and simple, the bullet having passed through.

"Can I ask any questions?"

"The fewer the better," said Bendyke.

"Then I shouldn't leave him in the drawing-room," answered the doctor drily.

Amos, declaring himself able to walk, they supported him up the stairs and deposited him in my bed. For the night, said the doctor, nothing more could be done. He would come around early the next day.

Bendyke turned to the two women and François. "We

must clear up the mess downstairs before we go to bed."

"In view of my not being allowed to ask questions, it would be most wise," said the doctor.

"You don't mind being left alone for a few minutes?" asked Dorothea.

"I'd like it," said Amos. Then, as they were about to leave him, the door held open by Bendyke, he cried out, "You'll come and see me, Nadia, won't you?"

Nadia ran across the room and bent over him, and only Bendyke's trained ear heard her whisper:

"I'll sit up with you all night."

When the last vestiges of blood had been cleared from the drawing-room, Amos's upper garments taken down to be burned, the Aubusson carpet rolled up and carried by Bendyke and François to the cellars, and François dismissed for the night, Nadia clutched Bendyke by the arm.

"Are you going to tell us what has happened?"

Up to now he had given but a garbled version of the affair, deeming it important that the tending of Amos's wound should be of paramount concern in their thoughts. For all they knew, Garcia was safe and sound in his hotel. There had been an encounter between the men on the quiet Croisette. Garcia had lugged out his Browning. A scuffle and a shot and Garcia had bolted like a rabbit. To-morrow would be quite time enough to take what proceedings they should think prudent.

"I've told you," he replied.

"Do you think I believe you?" cried Nadia, with a scornful laugh. "Would you, Mr. Bendyke Hamilton, the trusted soldier of fortune, have allowed an assassin like that to escape? Would you have made all this mystery about a little blood in the drawing-room? Bah! I can read behind your face. There is something you are concealing from us."

"I'm afraid there is, my dear," said Dorothea gently. "And we're bound to learn sooner or later."

He lifted helpless shoulders.

"Of course you will. I only wanted to let you have a more or less peaceful time to-night."

Nadia interrupted him: "A man's idea of peace!"

"Could I tell you before François and the Doctor?"

Nadia, a wraith in sea-green kimono, stretched out both her delicate and passionate hands. "What did I say? There is something to be told. What is it?"

"Well, if you will have it," said Bendyke, "Ramon Garcia's dead. Or he ought to be."

Nadia rushed to him, her hands on his shoulders, and looked haggardly into his face.

"Dead? And Amos killed him?"

"I don't know so much about that," replied Bendyke, in his matter of fact way. "The fight took place in Garcia's room. I was there. They were struggling for the pistol by the balcony on the sixth floor. The pistol went off and so did Garcia—over the balcony."

With her hands over her eyes and a "My God!" Dorothea reeled away. But Nadia stood quivering from feet to hair, in an ecstasy of exultation.

Dead? Really dead? He could not help being dead, thrown from that enormous height. And Amos had killed him! He had delivered her by one brave act, from the Thing that had made her life a horror! Through her lips did her barbaric ancestry speak amazing words in an abandonment of speech and gesture. Her eyes flamed like emeralds with the sun behind them. The wonder of her face glowed intense. Her passion reached the pitch of a Deborah. Amos had killed him, had killed him, had killed him!

It was Dorothea, with her sane English sense, and also

with her strong arms, who checked her. Nadia stared for a moment or two unintelligently into her eyes; then, a sudden shock, came the reaction of all that makes for modern civilization; and, after a few choking sobs, she collapsed in a little huddled heap upon Dorothea's young bosom.

"If I don't get back to the Beau Rivage before daylight, it might seem suspicious," said Bendyke Hamilton.

Dorothea nodded. Bendyke crept out without taking leave. If his main thought, as he descended the villa steps, was the perfect understanding between Dorothea and himself, who could blame him?

Into this melodrama did I plunge when I arrived in Cannes. Amos, though confined by his wound to the house, had insisted on transferring himself from my bedroom to his encampment in the studio. He had been up most of the day, sitting bandaged, in the sunshine of the drawing-room terrace. In a talk with him there, alone, I became conscious of yet further change in the boy. He had grown ten years older.

"Technically," said he, "I suppose I've committed murder. I've lain awake having it out with my conscience, and I think I've won. I hadn't any idea of killing him. All along it was in my head to make his face like a jellyfish and his body pulp, until he gave me satisfaction. I wish I had begun that way from the start. Anyhow, I thought I had him cornered, when out came his Browning. I wasn't conscious of the intention or the act of pitching him over the balcony. If we're to remain friends, Uncle David, you must believe my word as implicitly as the others do."

Of course I believed it; and I told him so.

"Therefore," said he, "I can't consider myself a murderer. I'm not going about branding my brow with the curse of Cain. I feel rather as though I have been an instrument chosen by Divine Providence for ridding the world of a venomous reptile."

"I don't presume, my boy," I answered, "to share in the counsels of Divine Providence; but, as far as a world-loss is concerned, I cordially agree with you."

To me, at first, the strangest thing of all was the bland silence maintained by the public authorities. Not an official whisper reached the ears of myself or my household. We were as immune from suspicion as our dear friend Mrs. Blennerhasset herself, who, on a day's visit to Cannes from Cap Ferrat, came in to see us. You remember that she was the witness of the first scene between Garcia and Amos, when the latter possessed himself of the Princess.

"Have you heard the dreadful news?"

Dorothea and I had come down to receive her.

"What?" said I. "Do you mean that Giralda is divorcing Howton?"

As Lord and Lady Howton were the dearest of old dears of Darby and Joans on the coast, my question was obviously playful.

"Silly!" she said. "I mean Ramon Garcia. You used to know him. Nadia knew him. I remember a funny evening when your nephew——"

"Oh, yes, yes," said I. "The South American——"

She burst in with her tidings.

"I hear he threw himself out of a window of the Palace a week or so ago."

I shrugged my shoulders as one peculiarly uninterested in the fantastic doings of Ramon Garcia.

"So the talk goes," said I. "The gossip only reached me on my return from England."

As to this smartest of women, so did I reply to a

score of other friends who came to me with great eyes and
a "Have you heard?"

After a few days of intermittent scandal, that was the
end of the matter. How the police envisaged it I have
no notion. There is nothing in France corresponding to
our public coroner's inquest. The Law makes its enquiries, of course, but in private, and in decency. Colonel Wigram's discreet investigations led him to the conclusion that the police recognized an act of suicide. There
was no evidence of struggle in the room. There had
been the sear of a bullet along the man's coat, and the
bullet had been found in the bedroom wall. The Browning, fully charged, save for one chamber, had lain a few
feet away from the mangled man. The obvious thing
was that he had tried a double simultaneous mode of
suicide, of which the first had been a failure.

And, in sober fact, who in the official, or even the social,
world of France cared one rap whether Ramon Garcia
was dead or alive?

To wind up the sordid story of the man, I may say,
that, from then to this day when I am setting it down, not
a word came to any of us concerning him. According to
French procedure, seals must have been put on his hotel
bedroom door. The police must have made the minutest
search among his papers and effects. What they found
they only know; but they certainly discovered nothing
that could compromise either the Princess Ramiroff or
the Marchese della Fontana.

He had come into our decent lives less as a man than
as a discordant blatancy. To me he had ever appeared
a creature unreal; one who had prodigiously stepped out
from some contemptible cinema drama and assumed the
roundness of human flesh. His psychology might perhaps have been an interesting study: but I don't think

I had speech with him on more than four or five occasions, on each of which he inspired me with disgust. I have made no attempt therefore to draw him otherwise than he appeared to me, namely, a vulgar Malignity set down in the midst of us.

If there is peace for such as him, well, in Peace may he rest.

Nadia, singularly quiet and subdued, remained most of the time in her room for a day or two after my arrival. I had little chance to talk with her. She pleaded shock and broken nerves. Then she insisted on returning to the Mont Fleuri. For our inner ring, all danger was past; for the social world, her visit to Dorothea was over. Besides, Amos, still an invalid, required better accommodation than the hard little camp-bed in the studio—to say nothing of the inconvenience to myself. More than any of us, she seemed to react to the tragedy. She went about pale and ghost-like, shunning us all. There were moments when hideous doubt crept into my mind; doubt whether, in spite of everything, she had not loved the dead man. Dorothea had told me of her outburst of savage joy when first she learned the truth. Yet it is a commonplace of psychology that the extremes of love and hatred meet. How else could I account for her pallid and affrighted welcome of freedom?

The car was waiting to take her back to the Mont Fleuri. She came down into the vestibule with Chouchou in her arms. She put out her hand:

"How can I thank you, dear David, for what you have done for me?"

I took the tips of her fingers and smiled.

"I am coming with you."

"Oh no. I could not think of it. You have to paint."

Amos, his arm in a sling, and Dorothea were there.

Said Amos: "Yes. Uncle David has to work. I'm doing nothing. I'll see you safely there, Nadia."

"You'll do nothing of the kind, you silly fool," cried Dorothea. "You're not going to be seen in public till your shoulder's better."

He made some exclamation of impatience.

"Dorothea is right," said the Princess. "No imprudences. I would prefer to go alone."

In her tone and her manner there was a touch of haughtiness that compelled our yielding. She kissed Dorothea affectionately, shook hands with Amos and turned to me.

"I can at least accompany you to the car," said I. And while we were descending the sharp flight of steps, I whispered: "When can I talk to you, Nadia? Up to now you have given me no chance. But you know that my life and happiness is in your hands."

"Yes," she said. "I know."

"Well then——?"

She did not reply. We had completed our descent of the steps, and there was the narrow pavement and Maxime, rug over arm, waiting by the opened door of the car. She entered, held out her hand for me to kiss. And so she drove off, an inscrutable sphinx.

CHAPTER XXIV

A CLOUD of depression hung over our evening meal. Bendyke Hamilton, who up to now had dined at the Villa every evening at my pressing invitation, had gone off somewhere with his friend Wigram. Only the three of us were at table. Dorothea, after a few attempts at sprightly discussion of my Academy pictures, which, according to annual routine, I should have to take to London in a week or so, abandoned the futile pastime. Amos ate stolidly, and spoke hardly a word. The end of dinner came as a relief. Amos lit his pipe, and sauntered on to the drawing-room terrace. Dorothea and I were alone.

"What does it all mean, dear? I can't understand it. Why should she have left us so strangely and suddenly?"

"You should know the ways of women better than I, my child."

"I only know that when a woman loves a man she doesn't treat him in that fashion."

I turned the talk, with a smile, for I could not reveal to her the anxiety that gnawed at my heart.

"You know then how a woman loves?"

She faced me half-abashed, half-daring.

"Yes, I do. And I'd go through fire and water for him."

"And he?"

"He'd do the same."

Our eyes met in our customary mutual exchange of humorous glances. She coloured a little.

"Of course, if you ask for it, you must have it. We were going to talk to you after all these worries had blown over. We're engaged. Any objection?"

"Only on financial grounds, my dear. It behooves us to be prudent."

"If we can't afford hot water to boil our eggs, we'll eat them raw," said Dorothea. "Anything else?"

There was nothing else. I have already told you my opinion of Bendyke Hamilton. She proclaimed me a dear, kissed me and switched back to Nadia.

"I could have beaten her to-day. She said good-bye just as anyone would do after a week-end visit."

"We all have had a tremendous shock," said I, and continued with a dissertation on tragedy and the sub-conscious self. "We must allow Nadia time to recover."

"I don't think Nadia's any kind of self cares a hang about the tragedy."

The horrible idea came into my head again. "Isn't it possible that she may have had some curious affection for the man?"

She stared at me open-mouthed. "My dearest, you're hopeless."

François brought in coffee. Amos, pipe in mouth, entered from the terrace; he shook his back like a dog, and we noticed the rain-drops on his coat.

"It's stifling," said he. "There's thunder about."

We became then aware, for the first time, of atmospheric, as well as moral depression. We drank our coffee in silence. A flash of lightning rocketed across the black gap of the open window and presently the thunder rolled.

"I can't stand it any longer," he cried. "I must go to her."

He was marching out at once. But Dorothea put her back to the door and bade him not be a fool.

"I'm going. I've a right to go to her."

"You're crazy," said I.

"I'm perfectly sane," he answered. "I tell you she is calling for me. Dorothea, let me pass."

"It's pouring with rain, and I'm sure you won't be allowed to have the car."

"You won't," said I.

"I can walk."

"And call on a lady, drenched to the skin?"

"I'll telephone for a taxi. I suppose I'm master of my actions?"

"Certainly you are," said I. "But it would be wise to know first what they mean."

"I don't understand. I'm going to see her, because I can't bear to be without her another minute. What's between her and me is none of your business."

At last had come the moment of the announcement or discussion that had hitherto seemed impossible. I turned to Dorothea. It may have been cowardly. But when a man in an abominable situation has to keep up his poor dignity, he seizes hold of any prop.

"You knew. You should have told him."

She replied quickly: "No, no. I couldn't. What you told me was in confidence. It was for Nadia——"

Amos looked from one to the other of us with bent brows.

"What should Nadia have told me?"

Dorothea was silent. I took a few steps about the room. Again I must repeat an often used phrase—my position was grotesque. At last I said:

"I ought to have put a stop to this long ago. But I

regarded your—your admiration for the Princess as a young man's folly without much significance——"

"You did?" he interrupted. "For what kind of a fool did you take me? I've often wondered. I had lived clean of women before I met her—and then—do you call what I've done for her boyish folly?"

The storm had surged nearer. The lightning was immediately followed by a deafening crash of thunder.

"Do you know why I want to be with her to-night?" he continued. "Because she's in deadly terror of this. With me there she wouldn't be frightened. I'm going, rain or no rain."

He pushed Dorothea gently from the door. I crossed to him.

"Stop, till you've heard me. I too happen to love the Princess."

He swung round, and on his face was almost scornful incredulity.

"You?"

Dorothea came to my rescue.

"He was right. I ought to have told you. He and Nadia have loved each other for a long time and are going to be married as soon as it's possible and decent."

He stood for a while looking wide of us, his shoulders swaying in their queer, bear-like fashion, and he passed his free hand over his stubborn hair, which no barber had ever reduced to sleekness. His eyes were dull with the pain of a wounded animal. Presently there flashed in them a sudden and dangerous light, and he drew himself up.

"Then what did she mean by it? I can't sleep until I know."

I said: "It's man to man now. What did she mean by what? You've got to tell me."

His fingers worked. "How can I tell you? Decent men don't talk of things——"

"They have to sometimes," said I, "when the happiness of decent men is at stake."

Dorothea put her arm round me. "Don't, dear. This is too dreadful. Nadia was only foolish and indiscreet. You know her over-excited nerves. Amos is exaggerating—things that Nadia thought nothing about——"

Amos flamed into fierce anger.

"Does a woman think nothing of kisses and passion and promises of everything? And why shouldn't she love me? Tell me that. I'm young, like her. I've got the world before me. I've killed a man for her sake. I've a right to her and her love. What have you got to say about it?"

He was young like her. Those were the words that pierced my soul. I let the material things that had occurred between them pass in a shudder. I could only throw out my hands in a helpless gesture and turn away. Dorothea opened the door and motioned him out. He stood on the threshold, drawing deep breaths; then, his kindly heart smitten by the sight of my dejected figure, he came across the room to me:

"If she had only told me she was bound to you! Why didn't she? That's what I'm going to find out. I've got to do it."

He left me. Dorothea followed him with woman-like remonstrance. What he would do was senseless. It was ten o'clock. Nadia would be in bed.

He was mulishly obstinate. The storm still raged, and she would be crouching terrified in the hotel. He put on hat and Burbery and, taking the key, went out of the house.

I sat holding in my hands my head over which the

universe seemed to have fallen in the shock of chaos. The possibility of Nadia reciprocating Amos's romantic passion had not found place in the most malignant of my dreams. Except for her aloofness from us all during the past two or three days, she had never given a sign that could betray the loyalty of her love for me. A thousand sweet and exquisite proofs crowded my mind.

For the second time, when speaking of the Princess, had he proclaimed his triumphant youth. The first was at Bradbury; then his oafishness had rendered his declaration ludicrous. Now, after a year's schooling, he had returned, a personage whose passion for a beautiful woman, younger than he, presented no aspect of the comic. Between Nadia and him there was but a separation of two or three years; between Nadia and myself two or three and twenty.

Dorothea came up and stroked my hair. I raised my hands and touched her arm. I heard her quiet voice.

"I feel sure, dear, that it will come out all right. Both of them have been off their balance. The night Amos came home wounded, she lost control of herself. I told you how she cried out hysterically and then broke down. It was I, and not she, who sat up with Amos. In fact I spent the night dodging in and out of their two rooms. Amos is only speaking wildly, dear," she assured me. "He had a touch of fever, the day after, and said silly things. He has taken those dreams for realities. Before the tragedy, nothing happened. She treated him as she has always done; you saw her before you went away. She was fond of him, of course; who wouldn't be? But only as her great bear."

She continued her theme of consolation, but I could only sit in the humiliation of bowed head and pat her wrist now and then to show how dear to me was her tenderness. But she brought me no conviction. "Kisses, passion, promises of everything." These were not distraught memories of dreams. They were not lies. From the lips of the man of unwarped honesty they were facts, realities, truths. They were things of youth's hot blood, far removed from the poetics of my middle-aged wooing. I remembered the evening when she had bidden me kill Garcia, and when, I having turned the matter into a jest, she had left the room in dignified anger. Perhaps if I had thrown him out of the window, I thought in bitter irony, after his rodomontade of an attempt to shoot me with an empty pistol, I might have received the reward of passion uncontrolled.

I must have raised a very lugubrious face, for the tears started into Dorothea's eyes.

"Oh, dearest, I can't bear to see you looking like that."

I tried to smile. "I can only yield to the law of nature. Youth to youth."

She would have none of it. "Who is young if you aren't? You're the youngest man of—thirty odd I have ever met."

I admired her brave mendacity; but I shook a despairing head.

Apart from its absolute content of years, age is extraordinarily relative. To the schoolboy of twelve, the sixth-form captain of cricket is a grown-up hero; the masters are creatures of infinite eld. To the septuagenarian the man in his middle forties is a youth with his foot on the early rungs of the ladder; to the girl of twenty, he can only be the member of a past generation. I recalled to mind an ancient picture, the outside illustration of a French comic paper, which represented a with-

ered nonagenarian wistfully regarding a young person of
opulent charms. And under it was written the legend:
"If only I were seventy-five again!"

Yes. The disregard of the relativity of age has been
the cause of many woeful tragedies.

Why, if the sap of spring had worked rejuvenescent in
my veins, had I not chosen some woman in her thirties?
To each other we both should have seemed young.

I gave Dorothea the benefit of these philosophic reflections to which she listened, with a sceptical smile on her
loyal lips. I wound up by repeating:

"No, my dear. Youth claims youth."

"And you're going to take the idea of Amos marrying
her, lying down?"

I nodded mournfully. With what kind of grace could
I go and plead with Nadia?

"If you don't stop it, I shall," she declared stoutly.
"Think of the lives they're going to lead together.
What have they in common?"

I might have asked my ingenuous Dorothea what she
had found in common with Amos when it had pleased
her to imagine herself in love with him. But I refrained.
I only answered:

"Youth. Youth."

"And after youth and youth have got sick of each
other—what's going to happen? Amos will turn out
eventually an Arch-anarchist or an Archbishop. And
she—what does he know about her? What do I know
about her? And, my dear, what do you know about
her?"

And indeed what did I know of the creature of charm
and rare elusiveness that was the Princess? At once
she was but a human fragrance and a tragic spirituality.

She was one who passes through the chambers of a man's soul and leaves them haunted. Was she not a woman for whom a man might more readily die than live?

Said my wise daughter, her honest brown eyes looking through me:

"What's the meaning of your portrait of her—the most beautiful thing you have done—your masterpiece?"

Said I: "How can I tell? I painted her as I felt her. That's all a portrait painter can do."

The merciless beloved went on: "And how did you feel her, as you call it? As the woman who would give love and comfort and cherishing to a man, or as a mystery, a wraith, a sort of sea-foam woman with strange thoughts and passions—such as you would never associate with a plump, commonplace young female like me, for instance?"

"You're a bit of a witch, my child," said I, "in spite of your plumpness."

"And if she's remote from you, the artist, with all your sensitive tentacles—what about Amos, who'll go at anything in life like a bull at a gate?"

We discussed the matter further, with long intervals of precious and intimate silence. The evening wore on.

Presently we heard the slam of the front door. We waited for a few moments; Dorothea ran out, leaving the drawing-room door open.

"Amos!"

"Yes."

She arrested him on his way upstairs. His wet hat and Burbery he had thrown on the hall table.

"Did you see her?"

"Yes."

"And what has happened?"

"Hell has happened," he cried. "Good night!"

He turned, fled up the stairs like a madman, according to Dorothea. She re-entered, closed the door softly behind her.

"You heard?"

"Of course."

"Well, what do you make of it? It seems, after all, as though she were loyal to you."

"God grant it," said I, very wearily. "We shall know to-morrow."

On the morrow I knew. Early in the morning François awakened me with a note marked "Urgent." I tore it open and read:

"DEAREST. I am in agony of spirit. How can I marry you when my heart clamours to be given to another? And how can I give it to another when he terrifies me? When I know not what unknown things his vast simplicities will require of me, or what his great hands will do if I do not follow him as he requires. I thought I loved you, David——" Oh, etcetera, etcetera, etcetera!—"So it is for the happiness of the three of us that I go out of both your lives. . . . I leave Cannes early to-morrow, by automobile, before you can receive this letter. I shall never come back again. Where I go eventually I do not know. Not to the imprisonment of my convent in Lincolnshire.— Are you aware that, as a widow, I inherit large estates in the Argentine? That is another reason, David dear, for me to fly from places where I am known. The Marchese is already making cynical proposals and offering his services.—Ah, my dear, my dear, do not misunderstand me. If I do not claim these estates they will be sequestrated by a rich government for which I care nothing. If I claim them, I can devote them—and I will devote them, David dear, every penny— to the needs of my compatriots outside of Russia. It will be something to live for. An aim not ignoble—— Oh, David dear, pardon your poor little Nadia, who pleads on her knees. If her heart was hers to give, it would be all yours——" And again, etcetera, etcetera, etcetera.

Well, that is practically the end of my story. What happened between Amos and Nadia on that last night

of their meeting I shall never know. Possibly in the
midst of all the primitive passions that drew them together, arose the mangled body of the dead man. The
only key I have is an admission he made afterwards to
Dorothea.

"All her love for me seemed to turn on the fact that
I had killed the fellow."

Possibly, I say—for who am I to know what passes in
my own soul, let alone that of others?—they stared
blankly into a mutual revelation. For her, with her Tartar blood, the dead man signified nothing; the live man
who had killed him, everything. For him, Puritan of
Puritan English, the swift, subconscious heave of his
enemy over the parapet signified, in spite of his pathetic
salving of conscience, something intensely tragic; some
burden infinitely terrible that his soul would have to
bear till the Day of Doom. She rejoiced because he was
a murderer. From her rejoicing he fled horror-stricken.
Hell had happened, he had cried.

Or else, he had lost control of himself and he had
threatened her, and she had been frightened. Had she
not spoken, in her letter, of her fear of his great hands?
His great hands at her throat. What else could her
words mean?

I shall never know—nor do I want to know.

Perhaps the first theory is nearer to the truth, in view
of his rapid evolution. The processes of his mind I have
had little chance of discovering because since then until
now, over a year afterwards, our meetings have been but
few. According to Bendyke Hamilton, his character
altered. He grew morose, introspective, self-centred.
He had lost his dream of reforming the Old World; but
none the less did he repudiate the suggestion of his re-

turning to Warraranga.   In a short time the young men
parted.   Amos went to Bradbury, where, as far as I can
gather, he had talks with the Bishop almost under the
seal of the confessional.   Tom wrote:

"The man of five-and-twenty started life with the
mind and the experience of a child of twelve.   He is
suffering now from the Shock of Life.   All remedial
measures have to be translated into the terms of the
religiosity that he inherits both from father and mother.
He is urging me now to smooth his entrance into a theological college.   When I see religiosity develop into religion, I'll begin to think about it."

Some time later came another letter.

"Confound the fellow!   I thought I was sufficiently
versed in the Cure of Souls to know my business.   Apparently I don't, and, to the making of my greater humility, I never shall.   Unknown to me, he has been going the round of the spiritual advisers of this many-sected
town.   I had told him, indeed, that if he could find
a better—well, a better place of worship than the Cathedral, he was free to go to it.   But I never expected him
to tackle the parsons themselves.   They are all good
fellows and sound divines: Congregationalists, Wesley-
ans, Methodists, Presbyterians, etc.; and no doubt they
did their best for Amos.   But in some sort of despair—
I can understand it—the exquisite Newman, with far less
cause, felt it—he goes to Monsignor Burnaby, the head
of the Roman Catholic community here.   Burnaby, besides being a priest and a Christian, is a very fine gentleman.   He writes me more or less to this effect.   'Your
nephew has come to me for spiritual guidance, or perhaps more accurately, for spiritual information.   I am
placed in a very delicate position.   Our Church dare not

reject would-be entrants.   What I have done is to give
him a letter of personal introduction to Father Somebody of Farm Street, London.   But it wouldn't be fair
of me not to let you know.'   So I tackled Amos, to the
very best of my ability, and all he could say at the end
was that he was going to find something somewhere, even
if he had to go to Thibet for it.   So he has packed up
his tents and gone to Farm Street."

Later again Muriel wrote me in her maddening Gothic
script.   Having little to do that day, I half deciphered
it.

"A dreadful thing has happened.   Amos has been received into the Roman Catholic Church——"

You must forgive me, but I failed to see the dreadful-
ness of it.   Except in an intellectual kind of way, I was
not vastly interested.   Why shouldn't Amos join the
Roman Catholic Church if he wanted to?   It's the most
democratic and the most gentlemanly communion in the
world.   It is a Fountain of Comfort to many million
human beings.   I don't think Muriel will ever forgive
me for my reply.

And, looking back at everything that I have tried to
set down here, it seemed a perfectly logical development.

Tom wrote also, after a while.

"I'm sorry for myself.   But so long as the boy has a
sure foundation, what does it matter?   Anyhow, Rome
is better than Thibet."

As I have stated above, over a year has passed since
the Princess Nadia vanished from my life.   I have never
heard from her. The Fontanas have sold the Villa
Miranda, with all that therein was, including what, I
presume in the Wild West phraseology, would be called

the gambling outfit, to the wise Americans; and they now live vaguely in hotels. Some time ago I met them in a Paris restaurant. I learned that Nadia was still in South America.

"Self-willed and visionary, like all Russians, my dear Mr. Fontenay," said the Marchese, "she will not put her business affairs into the hands of a man of the world like myself." He laid pathetic finger-tips on my shoulder. "And it's a matter of millions, millions——"

He dashed away a tear.

It is Christmas. Bendyke Hamilton and Dorothea, married some time ago, are with me. To marry her, he gave up his projected East African expedition, and Providence, so that he should have fuel wherewith to provide hot water for the boiling of eggs, has provided him with a Professorship of Unknown Tongues, at Cambridge. Also Dorothea's rag and bag shop seems to flourish. As far as I can make out there is a project afoot to buy up and tear down Claridge's Hotel and erect a bag emporium on the site. The pair are delightfully happy.

A day or two ago Amos stepped off from a Rome-bound train and spent the night with us. Outwardly, he was his gentle, shambling old self; nay more, he entered into our little jests with a newly acquired sense of humour. But, inwardly, I saw that he had progressed, or digressed, infinite miles from us. Now and then I caught his blue eyes set upon things in the vast distance. The man had undergone a stupendous change.

Leaving the newly wedded pair together in the drawing-room, we went up to the studio for a smoke and talk. I had forgotten that Nadia's portrait hung there in its beautiful Italian frame. He stood before it for a long time. Then he turned.

"I've learned many things since I left Warraranga," said he, in his simple way. "I've learned the meaning of that. You've got there all that matters."

He heaved a great sigh and pulled out his pipe. I cast a glance at the picture.

"I'm afraid my boy, we were both in love with an abstraction. These things can't be talked about. But it's all over. Let us shake hands and be friends."

He rolled in his chair. "Shake hands and be friends, Uncle David—with all the pleasure in life. But to me— she wasn't an abstraction. She was the incarnation of everything divine in human form. I went through a tough time. . . . Anyhow, that's all over for ever. I've conquered."

"My dear fellow," I laughed, "you're still the youngest thing on earth. Some sweet girl will sooner or later appear on your horizon——"

"Stop!" He rose with his arm uplifted. I want you to understand. In that sort of way women don't exist for me any longer. One has been enough—Oh! I'm not talking cynically. Very far from it. That's one reason why I'm ordering my life away from women."

I looked at him half-incredulously. Why was he bound for Rome?"

"You're not going into the priesthood, are you?"

He nodded. That's where, from the first, he had broken away from the Bishop, who held that you must first save bodies before you could save souls. His Church, said he, had taught him the wiser doctrine. He was on his way to Rome to enter one of the religious orders. At this I waxed indignant.

"In these days when men are needed to clean up the world, it's monstrous for a fellow like you to shut himself up for the rest of his life in a monastery."

He grinned in his old way.

"I'm not going to shut myself up. I'm going out into the world. But I'm a modest chap and I feel I need the guidance that the Order can give me. They've found out that I can speak when I'm wound up. I guess it's hereditary. My father was a bit of an orator, you know."

Well, to every man the dictates of his own spirit. Further argument was impossible. He added humbly:

"In this way I think I can do my bit, according to my lights, in cleaning up the world."

"And which is the Order?" I asked, although I had guessed.

"The Dominicans."

"You know the old pun: *Domini Canes?*"

He smiled: "The Hounds of the Lord."

"Well," said I, "the Lord speed your hunting."

And so, after all the comings and goings, the excursions and alarms, which at the beginning of this story I professed to abhor, I sat one day on my balcony, and taking to my heart the solace of the sea and of the Esterel's infinite beauty, I assured myself that henceforward my existence would be one of illimitable peace. I was happy, said I, on my cliff in the sunshine, because, at last, people left me alone. In my egoistic path, I found no block. I had my absorbing work, which seemingly, given health and strength, I could carry on for ever. I tasted the mighty freedom from responsibility for other folks' welfare. Cares neither black nor grey weighed me down. Nearing fifty I whistled blithesomely in my bath. In company I was reasonably jocund. Friends told me that I was the object of the Coast's envy; that on my cliff I lived unassailable, remote from the petty scandals of Casinodom; that there had been considerable stir two or three years ago over my painting of the Princess Ramiroff; that the Comtesse d'Orbigny had whispered that I was romantically in love with her; but that now, in the eyes of Cannes, I wore the halo of celibate beatitude.

I laughed away the far-off gossip. I accepted the envious estimate of my perfect, yet chaste and irreproachable hedonism. I agreed that I had everything in the world that a selfish and therefore a rational man could desire to make him happy.

Into that belief did I at times delude myself.

But there were others when I was smitten with such awful loneliness of soul that I was restrained, perhaps, only by my artistic fastidiousness and by hereditary sanctions strong in me as in Amos, from fetching in no matter what kind of creature, to comfort me and bring me mere human and intimate companionship. And then I looked at my picture of Nadia and wondered. And while I wondered, I lost myself in her mystery and her delight, and regret was poignant; and then, I turned away and began to wonder again. Had she married me, loving Amos; had she married Amos, turning me aside; on both roads lay untold misery.

And then, I took stock of my life. I had a great love once in all its bewildering fullness. In my work I had the meed of fame for which thousands of men have starved and crucified themselves and all those that were dear to them. Romance, sad though it was, had come to me in the early autumn of my years. I had ever hovering round me the love of the brave and beloved girl whom I cannot think of but as my own daughter. I learned that there was a new and tiny life groping its way into the jungle of the world. I had a strange and foolish hope, and I held out a tremulous hand in acceptance of the eternal wonder of the continuity of the generations of mankind. Providence had showered on me its tender radiance of beauty. Contrite, I repented of my ingratitude.

And then, on this morning of sunshine, in the serene beatitude of surrender, François brings me my letters, among which is one in a round schoolboy hand. I recognize the hand of Amos, ever a painful scribe, from whom I have not heard for many months.

He is very sorry that he has been forced to leave the Dominican Monastery or College or Institution, or whatever it is, where, after intensive training he was about to receive Minor Orders, because he could not believe in the Infallibility of the Pope. He had done his best and had listened to learned theologians who had presented to him all the horrors of Jansenism, but he could not stick the dogma. To "stick a dogma" is not the language of Formal Theology, but I let it pass.

He had been wandering about Rome, apparently at a loose end, and had been greatly attracted by the Greater Freedom of Eastern Orthodoxy.

He went on to say that after his emancipation from Dominican influence he had come under the spell of a personage whose name I could not read, but who seemed to be some kind of Russian High Priest. Pray forgive me, as one born in the worship of the Anglican hierarchy, for my ignorance of, or perhaps reprehensible indifference to, alien hierarchical systems. Anyhow, there he seemed to be caught and held by a gentleman possessed of a white beard and an indecipherable name ending in "-vitch."

"It was the Princess Nadia," said he, "who introduced me to this really remarkable man. The more I see of him, and of her, the more sure am I of my wisdom in cutting myself adrift from the Dominicans——"

I wasn't at all sure, myself. At any rate, they had taught the wild product of Warraranga to express himself more or less grammatically.

"My dear uncle," he went on, after a page or two— "Good God!" said I, "he has flooded me with twelve months' arrears of ink"—"don't think me a reed shaken by the wind of every doctrine. I'm not. I told you, when I first began to feel what Europe was, that I needed education, I realize now that all I have done has been experimental. I now have found Truth, thanks, in the first place to the Princess Nadia, who had put at my service all the influence at her command. Both she and the Archbishop"—it was the first indication that the High Priest with a name ending '-vitch' was an Archbishop—"have convinced me that the celibate life was not one decreed by the Almighty."

He went on in this strain. I held my head. What the deuce was he getting at? He gave me no clue, for with his characteristic abruptness he signed himself, "your affectionate nephew."

The clue was provided, after an hour of confused envisagement of the situation, by a telegram. It was dated, of course, the day before.

"Amos and I married to-day. Not my fault. I really could not help it. Forgive and congratulate. Nadia."

What on earth will happen to this pair of imbeciles,

I don't know. At any rate, it has nothing now to d
with me.

I give up the human problem.

I have no further interest in human things.

Yet, only the other day, there was a pink and whit
and fluffy thing, with less intelligence than a marmose
(and looking uncommonly like one) which was stuck in
my arms by Dorothea.

"Take the damn thing away," said I.

And the damn thing held my finger, and Dorothea
smiled with the smile of the Mona Lisa. And I said:

"Oh, all of you, have it your own way. Nothing in
the world—Art, Science, Philosophy, Love, Torture,
Dancing Teas, Death, Religion—nothing matters but
the propagation of the species. It's a Stone Age world."

Dorothea took the damn thing in one arm and embraced me with the other.

"At last, my dear, you've spoken sense."

I kissed her with mingled sentiments of urbanity, affection and humble surrender.

I have come to the conclusion that I know nothing
about anything.